MW01092399

V I R I O N

Mikki,
Nice to meet you!

M J   G R O V E S

Copyright © 2012
All rights reserved.

ISBN: 1478188812
ISBN-13: 9781478188810
Library of Congress Control Number: 2012912126
CreateSpace, North Charleston, SC

Cover photo:
Electron micrograph of influenza virus
United States Centers for Disease Control
C. Goldsmith and A. Balish

Dedicated to
Mary Korica Drexler
who taught me how to fly

TABLE OF CONTENTS

Noah and his family were saved…

…yes, but they were not comfortable, for they were full of microbes. Full to the eyebrows; fat with them, obese with them; distended like balloons. It was a disagreeable condition but it could not be helped, because enough microbes had to be saved to supply the future races of men with desolating diseases . . .

—Mark Twain, *Letters from the Earth*

VIRUS: IN VITRO

Directly or indirectly, every creature survives at some expense to others.
—Arno Karlen, *Man and Microbes*

An ingenious creation.

Extraordinarily efficient, profoundly adaptable, marvelously unpredictable.

Refined through endless cycles of trial and error, it has achieved a brilliance that cannot be attributed to the design of any human. Indeed if you believe that perfection reflects the hand of God, then God must be the author of this jewel; yet its destructiveness is surely the work of the devil.

It has no ill will toward humans, or anything else for that matter. In fact it has no will at all. No morals, no values, nothing so advanced as hatred. Killing is merely an incidental side effect of its primary purpose. An unintended consequence so to speak. Collateral damage.

If you could view it purely, objectively, you might be tempted to call it an exquisite machine, exquisite in the manufacture of death. But, you would be wrong. This is no machine; this thing is *alive*. And its instinct to survive is billions of years older than yours.

VIRUS: IN VIVO

DUYEN BA, VIETNAM
December 24

Hue Pham liked to waken early, before the sun, the village and the rest of her family. At this hour peace floated quietly on the delta and she longed to drink it in before the inevitable demands of the day engulfed her. Too soon, she and the other women would begin tending to the hundreds of chickens kept in pens behind the huts, whose sale allowed this village to eke out an existence from the mighty Mekong. Hue slid off the reed palette she shared with her husband, tied a scarf around her loose black hair and padded on silent feet past her mother, her uncle and her children. She stirred the embers of last night's fire, added a few sticks of dry wood and poured water to heat for tea, taking the empty bucket with her on the way out.

In the waning light of a full moon she could see tight vees of geese rising out of the mist that hung over the marsh, their honking a sharp contrast to the surrounding stillness. As she bathed at the water's edge she was alert to the familiar murmurings of the morning. When she first rose it was to the chirping of insects and the throaty croaking of tree-frogs, the music of the ebbing nocturnal voices occasionally pierced by the cut-off shriek of an animal that had just become prey. Just at sunrise the roosters would begin to crow, cuing the chickens into a chorus that measured the length of each day. As a child Hue would curl into a ball against the morning chill and try to anticipate each new note in the swelling symphony, rewarding herself with a smile at her cleverness if she was right. She found the passage of time had only deepened her connection to these layers of harmony, now inextricably entwined with pleasant memories of her youth.

Hue sat in contemplation on the bank of the river longer than usual, until the first rays of the sun cut across the Mekong interrupting her. She stood and retrieved her bucket, suddenly and unaccountably bewildered. With mounting foreboding she turned slowly back toward the village and felt goose-flesh rise, uninvited, pricking the back of her neck to her scalp. Walking first, then running, she dropped the bucket and raced toward the pens, her ears knowing something was terribly wrong faster than her brain could even grasp what. Later she would say she remembered thinking, hoping even, that she had lost her hearing, but she knew she hadn't because she was acutely aware of the sound of her bare feet thudding on the dirt, and the bucket clattering behind her. Hue rounded the corner behind the huts.

And froze.

The next sound she heard started deep in her own viscera and clawed past her lungs, erupting through vocal cords stretched taut with despair: the loss of a year's income and the certainty of imminent hunger were carried in the cry that arched over the delta morning, drowning out a sound Hue otherwise would have recognized as the buzz of a multitude of flies. Every chicken, every rooster was dead.

CHAPTER 1

"Shut down the Metro."

"It's too soon. We're not even sure we have an outbreak."

"You need to shut down the Metro," Michael Farrington repeated, leaning his lanky frame into the table at the crisis command center. "Now."

Mayor David Wilkins snatched up the advisory from the Regional Infectious Disease Surveillance System, the alert that had pulled his team together less than an hour ago, and glared at the words on the page. *RIDSS reports an unexpected spike in the number of people arriving at local emergency rooms in the past 24 hours with influenza-like symptoms. Several patients have been admitted in severe respiratory distress requiring ventilators. So far CDC confirms five patients are positive for avian influenza, type H5N1.*

Wilkins threw up his hands. "I'm closing down the city for five people? You've gotta be shitting me!"

Farrington accepted the tirade impassively. As undersecretary for Health and Human Services, he had known this wouldn't be easy when he issued the warning early this morning, the first of several planned disaster drills to be conducted in Washington and other selected major cities in the United States. All the participants at the table had known that RIDSS would test the national pandemic preparedness system with a simulation exercise, but no one had known when. For this run-through Farrington had crafted just the sort of subtle but potentially disastrous scenario they had all been afraid of. That he'd called the drill over the holidays hadn't improved any-one's attitude.

Wilkins huffed and turned pointedly to his health commissioner, "Do all these people have bird flu or am I gonna look like the world's biggest asshole in 48 hours?"

Commissioner Dowd pressed his lips together and said quietly, "I don't know. Possibly." He paused. "Probably." He paused again. "We don't have enough information."

Wilkins slammed his meaty fist on the table, jarring the coffee cups and people scattered around it. "Well damn it, this is all we've got to go on and I need some answers! Will shutting down the subway stop the spread?"

"No, but it will slow it down, Farrington replied. "We need to buy as much time as we can."

"Time for what? 'Cause I'll tell you what I see time for: time for every Tom, Dick and Harry who votes to remember to be pissed off at me in the next election. Time for every reporter who ever crawled out from under a rock to nail my ass to the wall with their fucking pencils."

"We'll run out of ventilators first," said Farrington calmly. "Every vent in Washington will be in use within 24 hours, and there are only a thousand in the entire country. If you contact suppliers immediately you can beat the surge and maybe squeeze out a few more." He turned to Dowd, "How many ultra-filtration masks do we have?"

"Enough for four or five days if they're used once; if we instruct people to re-use them we can stretch that out to maybe a couple of weeks." He shrugged his shoulders. "Everybody will want one."

"There are 500,000 doses of H5N1 vaccine in the national stock-pile," Farrington continued turning to the mayor. "Request what you think you need, but HHS will have the final say in distribution."

"Well that's you and your boss Michael," Wilkins shot back. "So why don't we stop beating around the bush and you can just tell us how much of this vaccine we're going to get. Will the pansy-asses on Capitol Hill try to save themselves, or will they actually send vaccine to their constituents?"

The mayor had hit a nerve: Farrington was unwilling to speak for his boss, Secretary of HHS Cyril Hunt, because he seldom agreed with him, and most of Washington knew it. For a moment no one moved.

Farrington's words, when they came, were as soft as Wilkins' had been loud. "Mr. Mayor, regardless of whether HHS supports your recommendations, we are charged to devise a plan for the district to deal with this crisis. Can we move on?"

"Alright," Wilkins said, folding his arms and sighing as he leaned back in his chair. "What else can we expect in the next few days?"

Farrington was impressed with the data the team had amassed and equally dismayed that they didn't know more. But they couldn't be expected to know more when they were preparing for bird flu with nothing but unproven hypotheses and the history of the 1918 pandemic to go on. That was all the information the world had. At best they could guess that the first wave of disease would sweep through the city within six to eight weeks and infect 20% of the population. Other communities in the nation and around the world would quickly follow, connected by travel and commerce. Multiple waves of illness would occur over the next one to two years. The virus would eventually burn itself out as it circled the globe, those who were unlucky enough to get the infection either recovering with newly acquired immunity, or dying in the process.

"Dowd," Wilkins asked finally, "How bad will it be?"

"Well, we'll be watching death rates day by day until we can answer that. It could be as low as two people out of every thousand. Or as high as 500."

"Shit." the mayor breathed as he looked around.

Now you're getting it, Farrington nodded as he watched the mayor mentally erase half the population. Couldn't politically buy your way out of that one.

. . .

As the room cleared out hours later, Wilkins sat at the conference table and rubbed his forehead. Farrington knew the man was just about to board a jet to Bermuda with his wife when he'd been snared by his cell phone into the drill. Fifteen more minutes and Farrington wouldn't have caught him; it would have been half over by the time the mayor landed. Even on vacation, leaders weren't on vacation, as Farrington was well aware: the phone rang, faxes poured in, the crises continued.

"Michael," Wilkins called out, motioning to Farrington as he was easing out the door. "How do you think it went?"

"Well, despite the holidays, you got all your key players to the table for the trial run. That's something," Farrington said, taking long strides toward the elevator.

The mayor rushed ahead to punch the button for him. "You're not gonna hold my pissing and moaning against me are you?"

"No," Farrington said, eyeing the mayor before he stepped on, "I'm going to deliver it where it belongs."

CALIFORNIA
December 29

Ken Culp spent the night in bed but never saw sleep. Keyed up since the phone call came yesterday afternoon, he had tried to go through the charade of slumber, willing his body to hold still for minutes at a time so as not to waken June. When he could no longer stand it, and well before morning, he slipped quietly out of the blankets and into his robe and slippers, escaping to the den where he was free to let the energy coursing through his veins reflect the possibilities exploding in his mind.

He had done it.

He had won.

Of course he had deserved to win; his work had merited the recognition for at least the last fifteen years. But inexplicably, he hadn't. Until now. He felt the familiar bitterness well up and chose to let it go: the most prestigious award in medicine, the Pritzker International Fellowship, belonged to him, Dr. Kenneth Wardman Culp. He was giddy with the excitement of it. Felt the aching in his joints melt away with the youthful vigor of a champion. Hard work had finally paid off, with power and validation from the scientific community he could only covet in past winners.

It was an effort not to shower and dress and drive to work hours before the typical start of his day, always at least an hour before anyone else arrived. Instead, he went to the kitchen and measured coffee into a filter, glancing at the clock and calculating that he would finish four cups before June awakened for her usual two, and still have enough for his thermos.

The liquid dripped hypnotically into the pot as Ken sat at the counter absently inhaling the aroma and indulging himself with an account of his path to glory. He'd dreamed of this moment from the day he entered research medicine as a Yale graduate over thirty years ago. Since then Ken had been on the forefront of the rapidly developing world of viral genetics at Crossfire Laboratory, a small privately funded institution in Silicon Valley.

Nearly single-handedly he had pioneered new ways of thinking about viral drift and shift, the processes by which viruses mutate from generation to generation. His experiments involved a specific type of avian influenza, H5N1, and showed promise in being able to predict and prevent a worldwide epidemic from the germ, which leapt periodically from birds to humans. In its current iteration the bird virus had not proven very contagious to people, but such a strain could erupt at anytime causing a pandemic. The Pritzker had been awarded for Ken's demonstration of a site on the capsule of H5N1 that enabled the virus to attach to mouse lungs, the closest tissue to human cells available for experimentation. The work had been brilliant he knew, but was still well short of his ultimate goal: to demonstrate that H5N1 was capable of *human* contagion. Despite years of effort, and tantalizing discoveries along the way, Ken had been increasingly discouraged with his inability to prove what he was certain was possible.

He shook his head as he thought about the long road, the self-imposed hours, the rigors demanded by the scientific method. But he had been tenacious. Single-minded. God knew his family would second that, and his body sagged as the unwelcome thought shot through him and stalled his reflection. Presently he drew himself up again and fixed his gaze beyond the walls of the kitchen. If there was a price to be paid for a grander vision then he had certainly been willing to pay it. He was not sure June had signed on for the life they had, but he was grateful to her for at least coming to accept it.

The sudden beeping of the pot roused him. Pouring a cup, he took up a position in his favorite worn chair, feet up on the matching and equally worn ottoman. Early in their marriage he'd treated himself to this extravagance, and he still appreciated it. The chair had been everything he hoped for, soothing his aching neck and back after long days hunched over the microscope. He knew the thing looked shabby, but the aging cushions had shaped themselves over time to his aging bones. "Ken, please, just let me recover it," June had pleaded repeatedly years ago. But he just couldn't countenance any change. "June, we're done talking about this," he had finally snapped, and that was the end of it.

Ken closed his eyes and relaxed his features into something resembling a smile as the chair wrapped itself around him. In this instant he refused admission to the worries that had been dogging him: there was no mother dying, disappointed in her last lucid moments by her son; no shrunken pittance of a retirement denying him a second chance at life; no elusive virus to taunt him. Rather, a visceral satisfaction spread through him as he imagined the award lifting his voice above the clamor of his colleagues; the endowment funding a super computer for the lab; the personal check made out to him, *him alone*, resurrecting his dreams.

As the adrenalin rush finally flagged, Ken entertained thoughts of an interview for *Science* or even *Time* magazine. His eyes began to dance under closed lids while waist-high fields of fluorescent green particles rippled around him. He was pushing through them intently, spreading them apart with his arms, looking for...

"Ken...Ken?" June in her housecoat gently nudged his shoulder.

He woke with a start.

CALIFORNIA
January 4

Nearly a week passed before Ken was free to publicly claim the honor bestowed on him. Trying to suppress his exuberance had only served to highlight his eccentricities. "Good morning!" he'd nearly shouted at the paper boy this morning from the darkness of the porch, frightening the young fellow out of his wits, so unaccustomed was he to any comment from the old man on previous rounds. Then, with a sudden inspiration, Ken had kept the boy waiting while he rummaged through his wallet looking for a five dollar bill as a tip. Finding only a ten and a one, Ken gave him the one, with a beneficent smile and a "Merry Christmas!" before he rushed inside and opened the *Examiner*, jubilantly confirming the publicity of his win and the formal ceremony that would later acknowledge it. The award itself, a fine, gleaming trophy, and the check, had been delivered yesterday by a representative of the committee.

Ken rushed down to the lab, late for the first time in his career because he'd been waiting for the paper. He strode in, beaming, cradling the Pritzker in the crook of his arm like a proud father.

"Why, Dr. Culp, you've been keeping this a secret haven't you?" smiled Carolyn, the receptionist at Crossfire.

"I was asked..." Ken trailed off, trying to explain the conspiratorial twist at the corners of his mouth these last heady days, the raised bushy eyebrows, the lightened step.

Carolyn hit the overhead intercom button as she rose from her chair. "Hey everybody, there's something down here you want to come see." The rest of the staff started to trickle in as she came around the desk to get a better look. Ken held the trophy in front of him, the silver replica of the earth gleaming in the shaft of sunlight that pierced the clerestory window. He felt the venerable weight of it too, tilting and turning it to show the lettering engraved in the equator: Pritzker International Fellow. June had warned him his fingerprints would tarnish the silver; he longed to rub his fingers over the deep grooves of the continents, the impressions of the latitudes and longitudes, but he restrained himself, trying to touch it only by the wood base. Was it mahogany, he wondered? Walnut? It was smooth and cool and heavy in his hands.

"What will you do with it?"

"I'm not sure," he said, as he gathered it back into his arms, unable to resist the urge to look again at the inscribed plate on its base: Kenneth W. Culp.

Carolyn piped up, "Dr. Culp, you keep that on your desk as long as you like, but when you're ready, that award belongs front and center in our display case." She nodded toward the large window in the reception area, littered with the modest past awards of scientists at the lab. Framed advanced degrees bordered the case, row upon row testifying to the extensive credentials of Ken and his staff. "I'll polish the glass and dust everything up in there so it'll shine."

He blushed at her fussing, shifted from foot to foot, yearning for the attention so long overdue, but quite unsure what to do with it. Slumping forward finally with the burden of his fame, he mumbled, Thank-you," and, "Thanks again," and retreated to the security of his office and daily routine. He had barely settled into his work before Carolyn's voice rang out. "Dr. Culp, call on line one." Ken looked up from the microscope and checked the time out of habit as he swung around in the chair to grab the phone. He usually hated interruptions, but he couldn't help but smile as he punched the button; he was determined to enjoy himself today.

"Dr. Culp?"

"Speaking."

"This is Marianne at PharmaGlobal calling. Hold just a moment please for Mr. Vaughn."

Ken had just enough time to acknowledge his irritation, new master of the universe, at being put on hold before J.B.Vaughn came on the line booming, "Ken! What an accomplishment! It's about time you got the attention you deserve!"

"Thanks...I...still don't believe it," Ken managed, master-of-the-universe instantly overwhelmed by the larger than life presence of J.B.Vaughn, CEO of one of the most profitable drug companies in North America.

"Of course nobody here is surprised!"

"Well...I was..." Ken said. "There's a lot of talent in the field...It's an honor just to be in contention." He was struck as the words left his mouth that, for the first time, this statement he'd made for years suddenly felt genuine.

Vaughn laughed heartily; "Nonsense! Your research has always been impressive. That's why you're on our team old boy!"

"Thanks. It's great to be appreciated," Ken said, overlooking the hollow fraternizing that usually grated on him.

"Say...let's do a little something at the next meeting...I want to make sure the committee knows about this."

"That really isn't necessary...but it's your call."

"So it is. So it is," Vaughn chuckled. "Well, I'll let you get back to saving humanity...while I get back to figuring out how to profit from it!" He chortled, and hung up.

Ken leaned over the desk to replace the handset in its cradle, struggling to be more flattered than disturbed. He shifted uncomfortably in his chair and thought about the place his credentials had earned him in the elite circle of consultants to the largest manufacturer of flu vaccine in the world. Periodically he was subjected to comments regarding the profitability of his research and they always lodged under his skin, niggling little burrs that picked at his contentment. It wasn't that he objected to the idea of profit in business, but he'd always disdained thinking of his research as a business.

Ken enjoyed nothing more than being in charge of the cool, pristine world of his laboratory. The purity of the science was the goal; to be recognized for the importance of his contributions was all the privilege he asked for or expected. There had been many times in his career that he couldn't believe how lucky he was to be paid to freely pursue his passion. But lately Ken had to admit that the notion his research could be profitable had become more important to him. He wasn't proud of this thought; in fact, he felt some shame just thinking it.

He clasped his hands over his chest and tilted back in the chair. Directly in front of his desk, through the wide glass partition that separated his office from the laboratory, he could see his research assistants fully garbed in their biohazard suits conducting the experiments he had meticulously designed. Ken was deriving tremendous satisfaction at the moment knowing that his work would continue today despite the reduction in his own productivity. He leaned forward to straighten the accordion of computer-generated paper he'd left on his desk yesterday. The latest sequence of viral genes generated from the mouse autopsy specimens taunted him as he folded the pages into their pleats; today was no different, he had so much more left to do.

Ken glanced at the clock again; it had been almost fifteen minutes since the last phone call, the longest uninterrupted stretch he'd had. As if on cue, Carolyn called on the intercom, "Dr. Culp, calls on line one and two." She continued helpfully, "It's your granddaughter on line two, so I told her to wait." In that instant he recognized how little this receptionist knew him; he reached for the phone and punched two immediately.

"Granddad!" Moira chirped. He felt a familiar blend of love and pride well up instantly as he soaked up the ebullience in her voice

"Hello my precious Moira. How is my little Fat Head today?"

"Granddad, you shouldn't call me that," she chided, giggling.

"And why not?"

"Because Mommy says people will make fun of me," she dutifully reported.

"They couldn't possibly make fun of you. You are the smartest little girl on the planet! Your head is stuffed so full of brains it's almost impossible for your neck to hold it up..."

She giggled again.

"...which is exactly why I call you Fat Head. But if you insist, that will just be our little secret name for you, and in public I will address you as Princess Moira, The Brilliant and Beautiful."

She dissolved into burbles at the thought of such an outlandish title. "Granddad, you made me forget what I was going to say!"

Ken played innocent. "Well, you'd better remember soon so I can end this dreadful conversation and get back to saving the world."

"That's it! Mommy said you won a prize! That's the best thing I ever heard! What was the prize Granddad? Did you win the lottery? Will you be on TV? Do you get to go to Hawaii? Can I go to?"

Ken tilted his head back and laughed, marveling at the delight he'd known since Moira's birth, thinking of how differently he'd responded to his own daughter Betsy. Betsy's childhood was gone and he hadn't even missed it. She didn't seem any worse for it, June had always provided for her, but he thought he should have done better. Maybe he still could.

Moira was an unexpected light in the tunnel of his life. The first moment he held her tiny wrinkled body in his arms wakened in him a taste for the simple pleasures of life. He thanked God for her skin of finest satin under his rough, over-washed hands; the haunting melodies he perceived in her plaintive newborn cries; the sweet scent of her milky breath as he took her in his arms after she nursed. In his new role as grandfather there were suddenly other things he wanted to do, and a pressing sense of the limited time in which to do them.

The prospect of spending the rest of his days at the lab no longer appealed to him: the work was nowhere near done and it wouldn't be, couldn't be, in his lifetime. He had begun to understand that he needed to pass the torch to the next generation of scientists. Avian flu was just one offender in a microcosm overflowing with threats to humanity. Despite enormous losses of life, as a species man had survived the periodic challenges. His was but a small effort in a much larger endeavor and he had been foolish to ever think there might be an end to it, a time when he could utter the word 'finished'.

In his post-Pritzker insomnia the path had become clear: his single mission before retirement would be to see his work on H5N1 used to create vaccines that were capable of saving lives on the grand scale necessary to avert a pandemic. In Ken's most cherished vision he would accomplish this in the next couple years and then retire to a life spent enjoying his granddaughter, and reclaiming the lives he had sacrificed along the way.

"Granddad?"

Ken suddenly realized Moira had been babbling on, requiring nothing more than a periodic "uh-huh..." or "really?" from him while he was preoccupied with his thoughts. The light from the phone call on hold had also blinked out he noted, bothering him not at all. Promising Moira a celebratory ice cream cone with sprinkles, he had barely replaced the phone in its cradle before the secretary announced another call. Still smiling, Ken hit the outside line and...regretted his action instantly. His investment advisor, Carter Skelley, came through in slick, calculated tones.

"Congratulations, Dr. Culp."

Ken sneered at the use of his professional title; the man had called him 'Ken' on all previous occasions.

"I understand the Pritzker is the most important award in your field. I'm proud to have such a distinguished client."

That was a situation Ken planned to rectify. "Sure. I'll get back to you," Ken spat out, and hung up. He knew exactly why the man had called and it wasn't to offer praise.

Ken was irritated with the quick change in his mood and furious with Skelley for causing it. Thirty five years of savings would have been enough, should have been enough, for him to have slowed down by now. Skelley's risky strategy had left his modest savings in ruins, had thrust an easy retirement out of his reach. He looked at his hands, the knuckles white from clutching the arms of his chair. Determined not to let anger cloud his judgment, he exhaled slowly and watched the blood return to his hands.

"Dr. Culp, your presence is requested in the cafeteria," Carolyn said, peeking around the door to his office. "Sorry sir, on such short notice we couldn't plan much of anything, but the staff wanted to celebrate."

"Be down in a minute," he said.

Ken stood and strode purposefully to a filing cabinet in the corner, unlocked it, and pulled out a manila folder from the back of the top drawer. He was through with following. He had done his time. He was ready to lead, using the full weight of his position and authority, his skill and knowledge, to make life unfold according to his plan. Today his newly defined aspirations would begin with a financial strategy that would restore his hard-earned wealth and see him retired at the pinnacle of a renowned career.

VIRUS: IN VITRO

Name: influenza type A, avian.

Description: eight pieces of protein, specifically: ribo-nucleic acid. RNA, wrapped in a shell.

Modus operandi: a savage intruder.

The immune system recruits a mighty army of antibodies, macrophages and white cells from the blood and lymph. Flanked by ancient genetic codes to identify, isolate and silence the invader, the flesh soldiers on.

But the body may muster all its defenses and still lose the battle. Early reports are not encouraging: perhaps one in twenty people will die, perhaps three out of four. It's an equal opportunity killer: pitched in the prime of your life, or at some weaker moment, it will steal into you, cloaked in the invisibility of air. Aerosolized droplets teeming with viral protein will settle into the lush mucus oasis of your respiratory tract.

Two billion years have distilled the virus into its current lethal state, but in all that time it never created its own shelter, or produced its own food. It cannot make you even the slightest bit ill, much less kill you, without your help. An accomplice to your own death, you will supply food, water, lodging. Fortified by you, the microbe will manufacture weapons of destruction that wreck your house so completely that your own immune system doesn't even recognize you. You will attack the very organs that support your life and drown in a soup of melted lung tissue and white blood cells.

Make no mistake, the virus does not escape unharmed: most of its weaponry and spawn will die with you, the host. Individual viruses are readily sacrificed to ensure survival of the species. Prior to your death, enough particles of freshly copied virus will be present in any number of coughs, sneezes and spittle to find new dwellings.

VIRUS: IN VIVO

DUYEN BA, VIETNAM
January 4

Hue Pham was miserable. First there was shock and grief in the village, but it was quickly replaced by grim determination. Then she and the other women had worked feverishly, their fingers bloody and raw, to pluck and gut as many chickens as they could before they rotted in the stinking pens. The men built large fires, and they had cooked the chickens and feasted on the carcasses, preparing for what must inevitably be a prolonged time of want.

The remains of the birds that turned putrescent in the subtropical sun before they could be cleaned or consumed were burned right in the coops, generating bedding for new fowl, when they could be afforded. Each family might buy one or two chickens in a month, trading for the scant crops that grew around their huts. Of course the new poultry could not be slaughtered, but must be raised for eggs to expand the population. They would need a rooster too. Under dire circumstances a neighboring village would loan a rooster for a while; one cock would do, and it would not be kept particularly busy. The village would pool its resources and purchase a pair as soon as possible. In two or three years they would recover. People would die before then, some of the new ones and some of the old ones: of the loss of calories, and of hope; of the futility that characterized their existences. It was part of the cycle. It was expected.

As if she were not miserable enough, Hue had taken a hard chill. She collapsed on her palette in the middle of a cool day in the delta, drenched in sweat. Her small children crowded around her, wanting for this and that. She could not help them. Her husband came to her side and she coughed on him. He brought their neighbors in to evaluate and minister. He called on her sister and brother-in-law from the next village to help care for her and the children. The attendants came and went, shuffling about with poultices and wraps, incense and incantations. She coughed on all of them, until she slipped into a coma and could no longer muster the strength to cough at all. Then all at once, Hue was no longer miserable. She was dead.

CHAPTER 2

CALIFORNIA
January 4

Ken returned from lunch and sat heavily in his chair, staring at the cover of the portfolio he'd retrieved earlier from the file cabinet. When he'd got his courage up he opened the folder and rested his forehead on both hands as he stared at the latest figures. Two hundred and twenty thousand dollars. *Oh my God*. He closed his eyes. Remembered a day a few years ago when he had transferred his savings to Skelley. The snake. He was embarrassed at the time because his hand had shaken when he signed the paper work authorizing the investment firm to convert over five hundred thousand dollars in CD's into cash to be invested under Carter Skelley's professional guidance.

Ken poured a cup of coffee and closed the blinds separating his office from the lab. He placed his feet carefully on the rim of a waste-basket, and stared at the walls. For the first time in his life he missed having a window to the outside world, yearned for something more than institutional paint and electron micrographs of viruses as a back-drop for his vision.

Ken had not given much thought to financial planning or retire-ment when he started his career. In fact he hadn't even considered the prospect of retiring until a few years ago. He loved his research and simply assumed he would continue to work, as both his parents had, until he was unable to do so, or dead. He knew June preferred him to plan for golden years filled with the pleasures of shared experiences, but he could never bring himself to participate in her quotidian notion. Until Moira.

Ken took a swallow of the lukewarm coffee and thought back to the day he'd been told he was going to be a grandfather. He felt a little guilty now that he had not been particularly moved by Betsy's announcement of her pregnancy. Certainly he had been happy for her and her husband Jake, but the news registered as just that, news. June had responded as a grandmother should, all agog, buying Betsy clothes, patting her stretching abdomen and fussing over baby paraphernalia in catalogs and stores. Ken assumed his usual inert posture in the family, mostly oblivious to the excitement surrounding him.

With Moira's arrival, no one, least of all Ken, could have conceived of his granddaughter's effect on him. At first his interest in the baby was assumed to be a temporary distraction from his intense schedule at Crossfire Lab. But the passage of time only increased his visits and his family's astonishment. Ken too seemed rather puzzled by the choices he was making: calling in the evening to see if he might baby-sit, stopping by on his way to work. If Moira wasn't in her parent's arms when he and June visited, Ken would drift away from the adults to look for her in her crib, or swing, or baby seat. There they would find him sometime later when they realized he was missing, leaning over her adoringly, captivated by the sound of her breathing, or the twitches of a smile that played across her face while she slept.

By the time Moira was a toddler, Ken had become a fixture in Betsy's house. They were having more dinners as a family now than Betsy could ever remember having growing up. Gradually the oddity of Ken's transformation wore off and the extended family resettled itself around the new dynamic, June and Betsy acquiring a previously unknown domestic radiance in the process.

Because of Moira he was ready to give June the retirement she had yearned for: the two of them taking Moira to places they had never been, Ken teaching her about the logic and beauty of science, nurturing her budding interest in all living things, basking in the sunshine of her guileless smile. Moira at six had more intellectual fire than anyone in his family since his parents.

He sighed, remembering long discussions at the dinner table as a child. His parents, Anna Wardman, medical ethicist, and James Culp, physicist, would periodically try to engage him by simplifying arguments on the concepts of irrational numbers, or the origin of quasars;

on the implications of when life began, or ended. His parents were normally rather quiet and unimposing so he was fascinated by the passion they exhibited during these times. One of them would assume the position of devil's advocate, and the discussion then became a debate. Even though their voices often became strident, there was never any acrimony, and when they had exhausted their arguments they simply smiled at one another and quietly resumed whatever activity they were previously engaged in, finishing supper, reading the paper, mopping the floor.

As Ken developed his own ideas of the world, his parents drew him into their discussions more and more. He was always more interested in the hard science of his father than the indeterminate ruminations of his mother. Mathematical puzzles, solving equations, analyzing the action of particles in motion: these things fascinated him, delighted his father. But he could never seem to find the solid ground he needed to join in his mother's philosophical musings. She loved wading in the murky waters of bioethical dilemmas, inherent human values, the essence of the soul. Ken had little stomach for these metaphysical questions.

Anna Wardman had remained professionally active well into her eighties when the early stages of Alzheimer's forced her to stop teaching, speaking on the lecture circuit, and writing. She was now living in a nursing home, near death at age 93. If James Culp had not died, he expected his father would have continued teaching indefinitely too: he was 59 when he was found at his desk slumped over the galleys of an article he was reviewing for *Physics*. Ken had had no reason not to follow their examples.

Like his parents, Ken was also a disciplined saver. His modest income at Crossfire would never have allowed his family an extravagant lifestyle, but neither did he or June crave one; they had few needs and inexpensive tastes. After he'd paid off his graduate school debts he had set aside a small amount each month for the future, although he carried only the vaguest notion what that future might be. He had been rather satisfied with his efforts until the last several years when he had discovered two unanticipated problems: that saving money was only one variable in the process of achieving financial security, and that retirement held far more interest for him than he ever imagined it might.

Shortly before Moira's birth, the Culp's financial security changed dramatically. Ken had enlisted the assistance of an investment counselor on the advice, nagging really, of June's family. "Ken, how's your portfolio holding up?" he'd been asked by June's brother at one of the gatherings of her side of the family he was always loath to attend.

"Uh...our...savings accounts...uh..." Ken stalled, looking worriedly at June for help, reluctant to discuss anything so personal, much less on a topic he knew so little about.

"No, not your savings," her brother interrupted.

"Oh...well...our C.D.'s..."

"No, Ken," he interrupted again, this time rolling his eyes at the others seated at the table. "Your stocks. There's a boom market coming. How far are you in?"

"Uh...we're...I'm..." Ken stammered. With no business background or training, his fiscal planning consisted of the reassuring sense that he was providing an adequate income for now and the foreseeable future. All of his savings was invested in bank CD's and life insurance policies.

"Nevermind," he laughed. "Ken, just a word of advice. Make sure you got some tech stocks. They're gonna go through the roof."

Ken had no intention of confessing that he didn't have any stocks, but privately June had attempted to defend Ken and reassure her brother by telling him that they were doing just fine with the CD's and the life insurance. June's brother had called Ken shortly thereafter, his voice thin with disapproval, and given him Carter Skelley's name. Ken felt rather sheepish about his lack of investment savvy in the glare of his in-law's judgment so he had dutifully placed a call to Skelley, and together, he and June had gone to the firm's office.

As they entered the slick, gleaming lobby of Skelley and Associates Ken felt awkward and ill-equipped for the event in his worn khakis, slightly wrinkled shirt and scuffed loafers. The furniture was ultramodern: armless chairs carved of sleek wood, glass-topped tables and metal-edged expansive desks, tiny canister lights illuminating abstract art arranged carefully on the walls, wide expanses of curtainless windows facing the sprawling, populous valley. Too-thin women in expensive designer clothes attempted to look busy answering the phone in hushed tones, or walking smartly to the fax machine.

Like the surfaces surrounding him, Skelley himself was all smoothness and polish in custom tailored pants with a starched, bright-white shirt and lustrous cordovan shoes. He extended his velvet hand to shake Ken's first, then June's; one was more limp than the other. He cordially offered them tea or coffee as he led them to his office where his jacket hung neatly from a carved gentleman's caddy behind his sumptuous chair. Ken stole a glance at June as they sat down. She was no more comfortable than he, her back rigidly refusing to conform to the cold leather of her seat. She clutched her purse primly to her abdomen, looking more than a little frowsy, the dullness of her capri pants, flowered shirt and mousy hair in sharp contrast to the buffed surroundings.

For the next half hour they barely heard what Skelley said, and understood even less. After answering some questions, they had simply agreed to his recommendations and left, feeling quite relieved that the ordeal was over. Ken had believed as they walked out the door that despite the discomfort of this meeting, he had killed two birds with one stone: June could tell her brothers that she and Ken had a portfolio, and he would no longer have to think about his future financial security. In this he was mistaken.

At first Ken had been impressed with the earnings statements, even though Skelley insisted he was achieving only modest growth, ("...Ken, you've only just begun to see the potential of these stocks...") Compared to his previous conservative holdings, Ken was amazed. More than once he congratulated himself for listening to his brother-in-law's advice.

Then came the tech crash. At least that's what June's brother had called it. He hadn't known anything about a crash, or how he was supposed to have protected himself or his savings from it. He never followed the stock pages or the financial news: that's what he thought Skelley was supposed to be doing. The weasel had called him before he got the statement in the mail and warned him with sugar-coated words about the figures, but nothing could have prepared Ken for the shock of opening the envelope. He actually thought he was missing a second page. A page omitted by mistake. Something that would say that the total funds in his account still added up to something close to what he'd had before.

At the time he was livid, with Skelley, with his in-laws, with himself for participating in this game. Where had it gone? It was more than just numbers on a page, wasn't it? There had been real money there. Who took it from him? His misery at the loss was compounded by his shame in not understanding it, and his guilt at having ever invested in anything more than what he knew, what he knew was safe. At least he still had the insurance policies. But they couldn't make up for this.

He was tempted to withdraw the money from Skelley immediately and put it back in the bank, but if he did that he'd have no chance to recover what he'd lost. June's brother had taken heavy hits as well. He was grim but spoke in cautiously optimistic code phrases of taxable write-offs, market rebound, and future doubling times. Ken called no one to complain. Decided in a moment of philosophical lucidity that it didn't matter. He could stay in research indefinitely. He could build his savings back up, and might never have need of it if he was capable of working until he died...like his father. The evaporation of his assets was just another academic exercise concerning irrational numbers. He thought his philosophical mother would have been proud of his transcending the concrete world of finance so handily. Had she been in her right mind, he might have called her.

June seemed to take longer than Ken getting over the damage. He had long since settled back into his routine at Crossfire by the time she reconciled herself to their loss. Ken did make one significant change however: he stopped all further automatic transfers of funds from his payroll to Skelley, and returned to his dutiful savings at the bank. He had not told Skelley he was doing this, and despite several attempts on Skelley's part to reach him, Ken had not spoken to the man again until today.

Ken raised his eyes to the trophy on his desk. He leaned forward and took the replica of the earth into his hands feeling its weight and its coolness. He ran his fingers reverently over the deeply engraved letters in the equator, marveled, as he turned it around, at the precision with which the continents had been etched into the gleaming metal. With satisfaction borne of half a lifetime of patience he drank in the bold formal script on the base: Kenneth W. Culp. He placed the globe gently back on his desk and took from inside his coat pocket an ivory envelope of heavy vellum. Sliding his fingers in he took out a check for two hundred and fifty thousand dollars made out to him. He gazed at his name in wonder. His award. His recognition. His achievement. The enormity of the accolade felt as heavy on his shoulders as the globe had felt in his hands.

This was his redemption. He had labored ceaselessly for the betterment of the human race, until now without the recognition his skill and dedication warranted. He had finally beaten the other contenders, some of whom he must now concede were pretenders. He had won by his dogged pursuit of excellence and he deserved it. He was a man whose research was both inspired and impeccable; he would leave a lasting mark.

And there was one more thing he would do, he thought as he ran his fingers with wonder over the Braille imprint on the check. With this money, he would buy his way to financial redemption too. Until now he hadn't believed it, but here, finally, was proof of his mother's perspective that there was indeed balance in the world. The highs and the lows evened themselves out over time. If you just waited long enough, you got your due. Ken replaced the vellum sheaf in his coat, packed up his things and left Crossfire early. It was highly unusual but his colleagues assumed that he'd given himself permission to celebrate by cutting out well before his customary time. They were right.

GUANGZHOU, CHINA
January 4

Lou Symington reached two fingers up to press on the bridge of her nose, applying steady pressure to massage the area just under her brow. She had been hunched over these data for days, looking for clues to predict the next outbreak of avian flu, and had come up empty-handed, unless she counted the headache she was feeling just now.

Leaning back in her chair she acknowledged the toll the virus was taking on her. She willed her muscles to relax as she practiced deep breathing to counter the stress. At the moment she longed for a whole host of things: a half dozen more field workers, a week of sleep, the prophesying abilities of a seer, and, as long as she was fantasizing, a good deep-dish pizza with an ice cold bottle of American beer. Floating momentarily on the thought, she imagined a decent guy sitting across the table sharing it. "Hell," she said out loud as she sat upright again. That was the problem with relaxing: it led to day-dreaming, and that led nowhere.

She sighed as she looked up at the stacks of paper that covered every inch of her small desk and filing cabinet, and grew from there, extending up the walls, taped and tacked, this way and that. Lou preferred to think of her environs as creative; more rigid minds had called her unorthodox approach a mess. On entering her office, some laughed and shook their heads in disbelief, others averted their eyes as if ashamed to witness the disarray, and some were obviously appalled. She didn't give a damn what anybody thought; she hadn't graduated summa cum laude from Wellesley and then Georgetown without knowing how to apply her intellect. She loved complex systems, daunting challenges. That was exactly why she'd taken this job as Chief of Infectious Disease Surveillance for the World Health Organization, evaluating seemingly unconnected events, seeking associations that only appeared to be random, but in fact were not. Lou found every bit of her brain power necessary, and her modus operandi perfectly suited to the task.

Lou was in China as part of a network of doctors stationed around the globe to monitor illnesses carried by animals and potentially communicable to humans. Her job was to track all outbreaks of avian influenza in animals and people in Southeast Asia, to isolate the exact sub-types of virus responsible for each outbreak, and ultimately to recommend containment, vaccination and treatment protocols for each episode. She smiled ruefully as she remembered being recruited away from arguably the best infectious disease program in the world at the Centers for Disease Control in Atlanta.

She'd let go a laugh after reviewing the job description presented by Dr. Makao Wataabe. "You're kidding me?"

"No," replied the Kenyan in cultured tones, "I assure you, I am not." Wataabe had been sent by the WHO from Geneva specifically to engage her interest. Surely her response was rather expected because, while the position was strong on goals, it was regrettably short on resources. Still, in the course of their acquaintance he had come to know her passion for serving people and no doubt his presence indicated his hope that she might agree to the offer after all.

Lou's incredulity subsided under Wataabe's steady scrutiny; since she'd known him, first as a professor, later as a friend and mentor, she had admired his brilliance, valued his gentleness and humility. Lou quickly composed herself so that he would not think she was ridiculing him. She needed no convincing on the mission; she was simply stunned by the utter disregard for the manpower, money and technology necessary to tackle it. The room was quiet as she grappled with her whirling thoughts.

"Dr. Wataabe...I am grateful...for the honor..." Despite their friendship, he had always insisted on calling her by her professional title; she accorded him the same respect. She sighed, searching for words in an effort to turn him down gracefully. "You know I believe in aggressively pursuing avian flu..." She stopped, lost.

Seeing her struggle, he nodded gravely, and gently withdrew his liquid brown eyes as he dropped his chin to his chest. He clasped his hands contemplatively in his lap and silence hung momentarily over them.

"I am sorry Dr. Symington," he said, squaring his shoulders and recapturing her gaze. "You are an outstanding physician. That is why I have come, to recruit the best." He paused and smiled kindly at her. "But I forget, you are also wise, and only a fool would pursue such a task without proper support. I shall continue to work for the resources necessary to address these issues, and perhaps someday we will have this conversation again, with different results. Please," he bowed his head slightly, "forgive me for asking."

He rose from the chair and offered his hand. He seemed to look straight inside her and she was unsettled by the admiration she read in his features. "We shall keep in touch in any case," he said, handing her his card.

She stood to shake his hand, uncharacteristically speechless. He smiled tiredly, turned, and walked away. Lou sank back in her chair and contemplated the framed poster of the Atlanta cityscape hanging in front of her, the brushstrokes of paint on the walls, the punctuations in the ceiling tiles.

She was still there, staring numbly, hours later. A hand that did not seem to be her own picked up the phone and dialed the number. "Dr. Wataabe," she heard herself say, "I'll do it."

CALIFORNIA
January 4

Ken's first stop after leaving Crossfire was Skelley and Associates, where he signed forms to liquidate all of his securities, directing the funds be sent to him at the office. This would take about five business days he was told by the stunned (*Really, how could he be stunned?* Ken thought) Carter Skelley. Two hundred and twenty thousand dollars.

Next he went to the bank and cashed in all of his certificates of deposit accrued over the last few years, after the stock crash, when he'd kept his earnings out of the hands of Skelley. One hundred and seventy thousand dollars. When the clerk handed him the check, he took the vellum envelope out of his pocket and placed it next to his award with great care, once more fingering with awe the pushed out nubbins that imprinted the numbers on both.

Finally, he went to the local offices of Charles Schwab. The receptionist directed him to a scrubbed young man at one of several work stations. Ken told the broker he wanted to open an account and purchase stocks.

"Yes, I know what I want," he told the man. By God he knew this time. No one else knew this business like he did. Why hadn't he taken advantage of his knowledge earlier? Everyone else was profiting from his work. Why shouldn't he profit too? The justice of his award had opened Ken's eyes. It was a sign of all the success that was within his grasp, and he was proud of himself for being here this minute taking advantage of it.

The broker was busy filling out forms as Ken slowly withdrew the cherished packet from his pocket. He removed the checks and gazed at them, struck for the second time in his life by how insignificant money seemed when it was just numbers on paper, wondering where all the actual, physical dollars that represented these figures lay, this numbered accounting of his life, his work, his dreams.

After a time he glanced up to see the young man looking at him expectantly. Ken slid the checks slowly across the desk with both hands. Ken felt a certain satisfaction as the broker's eyes widened. "How much would you like to deposit sir?"

"All of it. I will also be forwarding an additional check for $220,000 as soon as my account with another firm is dissolved."

"That's 420,000 dollars today and another 220,000 dollars later, for a total of 640,000 dollars?" the young man said as he finished a quick run of the numbers on his calculator.

"That's correct."

"What would you like us to purchase for you Mr. Culp?"

"Two stocks. Divide the money evenly between PharmaGlobal and Viraban."

•　•　•

Ken was giddy with delight as he left the broker. The Pritzker had resurrected his dreams, his dreams had become plans, and a moment ago the plans became action. He spotted a coffee bar across the street as he unlocked his car, and for the umpteenth time today decided to break with tradition by treating himself to a purchased cup of coffee when he still had some left in his thermos.

June had seen a lot of changes in him over the past several years but he thought he needed to pause just now adjust to the new experience of being master of his destiny; he did not want June questioning him just now as he had no intention of informing her of the financial changes he had made. She would be right back to telling her family, no doubt with some measure of pride, and then he would be in the same awkward position he had been before, with them rendering judgment on his strategy. He was not going to sign himself up for that again. June would not only be surprised, but pleased when he finally told her, something he would do after he had something to show for his efforts.

He relocked the car, crossed the street and entered the bustling shop, caught off guard by how busy it was. He looked at his watch; evidently Friday afternoons were popular with the coffee crowd. After perplexedly searching the menu, trying to reconcile the trendy lingo with his own vocabulary, Ken ordered a 'tall black', and took his purchase to the lone unoccupied seat in the place. The robust conversations surrounding him served as insulation more than intrusion and he was able to sink nicely into a chair and his thoughts.

Ken mused about what he would say to June if he did tell her.

He would have explained that by now he would have had enough money to retire if it hadn't been for Carter Skelley. He would have told her that he had been a fool all these years not to have considered the knowledge he possessed, and the connections he had, as valuable assets. He would have asked her to trust that he knew where there was money to be made in the current international focus on pandemic flu. He would have admitted to her that he should have thought about retirement when she wanted him to, years ago. He might have asked her whether she respected him less for seeking, finally, to profit from his research, but he was not sure he could face her answer if he detected evasion, or even tact in her response.

He would have told her he loved her and that he was doing this for both of them. And Moira.

VIRUS: IN VIVO

DUYEN BA, VIETNAM
January 6

Duc Trinh scooped two cups of rice from a rapidly disappearing store into a tin that would serve as a cooking pot on his journey. He tied a thong around the tin, double knotting the cord and double checking its security so as not to lose one precious grain. With a sturdy knife and a cup rolled up in a small red blanket for good luck, he said good bye to his wife and three young children and set off for the hamlet of his sister's husband's family, some three days walk away. She had married outside the village, to a man with somewhat better prospects than anyone in her own community. Duc had not envied the rise in status and income her new family had afforded; as long as he could feed his own family, he had enough.

But that had precipitously changed more than a week ago when the chickens died. His cousin, Hue Pham, had been lucky to follow them in death he thought. Daily Duc had found himself increasingly terrified by the looks on his children's faces, could not stomach their wide-eyed silent pleading for more food, could not bear the vision of gauntness that would soon replace the chubby cheeks. His wife was large with their next child. How would they feed it? She was losing weight rapidly; they both were, portioning their own spare servings into the children's bowls.

Death had been haunting his dreams each night, pursuing him with black wings and tongues of fire as he tore screaming, weeping through marshes and fields searching for food. He would waken from these nightmares quivering with fear and sit up to check on his sleeping family, needing to reassure himself of their safety before he could even begin to rest again. Many nights he did not seek sleep after such dreams, but lay still next to his wife searching for a way to escape the specter of famine.

On one such restless night he had come up with this plan: he would travel alone to his sister's village and beg her to take them in until after the baby was born. Duc's sister lived close enough to the city that he could hire himself out somewhere; he didn't mind if the pay was mean, better than to starve. If they agreed he would return to Duyen Ba to collect his family. He would have enough in a month or two to buy a few hens and they could return home with some prospect of putting food on the table. Until then his children and wife would be fed. In return, his family would do whatever was required to defray the cost of being kept. He would owe his sister and brother-in-law something after he got back on his feet, but he would make good on that.

In the stillness of the first morning out of Duyen Ba, Duc kept to paths roughly parallel to the river, using as his guide the outlines of huts built on stilts that were dimly visible in the early light. Soon he could hear the far off commotion of river traffic coming to life around the hamlets. As the day wore on he moved deeper into the delta, wading through the low spots of tributaries that crisscrossed the region where the Mekong spilled inevitably toward the ocean. He felt lucky to be going in the dry season; making this trip in the monsoons might have been more than he could bear. Gradually he found ease from his burdens in the cadence of his gait as he walked a familiar landscape that varied from marsh grass to protective jungle. By mid afternoon he tired, and ducked for a nap under a canopy of coconut palms, their fronds, big as houses, nearly drooping to the ground. He slept peacefully for the first time in days, awakening refreshed by a gentle breeze that stirred in him like a sigh.

Duc put in a few more kilometers then stopped in a tiny village whose fires he could see glowing in the twilight. The denizens shared both fire and sympathy as he told them of the devastation of the poultry. As it happened, one of their men, Tran Phu, and his young son had planned on leaving soon for some errands in the city. If Duc wanted to spend the night they would travel with him. He thanked them profusely and retired to a bed of thatch under the porch of one of the huts. At dawn the three of them continued on together.

It was mid morning when Duc began to chill. Within a couple of hours he was having trouble walking. He tried to keep the pace, but after a while even the boy was slowing his steps to wait for him. They could see he was not feeling well. He apologized profusely for holding them up and insisted they go on. They declined and held back for a while, hoping he would improve enough to continue; inconveniently, they were half way between two villages, and neither was close. Just past the midday sun, with the humidity rising and his spirits falling, Duc began to cough, progressing to violent spasms quickly. His companions were concerned but Duc convinced them he would be fine. Shortly thereafter, feeling guilty for delaying his comrades, he made a show of feeling much better, quickening his step and suppressing his cough. Soon he spotted a fork in the road and convinced Tran that this was the place his path would part from theirs and that they should go on without him. He would rest until he felt better, then proceed on his own, as was his original plan anyway. The father and son were persuaded and left him fruit and rice cakes so he would not have to cook his rice today if he didn't make it to another village by evening.

After they parted Duc collapsed into the arms of a mangrove tree at the side of the path, exhausted by the extra effort of pretense. He wakened as the late afternoon sun was angling in over the treetops. His rest had left him feeling, if anything, worse, and now he needed to make some attempt, despite his deteriorating condition, to get to the next village. He struggled to his feet, wheezing with the effort. A fit of coughing strangled him as he dragged down the path. He spat a wad of foamy, yellow phlegm, with generous streaks of blood, onto the muddy track. An hour of trudging, hacking and spitting saw him less than a mile further with no people or villages in sight. Crickets had begun their nighttime screeching in earnest. He looked about him; he was in mostly open marshland now and began to search for a suitable place to take shelter for the night. If he could find just a small tree or bush with low-hanging boughs the dew would not lay so heavy on him; that was Duc's last completely coherent thought.

He was chilling hard now, shaking uncontrollably as he stumbled off the path in the setting sun. Not too far away he saw a promising nook hiding in the waning light. As he neared he realized with gratitude that it was even better than it appeared from the trail: the thick brush was growing from a rocky outcrop which couldn't be seen from the trail. Duc crawled under the slight ledge of his sanctuary and covered himself with his little red blanket. He laid his head on his small pack and curled into a quaking ball as he fought the damp grasp of his fever and the approaching darkness. All through the night the strangling coughs that racked his slight chest could be heard by the marshland creatures nearby.

By morning, the delta had reclaimed its stillness.

CHAPTER 3

GUANGZHOU, CHINA
January 7

Lou wakened with a terribly stiff neck, her cheek pressed in a puddle of drool on the report from Thailand. Evidently she'd fallen asleep at her desk somewhere between Cambodia and Vietnam. It was dawn, not her favorite hour, and she was wrinkled, unwashed and hungry. She couldn't do anything about the sunrise, but she could remedy the other three problems she thought as she pushed away from her desk with both hands, freeing herself of the paper trappings.

Outside the air was chill and a light rain was falling. The stink of coal hovering over the Pearl River cut into her nostrils and she involuntarily exhaled to clear it. But the next breath brought more of the same, now mixed with the pungent aroma of a meat that wasn't beef, pork or chicken being grilled at a nearby vendor's stall. The sidewalks were just beginning to fill as she made her way toward the Bund and her tiny apartment in the business district that abutted the Pearl as it flowed through the heart of Guangzhou. She navigated around peninsulas of old men and young, seated or squatting at sidewalk tea houses for a morning cup and conversation, and smiled at the sidewalk vendors settling into their daily trades.

Lots of activity was already evident on the street: bicycles vied for road space with tiny cars and huge buses. A block ahead, two cabbies were pulled to the curb shaking their fists at each other over who had hit whom. In China the blame and the compensation took place right at the scene of the accident. Before Lou even got to them the police had come to dispense their highway justice. As she passed, one of the cab drivers thrust money in the face of the other, who gave him the Chinese version of a gesture that bore universal meaning.

A few more blocks and Lou rounded the corner onto a quiet, well, quieter, she corrected herself, side street. "Good Morning Dr. Lou!" said her neighbor. "You up early today!"

"Not by choice, Mr. Chan," she laughed, nodding her head in respect to her elder, and appreciating his ready cheerfulness. He lived with several other families in a small, ancient, walled compound of single-story clay and brick buildings arranged about a central common courtyard and wedged between new high-rises of shining steel. Mr. Chan had to draw water from a well in the center of the compound, while Lou and the other apartment dwellers had all the modern amenities.

"Maybe you got boyfriend?" he winked, "Keep you up late?" He scooped up the family's rooster, Ming, to pet him. Ming announced the day from Chan's arms. It was piercing, up close.

"Nope." she laughed again, clapping her hands over her ears and simultaneously side-stepping some chickens pecking at grain around her feet. "Don't even have time to work on that Mr. Chan." And she didn't. But she let herself wonder for a moment what it would be like to have the comfort and joy of a relationship again. She believed in love, but hadn't found it. Should she be looking, or was it supposed to find her? The only man on her radar screen right now was Connor Mackenzie, the Associated Press reporter she'd met a few years ago. He'd never asked her out, only asked her questions for interviews. But he seemed to be calling more often and his questions seemed less, well, necessary. He was charming, intelligent, and good looking, which could only mean there was something dreadfully wrong with him she had not yet discerned. He'd been attached when they first met, but she heard he was single now. She thought he was interested in her, but he lived in the U. S. How do you even start a relationship from continents apart? It was hopeless.

"Good fortune to you Dr. Lou," Mr. Chan called as Lou keyed into her building.

"And you Mr. Chan."

• • •

Lou showered quickly and changed. She wanted to spend the morning organizing her thoughts on the latest outbreaks of bird flu. She checked her watch: not even 8 a.m. yet. Breakfast at home? At her desk? She checked the fridge: not much there; smelled the milk. Ooops. Cereal was out as an option, unless she asked Mr. Chan to milk his cow for her: she considered this briefly out of hunger. No. Warm and unpasteurized was just too big a leap for an epidemiologist. She'd have to go to the store. Lou opened the window and stuck her hand out to check the weather, unsure if she was seeing mist or the ubiquitous Guangzhou smog, and inhaled the pleasant aroma of food cooking nearby. That was enough: she'd compensate for her bed-less night with a decadent breakfast. She could get her work done too: Lou called her assistant, Yong Wu, and asked him to meet her at her favorite café. She grabbed an umbrella, deciding to walk rather than deal with the thickening traffic. The restaurant was only a mile away.

Lou's route took her past a small park brimming with Chinese couples ballroom dancing to American music playing loudly on a boom box. They were completely heedless of passers-by, at first dipping in and out of a waltz around the terrazzo stones, and then bopping to a swing before she rounded the corner and lost sight of them. She was snapping her fingers to *Mack the Knife* as she slipped out of the morning mist and into the door of the restaurant where the tentacles of an enormous squid waved at her from an aquarium at eye-level. Adjacent to it were row after row of fish tanks, housing giant golden carp, and snails with their suckers stuck to the glass, octopi and anchovies, schools of smelt, lizards and crickets: lunch and supper for the patrons who would come and choose from the colorful, living display. Lou was unfazed; she took a booth in the back, away from the buzz of the locals and ordered a cup of green tea, while she waited for Yong.

Reaching over to the next table Lou picked up a copy of the international *Times* that had been left by another patron. A front page article featured the World Health Organization conference scheduled for today in Geneva. *Damn, I totally forgot,* she thought. Well, she could hardly blame herself; she had been preoccupied. Still, she couldn't believe she had forgotten: preparation of memoranda for the

WHO's Director Bueller had taken a big chunk of her time the past few weeks.

She noted the byline on the article was Connor Mackenzie's. He had called her last week wanting to be sure he got the criteria for pandemic flu right. The article in front of her was sound in its depiction.

"... *Webster's defines pandemic as a disease that affects a whole nation or the whole world. There are three conditions that must coincide to produce a pandemic, and historically these conditions are present at the same time only rarely. First, the virus, in this case influenza virus, must arise in a form that has never been encountered by humans; humans will therefore have no immunity to it. Second, the virus must cause significant illness in humans. Third, the virus must be able to spread easily between humans. Some scientists add a fourth criterion, that the virus cannot be so lethal that it kills all of its victims quickly or the virus will not have a chance to spread ... While it is reassuring that the convergence of these circumstances is uncommon, member nations of the World Health Organization are meeting in executive session today in Geneva to discuss just such a possibility ...*"

"Hey, Dr. Lou."

"Yong," Lou said looking up, motioning for the big man to sit.

"I brought the waitress with me, anticipating your voracious American appetite." He smiled at Lou and quickly ordered in Chinese. "Would you like me to order for you too?"

"No thanks. I'd probably end up with eel." She gave her order to the waitress, half in halting Chinese, half by pointing to the menu. A heap of scrambled eggs and bacon, toast and fried potatoes. "And watermelon," she exclaimed at the receding waitress, because it was more reliable in flavor than the orange juice, which she had repeatedly noted in China didn't actually taste like it came from oranges.

"You skip a few meals yesterday Skinny Minny?" Yong laughed, acknowledging Lou's figure despite her ability to put food away.

"Nope. All things in moderation, Yong, including moderation. Just fortifying myself for the demands of the day."

"Well, that order ought to last you a while," he grinned, then turned more serious as he pulled a piece of paper from his pocket. "Speaking of demands, I picked this up at the office on my way over."

It was a fax from their station chief, Binh Long, in Vietnam:

Dr. Lou,

WHO lab confirms H5N1 as the cause of the bird kill two weeks ago in the Mekong Delta (Duyen Ba). Per local authorities there is no reported illness or death of people in the village, but I have not had time to go there and conduct my own investigation yet.

Also received report this morning confirming cock-fighting roosters in Saigon positive for H3N3 flu variant. One young boy (works with the roosters---Dad is a handler) is hospitalized with a respiratory illness; lab work is still pending on the cause of his illness, but he is negative for H3N3 so far. No illness or death of any roosters or other handlers. But who knows?---the usual---everybody is so secretive. The government ordered extermination of all the roosters as a precaution, but the industry went underground to avoid the culling. They've just disappeared.

Please advise, how to proceed?
Binh

"We don't have enough staff," said Lou after reading the fax.

Yong nodded soberly.

"This is just what I was up all night thinking about," Lou continued, rubbing her forehead in frustration. "There's been a marked increase in flu outbreaks in the past nine months. We're battling local authorities who deny there's actually an increase, claiming it's just the WHO messing around where they're not wanted. Ruining their local economies. I'm sensitive to that, but you and I know that the increase in bird flu is real. The authorities can try to hide the information all they want; it's the farmers who are telling us," Lou insisted between sips of tea, "because you've worked hard to gain their trust. They call us now because they believe we might be able to help save their flocks and them. They can see it spreading firsthand and they're afraid. You used to spend all your time trolling the countryside for information when the outbreaks were few. Now I hardly know where to send you first."

"I know," Yong agreed.

"Add to that the explosion in new types of avian virus," she said, ticking them off. "November: H7N1 in massive poultry kills in Thailand and Indonesia. December: H9N1 in those geese in Mongolia.

VIRION

Dead by the thousands. Dropped right out of the sky. January: H3N3 in roosters. Where did that come from?" She asked, waving the latest fax in the air. "A new variant every month? The organism is changing and spreading so fast we can't keep up."

These were the reports Lou had been reviewing, looking for connections between the migrating wild fowl, which included turkeys, swans, geese and ducks, and the outbreaks in domestic fowl. She could identify no pattern in the kills or the variations in the virus, but as she looked at Yong's kind face she could identify his patience in allowing her to vent, and it calmed her. "Thanks," she said.

"No problem. You're right, of course," Yong replied.

"I had no idea when I hired you that you were such a 'yes' man," Lou smiled.

"Didn't you know? That's my middle name. Yong Yes Wu."

"Whatever happened to scientific debate? I need to have my ideas challenged so I don't screw up."

He laughed. "I think you have enough challenges right now. This morning I'm viewing my role as supportive. But, don't worry, if you need it, I can be a 'no' man too."

A steaming plate of soft scrambled eggs appeared in front of her. She smiled and thanked the waitress in Mandarin, "*shia-shia*," doing her best to get the inflection right.

"That's pretty good Lou," Yong observed. "You sounded Chinese."

"I don't dare speak much Chinese in public," she admitted. She would have preferred to blend in better with the culture, but learning the language required not only knowledge of the correct word to use but also the proper inflection. If you pronounced a word one way, it might mean 'good morning'. Pronounced with a different emphasis, the same word could mean 'friend' or 'well-water' or even 'horse's ass'. These linguistic nuances could make the simple ritual of trying to greet your neighbor in the morning a real problem. Lou had learned to restrict her usage to the few words she could confidently master. She picked up a piece of bacon and held it under her nose, savoring the smoky aroma before she bit into it.

"So, what's your best guess for the cause of the next pandemic?" Lou asked. "Are you in the H5N1 camp, or do you think it will be a new variant?"

"You can't pin me down on that one." Yong answered. "Confucius says…"

Lou interrupted with an arched eyebrow, adroitly trapping some scrambled eggs with her chopsticks. "Oh no. You're not going to give me the journey of a thousand miles thing?"

"No… Confucius says: 'Real knowledge is to know the extent of one's ignorance.' I don't know which virus is going to hit us," Yong said, "and like you, I'm not afraid to admit it. I will admit though that I find it fascinating, from a scientific point of view, watching this virus develop. I mean, who knows how long it took for the 1918 Spanish flu to mutate and incubate from a bird virus to a pathologic human form? Months? Years? Decades? Millennia? Or the Hong Kong, or the Taiwan? For the first time in history we have the tools to analyze the birth of a pandemic. But it's really just observation power so far. We struggle with the illusion of control with quarantines and culling and vaccination, trying to outrun it, trying to create the tools to avert a disaster. But can we? We're about to find out if that's possible."

"I'm trying to make it possible. I don't want to be a bad footnote in some future history book," Lou said ruefully. "If I could just get my arms around the jump in the human infections. All the human cases so far have been due to H5N1, and they *appear* to be transmitted directly from an infected bird. And it *seems* to take a big load of the virus and a lot of contact with the bird for a person to contract the disease."

"That's right."

"But what if I'm wrong?" She pleaded. "I was hired to try to avert the next human pandemic, and I feel like I'm failing." There had been a few cases recently in which it was suggested the virus was transmitted from human to human, fulfilling the third criterion for it to become pandemic. Lou was skeptical. She could come up with a host of reasons to discount the probability of human to human transmission in the reported cases. Patients lied all the time, for a variety of reasons too obscure to be anticipated by their physicians; no one could predict why or whether the patients would lie about exposure to fowl; the fallibility of any history given by any patient is appreciated by doctors the world over. Further, the victim may not have been aware of exposure. Poultry was everywhere in China: for sale, alive and dead, in the public markets, tucked under the clothing of pedestrians and people on buses, riding in the baskets of bicycles, floating serenely on ponds and squawking on the sidewalks. In China's chronically overcrowded conditions it was nearly impossible to avoid exposure to fowl. Plus, if the virus had been transmitted easily, they'd already be in a pandemic, and not just hypothesizing about one.

Despite the challenge, and her complaints, this was the aspect of her job Lou loved the most: epidemiology, the intersection between the practice of medicine and good, old-fashioned detective work. You applied science to the situation, but the conclusions depended on the infallibility of the evidence obtained. It was always tempting to infer, and nearly always wrong to do so.

"What if human to human spread is occurring Yong, but it's difficult? Just how close is H5N1 to developing easy transmissibility to, and between, humans?" She did not want to miss it, this final jump of the virus to pandemicity.

Yong shrugged. "Confucius says, wherever you go, go with all your heart. You're doing that Dr. Lou. No one could ask for more."

In silence Lou buttered her toast and picked at the rest of her eggs. The last strip of bacon she chewed and swallowed slowly, savoring this final bit of comfort. "C'mon, I'll give you a lift back to the office," Yong said when there was nothing more for her to finish, and they returned to the bustling streets.

SWITZERLAND
January 7

The conference room at WHO headquarters in Geneva was filling up quickly. Occasionally there was difficulty even getting a quorum for these monthly meetings, but there would be no danger of that today Michael Farrington noted as he passed the representatives of numerous nations gathering in the lobby after lunch. Director Hans Bueller had sent out a terse agenda in advance: the only topic today would be escalation of the pandemic threat of bird flu. The final item listed was a vote on policy: clearly none of the members wanted to be left out. Farrington slipped into a chair at the long mahogany table, across from the broad windows framing a superb view of the snow covered rooftops of Geneva and the picturesque foothills beyond. Men and women spoke in the hushed tones of churchgoers as they entered and selected a seat. Some jockeyed for a prestigious position close to the director. At most meetings Farrington had seen more competition for the seats opposite Bueller and nearest the door, for an easy exit in the event of an unanticipated soliloquy by one of the more long-winded participants.

Bueller began as soon as the bells outside chimed the hour, prompting the last person to sit and the whispers to quiet to expectant silence. "My esteemed colleagues, today I will present field data on the recent changes in avian influenza virus."

The chairman's remarks were translated, to those in need, through discreet earphones. "Bird flu continues to periodically cause crises in the fowl population, industry and economy of Southeast Asia, but our immediate concern is the implication that recent outbreaks pose for human transmission. Sorry," he said glancing around, "Some of you will need a refresher on the *virion*, the viral particle, to appreciate this new threat."

Farrington anticipated the segue. Many of the members were political appointees with no scientific background; it was critical that they understand the science well enough to make informed decisions. The WHO was an organization without a country; without the delegates spurring their sponsors back home to action, all WHO policy was just an empty promise. The director had to make sure that when the members left this room their knowledge would make them effective catalysts for change in their own nations. Malcolm, Bueller's secretary, drew the curtains and dimmed the lights as Bueller queued up the first slide.

"As some of you know, each influenza virus consists of a core of genetic material on the inside, surrounded on the outside by a capsule studded with two types of protein spikes, termed 'H' and 'N. These spikes are the grappling hooks the virus uses to break into a cell. It is the precise structures of these spikes that determine how well a virus can attach to, and thus infect, a host. If the virus is unable to attach, there can be no infection: the virus is essentially harmless.

He moved to the next slide. "The genetic core is composed of another protein which directs the formation of exact duplicates of the parent virus. Sometimes though, there is a problem in the process, and instead of an exact copy of the parent virion, viral propogation produces a mutation where the offspring are different than the parent." He scrolled through several examples of viral replication. These mutations may make the virion more able to enter human cells, or less able."

"Until now, what we have observed in avian influenza viruses are minor mutations like those seen here. These changes have not allowed the virus to grapple its way into human cells."

Now he used his laser pointer to direct attention to the altered progeny on the new slide behind him. "Large and abrupt mutations like those shown here however, are a much more serious matter. When the H or the N component of the shell of the virion, or the genetic core, changes drastically, the resulting mutant virus may be endowed with new abilities to infect other species, and be capable of far more destruction. The mutation results, essentially, in a new life form."

"There are fifteen different kinds of known 'H' spikes, and nine 'N'. For simplicity we number them in order. Each strain of influenza virus, whether human or avian, always includes one type of H and one type of N. Currently, only three combinations of H and N are capable of causing *human* epidemics: H3N2, H3N1, and H2N2." Bueller turned to his audience. "Stay with me," he said, "we're almost done."

"Until recently, only three different H and N combinations have caused epidemic disease in *birds*: H5N1, H7N7 and H9N2. We have monitored H5N1 the closest because not only has it killed the most birds, it has in rare instances infected and killed people... those who were in very close contact to a diseased bird. Even a minor mutation in H5N1 could make it as contagious to humans as it is to birds. This is not news to you. H5N1 has been, and will continue to be, a threat to humans. But, I digress...Here's the new problem."

The director hit the button for the next slide. The three known avian combinations appeared in bright white letters on a stark midnight background:

H5N1   H7N7   H9N2

With each subsequent click of the mouse a new date and avian virus layered onto the slide:

November: H9N1
December: H7N1
January: H3N3

"This, my esteemed colleagues, is the list of *new* avian influenza strains identified in bird outbreaks from Indonesia to the Russian Caucasus in the past 60 days. The H3N3, I might add, was confirmed just this morning."

Bueller turned off the projector, cueing the lights up and the curtains open. The breathtaking winter scenery was revealed once more, a serene and stunning contrast to the anxiety palpable in the room. Malcolm began passing out a data packet to each member.

"The first page is a visual of avian virus infections in people. Thus far, only H5N1 has been the cause of human cases, all of which have been confined to southeast Asia, eastern Europe and northern Africa."

"Following that you will find several pages of maps indicating flu outbreaks in birds in the past 24 months." Farrington flipped through the pages as Bueller summarized. He could tell at a glance there was a definite clustering of bird flu in Southeast Asia which was not a surprise, though the number of cases was noticeably higher than he remembered. What was also immediately prominent, but much more disturbing, were the number of far-flung outbreaks from the center, and three new colors of dots: red, yellow and green, that appeared now on the map, indicating the new avian H-N combinations in the past two months.

"Further on you'll find the death rate in birds associated with each H-N combination we've identified. It ranges from a low of 29% to an astonishing high of 94%. These extremely pathologic strains are evidence that these viruses are indeed new to the world, and not just newly discovered by us. They are infecting populations of animals that have no natural immunity."

Bueller paused.

"Eventually, my friends, that animal will be us."

CHAPTER 4

GUANGZHOU, CHINA
January 7

Lou glanced at her watch for the umpteenth time today: 9 p.m. The six hour time difference meant the meeting in Geneva was probably just beginning to get interesting. If it had been difficult in the past for Director Bueller to convince members that H5N1 was a threat to world health, persuading them to prepare for multiple strains would be even harder. Had she been right to advocate for this change he was presenting to the WHO members today?

Lou had been pressed for months by national governments, other scientists, and most recently her supervisors and the administration of the WHO to predict a pandemic strain. The world, represented ever more loudly by the press, seemed to be clamoring for H5N1 to have the official stamp of virulence by the WHO. Lou longed to provide answers; the task consumed her day and night. Some mornings she wakened with numbers and letters slipping away from her consciousness: 'H's and 'N's in jumbled sequences, 1's and 3's and 7's floating and falling. She wanted to identify the next pandemic strain as much as anyone. More. But she would not be led by foolery.

It was not a game of black jack. The closest to 21 didn't win. If you were wrong, nobody won, everybody lost. It was 21 or nothing. This was what she had tried to tell the people who pushed her, all the people who beat down her door wanting answers. There were days she was tempted to make up answers just to get the press or the Chinese officials, or her bosses off her back. But she didn't. Couldn't. Couldn't contrive responses she didn't believe in, couldn't prove. It was folly, arrogance, to construe interpretation of the available information, even if it were brilliant, as truth.

In preparation for today's board meeting Bueller had called Lou personally a few weeks ago after reviewing her recommendations. The administration at WHO was quite cognizant of the risks of inaccurate predictions, but they were also representatives of an organization that relied on its funding from the nations of the world, and those governments were holding WHO's feet to the fire. Political leaders needed something comforting to take to their constituents. In the best of circumstances this was a noble effort; in the worst, it was a thinly veiled attempt to divest the government of blame. National leaders wanted to know what vaccine to stock. Pharmaceutical companies wanted to know what vaccine nations were going to be advised to buy. Profit-driven corporations were not about to lose money flushing unused, unmarketable or expired vaccine stock. Ordinary people, frightened out of their wits by the prospect of a deadly infectious disease, were clamoring for the high tech solutions they had come to count on in life.

Lou had no patience with such nonsense. There was indeed a race against a biological ticking bomb disguised as avian flu, and every reason to anticipate such a virus could potentially cause widespread destruction. But premature predictions did not foster those ends. Policies based on faulty assumptions were more deadly than having no policies at all.

The barest beginnings of world efforts to cooperate on vaccine had focused on producing and stocking a single avian vaccine, H5N1, for human use because it had been the only strain to infect people thus far. Lou did not think this was an adequate basis for predicting H5N1 would ultimately develop pandemic potential. Over the past few months Lou had, against the more popular prevailing mob mentality, privately advised the WHO to pursue a program of stockpiling vaccine against multiple viral types, instead of just H5N1. The recent emergence of new mutants in the fertile breeding grounds of Southeast Asia, where animals lived in proximity to their owners, proved the wisdom of her logic: the virus appeared more likely than ever to take a form other than H5N1. Whatever virus acquired transmissibility to humans, it was a tossup whether ancient migratory patterns or modern commercial transportation would spread it most efficiently.

Lou knew that in the past few weeks her recommendations had been vetted by other scientists, physicians and epidemiologists in private phone calls and conference rooms around the world. She expected it, counted on it; the stakes were too high, the burden too huge for one person to bear. Unanimity under such conditions was not possible, but Director Bueller had informed her this week that WHO consensus was to propose adoption of her recommended new policy to the members today.

Lou looked at her watch again: 9:15. Minutes were crawling. Backwards. She stared at the phone. Contemplated biting her nails. Went to the bathroom. Connor was in Geneva and had promised to call her as soon as a statement was released to the press. Bueller wouldn't have a chance to talk to her until much later. She reached into her knapsack; maybe Connor had tried her cell. But she couldn't find her phone. Damn, what had she done with that? There was too much on her mind to make space for the little things like cell phones, car keys, sleep. She'd have to resort to calling herself to find it, listening for the tell-tale ring, and resign herself to waiting.

SWITZERLAND
January 7

Fresh snow was dropping in lazy, wet flakes outside the well-appointed headquarters of the World Health Organization. Connor Mackenzie was sitting in an overstuffed chair in the lobby trying to stay alert for breaking announcements from the boardroom, but the passing time and the falling snow had conspired such that he was now heedlessly daydreaming of skiing in the Alps. It was possible he'd even been napping. He had been reviewing WHO influenza tracking reports on his laptop in preparation for the news conference, and the sudden beeping of the low battery signal directed his attention back to the present. Sadly he acknowledged that his current assignment would probably not allow him time to enjoy the eight to twelve inches that was supposed to accumulate over the weekend; knowing this, he hadn't even brought his skis along for this trip. He leaned over and pulled the charger cord out of its case and plugged it into an outlet close by, moving the computer to an end table next to the chair to accommodate the cord. He had just pulled up the first draft of an article he had started in anticipation of today's meeting when the great walnut door opened and the first members emerged. Several headed for restrooms, others collected around large silver urns of coffee, tea and the requisite Swiss chocolate on the buffet. Connor gathered himself promptly and approached the director's secretary Malcolm, tilting his head quizzically as soon as he made eye contact.

"No Connor," Malcolm said, "we have no statement yet. Dr. Bueller wants to ensure everyone understands the reports prior to discussion and voting."

Connor certainly appreciated the difficulty in that task, having made a career as a journalist out of doing the same for the public. Connor leaned in a little asking Malcolm, *sotto voce*, "How's it going so far?"

"Off the record?"

"Of course." Connor cultivated the trust of the people who informed him, and this could only be accomplished with honesty. He would not print any direct quote without permission from a source. Adherence to this principle afforded deeper access into the heads of his subjects, allowed him to mine the subtleties of the issues. There were many sides to the complex topics he addressed; he tried to include all of them. Saw himself as a photographer of sorts: but recording the world he saw with words rather than film.

"As you would expect, the mood is intense," Malcolm said. "Bueller certainly has everyone's attention. It remains to be seen if the level of anxiety will support meaningful action."

"At least you have a full house today." Connor observed.

"Yes, no one wants to be left out of the loop." Malcolm tilted his head toward those gathered at the refreshment buffet. "They're hoping for more information than what they've read in our bulletins, perhaps a more optimistic interpretation than the scientists quoted in the press have suggested. At the very least, they all want a hand in the decision-making." Malcolm placed his hand on Connor's shoulder. "I'm afraid you're in for a long afternoon my friend."

Connor harbored no resentment for the wait; Bueller had his work cut out for him. Biological debates usually consisted of distinct and often competing perspectives. First, one had the facts, research-proven data that confirmed or disproved theory. Second, there was almost always 'soft' scientific data: research that had either not been conducted yet, or multiple conflicting data from the research that supported differing theories. Lastly, there was always individual interpretation of the data. This latter perspective was universally political and always problematic. Individuals in power made self-serving, expeditious decisions under the guise of government policy, frequently disregarding the hard science at their disposal. Historically this attitude had frequently hampered the efforts of organizations, public and private, bent on improving the health of populations at risk. Political expediency could severely undermine the effectiveness of such programs. Connor thrived on the people and the process. If he carried a torch, it was in the spirit of the word itself: as a means of shedding light on all the available knowledge that might be expected to inform his readers on a given issue. Those who recognized this feature in him, and had nothing to hide, saw him as an ally.

. . .

In a far corner of the room Michael Farrington was using the break to call his boss at HHS, Cyril Hunt. "No, Bueller hasn't requested a vote on anything yet, but you've read the reports; the WHO will be looking for a commitment to support preventive strategies in Southeast Asia."

"Well, you are aware of the president's stand on this." Hunt drawled, creating syllables where none existed. "The president has a certain disdain, Michael, for wasting federal dollars on private health care, at home or abroad."

Farrington was irritated by the man's intentional use of his southern accent to draw out the phrase. They had been over this subject repeatedly. The president's public response to bird flu paid lip service to preparing for pandemic, while privately he was openly skeptical of data that suggested such a pandemic might be imminent. Farrington felt sure that the president was getting poor interpretation of the science from his closely knit upper echelon whose sole focus seemed to be whether bird flu was politically correct to act on, or ignore. Current consensus appeared to favor 'ignore'.

The pandemic exercises conducted around the U.S. two weeks ago had emphasized the shortcomings of the nation's preparedness. Farrington had personally debriefed mayors of all eight participating cities and found them universally frustrated with the level of support they were anticipating from the federal government. Frustrated himself, Farrington had insisted, over Hunt's objections, that he be allowed to present the avian influenza data to the president himself, certain that the president would choose to be more pro-active once he had all the information.

Farrington had gotten his chance with the president but had been quite disappointed by his response. Other than a glimmer of interest in the purchase of additional H5N1 for first responders, the medical and public safety personnel activated first in the event of a crisis, the president had been cool to Farrington's advice. As he prepared for the trip to Geneva he had reluctantly concluded that either the president was so politically jaundiced that he was capable of denying the data in front of him because it did not suit his agenda, or he was incapable of grasping the national ramifications of an international infectious disease outbreak. Neither perspective was reassuring.

Farrington went on, prodding Hunt in hushed tones, "The United States will be looked to as a leader in this effort. Our participation, or lack thereof, will make or break the process." He paused, searching for something positive he could take back to the conference table. "The president said he was willing to look at a proposal from the WHO."

"What the president said was that he will consider the information as it becomes available." There was a pause. Farrington could picture Hunt taking a long pull between his overly full lips on the cigar whose pungent smoke he used freely as a screen and a weapon in his office. Indeed, he heard Hunt exhale pointedly into the phone before he continued, "I will remind you Michael, you are on an information gathering mission. Period. You will not commit the financial resources of the U.S. government or the president's endorsement to any policy at today's meeting."

Farrington was angry. Not surprised. Mute.

"Is that clear?" Three syllables turned into six. Somehow it helped to calm him, counting the syllables.

"Yes. Quite."

• • •

Connor noticed Farrington's grim expression as he snapped the phone shut. It wasn't rocket science to guess he'd been speaking with HHS secretary, Cyril Hunt, a committed mouthpiece for the party and the president in power. Hunt was not in the least fazed by international scuttlebutt that the leader of the strongest country in the world was somewhat of an embarrassment to mainstream scientists.

Farrington and the last of the attendees filed back into the room, taking their quiet murmurings with them. With the closing of the great door the lobby was once again utterly still. Connor checked his watch. It was well after two already and Malcolm had warned him that the real debate hadn't even begun. He realized with some disappointment that not only did he not have a complete article for tomorrow's paper yet, he still didn't have a good excuse for calling Lou. And he wanted to call her. More than that, he admitted, he wanted to go out with her. On a date. Not just to meet her for one of the sporadic interviews he'd arranged in the last few years, at first purely professionally, later, just to see her again. A real date. An I'm-a-single-man, you're-a-single-woman, why-don't-we-be-single-together kind of a date.

He could e-mail her he thought, with a flash of inspiration. He'd e-mailed her before. About science, medicine. Why not relationship? Connor flipped open his laptop, waited for his e-mail to boot up and hit, compose.

Lou,

Hmmm. Should he use 'Dear'?

Dear Lou,

Delete.

Hey,

No.

Hey Lou,

Definitely not. Delete.

Hi Lou,

I'd like to call and talk to you, but the meeting isn't over yet and I didn't want to bother you before I promised to.

Good God. Delete.

Hi Lou,

You've probably noticed lately that I call you with questions that are really beneath your level of expertise. This is because what I really want to ask you is something important, like are you dating anyone?

Delete. This isn't working he thought: if my writing were always this inept I'd be collecting unemployment.

Connor snapped the computer shut. Settled his lean frame deeper into the chair and pondered how this woman had gotten into his head. Realized immediately there was no pondering necessary. It was really quite simple: he'd been startled by a pair of the shapeliest legs he'd ever seen issue from the hem of a skirt, stretched out on the bed of a Paris hotel room. His hotel room. And hers. Of course she got into his head. He wouldn't be a card-carrying member of the heterosexual male gender if that first vision of her hadn't struck him immediately. And stayed. The bigger question was why it had taken nearly five years for him to get around to asking her out. That was pretty simple too: he'd been attached when he first met Lou. And by the time he became unattached, Lou had moved half a world away.

Five years ago Connor was a starving writer for *Biologica* magazine, just out of journalism school, living in a microscopic flat with his girlfriend in his home town of London. That relationship hadn't worked out, but they were still an item at the time he was covering the International Science Symposium for the magazine. He had a very limited budget for travel expenses and usually chose the thriftiest accommodations available so as to have more discretionary funds for other things, like food. At this particular conference attendees were offered the option of having a roommate assigned if they wanted to share a room. Connor had willingly applied for this alternative to forking over the cost of a single. He was an easy going guy; he could get along with anyone.

The meeting was in Paris and he arrived in the late afternoon. He registered at the conference reception desk where he was given a key and told his roommate had already checked in. The man's name was Lou Symington. To this day he wasn't sure if the room assignment was the result of a Frenchman's sense of romance, or if it was an honest mistake because the name was ambiguous. In retrospect there had been the rather obvious oversight on the part of conference organizers in requesting participants to identify their gender for the purpose of roommate selection.

Connor had keyed into the room to the sight of those fabulous legs attached to the distinctly feminine curve of a hip facing away from him on one of the two beds. In a split second he took in the hair cascading on the pillow, the heels discarded on the floor, the slender arm with a single bracelet glinting in the last shafts of daylight. He was immediately confused and exited quietly, returning to the lobby to correct the mistake. A quick check with the registrar disclosed that he had indeed received the proper room key; the light bulb of recognition flashed in Connor and the clerk at the same time: the name was the problem. A quick search of the hotel roster was done and revealed that the rooms were sold out. The hotel was more than happy to make amends by putting Connor up at a nearby pension. He had just accepted this offer when the body attached to the legs appeared next to him at the desk.

"I'll be with you in just a moment Miss," said the clerk solicitously. He raised his arm and signaled to the bell hop to order a cab for Connor.

"Yes, of course," she responded smiling.

"Excuse me," Connor had said stepping away. "Please take care of my colleague first." He was curious as to why she had appeared downstairs so suddenly from her state of repose.

"Oh, no," Lou had said, "I'm in no hurry. Please continue with the gentleman. I can wait." Excellent manners, Connor noted, for a woman who could have cashed in on her looks and her smile, particularly in Paris.

After nodding to the mademoiselle, the clerk had looked at Connor and shrugged, and proceeded to apologize for the mix-up saying he would notify the hotel manager of the error and expected some discount would be arranged for his inconvenience. "We will simply tell Mister, er... Ms. Symington her roommate did not show up and the room will be hers at no extra charge."

Lou perked up at the mention of her name. "Pardon me, did you say Ms. Symington?"

"Why, yes," the clerk responded.

"Well that's me. I'm not sure what you were just saying...I came down to report that someone just entered my room while I was sleeping.

I thought it must be my roommate but when I turned around, no one was there...I thought it might be an intruder. I came to see about having my room key changed."

Connor and the clerk exchanged glances. "I think I can explain," Connor said. "It seems you and I were placed in the same room by a simple, unfortunately incorrect, assumption based on your name. By the way, I'm Connor Mackenzie, reporter from *Biologica*." He looked into a pair of amused, discerning eyes.

"Pleased to meet you," she replied, "Lou Symington, epidemiologist at CDC." With long cool fingers she gave him the kind of firm handshake, neither too short nor too long, his dad had taught him.

"It was me you heard come in," Connor continued, "and when I saw what was... uh...clearly a...uh...woman...lying on the bed I, uh... left, figuring there was a mistake. I was trying not to disturb you. I'm sorry if I scared you. The clerk and I have been trying to correct the situation."

Lou shook her head and smiled, "Well, I've never liked using my full name, Louise. Maybe I'll rethink that, at least when signing up for a roommate. So which one of us needs to move?"

She was interrupted by the sight of the porter coming to collect Connor's bag and motioning him outside. She turned to see the waiting cab and placed her hand on his arm, restraining him as he turned to go. "Oh no," she exclaimed. "They don't have any more rooms here?"

The clerk nodded sheepishly. Connor would just have soon let it slide. It was a pain to have to commute but he really didn't see any alternative. That was the first but certainly not the last time she surprised him; she barely skipped a beat before offering another option. "It's very nice of you to give up the room, but unnecessary. After all, it was my name that caused the problem. If anyone should leave, it should be me."

Before he could object she continued. "But let's be honest here. I don't really want to stay at another hotel any more than you do. The conference schedule is packed, and trying to get back and forth would be a real pain. I brought appropriate clothing for sharing the room in any case. There is no reason I can't share it with you." He thought perhaps his mouth might have been hanging open just a little at this point.

"That's not necessary..." Connor started.

"You're right, it's not necessary. It's just...the right thing to do." And Lou had ordered the astonished bell boy to cancel the cab and drop Mr. Mackenzie's bag. Which he did. Precipitously. The clerk and Connor exchanged glances once more and shrugged, bowing to the young woman's assertiveness and incontrovertible logic.

It was those discerning eyes he mused later; she had summed him up as trustworthy in fewer than five minutes. That she was right about him only moved her up in his estimation.

•   •   •

Malcolm closed the door after the last participant re-entered the board room. There was the clink of ice cubes hitting glass as a few people poured water from the Bavarian crystal pitchers placed every few feet along the polished walnut table.

"One million doses of H5N1 vaccine were manufactured last year," Bueller began, "and I am pleased to report that half of these were recently purchased by the WHO. Unfortunately, thus far only a single pharmaceutical manufacturer has been willing to pursue vaccine production. The problem of course is that private business does not want to commit capital without a market for the product. The obvious danger to that approach is that if we wait until we have identified a highly contagious strain as a 'market' it will be far too late to begin manufacture. Further, even though the current H5N1 vaccine has been shown to be effective in producing an antibody response we can expect viral drift to occur in avian flu just as it does with conventional flu. Avian vaccine produced this year may not be effective next year."

"WHO has increasingly been pressured to predict which of these avian viruses will turn into a pandemic strain. The ramifications of such an announcement would be protean. I assure you that the World Health Organization's mission remains directed toward any and all measures possible to reduce the threat of disease. However, we have been, and continue to be, reluctant to make such a prediction due to the inadequacy of the evidence and the extreme mutability of the organism. I must emphasize here that the experts both within the WHO and without are divided as to the wisdom of naming a likely avian strain.

But, I digress." The director paused to take a drink of water, and get his thoughts back on course.

"The international inventory of osmavir, the only drug known to alleviate symptoms of the flu, is a mere 20 million doses. Remember, osmavir is not an antibiotic; it will not cure influenza like penicillin will cure strep throat, but it does reduce symptoms and death rates in those who have already come down with avian flu. Therefore, prevention of the flu by vaccine is critical."

"To this point the WHO has supported, indeed has called for, stockpiling of H5N1 vaccine as part of, and I emphasize *part of*, its program to mitigate the avian influenza threat. We have also encouraged pharmaceutical companies to enter into vaccine production and research into advanced vaccines that might be produced within a few weeks instead of the current several months."

"I am happy to report success to you today in several areas. At least five companies are actively engaged in the development of rapid vaccine techniques." There were nods and murmurs from around the room. "Several nations are now ready to sign an agreement signifying their cooperation to pool resources in the event of an outbreak." Bueller looked pointedly at Farrington: the U. S. was not one of them. "The WHO has also achieved unprecedented cooperation from the countries of Southeast Asia in quarantining and culling infected populations."

"Very impressive Dr. Bueller."

The director smiled at the delegate. "Our member nations, health experts and corporate allies must all be thanked for their contributions, but there is much left to be done." Bueller rose from his chair and placed both hands on the table, leaning into his final comments. "Avian virus clearly demonstrates the ability to change quickly," he said, pointing with one finger over his shoulder to the new variants that still hovered on the screen behind him. "We must endeavor to be as adaptable as our foe."

"To that end, the WHO makes the following recommendations:
1. That production of several new vaccine types begin immediately.
2. That member nations support these vaccines by encouraging corporate commitment to production.
3. That expanded stockpiles of small quantities of all vaccine types be maintained in nations around the world.

4. That until adequate vaccine can be produced to protect the entire world population, member nations will donate vaccine, or money to purchase vaccine, to the WHO for use in under-served countries in epidemic-prone regions as needed.

5. That production of osmavir be increased to meet future world demand. Member nations are asked to contribute medication to a front line pandemic response, supervised by the WHO and aimed at reducing illness, death, and the spread of disease."

The director sat. "Now, who is with us?"

CHAPTER 5

GUANGZHOU, CHINA
January 7

It was nearly 10 p.m. in Guangzhou, almost 4 p.m. in Geneva. Lou had stayed at her office all evening waiting for the phone to ring, which it hadn't. She wasn't sure if she was more eager to hear the results of the WHO meeting or to speak with Connor, and the embarrassment of this thought kept her from calling him to check on the status of the board. In frustration at the passing time and her distance from the events in the boardroom, she had worked herself into a fit of indignation over the anemic manpower and resources she and Yong had talked about over breakfast. Unable to contain herself any longer she called Dr. Wataabe in Geneva, expecting to vent to his voice mail as he too would be wrapped up in board activity today. To her surprise, he answered his phone.

"Dr. Symington, my esteemed friend," he said in cultivated tones, recognizing her voice.

"Is the meeting over then?" she asked.

"No, the director wanted to keep WHO staff participation to a minimum today so as not to have the appearance of strong-arming the members toward the new policies. I was asked to sit out."

"Dr. Wataabe," she blurted, her anxiety causing her to dispense with further pleasantries. "It is imperative that we double the manpower assigned to Southeast Asia immediately. The mutations we're seeing in animals significantly increase the chance that human cases will follow." Her speech became more strident with each remark. "Viral surveillance is totally compromised by our current level of staffing.

I've got terrific field assistants but they cannot be everywhere at once. And we need to be everywhere. Investigating all the cases. We can't afford to be waiting for the reports to come in. We've been reduced to stamping out brush fires as they're called in. We need to be out in the countryside dogging leads on every sick villager in communities near the outbreaks." She drew a quick breath, refusing to be interrupted. "There are so many farmers in remote provinces throughout the region that haven't heard the news of bird flu, or don't understand the threat. I've been in jungles in Thailand, Dr. Wataabe, on farms in China, and the rivers in Cambodia talking with these people. Life is so hard and cheap there could be multiple deaths in these places and no one would find it unusual enough to report. We have to be pro-active or we are going to miss it." She finished abruptly, her anger resonating in the distance between them.

There was a long pause during which she had the time and sense to be a little embarrassed; Wataabe was a gentle spirit and was undoubtedly flustered by her rant. But she needed manpower. Now.

"You are right," he remarked finally, calmly. "I too have been considering this issue and have discussed hiring more field workers with the administration. How many do you need?"

Well, didn't that just beat all? She was prepared to do whatever battle it took to have her demands met. In a really self-righteous moment she had thought about threatening to quit. Now she was all indignant with nowhere to go. It was just like her kindly Kenyan friend to diffuse her anger by agreeing with her. Hindsight informed her she should have given the man a chance before bulldozing away. Ire was wasted energy on this gentle man. If he had disagreed with her completely he would not have as much as raised his voice.

"Eight. Two additional people based in Thailand and Vietnam, two additional in southern China and four floaters."

"Floaters?"

"Yes. They'll go where they're needed. I must have the flexibility to move these people at a moment's notice. We have to hunt the virus, be right on top of the outbreaks and follow the human trails while they're fresh, trying to uncover any trace of pandemic potential. I'll continue to use Guangzhou as my base but I'll be traveling more extensively as well, keeping my finger on the pulse of the outbreak."

"What about Cambodia and Laos?" he asked.

"Their health systems are not organized enough to support field workers. Our people stationed in Bangkok, Hanoi and Saigon will have much more success relying on the infrastructures in Thailand and Vietnam as a base. But they'll have clearance to move freely into Cambodia and Laos, also Indonesia, as needed. The floaters will support all of our operations in Southeast Asia, moving about as needed. Unfortunately we will still be hampered by the archaic transportation infrastructure in the region, but hiring indigenous workers will at least afford familiarity with the local systems."

"I have already been authorized to approve two additional workers for you," Wataabe replied, "and I will pull money out of my own budget immediately to fund two more. I will approach the director general with your request for another four staff members, and I will not rest until we have supplied them. I will also work toward augmenting the travel expense fund for your region as it sounds as though you will need it."

"Thank you." Lou replied, her volume and frustration waning with her friend's response. "Our efforts to detect a pandemic strain are only as good as our field support. All the WHO policy and public relations campaigns in the world will be meaningless if we don't address the deficiencies in the information tracking process. I feel guilty that I haven't been aggressive in seeking reinforcements sooner. The events of the past few months have suddenly mushroomed and I can't help but think we are desperately behind already."

"I assure you I will have approval of the additional people before you have had time to hire the rest," he said.

"I'm sorry for blowing up Dr. Wataabe. You didn't deserve that." Lou was grateful that Wataabe's background kept him firmly on the side of research and the investigative process. Fortunately Director Bueller was also decidedly in the scientific camp, but there were many administrators at Geneva headquarters who held great sway in resource management who were less supportive of the underlying scholarship of their beloved programs. If the science was poor, Lou knew poor policy would follow.

Thinking about policy refocused her on the original intent of her call. "By the way, any news from the board?"

"No, not yet. I did see Mr. Mackenzie in the lobby speaking with Malcolm during the recess. Apparently nothing imminent is expected as I found Mr. Mackenzie ...uh ...resting in a chair shortly thereafter."

Lou laughed, welcoming the lightened turn of the conversation. "Dr. Wataabe, there's no need to candy-coat it. You mean napping! I've never seen a man with such a penchant for a nap."

"I am not prepared to say whether he was napping. It may have been that the brightness of the snow outside caused him to momentarily close his eyes as I was passing. Possibly he was deep in concentration, contemplating the salient features of the article he is composing. Perhaps he saw me coming and feigned sleep so as to avoid conversation with a tedious old man." Now they were both chuckling at the doctor's self-effacing tact, and the mental picture of Connor sleeping, probably with his mouth hanging open, in the plush lobby of WHO headquarters.

"I'll be sure to inquire about his level of concentration when I talk to him! Old man indeed! You are the most well-preserved specimen I've ever seen." While she was finishing with Dr. Wataabe, Lou's field coordinator, Yong, appeared in her doorway holding a piece of paper. She waved him in to have a seat. He was dedicated she thought, keeping the same crazy hours as she was.

"Just the person I was looking for!" she said as she snapped her cell shut. "Yong, I want you to hire two more people immediately. They'll be covering an area stretching from Hunan Province to Shanghai, so make sure they can handle the local languages."

"So soon? You're a miracle worker," he replied in impeccable English. Yong's grammar was better than most Americans and Lou was tremendously grateful for this skill, in addition to his ability to get to the bottom of a Chinese story. Each case report in the provinces inevitably followed a circuitous path, the Chinese tending to start any account at the beginning of the first dynasty, about three thousand years ago. It took a fair amount of patience and finesse to wind through a tale and get to the facts. It was one of the reasons she had insisted on using local talent and not importing her investigators.

"We're approved for four people Yong. I'm putting two here and two in Vietnam."

"That's great Dr. Lou. I'll get right on it." Yong stood up to leave, then smacked his forehead with his palm in the universal gesture for stupidity. "I nearly forgot." He reached out and handed her the paper he had walked in with. "This just came over the fax."

Local authorities report death of a woman in Duyen Ba. Symptoms suspicious for bird flu. Please advise. Binh

Lou popped her phone back open and called Binh, her station chief in Saigon. She didn't bother to identify herself. "What do we know about Duyen Ba?"

"Local authorities notified us this morning that a woman died there this week."

"Do we have a body?"

"Yes, for a change. They buried her in the village."

"That's lucky." Lou breathed. Cremation was common. "Do we know how long she was ill, what her symptoms were?"

"She had a cough. Otherwise, the details are sketchy."

"Do we know if it was the same village with the H5N1 poultry kill?"

"We do. It was."

"I'll get a flight first thing in the morning. How long will it take us to get down there?"

"A few hours. Depends on whether it rains. It's still the dry season, but you know that's just a comparative term in Vietnam. It still rains. Just can't predict. By the way, I know you usually like to ride a scooter but those tracks deep in the delta are just too bad to navigate if it pours, so we're taking my car. It's got four wheel drive and heavy duty tires."

"Fine, have it loaded and pick me up at the airport. I want to get down there as fast as we can. By the way, where are we staying?" asked Lou.

"Well, that depends. If we wrap up by late afternoon we can make it back to the main roads before dark and drive back to the city where your usual room at the Rex will be waiting."

"And what if we don't finish before then?"

"I will pack us a very nice, water-proof tent."

"Great."

SWITZERLAND
January 7

It was almost 6 o'clock before the participants emerged en masse from the boardroom at WHO headquarters. Connor had been repeatedly disappointed when a door had opened and only one person at a time exited, mostly to use the restroom, or occasionally as the afternoon wore on, to make a phone call. Each had returned. The thick walls masked all conversation. He might just as easily make out the sound of the snow flakes falling outside as anything he could hear emanating from inside the confines of the other room. He had at one point fallen asleep in the stillness.

Connor rose now and tried to gauge the outcome of the meeting from the looks on the faces of those issuing from the room but he found them inscrutable. A couple other reporters had shown up just before the usual closing time of the WHO offices, expecting to pick up a press release on the board's actions. They too moved toward the open door of the room, encountering the secretary who was motioning all of them in. Director Bueller was seated at the other end of the long table.

"Ladies and gentlemen, the executive committee of the World Health Organization met today to discuss the WHO's policies for containment, prevention and management of avian influenza. Particularly of concern are the patterns of increasing geographic distribution of avian fatalities, the concomitant emergence of new viral strains and the increasing reports of infection in humans. After exhaustive discussion," Connor noted the director's mien certainly reflected this, "the members have voted to table the policy recommendations of the WHO." Connor looked up sharply; this was not a good sign. "The issues are complex and the majority of members voiced a need to consult with their own health and government authorities before voting. Thank you. That is all." Bueller closed his laptop and stood.

"Excuse me, Dr. Bueller, is there a plan to reconvene any sooner than next month's scheduled meeting?"

"No Mr. Mackenzie," he replied sighing, "There is not. The members felt they needed ample time for consultation. We will meet in one month as scheduled."

"Will the WHO be releasing a statement of the policies proposed to the members today?"

"No. The organization believes it would be premature and perhaps counterproductive to do so."

"Thank you Dr. Bueller." Connor translated this last remark to mean that the director was not yet ready to use high pressure media exposure to arm wrestle the members into agreement. Prudent. It was a technique he could always employ later if needed.

Connor waited for the director to leave and the other reporters to filter out. Malcolm was collecting his papers and logging off his laptop. It had been a long day for him too.

"Surprised?" He asked Malcolm.

"Not particularly."

"Disappointed?"

"Most definitely." Malcolm had finished gathering his things and looked at Connor, shaking his head. "Why is it that the more urgently action is called for, the more we can rely on those who have power to shrink from it?"

They were both silent. There was no answer.

• • •

Michael Farrington exited the cab in front of his hotel on the banks of Lake Geneva and inhaled the crisp winter air. The snow had stopped and a crescent moon was rising in a clear sky not yet dark enough for the stars to pop out over the Alps in the distance. The valet welcomed him, bowing in a Swiss flourish of hospitality, but Farrington declined the open door and instead buttoned his wool topcoat and bundled his scarf, crossing the street to the pristine park that framed this part of the lake. A stroll along the wide promenade in the gathering twilight would do him good.

The policy changes suggested by the director had taken him, and he thought probably all the participants, by surprise. As he thought about it, the new recommendations made as much sense or more than the old, but they were decidedly a departure from the conventional thinking. He was still struggling to get his government to sign on to the previous recommendations to stockpile H5N1 vaccine and osmavir, and to donate both to the WHO for likely use in Indochina; he was dubious about his chances of success with the different approach outlined today.

The request for international support implied a significant financial commitment from the countries involved and it extended well beyond the discrete price of the vaccines and medications to be stockpiled. Inherent in the policy was the cost of research and development to produce vaccine faster, incentivizing private labs and subsidizing the creation of publicly held labs to make vaccine, contracting for the purchase of vaccine, absorbing the cost of expired vaccine, and in places like the U.S., covering the cost of litigation due to unanticipated side effects of receiving the vaccine.

Farrington paused to admire the giant flower clock as he strolled past, planted with evergreens and still functioning, its moving hands boasted, even in the winter. He dusted the snow off a bench with a view of the Jet D'eau, the tallest fountain in the world, flinging the crystal water of lake Geneva periodically nearly 500 feet in the air, and sat down to consider the extraordinary stakes. A problem of this nature had never been before the world community. While plagues had decimated populations and were often cited as changing the course of history itself, the modern day difference was that scientific advances had made it possible to know the enemy, had made it tantalizing to predict the threat, and had thrown down the gauntlet by challenging society to prevent it. Could it be done? No one knew. Humankind was the guinea pig. No consent necessary. Your presence on the planet confirmed your participation in a massive biological experiment.

Farrington wondered, not for the first time, if it was foolish to think we could avert disaster with our science and technology. From what he could discern from the all the evidence: fossils, geology, archeology, the current fever over global warming and over-population, water crises, severe weather trends: Mother Nature was a model of balance, the ultimate arbiter of excess. But this was not balance in the sense of equilibrium or placidity, but balance in the sense of things evening out over time. Natural phenomena were frequently cataclysmic in character and eons in duration. Wide swings in climate could be traced through the millennia, with periods of extreme heat being followed by prolonged ice ages. Continents collided, drifted and collided again. Ancient seas became modern prairies, and mountains were found at the bottom of deep ocean trenches. Entire populations of living creatures flourished then vanished, leaving only their remnants to the future. No, Mother Nature was no tranquil sea: she was an average of all her violence, a screaming roller-coaster ride of upheaval.

What of this virus then, he wondered? It had survived the challenges of earth far longer than mankind. In Earth's time-line of existence, Homo sapiens had been present for only the last micro-second of the history of the planet. Were we as a species kidding ourselves that we were here to stay? Did our superior intelligence qualify us as a suitable contestant in a battle with primeval organisms honed to perfection by virtue of their endurance through the ages? Was our complexity less an asset than a strike against us when pitted against simple creatures that had been around for millions or billions of years? Did the survival of the human race indeed depend on the existence and the favoritism of God?

Farrington had by now stood up again and circled the park along Lake Geneva twice to remain outdoors while he pondered these questions. The profusion of balconies along the wide boulevard facing the park were aglow with the comforts of evening as he wound his way back to the hotel. The air was not cold and he was thoroughly enjoying the snow glistening on rooftops and sidewalks in the soft light of the street lamps. Passersby smiled and nodded in complicit delight at the Geneva cityscape enfolded by the recently fallen flakes. Farrington had been criticized by more than one person in his past for being too contemplative. He could just as easily have suggested that a bit more contemplation would be useful for society in general and his critics in particular. The valet held the door open once more as he arrived at the hotel. Farrington caught the elevator and went to his room ready to call Cyril Hunt.

GUANGZHOU, CHINA
January 7

Lou spent the next few hours after her phone call to Wataabe restoring some order to the piles on her desk, grabbing the reports she wanted to take with her to Vietnam as well as a few of the recent

VIRION

scientific journals she hadn't had a chance to look at yet. Even if she didn't get back to the hotel the first night (and she fervently hoped she would, not being overly fond of the idea of spending a rainy night in a tent with or without her Saigon chief), there would likely be some time in her room on subsequent evenings to review articles and catch up on the research. She tossed her phone into her back pack and gathered her laptop and its paraphernalia.

She was loading up a small black vinyl case with test tubes, swabs and formaldehyde to collect samples when her cell rang. She recognized the number immediately as Connor's.

"Hi there," she said, a little breathless. "Long day?" She glanced at the wall clock: it was after midnight.

"Hi Lou," he replied, a smile clearly framing his voice. "Yeah. And without much to show for it." Lou thought he sounded pretty happy despite his complaint. Or was she inventing that?

"What's the official word?" she asked, trying to move beyond her girlish musings to something more significant, like her life's work.

"There is no official word. The members voted to table."

"Great." Sarcasm was the best response she could conjure. It was a discouraging, but not unexpected, outcome. Lou had been a guest at previous meetings. She knew how reluctant the members were to go out on anything remotely resembling a limb. Even, or perhaps especially, under dire circumstances they required consultation with their handlers, the people in power back home, wherever home happened to be. It might be months before they could get meaningful action. Considering that the biological experts themselves were having difficulty reaching consensus, it was not unreasonable to think the board members might also be. She just wished the political process could keep up with the viral.

"Not much of a story then?" she asked.

"Nope. It's already finished. I wrote most of the background while I was waiting. Turns out there were no guts to insert. Looks like I should have brought my skis," he said. "The snow looks terrific. What's it like there?"

"Chilly. Rainy. But I'm headed down to Saigon tomorrow where I understand it's warm. And possibly rainy. Common theme this time of year. I live in my slicker."

68

Connor suddenly lost himself in visions of Lou. He could picture her in her slicker: bright yellow, like the Morton salt girl's, with a hood. He'd seen her wearing it before. He could picture her in ski-wear too, and a bikini, even though he hadn't seen her in either of those particular get-ups. Back when they'd met they were both in other relationships. It was too bad because staying together for a week at the conference was the most time he'd gotten to spend with her and neither one of them had been free to explore the possibilities.

Though the arrangement was unconventional they'd had an enjoyable time as roommates. He found a great deal of amusement in their attempts to rise above the gender differences, both of them pretending that they were just sharing a room with a stranger as usual. Connor didn't know how most women acted but guys certainly didn't turn on the water to hide the sound of them peeing, or worry about what the bathroom smelled like when they came out. They didn't ask if it was okay if they kept the light on while they read for a while late at night or talk about who was going to use the bathroom first or who might shower when. For his part, he didn't drop his clothes on the floor, leave the toilet seat up or the bath mat down, he didn't leave his wet towel on the counter, and he tried not to snore, though he couldn't be sure of his success at that one.

Lou, he noticed, was an interesting study in contrasts. While he was doing his best to keep his half of the room tidy, at great expense to his manhood, she had clothing, shoes, tote bags, newspapers, journals and conference schedules flung about her space, some of it encroaching on his. But there was nothing disordered or disheveled about her personal appearance, and she was low-maintenance to boot; he'd never seen a woman spend so little time in the bathroom. Connor was relieved when Lou suggested he use the bathroom first in the morning, if Lou was anything like his girlfriend. But after he had showered and shaved and turned the facility over to her, he had flipped on the TV thinking he had all the time in the world to dress. She had come out of the bathroom in no time, looking fabulous, and caught him half-clothed. He didn't squander his time after that.

Each of them was busy with responsibilities that week in Paris, but they did find out they shared some common interests. Both loved to read, she favored non-fiction, he loved a good page-turner. They also discovered they enjoyed a variety of ethnic foods, movies that made them laugh, and skiing, snow for him, water for her. It had been a great week they agreed, as they parted company and exchanged e-mail addresses on the last day.

After that they had crossed paths periodically at meetings and with interviews on his international beat. Connor and his girlfriend split up sometime later and he found himself making up excuses to phone Lou. He found out through a few investigative calls of his own (what kind of reporter would he be if he couldn't tap into strategic sources for information?) that she was likewise free of her former commitment. They'd had lunch and dinner a couple of times in the last few years when he'd been traveling on assignment, ostensibly to discuss WHO issues, and recently they had been exchanging e-mails frequently, phone calls too. He hoped that soon they might get around to doing more than discussing biology together.

If Connor had known Lou felt the same way he certainly would have made an overture already, but she was pretty unreadable and intimidating. Always in control. A clear thinker and a woman who appeared to know what she wanted. He wondered if she wanted him. She'd probably say so if she did. That straightforward. Did he want to wait for that? Would she be offended if he got into her space by asking her out on a real date? He was not used to such self-doubt. He usually just said what was on his mind, took his lumps if that was the way of it, and moved on. Didn't suffer much from regret. What to do with this woman? And how in the hell to have a relationship with her in China and him living now in L.A.?

"Connor?"

Ooops. Pay attention Connor. How long had she been talking while he spaced out? "Sorry, lost you there for a minute," he said. "What are you doing in Saigon?"

"I was going because I wanted to investigate the H3N3 in the roosters myself. Before I even had a chance to pack for that trip we got a faxed report on a woman's death in Duyen Ba, the village that had the poultry kill a couple weeks ago. So I'm actually going to start there instead."

"Any details?" he asked.

"No, other than she had a cough." Lou said. "Hey, your voice just changed. You sounded just like a reporter there. Is all this off the record?" she teased.

"Really Lou, you offend me," he said with feigned indignation. "It's all off the record unless I call you as a journalist."

She laughed, "Well, if you're not calling me as a journalist, what are you calling me as?"

"A friend." *Oh my God*, he thought, *how lame was that?* "More than that," he continued staunchly, "A good friend." *Perfect. Lame times two equals twice as lame.*

Lou couldn't help it, she laughed again, listening to this man who strung together written words for a living tripping over the threads of a conversation. *I think he likes me,* she thought, then immediately felt a little sorry for him. She was difficult without intending to be, her assertiveness and self-confidence had a history of steam-rolling people, particularly the previous men in her life. If he was interested in her Connor would have to prove himself her equal. She wouldn't waste any time worrying if he had enough wherewithal to be half of a couple: she'd already spent too much time being concerned about how her intellect or mannerisms might bruise the egos of the men she'd dated. Lou was smart and direct, and had become over time decidedly unapologetic about either. There would be no more patching up of a partner unable to meet her on the strength of his own character.

A different man came through the receiver, interrupting her thoughts.

"What the hell Lou. I'm tired of beating around the bush. I like you and I'd like to go out with you. If that sounds too abrupt, if you're not interested, just tell me and I'll revert to my usual journalistic professionalism."

"Uh...give me a minute to think about that." He'd caught her off guard, came up to speed far faster than she anticipated. She thought there would be a lot more hemming and hawing before he got around, if ever, to asking her out. This was a new experience she thought, her curiosity piqued.

"Okay. I thought about it."

"And?"

"I'm interested."

Neither one could see, but they were both smiling.

Connor didn't even put the phone down. As soon as he disconnected he called and booked a flight to Saigon.

CHAPTER 6

CALIFORNIA
January 7

Ken eased his car to the curb in front of Betsy's house after he noted her minivan was parked in the driveway. He hadn't had time to fully extricate himself from the car before Moira came bounding out the front door to greet him.

"Granddad!" she exclaimed as she ran across the lawn, colliding with an overly large dog that belonged to them and appeared just as eager to see Ken as Moira was. As Ken came around the car he managed to angle out of the way of the mutt's intrusive welcome and sweep his granddaughter into his arms in one almost graceful motion.

"Sam! Sam! Get in here!" Betsy shouted good naturedly from the front door seeing the dog rounding a wide turn and advancing at full gallop for another go at Ken, whom she knew didn't appreciate Sam's charm. In a handful of great strides Sam took it all in and decided to opt for the circle-the-yard-until-I'm-tired routine rather that the knock-the-man-over act, thereby avoiding the mistress-sends-me-to-the-basement-until-after-supper consequence.

Ken never did understand why Betsy and Jake had to get a dog at all, let alone something as enormous as Sam. And slobbery. My God, the germs. Most of the microbes in the dog's mouth had not even been named yet. He had never allowed Betsy to have a pet when she was growing up for that reason: it was hard enough staying healthy without animals in the house. The dog was winding down in ever smaller circles as Ken and Moira walked up the yard. Betsy was holding the door open and leaning out to embrace Ken when Sam pushed his way around and in, giving Ken's right hand and sleeve a hearty lick with his great wet tongue as he passed.

"Sorry Dad," Betsy offered, shooing the offending dog off to the basement he had so conscientiously tried to avoid. As Sam was sent off to contemplate the depth and breadth of his doggie transgressions, Moira, stifling a giggle, took Ken's slimy hand and led him to the bathroom to wash up.

"Dad, can I get you anything?" Betsy asked as the two reappeared in the kitchen.

"No, thanks. Your mom will be expecting me home for dinner shortly. I just wanted to see how my little Fathead..." Betsy looked up sharply "...Oops...I mean how...Princess Moira the Brilliant and Beautiful...spent her day," he corrected himself with a wink at the named, grinning royalty.

"You know Dad, you can scar children for life with name-calling."

"Well, she hardly looks scarred Betsy. And it isn't name-calling. It's a complement. This little girl's head is loaded with highly active brain cells," Ken replied with a fond glance at Moira who was taking all of this in with interest, tilting her head toward each adult as they spoke.

"What if the other kids start calling her fat?"

"Well, she's not fat, so what does it matter?" Ken replied testily. "It's what *she* believes that's important. Anyway, I've never used that nickname in front of her friends Betsy, as I promised you I wouldn't the last time we had this conversation. Teach the child to stand on her own and nothing anyone else says will matter to her." Even before he finished the sentence he was aware he had unintentionally nettled Betsy, who still nurtured some defensiveness borne of the hurt of never being good enough to suit him. Ken tried to attenuate the sting of his remarks by changing the subject.

"Moira, would you like to do something with your old granddad this weekend? I thought maybe we could plan an adventure that would give your mom and dad a day off on Sunday." At this Ken looked at Betsy, his eyes expressing the regret his lips could not.

"Yes! Yes! Mommy, please?" Moira implored.

"Of course sweetie. You will need to make sure your homework is done before you leave. I can't count on your grandfather to get you back here much before bedtime," she said with gentle reproach. Ken immediately recognized and appreciated Betsy's kindliness; it was apparent she had already recovered and forgiven him for this latest wound. He hoped his belated recognition of the sins of the past and his current devotion to Moira would help to heal Betsy's needy heart over time.

Before he had time to respond, he was interrupted by Moira who had another thought that evidently required immediate expression. "Wait, wait! Grandpa, come and see!" And with that she grabbed his hand and led him running to the stairs. Bouncing ahead of him Moira coaxed Ken up, making a beeline for her room when she got to the top. By the time he entered she was proudly holding forth in one hand, for his examination, a turtle about the size of a pocket watch. Its head and legs were completely retracted, no doubt from the surprise of her precipitous intrusion into its turtle-dom.

Oh my God Ken thought, trying to hide his disapproval. "Another pet," he said out loud, forcing some enthusiasm into his voice. It took him a moment to recall what he had read in one of his journals; yes, now he remembered: salmonella bacteria had been found in turtles sold at pet stores. CDC had published a report on the risk a few months ago. Salmonella, for the children of America to take home and incubate. "Now Moira, you know you must wash your hands every time you touch your turtle," he admonished.

"His name is Clyde. And I have stuff right here that Mom got me Granddad," she said proudly, pointing to a pump bottle of anti-bacterial, water-free scrub next to the turtle's terrarium. "I had to promise to clean up after I played with Clyde or Mom wouldn't let me keep him." By now Clyde had poked his head out and was tickling Moira's palm with his tiny feet, working toward crawling off her fingertips. She put one hand in front of the other watching him crawl and peering all around and under him with the curiosity only a child can muster for a turtle.

After a suitable amount of time spent turtle-gazing, Ken navigated Moira through a thorough hand-washing with soap and water, and a squirt of the pump after that for good measure. "But Grandpa, you didn't need to wash," Moira pointedly observed as she took his freshly scrubbed hand and led him back downstairs. "You never touched him."

Back in the kitchen he and Betsy set about planning for Sunday. Ken would be driving to San Francisco for a board meeting of PharmaGlobal on Friday. He usually caught a flight out of the city after these quarterly meetings to visit his mother who was living out her days with Alzheimer's disease at a nursing home in Oregon. As was his custom now that she had no significant cognitive function left, he would dutifully stay by his mother's bedside all day on Saturday, and return home Saturday night. He always tried to plan something pleasant to look forward to the next day as the entire encounter was utterly demoralizing. This Sunday would be spent with Moira, and June if she wanted to accompany them. He could only hope his granddaughter wouldn't choose the zoo.

Moira piped up amid the adults' planning, "Granddad, can my friend Lucy come with us?"

"Moira, maybe that's not a good idea," Betsy interjected.

Ken tilted his head at Betsy. "I don't mind, Betsy. Lucy's a nice girl, whatever we do they'll have fun together."

"It's not that Dad. I just...um...I wasn't sure what to do actually..." Betsy paused, considering how to proceed. "Moira honey, go downstairs and check on Sam."

"Mom," Moira replied, feigning irritation as she headed for the basement, "If you don't want me to listen, just say so."

"What is it Betsy?" Ken asked when the door was closed.

"Well, I've been meaning to ask you how you felt about this. I've been putting Moira off for a few days about seeing Lucy because she and her family just got back from a trip to China. I know that's where some of the bird flu outbreaks have been. I wasn't sure if there was a risk of them bringing anything back with them."

"When did they get back?" Ken asked.

"Almost two weeks ago."

"Well then there's no problem with her playing with Lucy. There have been avian cases in China, but the number of human cases so far is minute. Most are animals spreading it to humans, and unlikely to be any risk for a family visiting the city, unless they spent their time in the poultry markets. Highly unlikely I would think. Plus, the illness appears to have an infection period similar to our usual flu, somewhere between two days and two weeks."

"So if they've been back for two weeks and no one is sick, I don't need to worry?" Betsy asked.

"Well, not about Lucy and her family," Ken responded. "But Betsy, the fact is all of northern California could be exposed tomorrow to a virus whose structure and very existence can only be predicted today in the broadest sense. These viruses mingle in other animals that birds encounter even more than humans: pigs, cats, mice, just to name a few. All this mixing between different species in the wild will eventually cause avian flu to mutate to a form that will be easily transmitted to humans. But we have no idea what that virus will look like, or when, or where it will hit."

Ken thought for a moment and said, "It's like trying to predict the next earthquake out here. We know that California sits on several major fault lines. Geologists can analyze historical data and note that a major quake occurs an average of every seventy years, but they can't predict whether the next one will hit in two years or a hundred and two. And they can't tell us which fault line will rupture, or how hard. But that doesn't mean they aren't working very hard to develop the technology that will allow their predictions to be more accurate."

Ken continued with conviction, warming to the topic he knew so well, pleased to have Betsy's attention. "That's what *I'm* doing with my research, trying to *anticipate* the development of the virus faster than the virus can actually develop. It's always a gamble, but an informed gamble. Man has an advantage over the germs because man can think; viruses are just tiny specks of protein, hardly even alive really. Our goal is to try to out-maneuver them. It's not only possible, it's been done, is still being done."

"Look at the smallpox virus for example," he said animatedly. "Because of medical research, it has been eliminated. It no longer exists in the wild. The only threat of smallpox to mankind anymore is from man himself. Vials of smallpox have been stored by labs for purposes of scientific posterity. The only way the disease could spread across the globe again is if some lunatic stole a vial and willfully released it."

Ken paused, satisfied; it always pleased him to talk about his work. Betsy smiled and sighed tiredly and Ken realized he'd probably given her more of an answer than she was looking for.

Moira took advantage of the lull in conversation to poke her head around the basement door, "Can Sam come up now? He's sorry." She looked behind her at the dog as if to confirm his sentiments. "Can I come back too?"

Ken glanced at Betsy who said, "Sure. Just keep Sam out of Granddad's way." Moira took her cue and sat quietly at the kitchen table while Sam, appearing contrite, slinked off to another room.

Ken went to the cupboard and pulled out a glass, filling it with water from the filtered tap. "Did you know that bird flu has been identified in flocks migrating throughout North America, including California's coastline?"

"You're kidding?" Betsy said, her voice thin with anxiety.

"No, of course I'm not kidding." Ken replied. "The virus here has not killed any birds, and has caused only eye infections in people who worked with the birds." He flapped his hands dismissively. "No one hears about these reports because they're considered veterinary oddities. And at best that's all they are. But at worst, any of the avian viruses, including those in North America, have the potential to mutate to a pandemic form. The avian flu epidemic currently *appears* to be arising in Southeast Asia, but it might just as easily start right here."

His words settled hard on Betsy. Fear had been creeping into her little by little as she read the reports of disease and death from avian flu, as she talked with her mother and friends about it, and watched grief-stricken relatives of bird flu victims on television. She looked at Moira, settled innocently in a shaft of sunlight on the kitchen chair, and wondered how she could survive if anything ever happened to her only child.

Betsy had grown up in the slightly paranoid Culp household, Ken always pointing out the invisible germs on ordinary surfaces. Over time she had grown rather complacent about the microcosm of viruses and bacteria, molds and mildews, because nothing dreadful had ever happened to her despite the repeated caveats of her father, the virologist. Of course she'd had the regular 'flu' before, knew the misery of the cough, fever and muscle aches in the years she'd forgotten to get her flu shot as Ken admonished each fall; nothing much to do for it but pain relievers and rest. But unless you were very old or very young, you just got sick for a couple weeks and then you got better. But bird flu was different: it was deadly, killing young, healthy people. And it scared her.

Betsy mulled these thoughts as Ken drank his water and washed his glass, then checked her fears for Moira's sake. "Well Dad, if it's us against the virus, then I'm glad you're leading the fight. I'm so proud of you." And Betsy walked across the kitchen and gave her father a hug.

CALIFORNIA
January 8

From his desk at PharmaGlobal's headquarters in downtown San Francisco, J.B. Vaughn commanded an expansive view of the Golden Gate Bridge and the bay. At the moment, he was contemplating the broad vista that stretched before him and thinking it a fitting reflection of the business he had strived to build. Still a relatively young man, (some day he was sure he would look back on his current age and think so), he had already made his mark in the cutthroat pharmaceutical industry as a CEO of considerable skill. The wealth he had acquired along the way solidified his impression of himself as a man among men.

"Mr. Vaughn, the members are in their seats," his secretary announced promptly at nine o'clock. Good. He liked to start on time. Vaughn closed the folder containing the company's production reports on traditional flu, pneumonia and Avimmune, the new vaccine against H5N1, and smiled as he walked down the hall to the board room: the timing couldn't have been better. Avian flu was all over the news with the Geneva WHO conference in the papers this morning, and his scientific expert was in the limelight for his achievements. Vaughn had already decided the outcome of today's discussion; making sure the committee arrived at the same conclusions had just gotten easier.

"Good morning. Good to see all of you," he boomed as he strode in. His secretary followed behind setting a mug of black coffee in front of him. His eyes swept the conference table, and he noted with satisfaction that no one was absent. With a barely perceptible nod from Vaughn his assistant retrieved a large carefully wrapped box from a table in the corner and placed it in front of him.

"I'd like to begin by congratulating our own Kenneth Culp on his being named this year's International Pritzker Fellow." Polite applause ensued from the dozen or so people in the room along with murmurs of approval. "In recognition of this tremendous honor I would like to present you with a small token of our respect and appreciation here at PharmaGlobal."

Ken stood and walked toward the head of the table shaking the outstretched hands that were offered on the way, appearing both proud and embarrassed. Attention was something he craved in the abstract but had a difficult time managing in reality. His work deserved to be noticed, but it was always so awkward to acknowledge. He rather slouched and nodded as he took the package from Vaughn, his hands dipping momentarily as he felt the burden of it, wrapped in sleek black paper with a plain silver ribbon. Vaughn, now with a free hand, gave him a congratulatory slap on the back. Ken glanced up at him making the briefest of eye contact, nodding further and glancing uncomfortably at him and the other members who were now applauding again. The corners of his mouth occasionally twitched as though he might break into a smile, but he didn't. Couldn't really. Didn't know how to enjoy the moment, no matter how much he thought he deserved it.

He walked back to his place toting the box, almost two feet tall and inordinately heavy for its size. Vaughn insisted he open it immediately. Easing the ribbon off, he carefully slid his finger under the taped edge of the wrapping without tearing the paper. He lifted the sturdy cardboard lid and cautiously extracted the bubble-packed object revealing a spectacular, hand cut, leaded crystal globe etched in clean beveled lines with longitudes and latitudes, the continents standing out in sharp relief and the whole sphere resting in the palms of two outstretched hands: an artist's striking rendition of the PharmaGlobal logo. Across the base, carved into frosted glass, was the company's motto: *The world is in our hands.*

Ken was not particularly a fan of art or knick knacks, but he was completely struck by the elegance and crafting of this piece. It was perhaps more beautiful, certainly it was more substantial, even than the Pritzker which had seemed to him of respectable heft itself. "Thank you." He murmured. And, "Thank you," again, not quite sure where to look, or what else to say.

As Ken rewrapped the gift and replaced it in its box, Vaughn noted with satisfaction that Ken seemed suitably impressed by the gesture. In fact he appeared to be nearly overwhelmed at the moment. That suited Vaughn just fine, "Let's move on to our discussion of influenza production lines."

"Currently, we the only makers of bird flu vaccine, also known as H5N1, which we have patented as Avimmune. Thus far we have engaged in limited manufacture of the vaccine because there has been limited demand. Governments have been supportive of the concept of prevention but loath to fund it. We have been able to sell all of our small stock of Avimmune to this point, but that alone is not sufficient sales to make this venture profitable. Quite frankly our investment has been a loss to date. But not one that was unexpected," he hastily added. It had been a risky decision, but Ken's arguments had convinced him that pre-emptive production of vaccine was a sound move. After all, it had a two year shelf life. As long as they continued with human influenza and pneumococcal vaccine at their main production lines while they developed Avimmune in the research facility, they had only the cost of materials to lose. And eggs were cheap. They were setting themselves up to be indispensable.

Vaughn continued, "Recalling our conversation at this table a year ago, if avian influenza is indeed a threat to the human population then it is also an opportunity for our company, indeed any company. Fortunately no one else has shown interest yet in this marginally promising venture. But, my friends," he said, willfully engaging each person with a direct look, "our monopoly will not last forever. Others will eventually patent their own versions of H5N1 vaccine."

"Avian flu has been increasing in both birds and humans. The press has begun to whip the public into hysteria, perhaps justified, perhaps not, over the possibility of pandemic. Governments are paying attention to the threat, real or perceived. The potential for large exclusive contracts to produce H5N1 vaccine is here and will last only until other companies can gear up for the sizable profit to be made. It is a window of opportunity I do not believe we can afford to miss." Vaughn had snared the attention of the business leaders with these comments. Now he threw out a hook to those in the group who favored an altruistic view of the company, "PharmaGlobal has been a world leader in saving lives with traditional influenza vaccine production; it is time for us to step up to the plate with avian."

"How much Avimmune have we produced?" asked a member.

"Fewer than ten thousand doses on our first attempt because the virus was so deadly it killed the eggs we were growing it in. We had to re-engineer the process repeatedly until we obtained a reliable yield." In fact they had experimented with the manufacture of H5N1 vaccine for almost two years in their small research plant before they'd been successful. The hurdles had nearly sacked the whole project, but they had finally not only created the vaccine but determined that the required new techniques could be transferred from the small research facility to the company's larger plant. Unfortunately the equipment would need to be substantially modified, entailing a significant expenditure of time and money. Nevertheless Vaughn was satisfied that with the infusion of PharmaGlobal's capital reserves, the company was capable of proceeding with full scale production of avian vaccine at any time.

"None of that first vaccine was sold but we did use it for testing to prove it stimulated a protective antibody response in people. Those really were our only goals at first: to successfully create the process and to prove that the product was effective. Mission accomplished." Vaughn paused to sip his coffee. "Last year we produced one million doses."

"What's the plan for this year?"

"Well now, that is a question," Vaughn replied, "and one on which I need your input." His board members had large enough egos that they didn't like being led to a pre-determined conclusion. Vaughn sought skilled advisors on his committee so he could tap into their brain power when necessary; finessing a rubber stamp of his strategy out of the same people was sometimes a challenge, but not insurmountable. If they didn't agree he could ram things through anyway, but that practice didn't go over well with the stockholders.

"We have been using our small research and development plant for Avimmune. One million doses are close to our maximum if we confine ourselves to that set-up. But if we were to replace traditional flu vaccine production at our main manufacturing complex with Avimmune we could make up to *sixty million* doses this year and still have time to switch back to one cycle of traditional flu shots after that for flu season." He saw a couple of mouths drop. He'd gotten their attention alright: generate bird vaccine to capture a monopoly market's worth of new profit, and protect the basic profit with a batch of the standard flu vaccine. It was not the first time he'd succeeded by taking this company into creative waters, and they knew it.

PharmaGlobal had been in the vaccine business for years, originally producing immunizations for several different childhood diseases, diphtheria, whooping cough, tetanus, polio, measles, mumps and rubella, as well as influenza. The company had suffered through downturns in the market when public panic about the safety of vaccines had not only reduced demand, but also increased litigation. Several pharmaceutical companies had dropped production altogether in the face of substantial jury awards for product liability.

Twenty years ago at the nadir of the company's performance, Vaughn was a neophyte CEO flush with confidence and swagger from his recent Ivy League MBA. He had, to everyone's surprise and the shareholders' delight, navigated PharmaGlobal through those rocky times while maintaining vaccine production. What he *had* done to mitigate the damage was to narrow the breadth of vaccine production. Instead of producing limited quantities of multiple vaccines he had steered the company into manufacture of just two lines, influenza and pneumonia. The economies of scale had helped the company stay afloat, and the rewards for persisting were substantial: after most of the drug companies stopped all vaccine production there was very little competition left. Suddenly PharmaGlobal was able to sell all of its stock of vaccine. Every year. Flu shot shortages, and years in which flu outbreaks were severe, could always be counted on to improve the following year's sales. Business had been great.

The main facility was capable of manufacturing 40 to 60 million doses of immunization every four to six months. Typically, pneumonia was made in the winter and traditional flu shots in the summer and occasionally fall, if the demand warranted. Full capacity was 120 million total shots per year in two to three separate batches, created on the same equipment at a large complex outside of San Francisco. When he had changed the output of the business from multiple vaccines to only two, the major operational consideration was whether the two vaccines were amenable to production on the same equipment and whether it was feasible to switch production back and forth between them. The answer had been yes in both regards. His team had designed the equipment and the process so they were specifically tailored to making only influenza and pneumonia immunizations. The profits PharmaGlobal had reaped since were largely due to his stroke of genius in producing both vaccines on one assembly line. It had saved on every aspect of overhead, from building space, to equipment, to utilities, to labor.

It was now January and the annual manufacture of the human influenza line was over for the season. PharmaGlobal would usually turn its production over to pneumonia at this point, having just enough time to get one complete cycle of pneumonia vaccine completed before returning to influenza production in May or June. If they began the manufacture of Avimmune now that would mean there would be no pneumococcal production this year. There had been shortages of pneumonia immunizations in the past, but the international inventory had been strong the past few years and there were other suppliers besides PharmaGlobal at this point. Anyway it was not Vaughn's problem if a shortage of pneumococcal ensued. He was under no obligation to maintain the status of world health; he was charged with running a business. And from that standpoint, he admitted he was concerned he would lose the predictable income from pneumonia vaccine, but he believed he would be replacing it with a far more lucrative product. PharmaGlobal could resume pneumococcal manufacture when the avian threat was diminished and the market for H5N1 vaccine was no longer hot.

"I would like to ask Dr. Culp to discuss the need for H5N1 vaccine" Vaughn said, purposefully using Ken's professional title to emphasize his credibility. He enjoyed playing this game, lining up his allies, voices of science, business and reason. Experts persuading experts. It was rather like chess he thought: positioning the participants a strategy he used to pursue his goals.

All eyes turned toward the newly distinguished scientist. Ken squared himself to face the other committee members, flushed with his recent acclaim. As he prepared to lead the discussion in this, his area of expertise, he felt just a pinch of disquiet that was not normally there, and wondered briefly about its cause. He cleared his throat a little in annoyance before proceeding.

"Contrary to popular belief, pandemic flu is not new. Viruses have swept the world periodically throughout human history, always starting first as localized epidemics. Modern technology has allowed us to investigate previous outbreaks of flu and has informed us that most of these epidemics have likely originated from animals. The most devastating modern pandemic, the 1918 Spanish flu, has lately been proven to have an avian virus as its source.

Avian flu is on the rise in bird populations with increasing reports of infection in the human population as well. To date, all the reported human cases are with the strain referred to as H5N1. It is impossible to predict whether H5N1 will ultimately develop pandemic potential, but I believe the evidence strongly indicates it will. This strain has already made documented leaps from human to human. Of course a truly pandemic strain would have caused much more widespread contagion than just the few cases reported so far, but it is only a matter of time before that occurs."

Ken paused to look around at the other committee members, some of whose eyes were glazing over. Trying to bring them back into the fold of understanding, Ken concluded loudly and succinctly, "H5N1 is the only avian virus of significance to humans."

Vaughn picked up the theme, "In the past year the WHO has called on governments to develop and stockpile vaccine. Mr. Kite, can you fill our members in on the political climate?"

Kite was assistant to the surgeon general under the last administration and one of two close ties Vaughn had in Washington. The other was a relationship he'd maintained with his college roommate, Cyril Hunt, for the past 40 years. If ever Vaughn had seen a man claw his way to the top through sheer will it was Hunt, who was now a member of the president's cabinet. Hunt was well aware of his own academic shortcomings, and precisely because of them he demonstrated impeccable loyalty to those who had the insight to see his value in other regards. Hunt had hitched himself to some mighty fine stars, and now Vaughn was along for the ride too.

Kite proceeded, "The nations where H5N1 has been occurring are some of the poorest on earth. They would love to have vaccine but can't afford it. Developed nations have been reluctant to act as protectors for the third world. Current thinking is that even wealthy nations must begin to stockpile preventive and treatment options because infection arising in these third world countries threatens all of us. The U.S. has been unwilling to commit resources until a specific viral target could be demonstrated. As Dr. Culp notes, the evidence increasingly points to H5N1. Soon, not only the U.S. but other world leaders will begin amassing vaccine to target H5N1. It is not clear whether U.S.-purchased vaccine would remain in the domestic supply or be sent overseas to high-risk areas of the world."

"What is the expected demand?" from one member.

"It could be as high as the population of the entire world if H5N1 becomes pandemic tomorrow," Vaughn answered with enthusiasm, which he hastily disguised as concern. "But the inquiries we've had in the last few months suggest we could sell all sixty million doses of Avimmune as soon as they are made."

"What's the shelf life?"

"Excellent question," Vaughn said. "Neither our quality control people nor the FDA will certify a vaccine for longer than two years, but practically speaking, if kept at the proper temperature, the shelf life of the product is indefinite." He shrugged, "Frankly anyone who has older vaccine on the shelf will use it under pandemic conditions rather than throw it away."

"How is it that we can use H5N1 vaccine that's more than a year old, when we can't use regular flu vaccine year after year? Isn't bird flu susceptible to alteration?" Vaughn was not pleased with the change in direction this question took. It came from one of the other academics on the board.

Ken looked up and got a nod from Vaughn. "You're correct in noting the easy mutability of influenza virus. The fact is we have no data on how H5N1 might respond once it contaminates the human pool. It might indeed mutate over time and it's a justifiable concern that vaccine we make for today's epidemic will not be effective or useful for tomorrow's."

"Then why would we make such a vaccine?"

"Because it is the best we can do at this point and because the world is clamoring for it." Vaughn interjected. For the last several months Vaughn had been debating the next step for PharmaGlobal. His gut told him that even without up-front contracts, PharmaGlobal would be able to sell all the Avimmune it could manufacture. Even without a confirmed pandemic strain the natural course of avian flu was playing into an immediate *perceived* need for H5N1 vaccine. There was no doubt that international concern was mounting, fueled by widespread attention in the press. Personal hysteria could not be far behind and would feed back into public hysteria. Nothing was quite as powerful a catalyst for profit as the combination. The world wanted a cure and he had it. It was a once in a lifetime opportunity and he was determined to capitalize on it.

"Do we have contracts?" another board member inquired.

"Not yet, but we're working on them."

"What if the virus changes while we're in production?"

"That's why we'll have the contracts. It won't matter. It will already be paid for." He realized as soon as he said it, that the remark sounded cold. He continued, "Of course PharmaGlobal is committed to remaining on the forefront of avian flu prevention in any case. Our plan is to continue to pour dollars into research and development, exploring new ways of manufacturing vaccine to be able to respond to changes in the viral particle. We will make millions of doses of whatever we discover the world needs."

Sometimes Vaughn's duties as CEO required that he tamper with the truth a bit. His advisors did not have to know that all the reserve capital in the business would be needed to switch the main plant production over to avian vaccine. There would be no funds available for research and development for one to two years. As the profits from H5N1 sales began to pour in, the original capital would be more than replaced---it would be hundreds of times more than his investment. Vaughn realized that by diverting capital away from R & D his company would not be competing for any chunk of profit that came from patenting a new process to make vaccine faster, but he had his gold mine right in front of him producing Avimmune the old-fashioned way.

Ken leaped back into the conversation with conviction. "The most important lesson from my study of this virus is that it is extraordinarily unpredictable. I agree wholeheartedly with maximizing PharmaGlobal's production of H5N1 because the evidence points to H5N1 as the next pandemic strain, but it is imperative that we keep our vision open to change over time." Vaughn nodded vigorously in agreement, quite pleased with the apparent spontaneity and enthusiasm of Ken's endorsement. "I support the mass production of Avimmune as the first step, not the end point, in this battle. We must continue research and development into faster methods of producing vaccine. It will be to our advantage to keep the company's ability to respond to the virus as nimble as the organism itself."

Ken looked at the CEO of PharmaGlobal. "I congratulate Vaughn on his commitment to meeting international needs and his ongoing dedication to funding research at PharmaGlobal."

Ken, wholly ignorant of the diversion of capital out of R & D, had corroborated Vaughn's statements without prompting. This was going even better than Vaughn anticipated.

"What about switching back to the traditional vaccine for next year's flu season? Will there be any problems with that?" asked a member.

"Our economies of scale will help us there," Vaughn replied, not clueing them in to the difficulty of altering the production lines between cycles. "Everything we do in our complex is geared toward large quantities and mass production. We'll have to sterilize and re-calibrate the lines, but we've proven in the past we are capable of that," Vaughn explained. "Further, if an H5N1 pandemic should hit in the next six months we will already be in full manufacturing status. In that event PharmaGlobal will continue to direct all of its production to Avimmune."

Vaughn made the last remark casually, but he knew he had dropped a second bombshell. Intentionally. Get them comfortable with the prospect of some change and while they were still a little off balance, continue to introduce new ideas. In his experience it took people the same amount of time to get used to one change as several, and they offered less resistance to boot. It was not only possible, it was prefer-able to press on with H5N1 vaccine for a second cycle in the spring/summer/fall due to the expense of having to reconfigure the lines in between each batch of traditional flu versus avian. If things went well with the incubation and harvesting of the virus, and Avimmune was still in demand, as it was quite likely to be, he could push out two cycles of avian between now and September and still possibly have time to generate one batch of regular vaccine for the late flu season next year. Or perhaps they would remain in the H5N1 business until the market died, leaving the manufacture of the less profitable traditional influenza vaccine to others.

Vaughn wanted his board to know it was possible to turn PharmaGlobal's entire operation over to Avimmune production if necessary. Perhaps even if it wasn't necessary, perhaps if it was merely profitable. A monopoly on a product in worldwide demand was an opportunity no self-respecting CEO would pass up. As far as J. B. Vaughn was concerned, this year PharmaGlobal would be making nothing but Avimmune.

· · ·

Ken left the meeting and headed to the airport feeling terrific. When he made the stock purchases with his Pritzker winnings earlier this week he had no idea what Vaughn was going to propose today. Ken had made his security choices based on what he knew as a virologist about H5N1's threat and the confidence he had in PharmaGlobal to fill a foreseeable need for vaccine. Vaughn's persona might be a bit over-the-top but his business management dovetailed perfectly with Ken's assessment of the significance of H5N1 virus. Ken was delighted with his purchase of PharmaGlobal shares; they were going to take off.

The other stock he had chosen, Viraban, was no less stellar. The U.S. company was, until recently, the exclusive manufacturer of the anti-viral drug osmavir, the only medicine shown to be useful against avian flu. Of course it was better to get the flu shot and avoid the flu altogether, but if you didn't have the shot, osmavir had the potential of saving millions of lives. It was somewhat effective as a preventive measure, and as a treatment to mitigate the symptoms of avian flu once a patient had been infected. Being unable to keep up with world-wide demand itself, Viraban had recently approved licensing the drug's patent to other pharmaceutical firms after intense international pressure to increase production. Viraban would not suffer from the competition: it was a solid old company that would stand to gain from every dose it produced. Its venerability and the nature of the product would make for soaring profits for the foreseeable future.

Ken chastised himself for his past worrying about the intersection of business and his research. He had not lost his objectivity in the process of purchasing these investments. Nothing had changed about him, or his research or conclusions. Today's meeting at PharmaGlobal proved it: his demeanor, interactions, discussion and decisions were as solid and well-reasoned as ever.

Ken was flying high well before he boarded the plane. He found himself looking at strangers, and nearly smiling at them too, as he walked through the airport to his gate. He was proud of himself for taking control of his life. For making financial choices based on his lifelong pursuit of knowledge, not someone else's: choices based on his hard work and understanding of avian flu. In doing this he was no less committed to success in his laboratory. The beauty of his investments was that they were now a part of his effort. His new portfolio, the one of *his* choosing, was as directed to benefiting the human race as his research. Not only was he using his mind to prepare for the struggle, he had placed his entire savings into equipping the world for it. The best work, the best decisions of his life were all feeding and flowing into one another. He was golden. Untouchable. Right with the world.

PORTLAND, OREGON
January 9

There is nothing on earth, Ken thought, as empty as the eyes of someone with dementia. His mother was lying semi-reclined in her bed, her arms drawn up to her chest, gnarly hands over top of one another, elbows swathed in batting, staring straight ahead at some indeterminate point in space. He could not help but think as he did his own portion of staring at the mindlessness of her inert form, that it was the most cruel and ironic of worlds in which we lived.

Here lay Anna Wardman, a lifelong student and teacher of philosophy, a lecturer of international renown in the field of medical ethics, a staunch supporter of choosing one's destiny, an advocate for the right to die. Here she lay against her will in this beige room with beige curtains and beige floor, her brilliant mind sucked away into the wrinkled flesh of a body that would not release her from being.

At least it was mostly against her will. It was true she had chosen this specific place to end her days, back before the disease stole her away neuron by neuron. But she most certainly, most adamantly had not wanted to persist in this state, dead but not dead. She had signed all the papers she was judged capable of signing before she arrived here, power of attorney, guardianship, living will. But in the ensuing time, the days they both knew would come, her guardian had been unable to act on her behalf, unable to exercise the authority his mother, if not society, had given him.

She had wanted Ken to take her life. She didn't put it that way of course. Anna's view was that Alzheimer's would take her life. What she wanted from Ken was just the help of a finite ending to the process of dying her disease had committed her to. She wanted no part of extended care after her mind was gone. She would have taken her own life but she knew as she got worse she wouldn't have the mental faculties left to do it, and to commit suicide while she was still able to function, she felt was premature. She shouldn't have to kill herself when she was still competent simply because this was the only time she was capable of carrying through with it. "After all," she said, "it's not that I want to die Kenneth, I just don't want to live in the extended terminal state this damned disease will cause. And I won't know it when I get there, only you will."

She was deeply disappointed that society had not found a way yet to help people with this terrible affliction. Toward the end of her career Anna had followed the development of right-to-die efforts in Oregon with keen interest. In fact she had been called on to participate in discussions of the law when it was being proposed as a ballot initiative. An academic and a professional, she never let personal opinions color her presentations, which were marked by balance, and respect for diversity. But there was no denying her relief in private that at least one state in the union was advanced enough to address the issue; it was the reason she had chosen Oregon to live out her final days.

Anna cherished some faint hope that the law might be tested over time in a way that would allow it to be used for Alzheimer's disease. It was regrettable, she thought, that people with Alzheimer's, or any slowly progressive form of dementia for that matter, would not be able to avail themselves of the right-to-die. Under the existing legislation, candidates for assisted suicide were required to meet three tests: to have a terminal illness with fewer than six months to live, to be mentally capable of making an informed decision to die, and to be able to take the fatal dose of medication by themselves. By the time people with Alzheimer's had fewer than six months to live, they could not meet either of the latter two criteria.

Anna was determined to leave as many possibilities open as she could. Even though Ken was not complicit, she hoped that watching her deteriorate might change his mind. She did not leave a stone unturned in assisting his potential metamorphosis. She joined the Hemlock Society and researched the various ways her life could be painlessly ended. She settled on obtaining a quantity of sedatives through her physician, who had no idea she was squirreling away the pills instead of using them as directed. After a couple refills she pounded the tablets with a mortar and pestle into a fine powder that would be easy to administer in a spoonful of applesauce, or mixed with a little water. With great care she typed out the directions and the expected timing of the results. (She would fall into a deep sleep; her breathing would gradually slow down and within a couple hours would stop. "Peaceful. Painless," she'd said. "Ken, can't you see?") Wrapping the instructions in a bit of plastic, she taped them to the bottle and entrusted the package to Ken, who accepted it as though it were a blood-soaked dagger.

His reaction notwithstanding, Anna was adamant that if Ken chose to assist her suicide, his action be covert; she would not have him subject to the archaic social justice system in America. Because of her advanced age, as long as he was not witnessed administering the medication, and was careful not to leave traces of the powder on her lips or tongue where they might be noticed by a staff member, no one would think to investigate the cause of an old woman dying in her sleep. She would be at rest, and he would be safe from prosecution.

He was supposed to dispense the lethal cocktail when she was no longer able to interact with the world, was without comprehension, beyond hope of recovery. That was most certainly now, Ken thought as he looked at her. It was not hard to see her deterioration manifested in quantum leaps when he visited only every four weeks. Day by day the downward spiral would no doubt have appeared more gradual. Still, he couldn't readily say when she might have crossed over the line she would have drawn for herself, was it one month ago, or three, or six? But he admitted it had happened. She was no longer living. She was dying.

Ken looked down at his own hands, turned them over. These were not hands he could imagine causing harm or pain, not the vector certainly for anyone's death. Not even if she had begged him. Which she had. He cursed the law of the land that would not allow her to make this decision herself, and have death dispensed by another's blameless hands. Someone clinical. Her doctor perhaps. A nurse. A certified death specialist. It didn't matter: somebody who had a professional contract with the patient and society to carry out this wish. But it was not to be. Without his action, there would be no premature end to her dying. His hands would be on it, all over it, if he gave her the potion, and he simply found he could not.

He had failed her. He knew it, and more to the point she knew it. Knew it before she went under. There had been times back when she still remembered who he was that he thought he could see blame in her eyes, but he knew it was his own imagining, nothing more than a reflection of guilt that he saw looking back at him, not her recriminations. Anna the philosopher would not blame him for his choice. As she had in his youth, she gave him the tools to ponder the dilemma, encouraged him to weigh all the arguments, respected his struggle. Accepted that he was not like her. Knew, in her last lucid moments, that if he were to take her life he would lose his own. Yes, she had begged him to consider her wishes. It had struck him to his core. But she had forgiven him in the same instant she realized it was not possible.

So here they were. Mother and son sharing the same corner for a few hours, breathing the same oxygen molecules, bathing in the same sunshine trickling through the bare winter branches outside.

He dozed.

And woke.

He had been making this pilgrimage every month for nearly two years and it never got easier. In more naive days he'd supposed at some point he would be less shocked by the deterioration, or at least more comfortable with the unaccountable stasis that supported her continued existence in the absence of every outward sign of life. She was a living mannequin. A withered doll made of skin stretched over muscle and bones.

Ken had read as much as he could about the illness, trying to cope with the horrifying changes in the dynamic, cerebral woman he had known all his life. Still, he was devastated the first time she didn't know who he was. He understood that clarity could reappear for minutes or hours or days in the midst of the utter bewilderment. He came to know that confabulation was a particular skill of those with Alzheimer's. With banalities and pleasant agreeableness the patient could appear to be perfectly normal. But a single probing question belied the mask of comprehension.

In hindsight he and June realized that Anna had exhibited the first signs of Alzheimer's about ten years ago: memory lapses, a few incidents of getting lost in what should have been familiar territory, misplacing first the car keys, then the car. These things were inter-mittent for several years and not of much consequence to anyone. Anna herself became concerned before anyone else and headed to the doctor about five years ago. The physician performed many tests and told Anna that Alzheimer's was the most likely diagnosis. His mother immediately started taking medication meant to delay the progression of the disease, and for a while the treatment had done just that.

Then, a little over two years ago, her symptoms began to escalate: she would not be dressed appropriately when they picked her up to go places, wearing a nice blouse, perhaps with pajama bottoms and unmatched socks; food had been found warming in the oven for days, she could no longer tell time, lost the concepts of now, and later. Once she came out of the bathroom crying because she could not get the 'hand cream' she had squirted out of the toothpaste tube rubbed in properly. Soon after, Anna was moved to the facility she had chosen: an Alzheimer's unit at a nursing home in Oregon.

At first his visits had been welcomed by her. Sometimes June would come too and they would converse as well as Anna's extant abilities allowed. Then one day he arrived alone and startled her. She was sitting in a chair looking out the window and demanded to know who he was when he entered the room, responding with a struggle when he tried to embrace her. Ken pulled back, unsure what to do. He drew up a chair and sat down directly in front of her, tilted her head up toward him and said, "Mom, it's me, Ken."

Still, no recognition.

"Your son."

Anna had peered at him for a long time afterward, the fright he had seen in her countenance visibly changing to bewilderment, then curiosity as she studied him. The words that finally came out of her were evidence of the intense struggle within.

"Yes," she nodded slowly. "You look just like me," spoken with unmistakable sadness, acceptance without understanding. Somewhere inside the tangle of remaining synapses, the woman she was knew that she should have known him, and also knew that the woman she had become, did not.

The end, he thought as he sorted through these memories, must surely be approaching. She had continued to swallow without choking, which might have caused pneumonia to set in mercifully. But the nurses had reported she was taking less nourishment recently, and there would be no feeding tube. No IV's. That much she was able to decree on her own.

Anna's eyes were closed when he rose to leave. He took her hand and stroked her hair wondering, before he departed, how many more times they would repeat this macabre dance.

VIRUS: IN VITRO

"The war against infectious diseases has been won."
—William H. Stewart, Surgeon General of the
United States, 1969

Come. Come closer if you want. Are you a voyeur? Do you want to see how it is? A dance some might call it. Or an accident. Or pure sex.

The carnal trespassers land separately and completely accidentally in the same moist, inviting territory. One invader, detestable guest, is familiar if unwelcome: it visits periodically, wreaks misery in its host, nurtures itself, replenishes its stock, leaves. The consort: a more perilous intruder, equally uninvited, nosing about. Each seeking, finding, succor.

They meet: a chance connection, anonymous hook-up. Violent beginnings, coverings stripped, insides laid bare, tearing themselves apart, blindly ripping, groping, grasping in the cytological void to find commonality. Pushing, pressing, twining 'round each other to the beat of a billion years of genetic code. The lovers crash together, and splinters of their former selves spin away uselessly. In a moment they are one, united, neither having been before. Inseparable. Unrecognizable. Something *else* than they were. From the crucible of the consummation, a new spawn, a reckoning none could divine.

What was, is no longer.

What is, was not.

VIRUS: IN VIVO

SOUTHWEST OF SAIGON, VIETNAM
January

Tran Phu and his son were having an easy journey to the city. The weather had been good, not too hot during the day nor too cool at night. It was the shoulder between the dry season and the monsoon and they encountered some light showers but no heavy rain. The weather was usually cooperative this time of year so Tran planned his errands as he was able around these expectations. His son was traveling to Saigon with him for the first time. He had been begging to accompany Tran for years but until recently his little boy legs would have been too slow. Now that he was beginning to show the growth that attended manhood, he could not only keep up fairly well, but would be useful in carrying supplies back to the village.

After they left Duc at the fork in the road, Tran and his son spent their first days sticking to the paths between the widely scattered villages encountering few people, camping alone off the paths at night as it suited them, making a bed of marsh grass, building a fire for their meal. As they got closer to the city and the routes that would become busier with people, bicycles and scooters, Tran purposefully steered them onto more circuitous, desolate tracks. He was carrying a good bit of money for the purchase of supplies and could not afford to lose the family's income to highwaymen who preyed on the peasants coming to town. He had been robbed more than once on the main roads, thieves ambushing him when the traffic had temporarily thinned or disappeared around a bend. Fortunately they had not hurt him on previous occasions; they usually didn't. As long as you gave up whatever you were carrying, the rogues had no reason to harm you. Enforcement of laws out here was almost unheard of. No one policed the vandals who crept out from the edges of the city long enough to do their dirty work; if they didn't do too much damage, they stayed under the radar. So, over time Tran had scouted out other ways into the city, figuring that the robbers were more likely to do their hunting on the commonly traveled routes. Thus far his logic in taking out-of-the-way paths had proven correct. It only added a little extra time to the journey; he thought it well worth it.

Tran's son was the first one to cough, two days after they had parted company from Duc. It was mid afternoon and they were still a little way from Saigon on a trail that wove through the last stretch of remote wetlands outside the city; they hadn't seen another soul since early this morning. The boy became increasingly pale and short of breath as he walked, his father increasingly concerned. Much to the boy's relief his father suggested stopping to rest in the meager shade afforded by some cattails growing out of a dry marsh bed a good distance off the path. Tran prepared a nest for them by tramping down the grass and laid his son's head, now beginning to flush with fever, to rest on his pack.

It was while the boy slept that Tran, sitting patiently beside him, began himself to cough. He tried at first to stifle the urge so as not to waken the sleeping boy but it was to no avail. Before long they were both wheezing and spitting foamy, bloody mucus that clogged their breathing passages and nearly strangled them. At one point he thought to leave his son and set off to look for materials to build a fire, warm some tea, cook some rice, but he found he was afraid to leave, as his son was now unable even to sit up to expectorate the increasingly viscous scum. He became alarmed with his son's labored breathing and the dusky color of the skin surrounding the boy's lips, which he did not think was wholly due to the fading light. Tran hoped that he might hear the rumble of a motor bike or the voice of a good man coaxing his oxen down the path. Ruefully he thought if he'd taken the main road even a ruffian would likely offer assistance after robbing him. But the only sound he heard was the murmur of a breeze through the rushes. He could see smoke rising in the dusk from village fires not too far in the distance, but they might as well have been beyond the sea as he was too overwhelmed now by his own weakness and uncontrollable chills to seek help. In the deepening twilight he stroked the boy's head soothingly, whispering words of comfort and prayer. As the sickness overcame him Tran lay down and tenderly curled his son's frail, shivering form into his own.

CHAPTER 7

VIETNAM
January 10

The plane banked over the sparkling blue-green waters of the South China Sea as the stewardess announced the final approach to Ho Chi Minh City. No one referred to the renamed metropolis by this moniker except entrenched bureaucrats Binh had told Lou, and evidently flight attendants, she thought. It was Saigon to the Vietnamese and Saigon to the rest of the world. She learned this on her first visit to Vietnam when she asked her colleague how he like living in Ho Chi Minh City. "No need to stand on ceremony Dr. Lou. No one will know what you are talking about. We are Saigon," he said proudly, firmly, as he inclined his head toward the skyline.

Lou was grateful for the speed and ease of the China Airlines flight, reminiscing as they made their final approach, on her first trip to Saigon and her knuckle-headed moment of stubbornness. Shortly after her arrival in Asia, when she did not yet fully appreciate the shortcomings of Vietnamese transportation, she had taken the train from Hanoi to Saigon against the advice of her WHO Hanoi assistant, a man she didn't know well. There was a bit of a language barrier between them, and the spotty communication, combined with her paranoia that he had pegged her as a spoiled American, caused her to insist that he book her on the train. It had taken thirty two hours on the *express* for her to travel fewer than six hundred miles. They had crept through the countryside, crawled along the mountains and dragged past the sea, belching black, choking smoke all the while from the wheezing engine. Bicycles whizzed by the sluggish train when they passed through towns. They moved so ponderously that small children, heedless of the dangers of the rolling steel wheels, were able to grab onto the car handles for a joy ride. Sometimes Lou's hard-headedness really paid off; sometimes not. This was a lesson she needed only once. When she first took this job, the WHO's only Vietnamese outpost was in Hanoi, but Lou had determined somewhere between two hours and thirty two into the train ride, that southern Vietnam, Laos, and Cambodia would be accessed through a new outpost in Saigon.

As Lou hauled her stuff through the airport and was greeted with smiles from strangers, she was reminded once again of how friendly the Vietnamese people were. With all the devastation of their country from the wars fought by French, Chinese and Americans on their soil, she would not have blamed them for coldness, or suspicion or outright anger toward foreigners. But there was none. "My people are," Binh had said, "forgiving. We are peace loving, and throughout history we have proven ourselves so repeatedly, when we have been left to our own destiny. We desire quiet lives of farming and industry and we have no quibble with those who do not obstruct our path. The war is over Dr. Lou, our spirits do not dwell on it. Of what concern is the past? We have only the present and the future to comprehend." Lou had been humbled by this absence of rancor. It was a feeling she was reacquainted with each time she set foot in the country.

Binh now spotted her schlepping her bags down the concourse. Back pack, duffle bag, sample case. She had just made it under the carry-on radar. "Dr. Lou!" he hailed, waving excitedly. She loved his enthusiasm, and she was eager for the extra set of arms. Packing light was not her forte.

"Good to see you Binh." She handed him the duffle and he made an exaggerated face under the weight of it.

"How long are you staying Dr. Lou? I only booked the room for three nights," he joked.

"I thought I had a tent, not a room Binh. I brought all the comforts of home," she laughed.

"It feels like it. You may need to ride on the roof once we load up. My car is not big like yours in America." She put her arm affectionately around him and gave him a good squeeze as they made their way outside, thoroughly embarrassing him in the process.

• • •

The drive to Duyen Ba was everything Binh had said it might be. The highway, as Binh generously referred to it, started off promising enough, paved or graveled for the most part. But twenty miles out of the city it had been reduced to a potholed dirt track, muddy in the low lying places where the last rain had not yet dried up. They shared the road with bicycles and pedestrians, motorbikes and small children leading enormous water buffalo. Colorful sacrifices of flowers, incense and fruit punctuated the green canvas of rice paddies at shrines along the road, serving as both thanks and pleas to the gods for good luck and a good harvest in these fertile plains. At Vinh Long they turned off the main route and dove into the heart of the delta, passing the active river market on this branch of the Mekong. Housewives in their nimble sampans negotiated for the day's supplies with merchants whose tiny boats were impossibly laden with thatched baskets brimming with the bounty of the delta: stinky durian, alongside sweet mangosteen, longan and litchi; bananas, papayas, and pineapple; orchids, and lotus and apricot flowers for tourists; and always rice, and fish. Lou wondered wistfully as she watched the lively display if she would ever have a chance to slow down and enjoy the culture of this country.

Traffic thinned considerably as they left Vinh Long, and the road became no more than a path. Binh sped along when there were no oxen or bikes, but he would occasionally send them bouncing and reeling, from hitting deep ruts and from swerving to avoid them. It was past noon before they found the village. They'd had to stop and ask the way a couple of times as they got closer. At the previous turn a man had sent his young son to navigate the last couple miles. They gave him a few dong for his trouble and he scampered toward home. Lou and Binh sat in the car just outside the small group of huts on the outskirts of Duyen Ba, eating some vegetables and rice he had packed for their lunch and taking in the lush scenery of the delta.

A few of the children and some of the adults had marked their arrival, and now approached with curiosity as they got out of the car.

Binh inclined his head slightly in respect to the eldest in the group and explained that he and the physician, nodding at Lou, wanted to speak to them about the recent deaths of the chickens. The two men conversed and agreed to begin at the livestock pens; it was best not to delve into the death of one of their human members immediately.

The ground inside the chicken coop was singed black from the fire the inhabitants had lit to cleanse it of the last traces of the rotting carcasses. There were loose feathers scattered all about the enclosure and a few new chickens, dirty from the ash, now roamed in the roomy pen. There still remained a powerful odor of chicken feces but the burning had attenuated its sharpness. Their guide was explaining that the new chickens were a gift from neighbors, for which they were very grateful. Lou noted his demeanor was sad but matter-of-fact. He did not appear to be overly disturbed by the questions Binh was asking or by the biohazard gear they had put on: masks, gloves, and gowns.

She and Binh did not need to take any samples from the coop; veterinarians had already identified H5N1 as the cause of the poultry kill. They accepted an invitation into one of the homes to talk with the elders, but politely declined the offer of tea as it would have necessitated removal of their masks. The elders sipped from earthen cups and alternated between contemplation and animated discussion in response to Binh's opening questions about the death of the woman in their village.

Hue Pham had been the mother of two young children, and had not had any previous maladies, according to her husband who had now been brought to the hut to speak with Lou and Binh. No one else in the village had been ill before, during or after her death. Her husband explained that she had worked hard with the other women in preparing the dead chickens for consumption, and they had all assumed her sickness was a result of the extra effort and the worry. He recounted sadly that he had no idea how severe her illness was. If he had known he would have taken Hue to town for help. But she died after only five or six days of coughing, struggling only at the very end to breathe. Now he didn't have food or a mother for his children.

With utmost tact Binh explained to the man that Dr. Lou was trying to help others avoid the same fate as his family. Even though Hue was gone she could help save lives by providing a tissue sample.

Exhumation was actually a common practice here but for personal, spiritual reasons, not for intrusive strangers. In any event it was early for an exhumation, but would he consent? Binh offered they could obtain what they needed with very little disturbance and rebury the body, or they could completely excavate the site for the family if they were ready to send the body on the next phase of its spirit journey.

Hue's spouse was silent for some time, then excused himself from the hut. When he came back, Hue's mother and uncle were with him. The three conferred quietly, before indicating that the doctor could obtain the tissue and that the body should be reburied. Once this had been decided, everyone rose and walked to the grave site where a conical hat, a pair of slippers and a carved tea cup lay on top of the freshly turned earth. The family said a few words and retrieved their loved one's mementos then retreated to their homes. Binh and Lou began the unenviable task of collecting a minute piece of lung tissue from a body that had been in the ground for several days.

"That should do it," Lou said, stifling what she hoped was her last gag, as she squatted to pack the vials of lung tissue into her bag.

"Do you want samples from anyone else?"

"No. No one else is ill, and they should have been by now if they were infected from the chickens, or even if Hue transmitted the virus to them before she died. It looks like Hue was the only victim here. Just make sure they know how to reach us if anyone else gets sick." She swung the bag over her shoulder. "We need to check on Hue's sister and brother-in-law." Outside Duyen Ba, they were the only people exposed to Hue, coming to help when she was sick.

"Their village is close the family told me," Binh replied. "We should be able to find it pretty easily."

"The only other thing we need to do is follow up on the young man who left...what was his name?"

"Duc Trinh."

"Yeah. Do we know where he was headed?"

"His brother-in-law's village, a few days walk from here. He's looking for temporary shelter for his wife and children. He's expected back soon to collect his family. Do you want me to try to find him?"

"If anyone else in Duyen Ba were sick, I'd have you go after him immediately. No, at this point it doesn't look like a contagious strain of H5N1. Just check on him in a few days when he gets back," Lou said.

After they loaded their gear back into the car Binh drew two huge sacks off the floor in the back. "I'll be right back," he said.

"Wait, let me help," Lou insisted. "What is it anyway?" she asked as they struggled toward the elder's hut, each under the weight of one bag.

"It's rice. I figured they could use it."

•   •   •

Connor got off the plane in Saigon and grabbed a taxi to the Rex Hotel. Built as a garage by the French during their occupation fifty years before, then converted to a hotel and used by the Americans as a center for operations and the press corps during the war, it was now a modest but pleasant hotel in the heart of the city. The clerk informed him that Lou wasn't registered but Connor knew the Rex was where she usually stayed because of its reasonable cost and proximity to the Ben Thanh Market, one of her favorite places to troll for meals. Her figure didn't suffer for it, but she loved to eat. Whether it was pizza or Peking duck, foie gras or fettuccini, she knew where the best flavors could be found, and for the best price too. He wondered where she might like to sit down for a meal in Saigon. He didn't think it would be very romantic to surprise her with a first date of noodles from a market stall.

After all, she didn't know he was coming. Neither did he, but before he'd finished pushing the disconnect button yesterday on their phone call, he'd made the decision. She'd given him the green light and he wanted to see her immediately. And he had the added benefit of being able to work on a Vietnam piece while he was here, as two stories appeared to be unfolding at the same time: the new H3N3 in roosters, and the death of the woman in the delta. He would do his own research while Lou was doing hers. If she was comfortable being a source that would be handy, if not, that was fine too. Connor was confident they could work out the personal and professional lines to be drawn. In fact, he thought with amusement, the professional obstacles would be considerably easier to surmount than the five year effort it had taken to acknowledge their mutual personal interest.

As he unlocked the door to his room Connor shook his head and wondered if he had lost his mind. Wondered if she was worth it. Decided within the three strides it took to cross the room that he must have thought so or he wouldn't be here. He deposited his things on the bed and returned to the front desk where he left her a note on his way out. He wished he could see the look on her face when she opened it, but then he wasn't even entirely sure she'd be here tonight. If he didn't hear from her he'd call the WHO office in the morning and find out if she'd made different arrangements. Knowing he needed to get his mind elsewhere until she showed up, he stepped out of the hotel with his notebook, tape recorder and umbrella, a hedge against the darkening sky. He flagged down a motorized cycle, driven by a cigarette-smoking, wizened old man, to take him to the mean alleys where the betting was heavy and the stakes high: Saigon's profitable cock-fighting district.

• • •

It was late afternoon before Binh and Lou finished interviewing Hue's sister and brother-in-law in a slightly larger village just up the track from Duyen Ba. There was nothing remarkable in their story. They and their children had lived in Hue's house for three days, caring for her and her family until she died. After the burial they had returned home uneventfully. No one was ill.

Lou had to consider that it had only been a week and a half since Hue had first exposed everyone to her cough, and the incubation period for traditional influenza could be as long as two weeks. However all of the suspected cases of human to human transmission of H5N1 had developed symptoms well within the first week of exposure. Assuming the worst scenario, that Hue died of avian flu, she apparently repre-sented a single isolated case of H5N1, like most of the others caused by a combination of factors which included poor resistance to the germ, and very close contact with the infected birds. Of course Lou reminded herself she still didn't have proof Hue had died of avian influenza; it might have been bacterial pneumonia for all she knew. It would be a couple days before the conclusive tests were finished. But regardless of the cause, there was no evidence of contagion at this point. The only unaccounted person was Duc Trinh, and he should be back soon enough. Then they could close the books on this case.

In the meantime Lou and Binh were sitting in the car trying to decide whether to make the journey back to Saigon. They only had about an hour of daylight left in which to cover a few more hours of bad roads before they got back to the city. Binh was willing to drive but he didn't look particularly thrilled with the thought. Lou was ready to capitulate and break out the tent when raindrops started to hit the windshield. Momentarily contemplating the canvas option, they looked at each other at the same time and said, "Let's go."

• • •

Connor stood in a narrow street in a seedy neighborhood on the outskirts of Saigon. The driver of the scooter had deposited him here, nodding repeatedly, in response to Connor's quizzical looks, that this was the place. His escort had then wheeled the motorbike handily about and taken off. Connor made a mental note not to pay the next driver until he was certain he was ready to stay. There were a few kids knocking around some open doorways, but otherwise the place was eerily deserted. Walking away from the main street, he poked his head into a few of the gashes that served as windows in the bamboo and rusting tin boxes lining the alley and saw nothing. A few empty crates. Broken bottles. Graffiti on the abandoned walls. The detritus of any slum in any city in the world.

As he walked he heard some hubbub coming from an open door up ahead. Peering in he saw men seated at small tables smoking and carrying on. The proprietor, wearing a filthy apron, saw Connor pause in the doorway and held up a bottle of the local brew from behind what passed as a bar, inviting him in with the gesture. Connor nodded and gave him a couple dong for the beer, taking a seat as he did so. Several of the patrons paused, took notice of him, his western face, and went back to their talk. In his best Vietnamese Connor asked the bartender if he spoke any English. Squinting through the smoke curling out of the cigarette that dangled from his lips he shook his head no. But after he finished wiping a dirty glass into a clean one with an oily, tattered rag, he came around the bar and spoke to one of the men at the table who dragged a stool over and sat beside Connor.

Jerking his head toward the bartender, the man said, "Giang say you want English," with a thick accent, but well enough to be understood.

"Yes. I was looking for the fights."

The man took a long drag on a home-rolled cigarette, then eyed Connor through the rising plume. Connor took the opportunity to advance his cause. He held up his bottle and motioned to the proprietor to bring another for his new friend, laying more dong on the counter.

"We are not supposed to talk."

"I see." He looked at the man's hands and saw they were covered in scratches extending up his forearms. Some appeared fresh.

"Are you reporter?" he asked looking sideways at Connor.

"Yes. But I am not writing today. I am just looking. I will not identify any places or quote anything you say. I am just interested in information." He tried to gauge the man's response to his honesty. He could have lied, but it would have been tough to be spontaneously creative enough to explain another reason a decently dressed Westerner would be in the slums today looking for a cock fight. "What's going on?"

In increasingly broken English with a few phrases repeated slowly for clarity, the man explained, "First some roosters die. Government close us down. Then police come and say roosters found in city will be killed. We take our birds. Hide."

"Are any more roosters dying? I mean not being killed, but dying?" he tried to explain. The man shook his head, no, but Connor wasn't sure he'd understood. He pressed further, "Are any handlers...people... men who take care of the roosters...are any of them sick?"

"No! No-body sick!" the handler declared vehemently. Then he paused for a time, considering.

"Mind sick," he said pointing with two soiled fingers gravely to his head and, "Spirit sick," the same fingers now touching his chest. "Our cocks fighters. Without fighting they not alive. We not alive." He hung his head down with this last remark and pushed away from the counter, trudging back to his friends.

• • •

Lou and Binh straggled into the lobby of the Rex close to ten. Binh wanted to be sure the hotel had space for her before he left; he hadn't made a reservation not knowing if they would make it back tonight. Assured of a room, Binh deposited Lou's duffle and took his leave. He would pick her up in the morning to prepare for a meeting with local authorities on the H3N3 outbreak. It promised, like most encounters with the Vietnamese bureaucracy, to be challenging. When it came to releasing information there was much red tape and little transparency in the system.

Lou was walking away from the desk when the clerk called out, "Dr. Symington, wait! I nearly forgot. I have a message for you." He reached across the counter and handed her an envelope. With her backpack in one hand and her suitcase in the other she had no way of opening it until she got to her room. She did not recognize the handwriting as she slid it into the pocket of her jacket: 'Lou' was scrawled on the front.

• • •

Connor wandered around the streets outside the hotel for a while enjoying the hustle of Saigon. He relished every opportunity to sample other cultures and because of this he never tired of the travel involved with his career. He was fortunate. He'd known many reporters who became resentful of the time spent away from home, especially as they acquired less intrepid spouses and children. Perhaps he would feel that way too some day, but right now he was still very much enjoying the lifestyle and couldn't help but think that a woman living on her own in a country as foreign to the American way of life as China might share his enthusiasm for adventure.

Could she be as good as she seemed? Attractive, smart, fun, straightforward. He could detect no artifice about her, no haughtiness. She had an easy smile and a sharp wit. Connor stopped himself short on the sidewalk nearly causing a collision with the people walking behind him; what was he thinking? He was here to ask this woman out on their first official date, not marry her. He hardly knew her and he was wondering if she would travel with him for the rest of their lives. *Whoa. What's got into you boy?*

It wasn't that he had any aversion to long-term commitments; in fact he thought of himself as the marrying type. He had just not met anyone yet who he could imagine spending the rest of his life with.

Until now. There it was again. An unbidden thought that flashed in his mind. Was it him? His age? Or her? Was she *it*?

He realized that in his reverie he'd been standing in front of a shoe store staring at the window display. He must have been there for a while because the clerks inside were pointing to him and whispering, giggling, as though perhaps this westerner had a shoe fetish. Connor smiled at the women and moved on, not the least embarrassed. He picked up a bowl of noodles at a street stall and headed back to the hotel where he hung around in his room for the rest of the evening, reading a little, writing a little, hoping Lou would call.

• • •

Lou keyed into her room, dropped her things immediately and peeled off her jacket making a beeline for the bathroom. She'd had the urge since they bounced into the outskirts of Saigon but refused to stop, preferring to live with her swelling bladder and the promise of a clean hotel bathroom over the squalor of a public facility, if one could even be located. She hadn't been quite desperate enough to opt for the bushes.

Feeling much relieved she rested her back against the cool porcelain and considered her next move. It was late. She was dirty, tired and starved. Which need to address first? She decided she was too exhausted to even pull her pants back up so she undressed and showered. By the time she came out of the steamy room fatigue had easily overtaken hunger and she collapsed into her bed totally forgetting about the note in the jacket she'd tossed over a chair.

CHAPTER 8

SAIGON, VIETNAM
Jan 10

Connor had called the front desk after midnight to see if Lou had checked in and was told she had, a couple of hours before. He confirmed that the clerk had given her his note and puzzled as to the reasons she might not have answered him as he stripped back the bedspread and climbed in. His sleep was fitful.

He checked the front desk for messages before breakfast and found none. He ate without relish, vacillating between hope, disappointment and anger as he tried to decide what to do with his day and whether or not to stick around Saigon. Maybe there was a screw up and she hadn't really gotten the note. Maybe the clerk gave it to the wrong person. Maybe she'd gotten it and was ignoring him. Maybe he had jumped the gun, scared her. Should he call her cell phone? Leave a message on her room phone? Or just leave town? Maybe this, maybe that. Why did it matter so much?

What the hell, he was here to write a story anyway. He might as well get some work done. He'd spend the day researching and writing and would make one more attempt to seek her out later. He didn't want to bother her now, no doubt she was working today: that's why she had come to Saigon. He'd go knock on the door of her room this evening and gauge her facial expression, her body language. If she was just leading him on over the phone he'd just as soon take his lumps now and exit this relationship before it even started. That would be too bad though, not only because it would mean she had been insincere, but also because he hadn't been able to discern that, and he thought he was pretty good at reading people.

• • •

Lou wakened with the sunlight pouring into her window and showered again to get rid of her morning bed-head. She skipped breakfast and grabbed her jacket on the way out, running to meet Binh who was waiting at the front of the hotel as planned. They spent the morning interviewing Saigon officials about the details of the rooster outbreak. Close to lunch time Lou fished around in her pocket looking for a stick of gum and pulled out the envelope. She looked at it a moment not quite placing its origin before it struck her that she'd put it there last night in her mad dash to the room and its modern toilet and had completely forgotten about it since.

Binh was holding forth with the authorities in rapid-fire Vietnamese as Lou discreetly opened the note.

Lou,

Thought since we confirmed our mutual interest there's no time like the present, so I hopped a plane to Saigon. Can I buy you a drink on the terrace as our first official date? Give me a call when you get in---room 421.

Connor

Wow.

That was fast. She wasn't sure she was entirely comfortable with the speed of his effort, but more pressing was the fact that she hadn't seen the message until this moment. Even if his eagerness was disconcerting, Lou would never have been so rude as to ignore him, and was appalled that he might construe her lack of response as such.

Nodding to Binh, she wordlessly excused herself from the room. The entire meeting was being conducted in Vietnamese anyway. She had been reduced as usual to gauging the tone of the conversation, the clues on the faces of the speakers. Binh would have to interpret all of it for her over lunch.

She pulled her cell phone out and dialed the hotel, asking for Connor Mackenzie's room. There was no answer, but at least he was still checked in. "Connor, listen, this is Lou. I am *so* sorry...I didn't get your message until just now...I mean the clerk handed it to me when I checked in last night, but it was late and I was tired and I didn't realize it was from you...and I somehow managed to stuff it in my...pocket on the way to the room and I had to go to the...well...I was so tired I just forgot it was there and didn't find it until just this minute..." She paused to breathe, realizing she'd been running on. She chided herself for sounding like a love-struck teenager, slowed down and continued her one-sided dialogue with the hotel answering machine.

"Anyway...I'm surprised...to say the least, but...I'd love to join you for a drink if the offer is still open...but only if we don't call it a date...I'm done dating...we...we'll have to call it something else...or maybe nothing at all...and since it's not a date, the rule is dutch-treat except if one of us makes it clear ahead of time...which you did...so... you can buy." She smiled. "This time."

"I'll be done late this afternoon. Call me on my cell or leave me a message at the hotel. I promise I'll check. Bye."

What did it mean that he had boarded a plane and arrived here within hours of her letting him know she was interested? Was he that desperate for a girlfriend? On the surface of it, his immediate presence seemed a bit over-eager, but from her other interactions with him he didn't seem to be the insecure type. On the other hand, she could interpret his actions as romantic: dashing off to court her as soon as the signal was given. As though she were a prize to be won. *Really? How... enchanting.* Did she want to be treated like that? She could take care of herself. Didn't need the glitz and glamour of a knight in shining armor swooping down to...to what? She didn't need rescued from anything; she loved her life. Didn't need it. But maybe, just maybe, she liked it.

• • •

Well I'll be damned Connor thought when he returned to his hotel mid-afternoon and heard Lou's message. He shook his head and laughed to himself; it was always a story with her. She'd had an entire conversation with his voice mail. He was glad he hadn't been overly indignant about her delayed response; that would have been an utter waste of his time and energy. This woman was entertaining if nothing else. Connor looked forward to spending the evening with her and decided to consult the concierge for a dinner reservation.

. . .

It was a bumpy start but they laughed about it that night over martinis on the rooftop of the hotel, which had a wonderful view of the Saigon skyline. Crossing from professional and acquaintance territory into the region of romance brought its own hurdles and they spent the next four days negotiating the terrain.

Lou had some definite space issues which she characteristically raised without apology. Even though she was thoroughly enjoying his company she was concerned that Connor not push her too far or too fast. She was not impulsive; in fact she was almost obsessively a planner and a plodder. She admitted that she felt a bit unnerved by his precipitous arrival, but she was having too much fun to hold that against him.

For his part Connor informed Lou he wasn't the least bit threatened by her need to set boundaries. Connor acknowledged his spontaneity and confessed to a need for space himself. He didn't appreciate clinginess and told Lou that her independence was one of the things that attracted him.

What he didn't tell Lou was that he was a patient man. If she was worth waiting for, he was not only capable, it was a test of his own skills he would savor. The more he got to know her the more he liked what he saw.

They worked during the days and spent the evenings cruising Saigon, building trust and a repertoire of shared experiences. There was no physical intimacy even though they both felt a strong attraction; Lou had never allowed herself to act early on her libido. When she was attracted to someone she had a hard time arbitrarily deciding how to stop kissing from progressing to sex, so she would give no signals to Connor that even made him feel comfortable putting his arm around her. She wanted to be sure that she wanted this man in her life before she let her guard down enough to even hold his hand.

Connor wasn't sure what was going on. He knew she was attracted to him, he could see it, feel it. She would look at him across the table, sizing him up, her gaze occasionally lingering on his lips, or moving to his shoulders or hands, almost daring him to reciprocate. But she kept a discrete distance when they were seated next to one another, not so far away that she was inappropriate, but not close enough to encourage casual contact either. It was damned awkward. He seized an opportunity to put his arm around her at one point when they were walking, ostensibly to guide her around a chuck hole in the pavement, and she gracefully slid out of his grasp as soon they passed the rut.

Lou was flying back to Guangzhou in the morning. It was their last night together and she would not stand still long enough to be kissed. All of their encounters had been in public places, she would not invite him into her room and she declined an invitation to his. They had finally parted in the lobby, Lou saying she was going to check her e-mail on the hotel's computer before she went upstairs. She had escorted him to the elevator and simply said, "Good bye Connor. I've had a wonderful time. I'm glad you came."

He rode the lift with his bewilderment and frustration. It was maddening. He was beginning to feel like a eunuch: four days and he'd barely touched her. No matter how difficult she was making this, his masculinity required that he make a move, even if she rebuffed him. He got off the elevator and walked to his room and called her cell phone.

"Hi."

"Hi."

"How are you?" he asked.

She laughed. "Same as I was five minutes ago...Why?"

"I just wanted you to know I had one hell of a time keeping my hands off of you all week."

Silence.

"Lou?"

"Yes..." *Wow. Polite, fun, romantic, intelligent, And a bad-boy too.*

"I'm sorry if I offended you, but I..."

"No... no, I'm...not offended...I just...well... you...took my breath away...I don't know what to say...except that you are full of surprises Connor Mackenzie...and so far I like them just fine." She got chills down her spine thinking she just might have met her match. "I need time..."

"I know and I'm not pushing you. But I just had to tell you how I felt."

"You know, even on the surface you are one interesting man. But what bubbles up from the depths of you is potentially even more fascinating." Lou smiled as she gave the guy some encouragement. "You'll be on my mind Connor."

"I'm counting on it."

VIETNAM
January 15

After Lou left Saigon, Connor decided to visit Duyen Ba himself. He reported regularly on the mass exterminations that had taken place in the poultry markets of cities throughout Southeast Asia, and had developed plenty of story lines from the urban dwellers' point of view. This time he wanted to explore a rural frame of reference.

Binh helped Connor hire a driver/interpreter. He and his guide were not as lucky as Binh and Lou with the weather. A downpour started just before they left Saigon flooding the low lying roads outside the city to a muddy mess. Worse, you couldn't see the ruts and holes, which caused them to do an inordinate amount of bouncing in the diminutive vehicle whose shocks Connor thought must have been left on the factory floor. It was a good thing they both had strong stomachs.

Connor was welcomed to the hamlet in the same way as Binh and Lou. He listened while the women talked of how they cared for the birds, how they had kept the chickens penned up as they had been instructed by the government, even though it was not their tradition to do so. Occasionally they would let the birds out to peck at scraps left on the ground from cleaning fish or corn, or any of the other digestible debris shrugged off from the village in the course of the day. Yes, they said, the birds might be out long enough to mingle with geese that passed through on their migrations, but the chickens were always back in the coop at night.

A few of the men lingered from their chores to lead Connor around the borders of the village, showing him the few fruit trees, the rice paddy, the burial place, and the landmarks defining the boundaries with the next village. Connor was reminded of the follow up Binh had asked him to do while he was here.

"Has the young man who was gone returned?" Connor reached into his pocket to retrieve a scrap of paper with the name, "Duc Trinh?"

The men shook their heads in answer. Through his guide Connor learned that they had been expecting him for a couple days now. He could tell by the looks on their faces that they were concerned.

"What would cause him to be delayed?" Connor pressed.

They looked at each other and put their heads down, clearly reluctant to answer. Then one of them spoke. He seemed to think that Duc might have been delayed by the weather, especially if it had rained farther north. The men picked their heads up and nodded vigorously to one another with this explanation. Another villager went on to offer that maybe the man's sister and brother-in-law had required help with some task before Duc returned to fetch his family. The other men nodded again, waiting for the translation to be made. Gradually they fell to hanging their heads once more. Connor's interpreter, aware of the group's now apparent symptoms of shame, patiently finessed a final hypothesis from a reticent spokesman: it was possible the young husband had been so frightened by the prospect of his family's starvation that he had run away and would not be coming back.

Connor was glad to have the information but troubled that he had caused the men to expose themselves. He knew that in their culture the dishonor of one man was the dishonor of the entire village. To be worried about Duc Trinh and his family was one thing, to reveal his likely disgrace to a stranger was quite another. Attempting to be helpful to them and to continue his investigation, he asked if he might be of service on his way back to Saigon. If they could provide some instruction as to where the man was heading or what path he might have taken, he would inquire as to his whereabouts. If there had been difficulty in Duc's getting back to the village Connor could offer assistance. The men seemed pleased with this offer and conferred once again, giving instructions to the guide on the location of the sister's village and the likely route Duc would have traveled.

After thanking the men and women for the interviews, Connor and his guide ate from a boxed lunch Connor had ordered from the hotel, packed up their belongings and headed out. They attempted to follow the path Duc might have taken as the villagers had instructed.

Unfortunately they had no picture of Duc but they had a fair description, and of course, his name. But names, Connor had discovered on previous trips, were fairly scarce in Vietnam and it was not unusual to have several people with the exact first, middle and last names in the same community. It would be challenging to locate, among all the villages they passed, where Duc might have been seen on his journey.

Compounding this problem was the difficulty he and the driver were having in gauging how far a walking man might have traveled on these roads before stopping for the night. Were there shortcuts they did not know? And would he stay in a village or camp on his own in the wild? Connor allowed his guide free rein with decisions on which way to go and where to stop. On several occasions as they jostled through marsh-grass-lined trails that were barely visible, or bounced over mangrove roots working up into the path or when Connor had to get out and push to get them out of a tire-sucking rut, they both questioned the wisdom of this plan. They stopped at every village they encountered for several kilometers thinking the area might be a likely layover point for Duc, and were just about to give up when they got a lead.

At the last hamlet the inhabitants had not seen Duc, but they reported that a neighboring village had sent two people on the road to Saigon about a week ago and they thought the men were traveling with a stranger who had stopped and stayed with them for the night. Connor and his guide got out of the car in the place indicated and made inquiries of a few children who at first raced up to them and then hung back shyly. An elder came out of a nearby hut and confirmed that indeed a young man, he could not remember his name, had stayed with them for one night over a week ago. He was on his way to Saigon. No, he paused and corrected himself, not to Saigon, to his sister's home in another town on the way. Tran Phu and his son were leaving for Saigon and they offered to embark a day earlier than they planned, to keep company with the outsider on their journey. It was more pleasant and safer, after all, to travel with companions.

"How were his spirits?" Connor asked. "Did he seem troubled?"

He was told that the man had seemed fine. He had spoken of the loss of the chickens with sadness, yes, but he was energetic with hope that he and his family would be welcomed by his sister and they would return to their village after the child was born. Connor found it interesting that names were of no importance, but the details of a story could be recited with vigor. The narrator related they had given the man a meal and some extra portion of food for his journey as they had felt compassion for his troubles.

"Have you seen him pass through on his return?"

The elder shook his head.

"How far did your people walk with him? Might we speak with them to see where they last encountered him? "

"You would be most welcome to speak with Tran Phu," the man said. "But he is not here. It has been ten days and he and his son have not returned from Saigon yet. It usually takes seven to ten days," the old man nodded toward the sky, "depending on the weather. They are expected back any time."

Until this point Connor was merely interested in what had happened to Duc Trinh. Wondered what story the man would have to tell if they found him. It hadn't occurred to him that there might be another reason for his disappearance unrelated to those cited by his neighbors. One that he and the villagers hadn't even thought of. Connor started thinking now. After a few pleasantries they thanked the man and he and the driver returned to the car and headed back to Saigon.

As soon as he got a signal, Connor dialed Lou.

"Lou, Duc Trinh never returned."

"What?"

"He was expected back a few days ago and no one has seen him."

"Interesting. Maybe he got side-tracked."

"It gets more interesting. He hooked up on the second day of his journey with two people from another village traveling toward Saigon."

"So?"

"They haven't come back yet either." Connor reported.

"Okay, you've got my attention. What else did you find out?"

"Not much. In Duyen Ba they tried to convince me that Duc might just be delayed, but then they admitted he might have abandoned his family. I admit that's what I thought too until I spoke with a man at the village where he spent his first night. According to this guy, Duc appeared to be in good spirits when he arrived, eager to get to his sister's and return to Duyen Ba. They had tried to persuade him to wait a day in their village because the other two people, a man named Tran Phu and his son, were not planning on leaving so soon, but Duc was adamant to keep going so he could get back home. Tran left a day earlier than planned to travel part of the way with him."

"Do we know the name of the town Duc was headed to?"

"Yes. My translator has it all written down, directions too. I thought I'd give Binh the information as soon as we get back."

"That would be great. I'll call him right now and tell him to get over there and investigate." Lou's mind was racing trying to figure out if the timing could be right for incubation of the virus. "Was anyone ill?" she asked.

"No. No one was ill in Duyen Ba when I checked in with them, and the man in the other village did not recall any illness when Duc stayed with them. He also denied that anyone in his village was ill."

"Thanks Connor. Good work. What's next on your agenda?"

"A hot shower and a cold martini. I might even find myself a Vietnamese spa and hire a fabulous pair of hands to massage the kinks out of my traumatized muscles. I about had to fold myself in half just to get into that car. I bounced from Saigon to the Mekong and back today."

Lou laughed. Having just been on that trip herself she could sympathize.

"I have to fly back to the states tomorrow to cover a conference in New York." Connor said. "I'll give you a call in a couple days. Let me know if anything comes up in the meantime."

"I will."

Lou called Binh immediately and relayed the information. He promised to start looking for Duc Trinh's sister in the morning. Lou knew from his sigh that he thought it might all be a wasted effort if the man had simply abandoned his family, but there was no way to know without checking.

CALIFORNIA
January 18

Retooling the production lines at PharmaGlobal's main facility was almost done. There had been a few additional kinks to be worked out, but things were progressing and they were on track to start making vaccine this week. After the board agreed to switch to Avimmune manufacture Vaughn had immediately initiated the conversion of the plant to avian production even though no purchase orders had been finalized with any of the organizations previously expressing interest. He had hoped to have the dollars up front, but if he was to make more than one batch of any vaccine this year he had to get moving. Proceeding was risky but it was more risky to wait. The more they could produce, and the faster they could produce it the more profit they would accrue.

Trying to evaluate the delay in orders, he'd called his old buddy Cyril Hunt at the department of Health and Human Services. "Just wanted to let you know we'll be rolling off sixty million doses of Avimmune by June. Hadn't heard back from you about how much your boss wants."

"The president is not jumping on the bird-flu bandwagon," Hunt had allowed. "Bunch of damn nonsense he says. But don't you worry, the party's dogging him...election year and all that...so you'll have an order. He's talking about five million doses of vaccine and some of that drug too, what is it? Osma-Fear...I think he calls it..."

"Five million? That's a drop in the bucket," Vaughn interrupted. "You can't even cover first-responders with that!"

"Whoa, J.B., whoa," Hunt stopped him. "As the president sees it, if this here cuckoo-flu is all hype, that's five million vaccines we'll be flushing down the national toilet. Taxpayers won't be too happy 'bout that."

"And if it isn't hype?"

"Well then," he allowed, "I guess you'll be sittin' pretty."

GUANGZHOU, CHINA
January 19

Lou was starting her day in the usual way, drinking green tea while she checked her e-mail. She missed a rich cup of coffee, but it was nearly impossible to find here. For a while she'd had coffee beans sent from back home, but it was a hassle and eventually she had simply fallen back on a 'do as the Romans do' philosophy. She consoled herself by noting that green tea was full of anti-oxidants which were ridiculously healthy for you; she had to remind herself constantly about its benefits because it suffused the palate like spinach water. Looked like it too, she mused, peering at the soggy green leaves floating loosely in the mug.

As she queued up her in-box she immediately noticed the arrival of the lab report from Duyen Ba. Opening the message she saw the results on the lung samples they'd obtained from Hue Pham. Under bacterial isolates it said: routine flora consistent with human lung, post mortem state. Scanning the page quickly she stopped when saw what she was looking for under viral isolates: *avian influenza, type: H5N1.*

So, Hue Pham had died from avian flu. Lou took a deep breath as she settled back in her chair and buried the hope she'd entertained that it might have been simply a severe, common respiratory problem that killed Hue: strep or staph pneumonia perhaps, bacterial lung infections that could be readily cured with appropriate antibiotics in developed countries but were still a common cause of mortality among the poor.

She scrolled through the mail, deleting the spam, and came across an e-mail from Binh. He'd spent the last few days looking for the town of Duc Trinh's sister. The information provided by Connor's guide had unfortunately been inadequate and the village he'd gone to was the wrong place; no one had heard of Duc or his sister. After exploring some of the neighboring hamlets equally without success, he'd finally been forced to return to Duyen Ba to obtain better directions. Binh fervently wished as he drove back to the hamlet that the young man had shown up by now and he could end his wild goose chase.

In Duyen Ba Binh was disappointed to learn Duc had not returned. After a second round of searching he eventually had been able to locate Duc's sister who was quite dismayed after she heard of her brother's plight. She and her husband would have welcomed his request to move his family in, but Duc had never arrived. Now she too was distraught that he was missing. She was adamant that her brother would not abandon his family no matter the circumstances. Binh had returned to Saigon and was unsure how to proceed.

On a better note he was happy to report that he'd been successful in hiring a new field worker, Mai Linh. She was Vietnamese and a recent graduate of a U.S. college, who had just returned to her homeland. Binh wanted to know what Lou thought he should do. Were the pathology results back yet? If they were negative there was no reason for him to continue this investigation. If there was further searching to be done, he would have to do it himself. Filing a missing persons report was nothing but a waste of paper in Vietnam. Did Lou want him to continue the search or stay in Saigon and train the new associate?

Lou mulled this over. It was true Binh might be wasting his time looking for a runaway husband, but this was also a loose end in a now confirmed avian exposure where there had been a death from H5N1. Chasing down every lead was exactly the reason she'd hired more case workers.

Binh,

Have your new hire spend time daily with poultry workers, restaurant employees, and city health officials. Tell her to acquaint herself with the hospitals and clinics and the popular healers around town. They'll become more comfortable with her face over time and be more inclined to speak with her if they notice anything unusual. She can also familiarize herself with the data on the outbreaks in Vietnam, Cambodia, Laos, and Indonesia, updating the charts in the computer with the new viral types. The details matter, and the more people we have aware of them, the more likely nothing will be missed.

Just received the path report-- Hue Pham died of H5N1. Dismal as it sounds, you need to head back out and find our guy, Duc. I'd start at the place he hooked up with the other two... (you didn't mention if they were back yet?) ...and see if you can't persuade them to retrace their steps with you. It's really unlikely that the young man carried any contagion with him as we've had no reports of additional respiratory deaths from the countryside, but, it's our job to prove it. Keep me posted.

Best,

Lou

CHAPTER 9

WASHINGTON D.C.
January 20

Michael Farrington was biding his time in the reception area of Cyril Hunt's office, having already been kept waiting twenty five minutes for his appointment. Hunt, he thought, was pulling a little power play meant to reinforce to Farrington his relative lack of importance to the White House in general, and Hunt in particular. If Farrington had thought in the same terms as Hunt he would have been angered by this overt display of arrogance; happily he was a different sort and refused to be either riled or intimidated by Hunt's shenanigans.

"Mr. Hunt will see you now," the receptionist indicated as she came around her desk and motioned Michael to the door.

"Michael, welcome," Hunt drawled as Farrington entered. "Grab a seat son and tell me about your travels. What seeds of discontent has the World Health Organization sown into your head on this trip?" he said tilting his head back and belching smoke from his over-sized Cuban cigar.

Farrington was amazed at the variety of ways the man could find to exude offense. He was also proud of himself for not taking the bait. There was a time in his life where the gall would have risen in his throat over such comments, but he was young then. Oh, to have the body of that man with the soul he presently possessed, he thought with passing wistfulness. He noted the sneer of the bloated toad sitting opposite him with studied detachment as he tried to generate some empathy as a means of tolerating the man's insulting demeanor. An insecure product of an unfulfilled childhood perhaps? Exemplary siblings outshining him, or worse, humiliating him? Unrequited love? Repressed homosexuality? The source of Hunt's affliction was unclear, and its explanation ultimately unessential to the task at hand.

Farrington had no taste for drawing this out with any small talk. "The WHO is advancing a new policy. We expected to be asked to stockpile H5N1 for domestic use and to contribute it to an international pool for third world countries."

"And...?"

"The WHO is backing away from that plan and advising a much broader pool of vaccines targeted at new permutations of avian flu as they arise."

"Why the shift? I thought H5N1 was being touted as the last horseman of the apocalypse." Despite the sarcasm Farrington knew he had caught Hunt's attention. Hunt took the cigar out of his mouth and leaned forward in his chair to tap off the ash.

"Well as the number of cases of human infection rises there's been an increasing amount of debate as to what form the virus will take when it reaches pandemic criteria. The discussants are divided into two camps. The first believes that since all the human cases have been H5N1 thus far, that H5N1 is the likely strain, even though its lack of contagion between humans has not made it pandemic yet. They believe we ought to be stockpiling H5N1 and the most aggressive among them even suggest inoculating the world against H5N1 now, before H5N1 achieves pandemic potential."

"No doubt that would be great news for the pharmaceutical industry," Hunt commented dryly.

"You're right Cyril, it's a gold mine. It's a race to see who can supply the product or the technology deemed most indispensable by health authorities." For once Farrington thought, he and Hunt agreed on something. "In fact I understand PharmaGlobal is rather counting on it. One of their advisory board members is a major researcher of avian flu. In a recent interview he suggested H5N1 vaccination of all residents of Southeast Asia."

"Yes, yes. What's the other view?' Hunt interrupted.

"...The second camp it seems has taken hold of WHO policy for the moment. Their theory is that the world is a vast laboratory for the mixing of avian flu with the human variant. Incubate all these viruses in a variety of species in the wild and eventually, with mingling and mutation, you'll have a pandemic strain. These scientists are concerned that H5N1 is just a red herring and that it has no more potential for achieving pandemic than any other avian strain. They worry that focusing on H5N1 inoculation will divert resources and attention away from identifying a real pandemic virus should it happen to be anything other than H5N1."

"Hmmph." Hunt belched, chewing agitatedly on the cigar.

"Let me see if I've got this right Michael," Hunt said leaning across his desk and into the phrase. "You're telling me that the focus on H5N1 is old news? The president is just getting used to the idea of building a supply of H5N1, and the strategy is already changing?" Cyril spat with contempt.

Farrington ignored his tone. "The WHO is pursuing targeted prevention combined with massive treatment programs. They are advocating for extensive research to revolutionize production so that new vaccines can be made within a few weeks, instead of several months. When vaccines can be produced in real time it will obviate the need to predict a pandemic strain. New immunizations will be made immediately. Until that happens the goal will be to contain the first outbreak through international cooperation. WHO sees wealthy nations providing a small but steady supply of vaccine in all identified permutations of the virus in the wild. As soon as pandemic flu is declared, all of the supply of vaccine would be made available to the population in the endemic area. Shipments of osmavir to those exposed would coincide with inoculation of those deemed most at risk. Governments would enact and enforce quarantines. Meanwhile every pharmaceutical company in the world would be set on making the vaccine for the confirmed strain so that when mass production kicks in, the correct vaccine will be produced, and not a vaccine that is mere guesswork."

Farrington had to admit that settling on any strategy was a scary proposition. One could understand the rhetoric that inflamed the debate. Scientists relied on data, and the data that existed could be interpreted in different ways. The fact was no one in the scientific community knew which combination of 'H' and 'N' proteins would construe themselves into a highly pathologic and contagious infection for humans. The current debate reflected each side's best guess. Not very reassuring, but the world had to make some choices. To do nothing was even more of a grim option.

Hunt was leaning back in his chair again, his head wreathed in smoke. The room reeked. "Interesting," was all he said.

Farrington thought it would have been appropriate for Hunt to ask him for his opinion, but he did not. Hunt puffed, exhaled.

"The president has been contemplating the purchase of five million doses of Avimmune from PharmaGlobal Michael. Might I remind you that your advice to him several weeks ago, when you insisted on a personal meeting, was to buy considerably more than that. What exactly do you think I am supposed to do with this new information?" It was a rhetorical question, uttered with disgust. "Do you think I can just march up to the president every other week and tell him his advisors have changed their minds? Do you think he wants to change his mind in front of the American public every time a scientist flies off on another tangent about how to save the world? This is not how the president of the most powerful country in the world conducts business."

Farrington snapped back, finally losing patience with Hunt's political protectionism. "You know Cyril, this problem defies black and white decision making. It cannot be reduced to a series of binary questions and finite answers. The most accurate thing we can say about the virus is that it is predictably unpredictable. I don't give a damn about your concerns to create acceptable political spin. I presume that's what the president and the party pay his handlers to do. I am here to relate to this administration the status, as perceived by the best scientists in the world, of one of the most complex biological challenges ever to face earth."

Farrington stood to leave. "You know where to find me should you want to discuss this. You are clearly resistant to serious deliberation at the moment. I can only hope someone in this administration has the foresight to see that whatever policy is decided on is the result of careful consideration of the available information. I would be happy to convene a group of experts for the president's benefit should you wish to avail yourselves of further input." And with that Farrington walked away.

Hunt raised an eyebrow and continued to worry his cigar.

"Ken," Vaughn said when his secretary finally got him on the line. One always knew where to find him, but Ken did not like to be disturbed and Vaughn did not like to wait. "Anything new going on in the world of avian flu?"

"Well, new cases are popping up almost daily. Bird migration appears to be spreading it east and south of Asia. But I would imagine you already know that, so, I guess the answer is, not much. That's an odd question from a man who makes it his business to have all the answers. Why do you ask?"

"Well, just double checking to make sure I'm not missing anything here. Orders for Avimmune are sluggish, considering the enormous interest expressed last fall."

"Can't imagine that's a problem. H5N1 is the only human player. Plenty of us are calling for stockpiles of vaccine. The orders are sure to follow."

"That's my take on it, but I don't like leaving any stones unturned," Vaughn announced. "Just being thorough. So, no recent contact from the WHO?"

"No. I wasn't really expecting any. I gave them my views last fall. Nothing's changed. Say, how's production going?" Ken asked.

"Terrific. Smooth sailing."

"Any breakthroughs at R and D?"

"Nothing to report there," Vaughn replied. He had laid off most of his researchers. If all went well they would lose less than a year in development. He was not concerned and there was no reason to concern anyone else. It was a business move.

"Genetic technology is the future of medicine and PharmaGlobal has a good chance of being at the top. Some great work has come out of your lab. That says a lot about what you value Vaughn."

"Yes..." Vaughn agreed. "Ken, have to go. Much to do. Give me a call if anything comes up." And he was gone.

GUANGZHOU, CHINA
January 22

"...Lou..."

"Yes...Binh?" There was lots of static on the line and she couldn't make out a thing he was saying, but the caller ID identified his cell. After a minute of scratchy cackling and a few unintelligible words, the connection was lost altogether. She received another phone call from him a few minutes later with the same result. He'd just have to get closer to a tower.

It was almost an hour later before he got through.

"Dr. Lou." He said urgently.

"Well that's better. What is it?" she said leaving small talk aside. It was clear he had something to say.

"I just returned from Bac Tho."

"Where's that?"

"It's where Duc Trinh stopped his first night on the road...the village where he met up with Tran Phu...the man and his son who went with him. I started back there as you said, hoping to speak to them. When Connor stopped there last week, they weren't due back yet, and no one was alarmed. But Lou, they've been gone over two weeks now."

"What?"

"That's right. No one has seen or heard from them. They were going to Saigon to pick up supplies. Several of the inhabitants have visited other villages looking for word of them but no one has been able to tell them a thing. Tran usually takes the back roads to avoid outlaws, so it wouldn't be remarkable for him not to have stayed in any villages on the way to or from town. Evidently he was robbed in the past and was carrying some cash this time."

"Wow. Not just one missing person, three. Two different villages. What do you think Binh?"

"Well, it doesn't sound good. Frankly at this point I'm more worried about foul play than flu. There isn't much murder in the countryside here. But maybe they were robbed and killed. At least we can probably throw away the theory that young Duc abandoned his family. Tran and his son certainly weren't having problems at home. Looks like something happened to all three of them."

Binh seemed genuinely distressed for the welfare of his country-men. Whatever happened to cause all of them to disappear was most likely not good, and he would not only have to find out what that was, but because of the extent of his professional involvement with the families of these men, Lou knew he would now be duty bound to follow up personally in each village with the bad news he was sure to discover.

"I have already notified the police. When I couldn't reach you from Bac Tho, I decided to get the authorities involved. I spoke with officials in Can Lai and My Tho, small cities on the main road back to Saigon. I gave them directions to Duc's and Tran's villages so they could get better descriptions of the missing people than I was able to give."

"How did that go?" Lou knew it would be an uphill battle to get the police to investigate. Even three lost souls at a time would not be enough to overcome the inertia that often characterized the local cops.

"About as you would expect. They were gruff, and noticeably under-whelmed with my concerns that something bad may have happened, and even less impressed with my insistence that their whereabouts were important as they are the subject of an avian flu inquiry by the WHO. Frankly, that may have been the final nail in the coffin of cooperation."

"I can call Saigon and pull some diplomatic strings to put pressure on the police to at least launch an investigation. How much of an effort they expend can't be guaranteed, but they won't be able to ignore our request for help completely. It does sound like our guys may have met with disaster, but you're right, it probably isn't the flu. You might as well get back to your work in Saigon."

"That's what I thought. I'll follow up with the police weekly until we get some closure," Binh replied. "Any other ideas?"

"No. Keep in touch."

Lou hung up thinking the whole thing was just too bad. Not only had Duyen Ba lost all of its poultry, a young mother had died, and probably also a young man trying to save his family from starvation. Even if the men had been murdered, Lou thought ironically, avian flu could still be identified as the instigating cause, having set the wheel of their troubles in motion.

Before she was ready to let the matter move to the back burner she forced herself to consider whether avian flu might yet be a more proximate cause for Duc's disappearance and that of the other two. Highly unlikely. Highly, she thought. But was it impossible? She had to take a closer look at the facts before deciding.

She pulled up her computer file on the case and started penciling in dates on her desk calendar as she reviewed the file.

December 24---Duyen Ba---poultry kill ---H5N1 documented as cause of death

December 31---Duyen Ba---Hue Pham becomes ill

January 4---Duyen Ba---Hue Pham dies---H5N1 documented as cause of death

January 5---Duc Trinh leaves Duyen Ba, arrives at Bac Tho that night

January 6---Duc Trinh leaves Bac Tho with Tran Phu and son

January 12 – 18 --- Duc and Tran expected back in their respective villages

January 22--- today's date. No sign of the missing men and the boy.

Next Lou pulled up reports she had filed on other human H5N1 cases to review the prodromal period, the time between known exposure to H5N1 and the onset of symptoms in the victim. This incubation phase ranged from two to fourteen days, with an average of eight. The time from illness to death from H5N1 was as little as three days and as long as several weeks if the victim made it to a hospital. For the patients who got well, the course of recovery was weeks to months.

Duc had left home twelve days after the poultry kill but, like the others in the village, he had handled the carcasses for four or five days after they died so he might have acquired H5N1 from the dead chickens and left Duyen Ba only seven days into the fourteen day possible incubation period. If he contracted H5N1 from Hue, he had not shown symptoms for at least five days after she got sick since he was still well when he stayed overnight in Bac Tho.

So, if Duc had contracted H5N1, whether from the poultry or from Hue Pham, then he had become ill after he left Bac Tho. But if that were the case, he should have had enough time to make it to another village for help. Even those who died from H5N1 had lasted a few days before succumbing. Surely he would have sought assistance. Or his companions would have pursued it. And, if Hue had transmitted a communicable strain of H5N1 to Duc before she died, why hadn't anyone else in Duyen Ba become ill? Duc had not been in as close contact to Hue as her own family, and none of them were sick. No it didn't make epidemiologic sense. If the virus were both communicable and pathologic, others should have gotten sick too.

Lou admitted she could not put it all together. There was nothing from the extant knowledge of H5N1 that could account for the current scenario. She concluded for the second time in the last hour that some unforeseen tragedy had probably befallen the men and hoped that the particulars would eventually come to light. It was unfortunate that the men had to encounter their calamity in the midst of an avian flu investigation. She would remain uneasy until she had a thorough explanation.

She was forced to draw her thoughts away from the missing men as there were other reports clamoring for her attention. She had received confirmation this week that the little boy hospitalized in Saigon with respiratory symptoms did not have avian flu, but a common childhood infection with RSV, respiratory syncitial virus. Interestingly, if the young fellow hadn't gotten sick and scared the bejeebers out of his mother, they never would have known about the H3N3 outbreak in Saigon. The cock-fighting industry was shrouded in secrecy; officially, it did not exist. Outside the rings, roosters and their handlers kept a low profile and officials turned their heads. Great case work on Binh's part revealed the father of the boy ran a cock-fighting ring, and his son was part of the everyday care and maintenance of the stable. Several roosters in the fighting community got sick, then died a few days later. The handlers quickly separated the animals and shut down the business on their own to avoid contagion. Within a week they had opened back up after no more birds had fallen ill.

It was shortly thereafter that the boy had developed a high fever, terrible cough and shortness of breath. When he turned blue, his mother, who had been trying all manner of home remedies to no avail, took him to the hospital. In a moment of panic she blurted out to the doctors that the boy had gotten sick just like the roosters. This remark brought masks and isolation gowns around the room, and a visit by health authorities and the WHO to the cock fighters who were, needless to say, unhappy with the attention. While all the dead roosters were long since eaten or burned, the veterinarians were able to collect blood samples from some that had been sick but had not died. H3N3 had been a surprise to everyone as it was the first time the combination had been seen in the wild.

At the moment H3N3 seemed to be a dead end. The Vietnamese government had, under advisement by the WHO, mandated the extermination of the rest of the cocks. The handlers of course had smuggled whatever birds they could out of the area before the culling, so the strain was likely here to stay. It was impossible to tell how virulent the organism was from a single isolated outbreak, but judging from the size of this one, its lack of major kill in the birds, and the absence of notable human transmission, it was not a player at the moment.

Lou moved on to considering the other two new variants. The first was H9N1, discovered in November as the cause of massive deaths of migratory geese in Mongolia. She had sent Yong out from their Guangzhou office to investigate that episode. He came back with long tales from area residents laden with conjecture on the significance of birds in flight dropping out of the sky before their very eyes. People had actually been injured by the falling geese. The events of the several days in which multitudes of geese were found lying dead across the plains or plummeting earthward from the heavens were described by the natives as portents for some catastrophe yet to befall them. The population was abuzz with rituals and prayers to appease whomever they thought they had offended.

The dead flock had been identified by the WHO as one typically migrating from southwestern China to northeastern Russia. There had been much interaction of the local people with the dead birds. Some had cleaned and cooked the fowl, grateful for the extra meat. Others had burned, buried or otherwise ceremoniously disposed of them as their spiritual leanings prescribed. Regardless of the disposition, there were no identified human cases and no other infected bird populations in the area. H9N1 was brand new, and currently moot.

The third variant was H7N1 reported in two separate places: a small kill on a farm in Indonesia and a large kill in rural Thailand. Lou did not have anyone free to travel to Indonesia; they'd relied on local reports and samples sent by the Indonesians. Lou had been trained that circumstances were related until proven otherwise, but thus far there was no indication of whether or how the two widely separated outbreaks were connected.

Possibilities were numerous. Migrating wild animals were the most likely source of any relatedness; however one would have expected more outbreaks in susceptible fowl along the flight path of whatever species was carrying the disease. So far there were none. The poultry markets throughout Southeast Asia were tightly packed breeding grounds for contagion, so contaminated birds could easily be spreading disease through licensed routes or black market smuggling. But again, there were no additional reports of H7N1 since December. Lastly, it was entirely possible that identical spontaneous mutations had occurred simultaneously in both Thailand and Indonesia. Possible, but not likely. As with the other new variants, no human disease had been reported.

Three new mutations in three months. She couldn't help but be fascinated by the profound changes the virus was making as she tracked it. The new variants had not demonstrated contagion among other bird species and no predilection for people. Nor had H5N1 developed reliable person to person transmission. Yet. But, left to incubate in pigs and mice and people and cats and swans and parrots and fish and ducks, any of these viruses, or another mutant, certainly could be the basis for a pandemic leap.

But which? Where?

Lou turned from her computer screen and stared out the window. She hoped that at some point in her life she could answer more questions than she asked. Why had she taken this job with its steady stream of problems without solutions? Ha! Another question.

Naming the enemy was a global priority whether it was correct or not. Everyone wanted to know what to fight, demanded to know. Beneath the rhetoric Lou vaguely perceived a sense of entitlement to the knowledge. And the media fed it. Most reporters had no idea how to question scientists or interpret the data they were given. They interviewed experts for their opinions without any competence for probing the fault lines of those thoughts. Her criticism was tempered with the knowledge that even scientists must hone the skills necessary to tease the conclusions from the evidence. In the field of epidemiology, as in most scientific pursuits, one started with an observation, or a set of observations, and whatever data already existed that might relate to the subject. Then one proceeded to offer an empirical hypothesis to account for the observations. To the extent possible, research was then conducted to prove or disprove the hypothesis. Without rigorous dissection of the research, there was no science, no truth.

In her own interviews she was always amazed that no matter how carefully she chose her words, trying to portray the influenza picture as the murky miasma it was, she came off sounding authoritative in print; the reporter never captured the shadings. With one notable exception, she thought: Connor. It was part of the reason they had become friends. She had begun to read his bylines after they met and was pleasantly surprised to see him dealing with subtlety. He asked questions that probed the weaknesses in arguments, laid bare flaws in extrapolating data, wrote articles that conveyed the nuances in the literature.

Lou had been so impressed with one piece on chicken pox that she called him to find out how he knew the proper questions to ask. She was sure if they taught that in journalism school all the other reporters would have been just as capable, and clearly they were not. Connor shared his love of science and his decision to obtain a bachelors degree in biochemistry. It was a non-traditional route to J-school he admitted but it had worked. Since then he found he was not satisfied as a reporter with the pre-packaged spam he was often handed by professionals. There had been far too many poor arguments advanced throughout history as gospel, and proven wrong, for him to be threatened by the mere presence of initials after a name: M.D., Ph.D., M.S. or M.P.H., it didn't matter to him. He would get to the bottom of what was known, and separate it from what was being guessed.

Lou was certain of only one thing: the most important response to avian flu was revolutionizing vaccines. A process that took a few weeks instead of several months was a reachable goal with the infusion of enough talent and money: charge scientists to make vaccine instead of the atom bomb, an inoculation parallel to the Manhattan Project for developing the atom bomb. With technology that could produce a vaccine within a few weeks, predicting the virus would become moot. In 1918 Spanish influenza killed more people than all the wars in recorded history combined. Yet war machinery was flush with funding, while armaments against the virus remained anemic. It was madness.

SOUTHWEST VIETNAM
January 30

The dog nosed her way over the uneven path, adroitly negotiating the ruts despite the continual side-to-side motion of her head as she tracked. Binh and his new assistant Mai had been scouring the territory north of Bac Tho for three days with a cadaver dog obtained from the Vietnamese military after much diplomatic wrangling by Lou. As far as Binh could tell the local police weren't helping them at all; they had encountered no one in uniform since they started.

"Aiyee!" Mai yelped. Binh turned in time to see her go down in a heap.

"Let me see...let me see," he said trying to calm her as she rolled in the dirt clutching her right ankle.

Tears streamed down Mai's face as he squatted down and gingerly took the ankle from her grasp. There was an unmistakable purple swelling starting at the junction between her leg and foot. Binh shook his head in disbelief. They had hoped to search another couple hours until dark, and the car was a good three or four miles back to boot. He sat down in the dirt next to her.

"You won't be walking on that anytime soon."

Mai launched into a full sob when she saw the look of resignation and fatigue on Binh's face: her stumble would cost them the rest of the day's work, and the pain she was in dissolved any effort she might have made to control her emotions.

"It's okay." Binh said, trying to soothe her, trying to figure out exactly how to make it okay. The dog had circled back to them by now, nose up in the wind, alternating between the handlers and the scent. Binh commanded her to sit, at which point only her snout continued to roam.

"Please tell me that was not a raindrop," he said under his breath as he stood up, hatching a plan that would not be improved by rain. He squinted at the sky and decided it was definitely coming, though it was just a wayward sprinkle he'd felt so far. He took a roll of tape out of his backpack and wound it around Mai's ankle to compress it, keeping the blood from leaking into the soft tissue spaces and causing more pain. He scooted her to the side of the path and placed her ankle up on both of their packs.

"That will help for a while. We'll probably have to loosen it later. Let me know if your toes start to hurt or go numb." He fastened the dog to her leash and handed it to Mai.

"Where are you going?"

Binh looked all around him and up at the sky again. "I'm going to look for some shelter for you before it starts to rain. Then I'm going to run back to get the car." He took off before she could object. He half jogged, half walked through the brush scouting for something more than reeds to protect his new associate when he saw a cluster of low, over-hanging rocks nearly obscured by the thick grass. He was angling in for a closer look when the wind from the approaching weather front changed direction. The odor hit him upside the head like a slap. He was on top of the body in the next instant, the violent gag out of him before he even recognized what had caused it. The retching continued as he frantically lurched about trying to find a space to clear his nostrils, his vision, of putrescence. At almost the same time he heard the dog barking distantly, back at Mai's side, as she too caught the scent.

An e-mail to Lou two days later read: "DNA confirms decedent is our man, Duc Trinh. Cause of death unknown due to decomposition. No trauma evident. Lung tissue sent to WHO for analysis."

GENEVA, SWITZERLAND
February 4

One month after the January board meeting Michael Farrington was back at WHO headquarters in Geneva as Director Bueller brought the reconvened members to order. The discussion was alive with input collected over the past four weeks from the delegates' experts and superiors back home.

"It would be a lot easier to commit to all of this if we were sure it would work," said one delegate.

"It is political suicide to send vaccine and drugs to the third world when there isn't enough for our own citizens," complained a member.

The man next to him countered, "It's also suicide to invite the outbreak onto your own soil by refusing to contain it where it starts. Donating vaccine and drugs is just good sense."

"Why not give H5N1 vaccine to everyone at risk? Why aren't we focusing on that?" from another.

"We shouldn't be making vaccine at all. It's a waste of money and time. It's all for show...to prove we're doing something. We have no idea if this is going to work."

"With air travel we're all going to be exposed before it can be contained anyway. I can certainly see the point of vaccine research. But wouldn't we be better off spending our money on treatment of people after they get ill? Shouldn't we be spending our money on osmavir?"

"Are we really capable of preventing a pandemic?"

And so it went.

"Reasonable people, well-informed debate," Malcolm told Connor afterwards. "A weighing of the costs of participation, versus the costs of non- participation in the WHO plan."

Farrington could only listen, having nothing positive to contribute from the U.S. He noted Bueller wisely did the same, allowing the discussion to wane, finally, of its own accord. Then Bueller rose from his chair at the head of the table and began, "It is a tribute to the honored place of modern medicine that these questions can even be asked today. To rely on antibiotics for the treatment of infections that less than a century ago would have resulted in certain death, to use artificial ventilation to rescue the victim of acute lung disease, to cut open the skull and remove a tumor from the brain, to replace aging blood vessels in a pulsating heart held by the surgeon's hands: all of these things we take for granted now. But none of them were proven interventions at the time. These measures were all the result of great thinkers working with the best available innovations of their time. They were not left on the shelf by either physicians or their patients because they might not have been effective. Trial, and yes, error, as well as research over time allows us to keep the best of our endeavors and dispense with the rest."

The delegates were looking at Bueller intently as he continued, "The population of the world, whether you like it or not, is the test group. Should we leave humanity to suffer the consequences of this virus simply because we are afraid to act? Those of us who are physicians take an oath: 'primum non nocere'; first do no harm. There is no foreseeable harm to our strategy; insofar as research or time causes us to reassess that conclusion, we shall be obligated as stewards of international health to adjust our plan. My esteemed colleagues, if there is no foreseeable harm in our acting, then history will not judge us kindly if we choose to throw off the burden of action simply because we are insecure about our ability to be successful. Be assured that regardless of our intervention, pain and suffering will accompany the next pandemic. Our best efforts at employing current technological tools can only hope to minimize the misery and deaths from such an occurrence, not eliminate them. The power to save every life belongs only to the supernatural. We humans are charged with saving as many as we can, and to do that we must move forward with the best knowledge available to us at this time."

Bueller placed both hands on the table and eyed each delegate at his table before proceeding. "Ladies and gentlemen, the measures before you require courage and cooperation to enact, resources to support, and speed to implement. With all due respect, it is time to vote. Do I have a motion?"

It was Farrington who spoke: "I move to adopt the recommendations of the World Health Organization as outlined." He was forbidden by the U.S. president from voting in favor of the resolution, but he damned well could make the motion: it made it a little easier for him to bear the shame of the official U.S. position. Farrington was relieved that the resolution passed despite his forced abstention.

Bueller issued an immediate press release identifying the new guidelines and affirming the board's commitment to work toward international pursuit of them. All the major news services carried the article the following day.

GUANGZHOU, CHINA
February 6

There was a noise, a dimly perceived but recurring, annoying clamor. Lou forced herself out of a dream and reached over to shut off the alarm clock but that didn't eliminate the disturbance. From her sleep-impaired state it took a few more seconds to comprehend it was her cell phone disrupting the night. She looked at the clock: 6 a.m. No one who knew her called this early. In her world this hour did not even exist. She flipped the thing open and said hello, or at least a croak came out approximating a greeting.

"Dr. Symington?"

She cleared her throat, "This is she." More intelligible.

"This is Ross Neelor, the technician at WHO's lab in Guangzhou."

"Yes Ross, what is it?" she responded leaning up on one elbow in the bed.

"I just finished analyzing the samples on Duc Trinh and... and...I thought you'd want to know right away," he said, a little breathless with the news.

"Yes...?" Lou pressed, sitting up further, waiting.

"Well, I've run and rerun the tissue but I keep getting the same results and it's puzzling. I'm not sure what to make of it."

"Ross, what did you find?" Lou asked sitting up entirely, losing patience with the young man's delivery.

"Well...I f-found...H5N1..." he started.

"That's it? You're puzzled about H5N1?" Maybe she just wasn't awake yet. Or he really was overly excited about having found something like the 500th case.

"No, I...I also found H3N2..." he got out before she interrupted him with,

"Oh... I see...Now that is definitely interesting." Avian and common human influenza in the same sample was indeed a new development.

This barely had time to register before Ross stammered, "...but that's...that's not all Dr. Symington...the sample also contains H5N2... I've been here all night...I ran it repeatedly...I couldn't believe it...But it's the same every time. I thought you'd want to know right away."

"What did you say?" Now she had both feet on the floor.

He repeated himself, this time without hesitation, "I've identified three viruses in the same sample Dr. Symington: H5N1, H3N2 and H5N2. I can't explain it, but I am reporting it," young Ross said authoritatively, finding confidence at last.

"Oh my God." She hung up the phone. "Oh my God."

Lou could explain it: H5N2 was a novel mutation, a brand new organism; she could almost feel her adrenal glands shoot the epinephrines out from both flanks with the realization. Within the course of two pulse beats her heart rate had jumped and she could hear the blood rushing past her ears. She felt like the turbocharged engine on a Porsche she used to own: zero to sixty in 5.3 seconds, a great asset if you were fleeing a predator, not very useful for critical thinking. Lou put the phone back on the nightstand. Sitting on the side of the mattress she placed the palms of both hands on her thighs and willfully slowed her breathing, allowing time for the ineffectual sensation to pass.

Minutes later she showered, dressed and headed to the office. It was not yet 6:30.

CHAPTER 10

Ken was sitting outside in the plaza of Cypress Arbor waiting for the nurse's aide to finish Anna's bath. His mother had been sitting up eating soft food from the aide's spoon when he arrived this damp February morning for his monthly pilgrimage. Anna stared straight ahead, no connection to the world apparent except the communion of her lips with the utensil. He watched her jaw move in rote circles, her tongue maneuver the pabulum inside her mouth, the Adam's apple rise and fall as she swallowed. What evidence of a compassionate creator was this? What deranged omnipotent being preserved this oral obeisance to a disintegrated mind? How did her soul, so adamantly opposed to this death, allow it? He contemplated such questions and others without answers as he sat trying to ward off the winter chill; he managed to steer clear of these ponderings back home, but it was hard to avoid them when he was here.

At least she had chosen the place, he thought in a futile attempt to assuage his guilt over her being here at all. Anna Wardman had been charmed from the moment she set eyes on Cypress Arbor. Ken and June had taken Anna on a two week excursion at her request, looking for a suitable place to move her as the Alzheimer's progressed. Anna was adamant that she participate in the decision and wanted to evaluate the appropriateness of the facility before she lost more mental function. They had driven from northern California into Oregon and checked out nearly every nursing home for four hundred miles. It was exhausting and depressing to Ken, but Anna's spirits were amazingly buoyed. She treated the trip as an adventure, a journey to a new and unexplored part of her life, even if the travel brochure was scary as hell.

The retirement community they eventually found was in Portland. They'd almost driven by it without looking because Anna didn't think she would want to live in the city. They ended up visiting the facility only because it was on their way to the motel and it was a little early for dinner which they wanted to have before they checked in. They went to Cypress Arbor more to pass the time than anything.

Perhaps it was because she had no expectations for it, or perhaps she was worn down with the effort and thereby more open to possibility, but it appeared to both Ken and June that it was love at first sight for Anna. The driveway was nearly hidden from the main street, and curved past some well-placed shrubs then through a cluster of the namesake evergreens before breaking into the open on the side of a well-groomed hill. There were several buildings grouped around a main courtyard which was filled with blossoming flowers and greenery, and people strolling or sitting contentedly on benches. Anna had turned this way and that in the car as they had driven up the hill, her neck surprisingly mobile despite her arthritis. She had remarked, "Oh..." with wonder, and "Oh my..." around every bend in the drive, delighted with each scene as it appeared. She had jumped out of the car with more vigor than she had exhibited in months, as soon as Ken parked.

"This is *so* lovely. I'm *so* glad we came here. Are we still in Newport?" she'd asked. It was like this; she would carry on entire conversations without apparent confusion and then insert something that made you wonder if she really understood anything. Newport was yesterday. They'd driven all the way up the coast looking for a place by the sea, but nothing had moved her.

"No Mom. We're in Portland."

"But I don't think I'll like anything in Portland," she said dubiously.

"Well, maybe you won't, but that's where we are."

"Really?" She looked around with surprise, taking in the meticulous landscaping and the towering cypresses which all but obscured the dimensions of the city beyond. The grounds and the buildings were exceedingly well situated to convey a country setting. "It doesn't look like Portland to me." She had smiled then and taken June's proffered arm to walk to the main entrance.

Since they hadn't called ahead to arrange for a tour it took a little while to find a staff member to assist them. Anna seated herself in a chair by a window overlooking the expansive hillside and the trees, and remained motionless there, her hands folded over her purse, until the guide appeared. The residential director offered Anna a wheelchair for the tour, which she refused. In her former mind she would have been offended by the implication, but with the exception of those times when her perception was at total odds with reality, Alzheimer's had given his mother a more charitable disposition. It wasn't that Anna had ever been a shrew, but the crankiness that the simple tasks of living can sometimes elicit seemed to be evaporating along with her cerebrum. When she wasn't confronted by a flagrant contradiction to her comprehension or functioning she was eerily pleasant to be around.

They ended up spending a few hours at the facility which offered multiple options for residents, from independent living in condominiums to short-term nursing care and comprehensive extended care. What had sealed it for Anna however was the dedicated Alzheimer's unit. Ken had explained to the guide, out of Anna's earshot, what her diagnosis was, and the guide was uncertain what to say when Anna asked to see the unit; it was rare to encounter a patient so open to previewing her destiny. For Ken it was a sign that his mother was still able to periodically engage her considerable faculties. Viewing the Alzheimer's ward was emblematic of the curiosity she'd exhibited all of her life. His heart ached watching the peaks of her intellect juxtaposed with the nadirs of emptiness.

After the tour Anna told the woman matter-of-factly that she didn't want medical treatment as her condition deteriorated. Ken nodded and said that Anna had already filled out powers of attorney, guardianship and the living will that California law recognized. Their guide went over Oregon's choices regarding feeding options, naso-gastric tubes, IV's, 'do-not-resuscitate' orders, even mammograms and flu shots. The patient was free to decide what she wanted as long as she was competent to do so. Anna smiled sweetly at the nurse, and more pointedly at Ken, and said, "My son knows what I want."

The tour and the questions were over. The room was still. Dust motes hung in the last shafts of sunlight piercing the window. Anna was now looking intently at her lap, June somewhat anxiously at Ken.

The guide had been through this often enough to feel comfortable with the family's discomfort. No one spoke or moved for minutes. Finally Anna picked her head up and looked directly at Ken, saying in a clear voice, "Kenneth, this is where I choose to die."

They made arrangements to return the next day and carry out the administrative details. If Anna elected to move to the facility soon she might enroll in the assisted living unit where she could still maintain some independence. She could take all of her meals in the common area; a nurse would administer medication as directed and an aide would monitor her ability to dress and groom herself. She would be transferred to the Alzheimer's unit as she, her doctor and her family thought appropriate. Ken looked at Anna and shook his head. None of them were prepared yet to decide when Anna would move in.

But they were able to formalize Anna's wishes in anticipation of her moving there eventually. She chose to dispense with all preventive testing and treatments except the medication to slow the progress of the disease. She said, "No," to routine blood pressure checks, to weighing herself, and blood drawing. "No," to Pap smears and mammograms and flu shots. Ken asked her what the harm was in a flu shot, pointing out that while she was still coherent she probably wouldn't want to be sick. She replied in a snap that pneumonia was a friend to the elderly, and if she was lucky enough to get the flu and die from pneumonia instead of a slow miserable death from her disease, she certainly wasn't going to do anything to stop it from happening.

The nurse performing the intake exam paused at that point and informed Ken and Anna that Cypress Arbor was an influenza surveillance site for the CDC and that all patients with fever and cough were reported to CDC as part of their tracking program. All residents were subject to flu surveillance for the good of the entire facility.

"That's interesting," Ken observed. "It never occurred to me an extended care facility would be a surveillance site. I'm impressed." The nurse nodded and further explained that Anna would not be forced to take the vaccine and that declining a flu shot now did not preclude her from changing her mind later.

The stiff wind now blowing through the cypress trees cut through Ken's clothing and his reminiscing. Shoving his hands deep into his overcoat pockets to warm them he discovered the small stuffed animal Moira had sent with him. She had not had a close relationship with Ken's mother because Anna had been increasingly disabled in the years in which she and Moira might have forged such a bond. Nevertheless the child had developed an affinity for her and asked about her after each of Ken's visits, sensing that the subject was important to her grandfather. Moira had taken the fleece teddy bear clasped to her chest last week as she sat in Ken's lap, and pressed it into his hand. She made him promise to deliver it to Anna on his next visit, and he had dutifully obeyed. Moira would definitely ask about it and he wouldn't let her down or lie to her.

The nurse's aide, he realized, was waving to him now from the open door of Anna's building. He rose to acknowledge her and made his way back to Anna's room. They were in the middle of flu season now and he noticed a few rooms with masks and gloves outside the doors. He wondered in passing if the patients were being isolated for influenza or something else. Anna had shown no signs of illness despite her not having a flu shot for the past two seasons.

Ken had been receiving human influenza shots annually since he was in graduate school. Because of his research he was one of only a few people in the world who had also been vaccinated against H5N1 during PharmaGlobal's human testing on the effectiveness of Avimmune. After the vaccine's proven safety in mouse trials, he arranged for his lab assistants to have the opportunity to obtain the immunization in the human trials. Not all of them chose to take it despite his advice. Some were reluctant to count on its safety, and some felt the biohazard precautions at Crossfire were more than adequate for prevention. Ken didn't agree with their varying assessments but it was no matter to argue about. Their risk was their own and he would be guiltless if they contracted the disease. As the risk of pandemic mounted he only wished he could have had his family immunized with Avimmune, but the strict testing protocols made no allowances. The vaccine was simply not available to the public yet.

Ken entered Anna's room and spoke with her aide for a few minutes while she finished straightening the room after the bath. He took the teddy bear out of his pocket and set it on the stand next to Anna's bed, in front of a framed picture of Moira. The aide commented on the kindness of the little girl's gesture and promised to keep it close to Anna. Ken pulled up a chair as the aide withdrew, and settled in for his monthly vigil.

SAIGON, VIETNAM
February 16

After Duc's body was discovered, the WHO was able to bring enormous pressure on the police in Saigon to conduct a search for Tran Phu and his son. Local authorities in towns from Bac Tho to Saigon were sent to scour the countryside. Hospitals, rooming houses and brothels inside and outside of Saigon were turned upside down looking for the two.

Tran's body and that of his son were found less than a week later. At least it was presumed it was they because there were two corpses, one smaller than the other, curled together in extremis, lying in a marshland. The victims were being matched with DNA to prove identity. Lou had already called young Ross at the lab to warn him lung samples were on their way. It took nearly three days to process the tissue; Lou waited anxiously the whole time.

CALIFORNIA
February 18

Ken reluctantly rolled over in bed and looked at the clock: not even 5:00 a.m. yet. But there was no sense fighting it, his eyes had flown open a few minutes ago and he knew from recent experience he would be unable to will himself back to sleep. He scuffed past June's sleeping form earlier it seemed each morning, responding to some internal buzzer intent on reading the *Chronicle* before work. Lately the news had contained a number of avian flu developments and he found he couldn't concentrate for the remainder of the day unless he knew exactly where the world stood.

Even as he made the ritual trip to the front door, it irritated him that there was so much to read these days in the lay press about bird flu. Not that it wasn't important, it absolutely was, but it had been important for the last several years and was only now garnering the attention it had warranted for some time. It was disingenuous. The media had been too busy printing entertainment instead of news. Now that bird flu was entertaining they were interested. But they still weren't thinking or questioning. Just miming. Qualified and unqualified people alike were spouting their opinions on the pandemic threat and the media made no effort to separate the wheat from the chaff. Even the WHO needed to be called to account for dropping the ball on the most recent case in Vietnam. But no one was challenging them Ken thought with disgust.

Nearly two weeks ago, after the discovery of H5N1, H3N2 and H5N2 in the same Vietnamese victim, Ken had expected to see a bulletin from Geneva calling for widespread H5N1 inoculations in Southeast Asia. In Ken's mind it was clearly the combination of H5N1 with the H3N2 that led to the new strain. Preventing H5N1 in the indigenous population would reduce the likelihood of similar mutations.

But there had been no such advisory. In fact in the very same week, Ken had been astounded to read of the new recommendations endorsed by the WHO regarding vaccine production and stockpiling. To his shock and consternation the board was not suggesting massive stockpiling of, or vaccination against, H5N1. What they proposed instead was preparing vaccine in a variety of H and N configurations to cover as many strains as possible.

Ken padded through the living room quietly, turning on just enough light to manage the darkness. As he reached to retrieve the paper off the porch the smell of coffee wafted past him, already steaming from the pot June had programmed for him last night. She, more than he it seemed, could anticipate his increasing restlessness. He unrolled the bundle and today's super-sized letters jumped out at him: *H5N2 in Vietnam: Pandemic Strain?*

He ran a hand through his hair as he reviewed the outbreak. The article this morning added two more victims who had been traveling with the first man, identified two weeks ago as Duc Trinh. The current victims, a father and his son, only had evidence of H5N2 virus. The dates of death for all three victims were unclear due to decomposition, but the location of the bodies and the absence of symptoms prior to departure suggested that the all of them succumbed rapidly.

Ken could hardly believe what he was reading. A period of only two or three days between exposure to the virus and death? It was unheard of, even in the infectious disease world. The strain must have superb contagion and unparalleled lethality. It was the worst possible combination. But then what had happened to it? If it was that effective in killing why hadn't an epidemic started in the region? He answered his own question before he had finished forming it: the virus was too lethal to sustain itself. It had died with the hosts. Simple but stunning. A highly pathologic organism in theory could self-destruct, but no one had ever witnessed the phenomenon before.

Interesting that it was H5N2. What did it mean? And what would the WHO do now? He was having more and more difficulty understanding them. Ken had been interviewed by Makao Wataabe in November and had told him in no uncertain terms that H5N1 was the only current threat. He strongly advised immediate commencement of vaccination programs targeting the entire population of Southeast Asia, as rapidly as manufacture would allow. To be sure, Ken had either suggested or agreed with all the other bullets presented in the WHO's new recommendations: the development of rapid vaccine technology, the stockpiling of osmavir, the cooperation of developed countries in meeting the avian prevention needs of the underdeveloped, but he was floored that widespread H5N1 immunization had been cast aside in the final policy.

Ken folded the paper in disgust. Today's headlines changed nothing in his mind. If the original victims had been inoculated against H5N1 there would have been no opportunity for them to have incubated or mutated the H5N1 virus to H5N2. H5N2 had killed two people, H5N1 hundreds of people, millions of fowl. He believed members of the WHO board were hesitant to support H5N1 inoculation because they did not want to underwrite the substantial costs of prevention in the third world, construing these people to be "surplus" populations. If their own citizens had been threatened by encroaching avian flu, the wealthy nation representatives of the committee would have signed up for Avimmune immediately he thought bitterly. From Ken's perspective the new policy reeked of cowardice and parsimony, and political expediency.

Last week, when he could stand the boiling inside him no longer, Ken had finally called Director Bueller himself, taking him to task for the new guidelines. "How could anyone argue with the dominance of H5N1 Hans? Hundreds of people have contracted it, and the fatality rate is close to 100%. We have H5N1 vaccine available now and precious time is being wasted by not using it. The WHO, the very organization that should be protecting world health, is sabotaging it with this new vaccination policy."

"Ken there is certainly more than one conclusion that can be drawn from the evidence," Bueller had said, trying to soothe him. "There have been multiple new strains cropping up in the past few months, including H5N2 just this week. These developments favor several vaccines instead of just one. No matter what vaccine is made now, it might be wrong. We have to cover more bases."

"Right now, when the threat is right in front of you, you are covering no bases Hans. Not to use what is available simply because it might not be perfect is wrong. It's all a matter of degrees," Ken countered. "If all vaccines might be wrong, why are we making anything at all Hans? Why not wait around for the actual pandemic to occur and then make vaccine?"

"Ken, you and I both know that is exactly what may happen. But it would be foolish not to try to pre-empt the bug. We simply have more chances of being right with more than one vaccine. We need multiple production lines running multiple strains until we develop the ability to turnaround production of vaccine in two weeks instead of six months. The reason H5N1 is the only vaccine in existence is because there hasn't been the political or corporate will to advance any other. Governments won't invest in medical care the way they do in defense spending, and business won't respond until the profit margins are certain. The approval of the WHO board will bring new private and government researchers and manufacturers into the picture. This is what the world needs now."

"Where is the harm," Ken asked, "in using Avimmune until another virus demonstrates greater human activity and another vaccine is available to counter it?"

"Ken," Bueller sighed, "You know perfectly well there are several potential harms, not the least of which is that the clinical trials of H5N1 were carried out on an extraordinarily small test group."

"There were no significant complications." Ken stated.

"There were only 500 people tested!" Bueller was not giving him an inch on this one. "If there were a fatality rate of 1 in 1000 from the vaccine, 500 test subjects wouldn't show evidence of it, but when we vaccinate 100,000 people, suddenly we have 100 deaths. That's almost as many as from the virus itself!"

"That's nonsense. No vaccine has that high a complication rate," Ken protested.

"That's true of the vaccines we've developed historically Ken, but that is no guarantee of Avimmune. Even if the rate of problems is as low as one in 100,000, if we start injecting the billions of people in Asia we'll have thousands of deaths, or whatever other complication the roulette wheel spins out, because the fact is we don't know what the potential harms are from the vaccine itself." Bueller was building some steam of his own now. "If we identify an avian strain that meets all three pandemic criteria, then it will be worth the risk to use whatever vaccine we have been able to manufacture, but until then, I will not be endorsing the widespread empiric injection of any vaccine."

It was a difficult conversation for both men, each of whom was full of integrity, concerned for the welfare of the people, and convinced he was right. They finally concluded the exchange in an uneasy truce whereby both agreed the damn virus was unknowable at this juncture, the situation remained dynamic, and that all parties involved in efforts to penetrate the organism's secrets needed to continue to communicate. Prior to ending the call, Bueller assured Ken that his advice had been invaluable in the process of formulating the recommendations, even though the committee had ultimately decided on an alternate strategy for vaccination.

Bueller's parting attempt at flattery was ineffective. Ken felt the man's words like solid blows. He was the most prominent researcher in avian influenza, knew H5N1 like the back of his hand, had just won the Pritzker for God's sake, and his ideas, his opinions were of no consequence to those making the most important health policy decisions on earth. The derision of his professional credentials by the WHO was a bitter enough pill to swallow without the additional knowledge that the advice he had given to PharmaGlobal, sought and heeded precisely on the basis of those same credentials, might cause the company and his recent investment in it to falter.

Ken couldn't believe that his dedicated pursuit of the avian virus could blow up in his face so quickly. Nothing about his research or the viral threat had changed. How could the people in charge at the WHO be so fickle, so cavalier with the evidence and their power? Where were all the other reasoned scientific voices that had matched his calls for H5N1 prevention not so long ago?

At the time he was interviewed last fall he had made the best recommendations for world safety that the current state of affairs would support. When he called for H5N1 vaccination he hadn't even remotely entertained a thought of profiting from that knowledge. His choice to invest in PharmaGlobal had come months later.

For the past ten days the actions of the WHO and his conversation with Bueller had nearly paralyzed Ken's ability to think or act. He wasn't sure what, if anything, he should do, or say, and to whom. He played scenes over and over in his mind looking for flaws in his logic or actions, and could find none. He evaluated his research: it was solid, stood on its own, untainted by the WHO's snub or by his investments. He evaluated the evidence on H5N1: it was still clearly the major avian player. He evaluated his stature: it was perhaps compromised in the view of those who disagreed with his call for H5N1 inoculation, but that was no means the entire world. The jury was still out on who was right. He could hold his head up without the endorsement of the majority of his colleagues; heaven knows he had done so before the Pritzker. If fame was short-lived, so be it. He could live without it. He had for years.

Ken had to admit what he was having the most trouble with at this moment was insecurity about the effect of WHO's policy on PharmaGlobal. He wished just for a moment that he had not transferred all of his money there. Then he remembered he hadn't, and sighed with relief at his foresight. Half of it he had placed in Viraban, the maker of osmavir.

He reassured himself that PharmaGlobal was an outstanding company with an excellent record, a proven CEO, and more products to sell than Avimmune. The company might not put to use all of its H5N1 but it would switch back to human influenza in the fall, and the top notch R & D team always had the potential for a breakthrough in technique that would put the business on track for solid gains. He was appalled at the thought even as he had it: he was thinking like an investor and not the scientist he was. Well, he argued back at himself, the fact was he was an investor too and there was nothing the matter with that. No one else was looking out for him and his future. If he didn't do it, it wasn't going to happen.

Back and forth he went these last several days, debating, proselytizing, justifying, reassuring the voices in his head. In the end he decided that nothing more was the matter with him than a bruised ego. His financial status was fine. He'd checked the stock pages on both companies, a habit he had never subscribed to even after he'd made the purchases, and both shares were up slightly from where they were when he'd bought them almost two months ago. He was being paranoid about the stocks because of his past experience with Carter Skelley. This was different. He was in charge of his future now. H5N1 virus was not going to go away. There was plenty of time for PharmaGlobal to sell its inventory.

After he sorted all this out Ken concluded that the world was indeed a dangerous place, full of peril, and that he remained a committed voice in the struggle: an informed, credible defender of man's right to benefit from the best data available. He rededicated himself to being an advocate for the best science and the best evidence in the field, and reconfirmed in his mind the soundness of his own considerable intellect in interpreting and defending the same. Whether he stood with the minority or the majority he determined he would be heard, as all voices in the polemic were critical to the outcome. He resolved to carry on with renewed vigor and confidence in his work.

Forcing himself out of his preoccupation with these thoughts for the umpteenth time in the past couple weeks, Ken returned to the present and the new information in front of him.

Of what significance was the appearance of H5N2?

He mulled it over for a long while and ended up with this: H5N2 was a non-player. It was lethal and contagious, but it was gone. Viral suicide. What wasn't gone, was still there, and had *created* the new spawn was H5N1. It made no sense to go after the offspring, one needed to go after the parent. H5N1 continued to be *the* threat and he was going to do his damned best to prove it in the lab. It was the only way to help.

WASHINGTON, D.C.
February 23

Farrington sat opposite Cyril Hunt in the secretary's office, reluctantly inhaling cigar fumes. Perhaps the man's judgment was as clouded by the smoke as his face, he mused. He wondered if his own faculties were faltering; he was hearing things he thought must be hallucinations.

Hunt had informed him the president was going to ask Congress to pass legislation providing tax incentives for private industries willing to produce vaccine and work on new methods of production; he would also convene a task force to evaluate the adoption of quarantine laws. Great Farrington thought. Legislation and committees. Spread the responsibility out. They would be well into the next century before anything was agreed on. A move that was politically safe and totally ineffective. Farrington tuned back in.

"...In a magnanimous display of international concern the president is also willing to send one million doses of vaccine and osmavir to the WHO for use as it sees fit in the third world..." Hunt was saying.

"That wouldn't cover twenty percent of the population of any major city in Southeast Asia Cyril and you know it," Farrington interrupted.

Hunt continued, unperturbed, "...The federal government will also reserve one million doses of each for U.S. medical first responders and the military." The king's minion, dispensing royal favors.

All of it was inadequate. Totally inadequate. "This won't make a dent in our pandemic readiness," Farrington protested.

Hunt waved his objections aside with a plume of smoke. "...the president's plan will encourage purchase of inventory by the states..."

Michael interrupted again, "By the states? You mean the United States?"

"Michael, do not be purposefully obtuse with me," Hunt slavered around the cigar. "The states, as members of the United States, will purchase the vaccine for themselves."

Farrington was nearly stuttering with incredulity, "...And...and what funds will they use?"

"State funds Michael. Get hold of yourself boy!" Hunt commanded removing the stogie from his mouth, spitting the words out. "This isn't rocket science. The states are in a better position to prepare for the needs of their residents. We don't want or need a one-size-fits-all program managed by the bloated bureaucracy of the federal government here. We will just add one disaster on top of another. Need I remind you of FEMA's response to Hurricane Katrina? What was called for then, and is called for now, is federal *coordination* of state sponsored plans. Federal authorities will determine what modes of prevention and treatment are acceptable and the supplies will be purchased, stockpiled and distributed by the states," Hunt said, punctuating the air with his cigar on each point.

Farrington leaned back in his chair to give himself time to take it all in. The man was dead serious. Hunt had just outlined a plan for the U.S. to follow the WHO's guidelines in theory, but it was so cleverly structured that the result was in fact almost complete non-compliance. The breathtaking disregard of international policy and national well-being necessary to conceive of such a plan, and the arrogance in launching it, bespoke a capacity for negligence in the administration that Farrington could not comprehend.

"Why Michael, you look like you've seen a ghost." Hunt taunted.

"Let me make sure I have this straight," he said, his lips stretched tautly. "The federal government will encourage the production and stockpiling of multiple avian vaccine strains, as well as stockpiles of osmavir, and research into faster vaccine technology."

"Exactly, just as the WHO guidelines suggest." Hunt nodded with as much glee as his jowly, cynical face could register.

"The guidelines include providing the financial wherewithal to accomplish the ends!"

"That will be provided by the states." Hunt responded palms splayed, flecks of ash falling from the cigar.

"That's bullshit and you know it! It's another unfunded mandate! Individual states don't have the money, the brain trust or the coordination to tackle a problem this big. Whatever happened to the 'United' part of the United States? It isn't a loose federation of states, it's supposed to be *united*! We are at war and you're sending the states to battle! Avian flu isn't a local problem. The cowards at the top of this garbage heap haven't got the guts to use federal dollars to protect this nation from a health threat greater than any other danger man has ever faced. No, they are sadly and ineffectually mired in the last century spending our money on war toys instead. The only ploy you haven't trotted out is a faith-based contingent to underwrite your excuse of a program. You guys have made a career out of this kind of crap, only this time you're not messing with an electorate who isn't going to notice, you're not just feeding your fat cats in business anymore. Katrina will look like a walk in the park; multiply that debacle across every community in America and this administration's reputation goes down in infamy. Not to mention the rest of the world. It will be survival of the fittest and who knows who will end up on top when it's over." Farrington paused from his rant and considered his next move. Hunt and everybody around and above him in the White House staff had deserved to hear it, but they probably wouldn't.

"You know Cyril," he said after a moment, "I thought we were on the same team."

"But we are Michael. We are," Hunt drawled. "If this president doesn't succeed, you don't succeed."

"Succeed? I have tried every way I know to bring reason and purpose to the avian flu policy of this country, and the response of those in power is heedless denial and self-delusion. You think I'm going to hang around this administration to *succeed*?" Farrington asked incredulously. "I have already failed. In my wildest imaginings I cannot conceive what fairy tales you tell one another to so glibly write off the world's experts in health care."

Farrington took a deep breath and slowed his speech purposefully as he continued, "There are many measures of success Cyril, and I intend to distance myself from your version of it. I will have to live with my own failure; I choose not to live with yours and the president's." Farrington stood from his chair and reached across the desk to the ashtray where Hunt's stogie was smoldering; he picked it up, looked at it with disgust, and crushed it out before walking away.

CHAPTER 11

CALIFORNIA
March 5

The cloud cover was thick over the San Francisco bay and had been for days. Reaching through the windows, the gloom had crept into the well-appointed executive suite, and hovered about the desk of J.B. Vaughn. He inched up the rheostat on the light switch trying to wash the murk away with incandescence. All he succeeded in doing was causing an intense glare to appear on the figures spread out before him, and it was giving him a headache.

He had problems.

PharmaGlobal was nearly two months into production of sixty million doses of H5N1 and thus far he had contracts to sell fewer than 5 million vaccines. Vaughn had been puzzled in late January when he hadn't received any signed orders yet. The customers who'd expressed interest in the fall were still concerned about H5N1 but were reluctant to act and he'd been unsuccessful at the time in figuring out what the encumbrance was.

Then, four weeks ago, his heart had stopped cold reading the front page article on the new guidelines from the WHO. New policy. Multiple vaccine strains. Everything clicked. That's why the interest had dried up: WHO had been restructuring their response to avian flu. Why hadn't Ken known about this? He'd been on the phone immediately demanding to know what was going on. Ken had sounded shaken when he finally returned Vaughn's call late in the day, but had assured him there was no consensus among the experts on the new policy. Ken considered WHO's move to be folly. He was outraged that

H5N1 was not being pushed and vowed to continue to make the case for immunization.

Vaughn had spent the month since then trying to drum up business. He had Ken calling other experts and politicians across the country to stir the debate, and he had followed up these conversations himself trying to fan the flames of the hysteria that had convinced him from the beginning that Avimmune production was a good idea. The panic was still there but his contacts were largely afraid to deviate now from what WHO had recommended. The more he learned, the more he realized none of the authorities could agree on anything except that the occurrence of pandemic flu was inevitable. Every consultant he spoke with or whose comments were reported in the press had a different concept of the best strategy. It was a nightmare, for the public and for him.

As though the political and scientific dilemmas weren't bad enough, the production line had run into a snafu: it was taking significantly longer to incubate the virus than originally planned. His team had informed him last week that the current batch of virus was developing sluggishly; it would be at least another six or seven weeks before they could proceed to harvesting the virus. Converting the live virus into killed fragments and refining those particles into pure protein was expected to take another two months. The last phase, aliquoting the doses into vials or pre-filled syringes for distribution, would take one additional month, if everything went well. Vaughn had originally factored a one-month delay into his best-case-scenario five month cycle, thinking he had been generous with this contingency. But he had not counted on using up that cushion, and more, in the first two months.

By his original estimation the vaccine should have been ready by June. He accepted that making H5N1 at all would put him a little behind in traditional fall flu vaccine production, but he would still have been able to take advantage of the late season market. Of course, back when he had contemplated this course he thought the call for Avimmune would be so strong that PharmaGlobal could continue avian production indefinitely, until the demand died down.

Vaughn leaned back from his desk. With a delay right out of the starting gate he was looking at August or even September before the vaccine would be ready. If he sold fewer than ten percent of the projected H5N1 he would also be sitting on a lot of inventory that might never be sold. Cash flow would be dismal for a while, but the vaccine had a shelf life of at least two years. Hell, he wouldn't destroy it even then: in an epidemic people would be so desperate he could unload even expired vaccine at top dollar. The FDA was ridiculous with their expiration criteria anyway; provided the products were kept at the appropriate temperature they remained reliable in potency long after their official expiration date.

It was clear that PharmaGlobal would not have time to crank out any traditional flu vaccine for next season. They could still return to pneumonia vaccine production in the fall and at least begin to replenish the corporate coffers, but the company would be cash poor for a while. One thing Vaughn was sure PharmaGlobal was not going to do was to return to a fractured policy of multiple small lines of different vaccines. There was no way for a company this large to be efficient at anything but mass production. If it could not be made in quantity, PharmaGlobal was not going to be making it. WHO could stuff their policy; his company was not interested.

Vaughn sighed with resignation and disgust. There was no way around it: the stock was going to tank and the shareholders would be very unhappy. It wasn't going to be pretty but it wouldn't be the end of the world; PharmaGlobal would make it. He had brought the company back from worse straits.

Then too, he thought as he tapped the papers neatly back together, all the WHO policy in the world couldn't stop a real pandemic from happening. If Ken was right about H5N1, PharmaGlobal would still be selling a lot of vaccine.

SAIGON, VIETNAM
March 6

After getting the lab confirmation of the H5N2 found in the three corpses, Lou had flown to Vietnam to explore whether there had been any further spread. Mai and Binh drove back to the countryside and collected blood samples from the two villages the victims came from, looking for evidence of H5N2. Lou wanted to rule out the occurrence of a milder form of disease in any of the other inhabitants which might have become more lethal in transmission to the men who died. Mai and Binh also stopped at additional hamlets along the route where the dead men had traveled and took samples both from poultry and people.

Lou spent her time with an interpreter in Saigon combing every hospital and clinic for reported illnesses and deaths due to respiratory causes. She obtained blood or tissue from such patients to check for H5N2. To evaluate the animal reservoirs she visited the prominent veterinarians in and around Saigon looking for evidence of poultry epidemics. Within ten days the exhaustive search was completed and the results back.

"Here are the last reports Dr. Lou," Binh said, handing a few faxed sheets to Lou, and taking a seat next to her at the scratched teak table in the cramped Saigon office.

She poured some jasmine tea from the pot and sipped it; it was like drinking flowers: a tonic for the exhaustive work they'd completed.

"Well?" Mai asked.

"Nothing," Lou said, placing the reports on the table. "No one else, and nothing else we've tested has evidence of H5N2."

"A dead end." Binh said.

"Thank God," said Lou. "Can you imagine the consequences if this bug had been born in the city instead of a dirt track in the wilderness? The same mutation occurring in Hanoi, or Bangkok or Guangzhou?" Lou shook her head at the thought. The loss of life was incomprehensible.

"We dodged a bullet."

"More like a nuclear explosion." Lou said, leaning back in her chair, twirling a pen between her fingers. "Still, it's fascinating isn't it?" She looked at her colleagues and saw the macabre interest reflected in their faces, the same curiosity that made you unable to take your eyes off a bad accident. "It's always been a theoretical possibility: an organism so lethal it self-destructs."

"Would you say H5N2 fulfilled pandemic criteria Dr. Lou?"

"The scientific community will probably debate that question for years Mai. As a spontaneous mutation between human H3N2 and avian H5N1 it certainly fulfills the first criterion: a new organism for which the natural population has no immunity."

"It also fulfills the second condition," Binh added, "It caused significant illness…in these three cases, death."

"But it's the third criterion that's the conundrum," said Lou. "Duc readily transmitted H5N2 to Tran and his son, but all of them were incapable of transmitting it further because it was so lethal it killed them before they had a chance. So it was highly communicable in the short-term, but in the long term, in that moment, in that place, it was not."

"Its deadliness was suicidal," Binh observed.

"But there was also luck," Lou added. "We don't know how many people the victims might have encountered on their journey. With as lethal as H5N2 is, and the evidence of all our negative reports here," Lou gestured at the papers strewn over the table, "there is no doubt in this case that there was no direct contact with others on the road. But if these men had lodged in any villages along their path, after they had come down with symptoms but before they died, we'd probably be witnessing an entirely different story. There would have been enough contact around a common cooking fire, or in people coming to the aid of the ailing men, to have started a much more widespread outbreak, despite the lethality of the bug. We probably could have contained it with quarantine, but with just a little luck H5N2 might have had made it into Saigon."

Mai and Binh nodded soberly in agreement and silence hung momentarily in the room.

"It's humbling," said Lou, "the power of this tiny piece of RNA that has to be magnified 50,000 times just to be seen."

CALIFORNIA
March 12

Seated, Ken scooted in his chair to the file drawer at Crossfire, pulling it open and adding four more articles he had clipped out of professional journals to his folder on human H5N1 infections. Victims had been reported from Russia to Africa; from China to Europe. In several cases there was no obvious evidence of bird contact. He also kept a folder on veterinary articles. Millions of birds had died from H5N1 or been killed by authorities; tens of millions more had been vaccinated.

There had been rare occurrences of new strains in the wild but nothing that compared in scope to the frequency or lethality of H5N1. The WHO and authorities in stricken areas were calling for the immunization of poultry to H5N1. He could not understand why they refused to apply the same logic to people.

Ken filed all his articles first thing in the morning now: it was easier to keep up that way. Gave him some time to contemplate and review the crisis before he had to engage in the perfunctory duties required of him each day. He felt more pressure than ever to know everything he could know about the activity of avian flu, and how the press, public, WHO and other professionals were responding to it. It was war and he was engaged.

There were other stories he cut out, largely from the newspaper, profiling the range of uniquely human responses to it. These Ken kept in another file. He flipped through the folder and perused a few, offended all over again by the cutesy titles that mocked the seriousness of the subject. "Fake Flu Fools Farmers," in *USA Today*, claimed China had become the source of cheap, bogus avian vaccines being marketed to worried owners of bird stock. There was no telling how many animals had actually received real vaccine and how many had gotten the impotent knock-off. He thumbed through recent articles on the spread of panic over avian flu. In, "Fowl Deeds," clipped from a *Parade Magazine*, the author reported people were killing their neighbors' healthy poultry out of fear of disease. International residents and businesses were leaving Southeast Asia in droves according to the *Examiner's*, "Panicked Populace in Flight." *The Wall Street Journal* reported economies were collapsing from the widespread culling of fowl, and poultry workers were hiding their stock from the authorities so that if H5N1 was discovered they could protect their inventory from immediate destruction. In, "Got Osmavir?," *Time* magazine's cover story a week ago, affluent nations of the world were hoarding the drug in such quantities that the sale of it to those countries had recently been banned by the manufacturers, who were trying to reserve inventory for other regions most in need. Ken shook his head, ran his fingers through a shock of thinning gray hair as he sat looking at the open folders in his lap. Not only was avian influenza exploding, the world was falling apart reacting to it.

He replayed in his head multiple conversations he'd had with Hans Bueller over the past few months. Each time they seemed to drift further apart in their opinions. "If Duc had gotten the vaccine he could have fought off the H5N1 infection. It wouldn't have been around long enough to mix with the H3N2 and mutate." Ken had argued.

"Ken, Duc could just as easily have taken a traditional flu shot for H3N2, readily available and with a proven safety record, and had the same advantage," Bueller countered. "It's much more logical to immunize the region for H3N2. In fact, we have been working with Chinese, southeast Asian and African authorities to ramp up traditional flu shots just for that purpose."

"Then you agree with me!" Ken had boomed. "If you're trying to immunize against H3N2 to prevent mutation, you should also be using Avimmune for H5N1!"

"Avimmune does not have a safety record Ken. We've been through this."

"Hans, in the history of medicine there has never been a vaccine with a serious safety issue and you know it. What we don't have is the luxury of taking the time in trials to prove it. H5N1 has a proven safety record, if limited. I've taken it; so have most of my staff. We're the only people in the world who will be immune when H5N1 hits. It's not right!"

"Ken, the risk-benefit ratio of a vaccine untested through clinical trials is unacceptable when spread out over the millions of people you're suggesting we give it to. Unless H5N1 actually becomes pandemic, it is an unacceptable risk at this time to immunize the public preventively."

"That sounds like a cowardly decision wrought by WHO's legal department instead of an informed one made by your medical advisors."

"That's utter nonsense and you know it," Bueller replied.

"Perhaps you should let the public decide," Ken fired back. "Maybe they'd be standing in line to take that risk."

"The public is in no position to judge this. They're scared to death. They'll do anything, whether it's been proven or not, if they think it will help."

"Well then maybe they're smarter than we give them credit for. In this case being willing to take a risk may save their lives." Ken continued with acerbity.

"Ken, no one has all the answers," Bueller said, exasperated, "but it is our job as the most well-informed scientists in the field to sort through all the evidence and provide the best advice we can. We can all agree that there is an obvious threat of H5N1 to poultry, and we are aggressively tackling it with immunization, culling and quarantine. However, there is no such immediate threat to people, only a potential threat, and that threat is not clear enough to warrant immunization with a single strain at this point. What is mandatory is further preparation, which needs to occur for a variety of strains, each new one as it pops up, and even those that haven't yet occurred. As the Duyen Ba case dramatically illustrates, we don't know where the ultimate threat lies. It defies prediction: ultimately we do not know what the organism will look like or where it will come from. To think otherwise, frankly, is hubris." Ken listened to the director's arguments, but remained unmoved.

"Ken, look, we're on the same team; we both want to protect the world from avian flu. But let's have a reality check," Bueller implored. "Our disagreement about vaccinating against H5N1 is entirely moot until we have the resources to support such a plan anyway. And we don't. Even if we wanted to immunize the entire world against avian flu right now we couldn't. WHO has less than a million doses of H5N1 vaccine on its shelves, half the entire world stock of it. We have funds to purchase an additional 2 million doses, and some vague promises from a few nations to provide maybe another two million doses from the next batch of vaccine that *isn't even finished* yet."

Bueller continued, "PharmaGlobal tells us they will have sixty million doses ready. When? In August or September. That's months from now! Even if WHO had the funds to purchase all of it, and we do not, that quantity is nowhere close to enough to provide significant protection in southeast Asia let alone for the planet. There are seven billion people in the world and most of them live in areas where pandemic is most likely to originate. With such limited resources we can't just start giving H5N1 willy-nilly. We have to target populations most at risk."

"You have to start somewhere Hans. Start in the communities with significant poultry exposure."

"Ken sixty million doses would barely make a dent in the populations at risk."

"Then order more!"

"We can't get financing to order what's available now! Don't you see? No one wants to commit money to an uncertain cure."

"If WHO labeled H5N1 as the pandemic threat...people, businesses, governments...would be flocking to fund you. That's what's happening with osmavir. Production has been boosted logarithmically since it's been touted as an effective treatment."

"Yes, and the wisdom of *that* is debatable as well," Bueller sighed. "You know as well as I do that we don't know how effective osmavir will turn out to be under actual pandemic conditions, whether the virus will become resistant, or require higher or longer dosing than we've planned. But we felt it necessary to include it in our strategy because it's the only treatment available. We're very uncertain here that the cost of stocking it is worth the benefit."

"It's the same for Avimmune," Ken said trying to ram his point home. "In the absence of alternatives Hans, the benefit need only be *likely* as opposed to certain to recommend it."

"But it's not the same Ken. Osmavir, if it works, will presumably be effective against any avian strain. Avimmune will be effective only for H5N1 virus, and continuing viral shift and drift may make whatever is produced by PharmaGlobal in August of this year ineffective by August of next year. Even worse, if the pandemic is caused by some other strain, *H5N1 vaccine will have no effectiveness*. We just witnessed three deaths from H5N2 for God's sake. No one could have predicted that a month ago. There is no certainty that H5N1 will become a lethal strain. No, Ken. If we were to advocate for nothing but H5N1 vaccination now, nothing but H5N1 would be produced, no incentives would exist to manufacture anything else. And research into faster means of production, which you and I both know is the only basis for real hope, would languish as industry threw all its resources into cranking out as much H5N1 as possible."

Ken persisted.

"Ken, look," Bueller said. "I have another call. I have to go." And he'd hung up, leaving Ken to stew.

Ken sat sullenly at his desk now, still stewing, days later, every day. He'd spent his whole life predicting and chronicling the shift and drift of viral proteins in the laboratory, had been responsible for the development of avian vaccine for people and won modest to coveted accolades along the way for his efforts. The single agent available for prevention was being manufactured in a facility he helped to advise not fifty miles away, and *it was going to waste*. Within a few more months sixty million doses of Avimmune would be ready for worldwide consumption and most of them were going to sit on a shelf in a refrigerated warehouse in California. There would be no public distribution. No clamor. He couldn't even obtain it for his family. No one would stock it. The error of it was criminal.

The frustration in him boiled over into his work and family life. The burden of his apparent professional impotence loomed large in personal interactions. He ordered June around, snapped at his coworkers, and had Moira in tears more than once crankily objecting to childish behaviors that ordinarily delighted him. He had been ashamed by his acrimony but seemed unable to stop himself. The more powerless he felt in the international realm, the more he attempted to reassert control in the parochial.

His gall rose further as he considered the additional toll this ill-conceived WHO policy was having on his investment in PharmaGlobal. He was trying not to obsess about it, but the price of PharmaGlobal stock had recently dropped thirty percent, a loss he hoped would be temporary. Ken clung to a belief that those in power at the WHO would eventually come to their senses as the disease toll mounted, and order widespread Avimmune inoculation. His investment would rebound.

At least, Ken thought bitterly as he closed the drawer and scooted back to his desk, his Viraban stock was doing well. There wasn't a single dose of osmavir lying on a factory shelf; the demand far outstripped the supply and would indefinitely. Despite the fact that there were several manufacturers of the drug, there was essentially no competition because each could sell as much product as they could make. Viraban was flying high and would only go higher. At this point though, his success with Viraban was only offsetting the losses at PharmaGlobal. He was no closer to retirement.

Trying to clear his mind, he made a concerted effort to return to his work. He scooted his chair up to one of the most advanced electron microscopes in the world and peered through the eye-piece at the latest specimens of mouse lung he was attempting to infect with H5N1 virus.

165

It took a magnification of nearly twenty thousand times just to begin to see a virus this small. To get the best views of the offending particles he would have to crank the power closer to eighty thousand.

This particular experiment had been running for over two years. Ken had supervised various manipulations in the virus' shell, cleaving or adding small sections of protein to key attachment areas. The newly 'drifted' virus was then injected into mouse cell cultures and allowed to incubate to ascertain infectivity. The results were apparent under the microscope: if the virus was able to attach easily, the interior of the cells would be loaded with particles; if not, the viruses clumped harmlessly in the spaces between the cells unable to gain entry, non-communicable, and essentially benign to the host.

Ken usually lost himself in these studies. Under the spell of the microscope he entered the world of the tiniest known life forms, and despite the number of years he'd been doing this, it never failed to mesmerize him. Occupying his full visual field now was the green glow of electrons bouncing through the heavy metal grids implanted in the sample. This refraction allowed for the tremendous magnification power of the equipment. Ken scrolled around the slide from side to side, and up and down in a precise pattern honed by years of practice. Any observer looking at his face as he assessed the specimen could have seen the disappointment register. Another failure was written now in his falling brow, the slackened cheeks. If he could demonstrate proficient infectivity by H5N1 in mice, he could prove the final mechanism for its development into a pandemic strain. He could persuade the non-believers that H5N1 was indeed in a pre-pandemic phase and wake them up to the importance of immunization.

But it was not to be today, and Ken found himself distracted from his work once again. Rolling around in his brain at the moment, like a pinball bouncing off the walls of his unrealized expectations, was his disillusionment with J.B. Vaughn. He couldn't believe the man had lied to him and the board about gutting the research department.

A grim but determined Vaughn had delivered a somber report at the board meeting last week. He spoke of the production delays and the new timetable of August for completion of the vaccine. This was the first Ken had known about the problems with production although he was well aware of the dismal sales contracts. And Vaughn had exploded in response to a question from a member regarding returning the facility to smaller batches of multiple avian strains. "As long as I'm at the helm, PharmaGlobal will *not* be returning to a program of small batches of multiple vaccines! The turnaround in this company's profits was achieved by thinking on a grander scale. We are not going to go backwards in our long-term view to make up for a short-term problem."

"Multiple vaccines are not the way to go anyway," Ken offered, supporting Vaughn, trying to help. "H5N1 is the player, the only major player. When the pandemic hits, we'll be ready with Avimmune."

"Ken's right." Vaughn said.

"How's it going in R & D?" Ken asked him, looking for something positive to move the discussion toward.

"It's not on the agenda today," Vaughn replied, his voice rising again. "Let's move on…"

"But it's always on the agenda," Ken interrupted. "That's really where we shine, being ahead of the curve," he nodded as he looked around at the other members. "That's why we have Avimmune. Thinking ahead. Researching what's next. Coming up with solutions to problems before the problems have even occurred. Surely there's time to tell us briefly Vaughn---any breakthroughs on rapid vaccine techniques?"

"No. There is nothing to report. Moving on to our fall schedule…"

"Wait. *Nothing* to report?" Ken cut him off once more.

"No," Vaughn said fixing Ken with a look that dared him to interrupt again.

Ken persisted. Quietly. Innocently. "Why not?"

"It's about cash flow." Vaughn responded. "It's not on the agenda because there is nothing to report."

"Cash flow?" Ken was baffled. Appalled. Angry. Did everything in the world boil down to cash?

"R & D is temporarily shut down to provide the cash necessary to retool the production lines to make Avimmune. There will be no R & D report until they are up and running again, probably sometime this fall."

"You sacrificed research for production Vaughn? I can't believe it," Ken replied, his vocal cords taut from betrayal, disappointment. "The research informs the production. It's necessary to it. I don't remember your telling me, telling us, that it was a choice between Avimmune or research."

"Might I remind you the day-to-day operations and decisions in this company are mine!" Vaughn countered, startling Ken and everyone else with the vehemence of his reply. "I took PharmaGlobal from near bankruptcy and turned it into one of the most profitable pharmaceuticals in the world."

Vaughn paused, lowered his voice again. "You need to trust me on this. It was a necessary call."

Ken felt himself inexorably withdrawing from the meeting after Vaughn's revelation. He was vaguely aware of the buzz and trip of voices in the room, could see things if he chose to look, but he was no longer part of the congress. Lost in himself, he was surrounded now by a deepening sense of unreality, of events spinning out of his control. Of things happening that shouldn't be, of people behaving in ways they couldn't be. Of words being spoken and promises broken.

He was searching for explanations. For something to hold on to. Everything he had worked for, all he was trying to do, seemed to be turning to ashes around him. He was a smart man, brilliant even, he allowed. Hard working. Dedicated. Tenacious. Respected. Zealous in his pursuit of knowledge and understanding. What was happening when every person in his life let him down? First Bueller, then the WHO, now Vaughn. Who could be trusted to do what was right? Was this all that humanity could expect from its leaders? Cowardice? Mediocrity? Lies?

No. No. And no.

Staring into the foggy bay that morning at PharmGlobal and disconnected from the babble around him, Ken had a sudden, clear vision of what his life meant. He saw that he could only be responsible for himself; that he could not be held to account for anyone else's shortcomings or failures. His power lay in the courage to act on his own beliefs, whether anyone supported his efforts or not. He would persist in his personal mission to aid society in any way possible and, regardless of the outcome, he determined he would be at peace knowing he was doing everything he was capable of. He would not rely on the vagaries of other institutions or people to validate his ideas or to accomplish what he alone could do. If no one else could be trusted, if his was the sole remaining voice of honesty and reason, so be it.

Fortified by his day-dreaming of these recent events, Ken gathered the tendrils of his floating thoughts and returned to the cocoon of Crossfire and the present. Using a pair of fine forceps he pulled another slide of mouse epithelium from the case of fifty he had yet to evaluate and placed it under the microscope. He took a swallow of cold black coffee and folded up this morning's partially-read newspaper with its clipped areas flapping, and threw it in the garbage. He never saw the article in the business section about the whistleblower at Viraban.

VIRUS: IN VIVO

LONGZHOU, CHINA
May 1

Chu-Wei squinted into the sun just cresting over the fish pond. He tucked a rice cake and a piece of dried fish into his pocket and jumped off the front stoop of the hut. The air still retained a breath of its pre-dawn coolness as he trudged past Anh-lee, the water buffalo who tilled and harvested the rice paddies for the Chu family three times a year. A slight skip appeared in his step, one of few perceptible indications of his childhood, as his mind wandered to the games he would soon play at the neighborhood festival. The village elders hadn't announced a date yet, but with the birth of a son in the community, there was always a celebration, with extra food, sweet treats, friends to play with, and most importantly a whole day off from his usual chores.

Indeed, his pace slowed again as he contemplated, from a ten-year-old's point of view, the combination of conditions that would make his life challenging today. It was hotter than the hottest he could ever remember for many days now in a row. His little body would sweat, and he would need to draw an extra bucket of water just to quench his own thirst. The grass all around him was parched, and the rice paddies low on water from an unseasonable lack of rain. He must not only drive the ducks from the fish pond to the paddies so they could do their job of chewing up the weeds making their way through the tiny rice shoots, he must also haul water for the pigs and chickens and the rest of the household. When there was rain, water collected in barrels at the hut, and in drinking bowls in the wire coops that housed the livestock over the fish pond, so there was no need to tote it. But today he would have to get the large buckets out of the shed and wear the cumbersome shoulder harness, which was really made more for a man than a boy, and scoop the water out of the pond to pour into the pigs' and chickens' bowls. He would trudge several times far up the meager stream to collect water for the household: his parents, himself and Anh-lee.

Once, not long ago, he had lied to his father saying he had filled the water bowls in the livestock pens, but his father had gone to check and found the bowls empty. His papa scolded him severely for mistreating the three pigs and seventeen chickens, all of whom were named and treated as members of the family for their important contributions to the Chu's life. "Our chickens and pigs must be fed and watered daily, just like you!" he thundered. "We depend on their health to survive! Do you not see that the chickens must eat and drink to lay eggs? That the pigs cannot fatten without this? Why, we even need their waste to drop through their cages over the pond to feed the fish. The fish grow bigger from this and make even more fish, and we can sell them at market for more money! I hope I have not had a son who can grow up to be such a fool as this!"

His ears as well as the backs of his thighs still stung from the memory of his father's rebuke. Chu-Wei was a good son; he would never again slough his chores. But he determined to make his drudgery more fun, and allowed himself to go back to happy thoughts of sweets and friends and games, as he drove the ducks with his bamboo staff from their nightly rest at the pond to the paddies on the far side of the field.

CHAPTER 12

PORTLAND, OREGON
May 6

Anna Wardman had not been out of her bed for months. While the Alzheimer's had eaten the fabric of her memory like moths a sweater, it had spared her body for quite a long time. Even as recently as this winter she had been capable of sitting in a chair for a few hours a day. Last fall she was still walking with stoved-up joints down hallways that were new to her every day, an aide supporting each side.

Whether it was arthritis in her old bones, or the Alzheimer's disease excavating deeper and deeper ruts into her grey matter that affected her ability to move, was only of academic concern. For some time now she could not be removed from the bed. But she could be turned, and required this every two hours because she had developed gaping bedsores despite the nurses' best efforts to prevent them.

Apparently one weekend Anna had been overlooked on the routine turning schedule, and the oozing decubiti had appeared almost immediately, creating raw, seeping maws out of the delicate places that used to contain her elbows, heels and tailbone. Once the devitalized, pus-prone spaces opened, it was very difficult in her chronically immobilized and otherwise debilitated condition to get rid of them. Anna had had her sores now for six weeks. They ranged in size from one or two inches on her feet and arms to as large as a saucer over the withered flesh of her buttocks. Furthermore, even the act of being flipped over in the bed regularly was now threatening to break open new areas of decay over both hips.

Ken had seen the wounds on his mother's extremities and had no intention of viewing those on her buttocks. Part of her daily regimen was the application of moist dressings which were left to dry under a therapeutic light to encourage healing. Inadvertently he entered the room as the nurse was setting up the treatment. Anna was a modest woman and would have been chagrined at her exposure. Ken averted his eyes and attempted to exit the room but the nurse blocked his retreat, eager to show him just how *great* the lesion over her sacrum looked. Before he could object she had whisked away the dressing revealing the hideous sore. From Ken's perspective the nurse exhibited an enthusiasm for the clinical status of the chewed up bloody tissue that was unwarranted; maggots crawling through rotted meat could not appear worse. He restrained a gag and removed to the other side of the bed as hastily as he could manage without alerting the nurse to his discomfort. No doubt disappointed by his lack of excitement for the progress of the decubitus, Anna's nurse replaced the dressing, directed the heat lamp to the site, and left Ken alone.

He controlled his physical reaction fairly quickly, but his anxieties, he found, were not so easily assuaged. His mother did not appear to be in pain from these putrescent corruptions, but how could he know? He had heard tales of other people with bedsores. Conscious people. They were extraordinarily painful he thought. Was she not feeling it? Or was she in terrible misery with no mechanism left for her to express it? Did pain have to be part of her drawn out dying? If *she* wasn't feeling it, he certainly was. He had hoped she would die peacefully, of natural causes. Was this natural? My God, he decried the cruelty of it.

Tomorrow she would be ninety three. Ninety three years of life; perhaps ninety of living, she would have said. How much more could she stand, or he? She had known it would be like this, despite Ken's naïve objections. Predicted it. Dreaded the inhumanity of it. The loss of soul. The grotesque distortion of self wrought by the disease on the long, slow march toward death. If, in some nerve cell still functioning in her brain, she had any awareness of her plight at this moment she would be so angry. Angry at the waste of time and money spent dying, angry at her inability to either live properly or die quickly. Angry at the doctors for not being able to help her live. Angry at Ken for not being able to help her die. He hung his head in shame.

Even abhorring the path in front of her Anna had admitted she could never have taken her own life. In lucid times, with Anna recapturing all the skills of analysis employed in her lifetime, they had discussed her wishes, debated them. She articulated that she simply did not want to live when she was no longer cognizant of her surroundings and unable to perform basic nutritional and toilette functions. She acknowledged she didn't want to miss one moment of purposeful thought, and wasn't sure *when* to draw the line between the knowing and the not knowing. She would have to be lucid to take her own life and if she were lucid, Anna explained quite rationally, she would not be ready to die. Anna had studied Alzheimer's; she knew there would be months to years of dying with it, after the years when you lived with it. Someone else would have to help her take her own life when she was no longer capable of doing it for herself.

"How can you ask me to make that choice for you?" Ken had pleaded with her. "If you can't know when your last lucid moment will be, how will *I* know when your personal experience of the world is no longer meaningful? What if you still have awareness in the midst of your Alzheimer's? What if there is some satisfaction of living even in your coma? Something you are unable to communicate? Mother, it is too much to ask."

The words haunted him, chewed at the fabric of his being. As he looked at her now, the stark reality of her lying in front of him in the bed was a sharp contrast to the muddy condition of his mind. He craved black and white, but his thoughts were shrouded in grey. He was having trouble telling right from wrong and bemoaned this difficulty; things had seemed so clear to him before. He was lost, he admitted. Everywhere. Not just here at Anna's bedside. She had become another obstacle to his struggle for clarity. Another example of his impotence.

How could he reconcile his beliefs and still be a good son to her? She deserved this from him he thought, as remote memories of her tenderness toward him as a child pierced him like an arrow. Looking at her so vulnerable, so passive in the bed, he was plagued with doubt. Awareness, if it existed for Anna, was nothing more than agony now, trapped in the failed mind, the failing body. In pain. Was she watching him even now, testing him, pushing him to the limits of his convictions? His head sagged into his arms resting on the cold steel side rails of the bed that separated them.

"Oh Anna," he said weeping softly, "I'm so sorry."

VIRUS: IN VIVO

LONGZHOU, CHINA
May 7

It was too bad really. Chu-Wei's mother knew how eagerly her son had looked forward to the celebration, so he was more distressed to be sick today than he might have been on any other day of the year. But here he was this morning with flushed face and burning hot skin. She had to keep him home. She attended to him all day, brewing tea and applying cool cloths to his forehead. He sniffled a bit and asked if he couldn't go to the party just for a little while, insisting in a scratchy voice he felt fine. His mother was not swayed.

She cooked while she nursed him, preparing dishes to be shared with other families at the festivities. He pined before the events even began, mourned in anticipation of all the fun he would miss. It nearly broke his mother's heart. He was such a good boy. In the afternoon she sat down with him and began to tell stories, thinking it would take his mind off the gaieties that were becoming increasingly audible outside. He smiled wanly at her after she told one of his favorite tales of the dragon king and the magic pearl. "Mother, I am sleepy now," Chu-Wei said as the noise of the celebration grew louder. He lay his head on the pillow and blinked at her with heavy lids.

"Alright son, you look like you need to rest. I will take the dishes to the courtyard and then return.

"Don't worry mother. I will sleep. You don't need to stay with me. I'm not an infant like the one the party is for. You make me feel like a baby sitting here, watching me."

She stroked the boy's hair and smiled. "Well, I see. You're all grown up then. Alright, I'll stay for a little while and then return to check on you. There is water here," and she showed him the pitcher and his cup next to the bed. "I will not be gone long." Taking up the heavy pot she walked outside and called for her husband to fetch a second pot and hurry along. Chu-Wei's father appeared in the doorway and noted him napping peacefully. He paused over the child, looking at him with tenderness before he picked up the kettle and left.

Chu-Wei waited for the sounds of their footsteps to disappear then climbed off his cot and peered cautiously out the window. His friends were milling about within sight and he was able to get their attention by waving his arm. One of them had come by earlier to see if he was ready to play, but he reluctantly informed him that his mother would not allow him to attend any of the merriment. They had plotted then to meet after his parents left, hoping to have at least a little time to play. Chu-Wei did not feel his best it was true, but he had felt worse than this on many days and still had to do chores. Why shouldn't he be able to have fun on this holiday?

The boys stole around the house, hiding Chu-Wei among their youthful bodies as they ran to the duck pond to throw stones and cool off in the late afternoon heat. They frolicked for a while, giggling and wrestling in the dirt before jumping in the water to rinse themselves. Chu-Wei realized he would be wet if his parents came back soon so he reluctantly got out of the water before the other boys to dry off, and was stalking crickets in the tall grass at the edge of the pond when he spotted the lifeless duck. It was not one of their flock, he recognized immediately, and it looked to be recently dead because there was some fresh blood oozing from its bill onto the reeds crushed under its body. With excitement he hailed the other boys, still splashing, to come see his find and they took turns prodding it with a stick and dancing around it and squealing before one of them dared another to drink its blood.

Shrieks and gasps followed, with the boys' taunting escalating from dares to double dares. They poked further at its carcass, now muddy from their intrusions, and circled it, peering more intently. Gradually they settled down. The duck was now placed between them in the center of a circle they had formed sitting cross-legged, knee-to-knee, in the rushes.

In a somber voice one of the group started a story of the fabled hero, Yi, and the elixir of immortality. The boys' attention was rapt as the narrator told of Yi's great courage and strength in rescuing the goddess Chang'o, and of how he slaughtered a vengeful god who had taken the form of a wild goose, and drank his blood to achieve immortality. At this juncture the storyteller solemnly took up the limp body of the duck and placed his mouth over the bloody bill and sucked. Smears of dark purple stained his lips and cheeks as he passed the duck to the boy next to him.

The child next in line, not completely convinced by the narrator's account, protested, "This is a duck, not a goose. What if it isn't a god?"

"If it is and you don't drink, then you won't be immortal like the rest of us." And without warning the storyteller snatched the duck out of the contrary boy's hands and handed it to the next one, challenging him to cast off eternity so glibly. One by one all the boys took their turn and all five drank, the formerly reluctant boy grabbing the duck off the dirt where it had been cast by the last boy, and taking an especially dramatic pass at the gory bill.

When the impromptu ceremony was over, the children, still gathered in a circle, were grimly confronted by the bloody streaks on their faces and the sharp metallic taste in their mouths. Without a word they stood and went back to the pond to wash.

The light banter of their play had been lost. They found their newly acquired immortality weighed heavily on them, and soon after that they disbanded, Chu-Wei saying he needed to be back in bed before his parents came home. With the burden of eternity in front of them, they rejoined their lives on earth.

Chu-Wei was fine the next day. Out of bed, doing his chores as usual. Five days later all the boys except Chu-Wei were ill. He went to their homes to visit them as one after another they took sick with fevers and coughs. A few days after he visited his ailing friends, Chu-Wei became sick again. And he wasn't better the next day.

177

CHAPTER 13

CHINA
May 17

The report came to Lou at her office in Guangzhou via telephone from an alarmed physician at Nanning City Hospital. Yong had taken the call and brought her on the line as soon as he realized the gist of the message. In very broken English the doctor proceeded to explain that he thought he had two children with avian flu and that there might be three more children from the same community with the disease. The hospital was sending a doctor and an ambulance to collect the others from their homes in Longzhou but it would be several hours before they knew the extent of additional involvement in the farming hamlet.

Struggling mightily to keep up with the doctor's speech pattern, Lou asked him to speak in his native Chinese and had Yong translate. It took about twenty minutes to gather as much information as the doctor had, which included the fact that some of the boys had been playing with a dead bird. Lou thanked the man and told him WHO would send a physician knowledgeable in avian influenza management to Nanning as soon as possible. He was quite relieved to hear this as the boys were not doing well. She promised she would keep in touch with him and gave him her cell number to contact her immediately with updates on the children.

It was mid-morning in Guangzhou, the middle of the night in Geneva when Lou telephoned WHO headquarters to enlist medical assistance for the boys in Nanning. Even without documentation, the evidence that the children had avian influenza was compelling. She didn't have the luxury of waiting for lab confirmation to act. Veterinary experts would be called to assess the bird if it was still available, but she wasn't overly optimistic about that; people often ate the evidence, and what they didn't eat they burned.

Lou alerted officials in Nanning and Longzhou that quarantines were to be set up at the perimeter of the boys' village for all livestock and people. The only persons allowed in or out were to be sick individuals and the ambulances sent to assist them. This was the first quarantine imposed in this province, and in Lou's experience it was best to involve bureaucrats at different levels of society: knowing someone else was watching them helped to effect compliance. Lou could only cross her fingers and hope that the level of cooperation in the community exceeded the level of corruption. One never knew.

Lou had pulled some diplomatic strings to get access to a pilot and a small enough plane to land on a strip close to Longzhou, a small town by Chinese standards nearly four hundred miles away. If she'd taken a commercial flight she would have had to go through Nanning and then drive another hundred miles to the village. Too much time would be lost. This was the largest cluster of avian influenza yet. Five cases potentially. One community. Yong arranged for Longzhou authorities to meet them at the air strip and drive them to the village. Lou and Yong each sped home, quickly packed a bag, and drove to a private airstrip used chiefly by the rising corporate leaders of southern China. They took off fewer than three hours after the doctor's call and were landing in Longzhou ninety minutes later.

• • •

Connor got the call from the Associated Press with the breaking story in Nanning while Lou was in the air. He was working in the Congo, investigating a recent Ebola virus outbreak. The story was nearly finished. He debated whether to fly straight to Nanning or to Guangzhou first. Guangzhou had a first rate infectious disease hospital. If the victims were in serious condition it was likely they would be transferred to the specialized institution.

Lou typically would have called to let him know of a story like this. They had been in touch via phone or e-mail nearly every day since Saigon. That she hadn't reached him meant she must not have had time. He tried to call her and got the standard 'out of service area' message. In the end he decided to get on the first plane he could to Guangzhou. Flights into and out of Africa were not especially frequent; just getting to mainland China would give him more options than he had here. Once he got to Guangzhou he could reassess the situation, which would be several hours further along by then, and determine how to proceed.

He checked out of his room and spent the next couple hours in the lobby reading through the international papers until it was time to leave for the airport. The front page of *The International Times* claimed that a new scandal brewing in the pharmaceutical industry threatened to affect avian flu preparedness. The largest maker of osmavir, the U.S. owned company Viraban, had been accused of fraudulent practices in its manufacture of the drug.

A long term employee had gone to the FDA claiming that Viraban had knowingly and deliberately diluted one of the key ingredients of the drug, to boost production. Apparently star anise, the herb from which the key ingredient, shakimic acid, was derived, was in very short supply. There being no other source for the substance and no substitute, a few employees at the company, including the president, had decided to stretch the acid by cutting it fifty-fifty with an inert ingredient. They were able to crank out twice as much osmavir from the altered anise, a fact which caught the attention of one of their engineers who discovered the ploy after conducting some discreet detective work.

According to the newspaper the company was in official denial mode, but the whistleblower had brought enough evidence with him for the FDA to temporarily suspend Viraban's production and sales pending the results of an investigation by the justice department. Fifteen million doses of osmavir were being pulled from drug store shelves and government stockpiles immediately; five million new doses a month of the drug were now in limbo.

There were a few other items that piqued his interest on the inside pages. The German government had decided to proceed with state-sponsored manufacture of H5N1 vaccine and were planning to provide enough to inoculate all eighty million of their citizens. Twice. It was a point of debate in medical circles whether a single dose of vaccine would be adequate protection and the Germans intended to err on the side of caution by administering two shots per person. The state would be taking over a production facility that normally produced immunizations for measles, mumps and rubella to achieve this goal, and world health authorities were concerned about ensuing shortages of these basic pediatric supplies as a result. Germany expected to have the H5N1 produced in six to eight months and all Germans vaccinated in double that time. The chancellor announced that after they had completed their national goals the facility would be turned over to vaccine production for international consumption. The Germans evidently saw their strategy as beneficent to international health as it was practical for their own; the rest of the world was taking a dimmer view.

Connor had to at least give the Germans credit for honesty. There was no getting around the suspicion that the richest nations in the world were apt to hoard as many of the tools to fight avian flu as they thought they could get away with.

A case in point was another article buried in the business section. There were only two makers of respiratory masks with fine enough gauge mesh to prevent influenza virus transmission. One of the makers was European owned, the other, American. Neither company was selling many of its masks outside of its own national union, raising the ire of all the other countries attempting to purchase their own supplies. To make the matter more interesting, India furnished the raw materials for the masks and housed the factories that produced them. Yet the international ownership of the factories meant that sale of the masks was being withheld, even from India. Indian authorities took a dim view of being closed out and had confiscated the inventory and taken over operations until an agreement could be reached with the international owners to provide the finished product not only back to India but to other nations who had been frozen out.

The *Times* even featured a special insert on avian flu and China, the country with the highest population and arguably therefore the most to lose in a pandemic. They were aware that just their sheer numbers meant they could count on no one for help. Fortunately their manpower had proven extraordinarily resourceful over time in the ability to create a knock-off of nearly anything. The Chinese were hard at work making duplicates of all manner of things that were in short supply: from syringes and intravenous bags to vaccines and ventilators. Unfortunately, in China quantity was often more prized than quality with predictably uneven results. The recent discovery of millions of doses of fake poultry vaccine administered to chickens throughout the eastern provinces had seriously undermined China's credibility. But Connor felt himself cheering the Chinese on: they had more of a will to succeed, it seemed to him, than his own leaders who were hopelessly mired in grandstanding. The world had an additional measure of hope if China could do for flu prevention and treatment supplies what it had done for the ball point pen and computer chips.

On the editorial page the United States was being roundly criticized for its fragmented approach to the pandemic threat and its refusal to marshal its power to address it. The author took the American leadership to task for a host of sins: its paltry financial commitment to vaccine research, its reliance on corporate entities for innovation, its miserly contribution to vaccine and drug stockpiles for unrestricted international use, and not least, its recent abdication of responsibility to state and local governments for planning flu response strategies. None of the author's accusations were new, but the tone of the debate was increasingly vitriolic as the public perceived the crisis looming larger.

Connor glanced at his watch and folded up the paper, uncharacteristically relieved to be done with it. Reading the news had long been a pleasure for him but sometimes the intensity of it required some concerted redirection of his thoughts afterward to preserve peace and balance in his life. He had a few minutes before he had to leave, which he used for a brisk walk around the grounds of the hotel to clear his head and shift gears before stepping into a cab for the airport.

He was eager to see Lou again, and his thoughts distracted him as he negotiated his way through the airport crowd and boarding rituals. She was one of the most independent women he had ever met, certainly the most free-thinking, self-confident, headstrong woman he had ever dated. There was a time in his life when that particular combination probably would have put him off despite her looks. But that wasn't happening; he was damned attracted to her. He threw his luggage into the overhead compartment on the plane, thinking how different it was with Lou. She needed time; he was giving it to her.

Connor nodded pleasantly at the stewardess as he passed her. He'd been courting Lou by phone and e-mail, nurturing common interests and celebrating amusing differences. He'd been to China twice in the last two months on assignments, planning his reporting schedule around flights through Guangzhou when possible. It left him a day or two each way to plan some real dates with her. With the frequent travel involved in his work he'd found it entirely possible and surprisingly enjoyable to conduct a long distance romance. But he would be grateful if they could cut the distance by a continent or two.

Connor settled in to his lap belt contentedly and plugged in a set of headphones for the trip, closing his eyes and scrunching sideways into an almost comfortable position against the window. The corners of his mouth curled into a barely perceptible smile as the jet took off.

•   •   •

By the time Lou and Yong arrived in Longzhou the remaining three children were enroute to Nanning General Hospital. Wearing microdense masks Lou and Yong interrogated the families of all five boys who were sick. They received the same story from each of the parents on the escapade with the duck. Chu-Wei, according to all interviewed, had not participated in the blood sucking because he was sick and in bed that day. It appeared he had gotten ill from visiting the other boys after they got sick.

The duck had evidently received an impromptu burial by one of the children a few days after the boys' ceremony, and no one had really thought more about it until two of the children became so sick that they were rushed to the hospital. One of the parents, alarmed about the possibility of bird flu after hearing his son's story, had gone out and found it, saving it for the authorities. Yong double-bagged it in a biohazard sack for testing. They took blood samples from the families and the livestock before returning to the police vehicle they had arrived in to regroup.

Removing their masks they began to pack up their supplies. "Looks like we may have another case of person to person transmission, huh?" Yong asked soberly.

"Maybe," she replied, biting her lower lip as she thought for a moment. Lou loaded the sample case into the trunk. "We should leave these people some masks to wear for the next two weeks. If person-to-person transmission occurred there could be others incubating in the next two weeks. They'll have infected one another before we have any results back and they may want to protect themselves. Quarantine only protects the outsiders. It's the least we can do. So we don't waste the supplies, go back in and explain the risk and distribute a mask to those who want one." Lou tied her own mask back on and picked up her notes.

"Where are you going Lou?"

"Back to talk to Chu-Wei's parents. I'm not sure I asked all the right questions." Lou said as she strode back through the quarantine line.

● ● ●

Lou tried to reach Connor on the way back to the Longzhou airport. It was the first time she'd had a moment to spare since this morning. He didn't answer, but on checking her own messages she was pleased to hear that he had called her.

"Hey Lou, heard about the kids in Nanning. I'm about to hop on a flight to Guangzhou. I'll be camped out at my usual room around the corner from your apartment. Let me know when you're coming back and I'll pick you up at the airport."

Maybe it was time for him to camp out in her room Lou thought with a combination of anxiety and delight that surprised her with its swiftness. She flipped her phone open. Left a message. "Hi Connor. Maybe I'll let you kick my butt in Scrabble when I get home, or you can set yourself up for another trouncing at backgammon...I'm on my way to Nanning to check on the boys. Not sure when I'll be home... I miss you." That was really all she had wanted to say she realized as she hung up: I miss you.

Lou snapped the phone shut, wishing he lived closer, a lot closer, so there wasn't this constant pressure when he was in Guangzhou to figure things out. Connor was different than the others she'd been involved with. Sure of himself without the concomitant enormous ego. Comfortable in his own skin and not threatened by her assertiveness or intellect; he could hold his own in a debate, but had no need to win an argument. He was a thinking man, not given to rapid fire diagnosis and action, as her training and work required; he enjoyed gathering information from many sources and then contemplating the relative value of each before arriving at his own conclusions.

Frankly, Lou wondered what was wrong with him. She hadn't found any flaws, annoying mannerisms, cloying character deficits. Yet. She had been a little concerned that he might suffocate her with attention, flying off like that to see her right away in Saigon. But she had given him clear signals to back off, and he had. His ability to stay away made her want him back. And he was good looking to boot: she certainly wouldn't kick him out of bed for eating cookies, as she and her girlfriends used to joke about sexy men. Imagining him in bed made her realize she had to sort him out quickly because she was finding it more difficult each time they were together to hide her attraction. She could tell he was holding back out of respect, but she saw the hunger in his eyes. Sometimes when she looked at him, she caught him smiling bemusedly at her, as though he were undressing her in his mind. The thought of it sent a pleasant chill down her spine and lodged in a place that had been quiet for too long. Something would have to give. Soon.

I can't believe I'm fantasizing about this guy right now, she thought as she climbed back into the four-seater prop plane. She forced herself back to the present. There was a potential crisis unfolding around her and she was, of all things, falling in love. It was really incredibly poor timing she thought with a sigh.

CALIFORNIA
May 19

Two headlines screamed at Ken from the front page. Sitting at the kitchen table with June puttering around him, he began to wildly skim each piece, unable to focus on either, the implications of them like gasoline on the fire burning inside him. He dragged his eyes from the paper and forced himself to look at June, tried to hold on to the normalcy of her putting the glasses from the dishwasher into the cupboard, oblivious to him and his agitation. He wanted to set the paper down, arm himself with reason before he attempted to read, but his trembling hands would not release it, and the words on the page, side-by-side dragged him in again like a magnet: *H5N1 Strikes Five Children in China* and *Viraban Subject of FDA Probe.*

Surrendering, Ken lost himself in the first article. He read about the boys, between nine and eleven years old, who were on their way from Nanning to the Infectious Disease Hospital in Guangzhou due to the severity of their conditions. The WHO had determined the probable source of the infection for four of the boys was direct oral contamination from a species of migratory duck. Parents of the fifth boy reported he had not been in contact with the duck, but had visited his friends repeatedly after the onset of their illnesses. According to the reporter, person-to-person transmission was presumed to be the source of the fifth boy's infection.

"Presumed! Indeed! What are they waiting for!" Ken shouted at the newspaper. June was so startled by the outburst she dropped the can of coffee she'd been holding, spilling grounds over the counter. She wheeled around, her hand at her chest, and saw Ken's crimson visage still directed at the paper.

"Ken, what's the matter?" she asked.

Interrupted by June, Ken appeared not to realize he had spoken aloud.

"I...I'm sorry...I didn't think...I didn't know I was..." he stammered.

June, walked around Ken's chair and placed her hands on his shoulders. "Ken," she said searching his eyes, "What is it? I've never seen you so...agitated. You're not yourself lately."

Ken met June's gaze, then looked away, out the window, unable to withstand her sincerity. The sun was shining in an impossibly azure sky, but it only threw shadows on his heart. He was so ashamed of what had happened, was happening to their nest egg for retirement, so uncomfortable with the fact that he had not told her of his plans before he had made the changes. He was miserable with keeping it a secret, and now he couldn't tell her until he made things right again. Worse, he'd been snapping at June out of frustration with everything going wrong. It wasn't her fault that no one but him could see that H5N1 was *the* pandemic threat. She wasn't to blame for the stockpiles of vaccine that would be sitting unused on the shelves of PharmaGlobal. June didn't gut the research program or lie to him about it like Vaughn had. But Ken was lying to her. Or at least not telling her the whole truth about what was bothering him.

They had never been two people who shared every fleeting emotion with one another because they considered such drama unnecessary. But they had always included one another in matters of importance, and Ken had never carried the burden of withholding anything from her before. He hadn't thought of it as lying at the time. He just didn't want to worry her and he didn't want her running off to tell her brother about his investments. Now he was in the terribly awkward and uncomfortable position of not being able to tell her at all. He just couldn't face her disappointment. Not now. Not with everything else.

"I'm sorry June," he said, contrition in his voice and his heart, even if he couldn't meet her eyes more than fleetingly. "You're right, I haven't been myself. I'm very upset about this whole avian thing. I can't get anyone to listen to me. There's another case," he gestured with the back of his hand to the paper lying in front of him, "of H5N1 with person-to-person spread. This time it's five little boys in China. It makes me so mad that I'm unable to help. I think about Moira when I read about these kids, and how upset I would be if she got sick from something that could have been prevented." His voice was rising with each sentence. "Every case of H5N1, every death, is on the hands of those who are dictating and following this inadequate policy. There is no excuse for withholding vaccine! Heaven knows, we can't help everyone...we don't have enough yet, but we should be helping as many as we can. Instead of funneling government *war* chests into *killing* people, we should be using our resources to save lives!"

Realizing he was shouting again, Ken stopped his tirade and sighed heavily, shaking his head at June then dropping it into his hands. "I just do not understand."

June put her arms around the man she had loved and tried to understand these many years, holding him and stroking his head. He always worked so hard to do the right thing; it was a constant burden to him. June thought of his flaws, they were small really, not much to complain about; they all boiled down to devotion to his work. It had been difficult for her and Betsy to constantly take a back seat to Ken's research. But he had never mistreated them. He had a much broader view of his purpose in the world, and she respected him for it. He was a good and decent man and, God-willing for she had been praying for it, he was becoming a better husband and father with time, and heaven knew no more dedicated grandfather.

As June comforted him Ken's eyes opened to the discarded newspaper lying on the table and the headline of the second article about Viraban that had captured his attention just minutes ago. His shoulders sagged as June let go her embrace and resumed her puttering in the kitchen. Ken took up the print and read on.

• • •

The same morning, as soon as he got to Crossfire, Ken placed a call to Michael Farrington, one of the few professional people he still respected. They had been allies in alerting Hunt and other Washington policy wonks on the importance of stockpiling Avimmune and osmavir. There was none of the usual political sleaze about Farrington and Ken wanted some straight answers.

"Michael, Ken Culp here."

"Why, yes, Dr. Culp, what can I do for you?"

"Michael I'm looking for some insight into the government's position on H5N1 vaccine."

"Really?" Farrington responded, "So am I."

"Pardon me?"

"Sorry. I shouldn't have said that. It was a flippant and inappropriate answer to a reasonable question. I've become quite cynical since I resigned my post."

"You resigned?"

"Yes, sorry. I thought you knew." Farrington explained, "I got tired of bucking the system. Couldn't make anything happen despite my best efforts. In the end I decided the only thing I could do was to dissociate myself from this administration."

"I'm sorry. I had no idea you quit."

"Spinning my wheels. Couldn't do it any more. Damned aggravating son-of-a-bitch I had to work through to get to the president. I'm not sure anything I said to that man made it up to the Oval Office. Although I have to say I didn't fare any better presenting my case to the president directly. The scuttle I'm picking up in D.C, although no one will admit it, is that the world could stand several million fewer people. Third world nations don't have enough of anything to go around. Why should we bail them out? Just so they can continue to reproduce, foment resentment at our wealth, and drag the rest of the world down? You know what else? These guys talk about a pandemic like its nothing more than the latest brouhaha from the hand-wringers of the world, the same people who brought you Y2K, the crisis that never happened."

"You can't be serious."

"I'm sure as hell serious. And I'm mad. I'm mad at the press too. Instead of hounding the president on why we haven't funded research, on why we haven't fully opened up the patent on osmavir, on why we haven't sent stockpiles of vaccine to Vietnam or China, they just come to their press briefings and ask trite questions and write, 'Yes, sir,' and 'Of course, sir,' like a bunch of dutiful little stenographers instead of the penetrating intellectuals they are supposed to be."

When he called, Ken had hoped to have an intimate conversation with Farrington, cashing in on their previous relationship as allies in policy, but even Ken was taken aback by Michael's rhetoric. Ken could only conclude Farrington's anger and disillusionment were as profound as his own, and he respected the man in even greater measure than he had before.

"What can we do about it?" Ken asked, eager to do more than just complain about how poorly things were going.

"Well, I don't know. It's discouraging. Each of us has to do the best we can. Whatever we are capable of I suppose. I'm working as a consultant, trying to help states pick up the ball the federal government has dropped. We have to keep at it Ken. I've tried at the top and failed. I'm going to the middle layer to see if I can make a difference there. The federal government may have to be shamed into acting. Is profit the only motivation for saving ourselves? Sorry, that's not my idea of utopian society." Farrington stopped abruptly, seemingly out of ideas. There was a moment of silence between them. "I'm afraid I've chewed your ear off Ken. I'm sure that was more of an answer to your question than you bargained for."

"No, not at all Michael. I certainly understand your frustration. In fact, I'm relieved to hear it. I've been thinking I'm the only one who sees the problems here. I'm glad I'm not alone." Ken paused. He had one more topic to explore.

"Michael?"

"Yes?"

"I...uh...wondered if you knew anything about the Viraban case?"

"Well, there are people claiming this whistle-blower is a communist or a terrorist, but between you and me, Viraban is up to its eyeballs in excrement right now and the water in the toilet is still rising."

"So there's some truth to it?"

"Another blow to pandemic preparedness I'm afraid. I understand there are video tapes of the chief engineer explaining to a supervisor just how to prepare the ingredients for manufacture. Someone rewrote the manual and adjusted the equipment to dilute the active ingredient to half-strength to save money: evidently the acid they use is getting harder to come by and more expensive as demand increases. The supervisor was hired specifically because he wouldn't have known the difference in the mix. Looks like the CEO had a hand in crafting an early retirement package for the former super just to create the opportunity to make the change in personnel. The FDA seized samples straight from the factory line and the warehouse prior to shipment. Everything they've tested from the past nine months is sub-potent. And it's identical. So there is no way to claim it was a single batch accident. Unfortunately for all of us, Viraban is going down."

CHAPTER 14

CALIFORNIA
May 19

Ken wished someone would pinch him, hard. Waken him from this nightmare. He dared not look at the stock pages. He'd brought the remnants of this morning's paper with him, and it sat on the corner of his desk daring him to open it. He stared back, refusing to acknowledge its power. He would not look. It didn't matter. It would be terrible news and it was only going to get worse. It was only money. Numbers on a page. He still had his house, his wife, his work. And Moira. It was very simple really; he was back where he started, a devoted scientist in his laboratory researching cures for humanity: Plan A. Up until Moira was born, it was the only plan he'd ever had. He could return to it. He would have to.

He would have no retirement, no halcyon years of leisure spent in the radiant aura of his precocious granddaughter, the child he never had. Or more accurately, the child he never appreciated. It was too ironic, too unbelievable to be happening. His mother would have had a heyday analyzing the twists and turns of his path had it been an outsider's life she was contemplating. For Ken she would have tried to be a mother first and given him what every child in trouble needs from a mother: sympathy. He wished she were here; she would have kept his confidence, he could have told her everything. But thinking of her only worsened his misery; it was another place he had failed.

How could he have ended up so wronged when he had always aspired to do right? He was tearing at his hair as he sat overwhelmed at the desk in his lab. He had the mini-blinds separating him from the laboratory pulled shut nearly all the time now because so much of his day was spent agonizing over the obstacles that loomed large in his path. He could hardly stand watching his assistants scurrying about their experiments when he felt it was all so futile. He hadn't been able to alter the virus to attain infectivity. He hadn't been able to convince the world to inoculate against H5N1. He hadn't been able to be a proper husband or father or son. He could have been a good grandfather but that opportunity would be lost to him as one financial debacle compounded another. He was certainly a failure at managing his money. His work would literally consume him as he died trying to make a living. His family had observed as much over the years, and in moments of frustration had railed against his commitment to his research. But they were too kind to take any pleasure from his misery now, if they had known. And he would not tell them.

Moira would grow up fine without his doting. June and Betsy might wonder why he stopped talking about, or planning for, retirement. But they would never know. He would retreat into the microcosm of the cells magnified umpteen thousand times under the scope, the pristine plates of sterile petri dishes, and the virion capsids with their H and their N spikes, the twisted strands of RNA lurking within. His family would just think of the past few years as a pleasant bump in the otherwise uneventful home life of Kenneth Culp, dedicated scientist.

He had never known such despondence.

CHINA
May 20

It took her three days, but Lou finished her investigation in Nanning, including making arrangements to transfer all five boys yesterday to the Infectious Disease Hospital in Guangzhou, a state of the art facility more capable of dealing with their illness. Fortunately the attending physician who first saw the boys had a high index of suspicion for avian flu based on their presenting histories and physicals. The doctor had ordered isolation precautions immediately and no one but the emergency personnel had been exposed. The three nurses and one doctor who saw the boys first were to be quarantined for two weeks, as were the admitting secretary and the two orderlies who wheeled the children to have their x-rays. There did not appear to be any other potential exposures in Nanning. The ambulance attendants sent out to collect the other three boys had worn masks and gloves and were not at risk. As they had already cordoned off the children's village, the isolation of Longzhou was taken care of. If a person-to-person strain was involved the only stones left unturned were the parents who had accompanied their boys to the hospital. They had been ordered to wear masks from the time the boys were admitted in Nanning, but some additional arrangements would need to be made in Guangzhou. They would need to remain in isolation both from their children as well as from the public in case they were already incubating the virus. It would be two weeks before they were confirmed free of disease.

Lou dialed Connor from the makeshift office Yong had set up in Nanning hospital to let him know she was returning to Guangzhou. He did not try to conceal his pleasure at the prospect of seeing her and told her he would pick her up at the airport.

After speaking with Lou, Connor spent the next hour editing his story on the boys' condition, garnered at this point from long-distance interviews with the chief hospital spokesman in Nanning, and a few of the parents who had already arrived in Guangzhou. He would not be allowed to see the boys at Guangzhou Infectious Disease Hospital; all contact had been restricted to essential personnel due to the boys' potential infectivity. Connor was told all the children had high fevers and terrible coughs. Of the first two who came to the hospital, one was already on a ventilator and the other was close to needing one, struggling mightily to breathe. One of the other three boys appeared to have developed meningitis, losing consciousness somewhere in the air ambulance between Nanning and Guangzhou. The last two were still breathing without difficulty except during coughing spasms which were frequent; they were very sick, but easily aroused and able to communicate.

Connor did not trouble his interviewees for long, knowing they were beaten down by their worries, but he did manage to speak with Chu-Wei's parents a little longer. From outside the glass of an isolation booth he asked them over an intercom what manner of illness kept Chu-Wei in bed while his friends were playing with the duck. Mrs. Chu told him of the fever and malaise and her decision to keep him home that day despite the village festivities.

"Festivities?"

"There was a celebration in the square," Mom explained. "He wanted to go very badly to be with his friends but I made him stay home."

"So you were there with him?" Connor asked.

"Yes, I was there all day cooking, and ministering to him, making tea, sponging his face, telling him stories to take his mind off things," Mom said wearily.

"In the afternoon we carried the food pots to the pavilion," added Mr. Chu helpfully.

"So Chu-Wei was left alone?"

"No. Not really," Mrs. Chu responded. "Not for long. He said he was tired and wanted to sleep. I was back soon. Maybe an hour, maybe two, later. He was still asleep."

Mr. Chu added, "Yes, he was sleeping before we left. I stood over his bed and watched him breathing so peacefully. I felt sad for him not being able to play. He was so looking forward to the day,"

"How long was he sick?"

"Oh he was fine the next day," Dad responded. "He went back to his chores the very next morning."

Mom emphasized, "He was hot only for a day, and then fine again... until he visited the other sick boys. Chu-Wei heals very quickly," she said, trying to convince herself as much as Connor. "We have sound bodies in our lineage," Mrs. Chu clapped a hand to her sound breast in saying this. "He is strong..." Here she turned to her husband and broke into tears as he took her hand.

"My wife is very upset."

"Of course," said Connor. "I understand. Thank you for your time. I hope for your son's rapid improvement." He rose and made his way out of the hospital and into the Guangzhou night.

Connor quickly dialed Lou. "Hi," he said. "Glad I caught you before you took off. Wanted to check this detail before I filed my copy. Did you talk with Chu-Wei?"

"No. He's too sick. Just his parents."

"Me too."

"What do you think of their story?" Lou asked.

"I think they're telling the truth as they know it. I'm not sure they know it though. Sounds like a ten-year-old's fib to me."

"That was my gut feeling too. Especially after I talked with two of the other boys. They don't look me in the eye when they say Chu wasn't with them at the pond. I doubt it's person-to-person transmission Connor, I think Chu just took a tad longer to incubate the virus and show symptoms, but I've got to proceed as though it's person-to-person until we prove it's not. Maybe I can wear the boys down to the truth eventually, but right now they're too exhausted with the illness to push it."

"You sound pretty exhausted yourself."

"I am," she sighed.

"Just come home. I'll be here for you."

•   •   •

It was a little awkward, but just a little.

Connor was in a taxi waiting at the private hangar when the little plane rolled to a stop in the heat of an early Guangzhou afternoon. He jumped out of the cab when he saw Lou emerge, stepping carefully on the wing. By the time she started to lower her foot from the last step toward the tarmac he was there, supporting her waist as she stepped backward. He turned her around and held her close saying, "I'm so glad to see you." The wind blowing across the stretch of runway caught her hair, whipping it into her face as she pressed into the warm recess of his neck, scented a little with this morning's aftershave.

"I'm glad you're here," she replied, and pulled her head away just enough to look him in the eye.

It was a quantum leap. With that embrace and the acknowledgement of their desire to be with one another they had moved to a new level of comfort and exploration in their relationship. Lou reached up to take her backpack from Yong and flipped it over her shoulder while Connor took her bag in one hand, and her hand in the other. They walked to the taxi looking for all the world like two people in love. Yong smiled as he watched them. He was very happy for her.

•   •   •

They were oblivious to the traffic, talking about the weeks they'd been apart and the latest bird flu outbreak, and were surprised when the cabbie pulled to a halt in front of Lou's place and flung open the door. Lou keyed into her apartment with Connor right behind. He wouldn't allow her to carry anything, toting everything of hers and a backpack of his own in. She was glad to be home and suddenly exhausted with the effort.

Connor placed her things on the couch, turned her around and took her in his arms. "You need to rest."

"Yes, but I want to be with you too."

"There's time for that," he said, brushing some strands of hair from her face. "I have a plan, and your only decision at this moment is whether you want a shower before or after your massage."

"A massage?" she asked. "Have you hired a masseuse?" She pulled away a little, and craned her neck around the apartment as though he'd hidden one somewhere. "I'm not sure I can handle that. They'll massage your breasts and everything else you own in China," Lou said laughing. "That's a little beyond even my sense of adventure."

Connor laughed too. "I'm your masseuse, and while I admit I did consider your breasts, I was thinking more of here," he said, kissing the side of her neck. "And here," kissing her temple, "and maybe your back, and your legs, and your feet," he finished, punctuating each word with a kiss on the soft spots framing her face.

"You'd do that for me?" she sagged in his arms a bit at the notion.

"And your breasts, if necessary."

She laughed again, giving in to the comfort of his caresses and the fatigue. "I'll shower first."

"I have a bottle of chardonnay," he said, releasing her. "Let me pour you a glass to take with you."

She watched in astonishment as he retrieved a bottle wrapped in ice bags from his backpack, pulled out a corkscrew and opened it. He had left nothing to chance. Connor handed her a glass. Smiled. "Open the door when you're comfortable."

"You're going to knock me out," Lou said.

"Good, because a nice long nap is next on the list of how I'm going to take care of you today."

Lou was so tired she could barely pick up her feet, yet it seemed she floated rather than walked to the bathroom. She was over-whelmed by Connor's thoughtfulness, or maybe, she told herself, it was just the fatigue. She had tears in her eyes as she stepped into the warmth of the shower. Not since her mother had anyone taken care of her before.

A sip of wine before and after the shower had the effect of nearly putting her in a coma by the time she put on the beautiful green and gold silk robe she had picked up for a song the first month she'd been in China. Lou ran a quick comb through her hair, splashed some lotus blossom on her shoulders and peered at her legs: she was grateful she'd recently shaved. If she hadn't been so tired she might have been too nervous to relax after she opened the door and lay down and Connor began to massage. But the combination of wine and weariness allowed her to melt into his amazing hands.

"Where did you learn how to do this?" she asked.

"It was one of my fluff college classes," Connor replied, stroking her calves, firmly in one direction, then lightly in the other. Back and forth. Mesmerizing. "I've been able to do a lot more with that class than the pottery class I tried. My mom got a lot of deformed pencil holders out of that one."

Lou smiled. "I took belly dancing."

"Really? I'd give an undisclosed portion of my anatomy to see that."

"I wasn't very good." She laughed and patted her middle. "No belly."

"Don't tease me anymore with that vision. I'm trying really hard here."

He was silent after that, stroking her neck and shoulders, hands and arms, all the places he had promised. Despite her exhaustion Lou found herself wishing Connor would do… more. The rhythmic motion, the warmth of his hands, the scent of his aftershave as he leaned over her and into her muscles had every cell in her body on alert. If she had been another kind of a woman she would have spoken, invited him into herself. But she just couldn't. Didn't know how to say what she needed. She hoped he would figure it out.

He finished by taking her earlobes between his fingertips and rubbing them gently. Then he kissed her on each one.

"It's four o'clock," he said looking at his watch, wiping the excess cream from his hands with a towel in his lap. "Time for your nap. I'll be by at seven to pick you up for dinner."

Connor stood and turned rather awkwardly, trying to drape the towel in front of him as he exited the room; Lou's eyes were closed and he hoped she hadn't noticed. He was determined to let her make the first move, was doing everything in his power to lead her there, but he hadn't factored in the rather noticeable hard-on he'd gotten from stroking her.

After leaving her apartment he called Yong, intent on the next phase of his plan. "Yong, I'd like to take Lou somewhere special for a day or two. Any suggestions?"

"Sure Mr. Mackenzie. I know just the place…all the lovers go there…sorry, perhaps I spoke out of turn?"

"No," Connor laughed. "I guess it's pretty obvious."

"It's a park about an hour north of here by train…Very interesting rock formations…Great for walks…Some of the hotels have hot springs. I'll make a reservation for you," Yong offered.

"Okay. That would be great Yong. But, two rooms, not one. I don't want Lou to feel pressured."

"Okay. Two rooms it is." Yong smiled as he hung up. He was pretty sure they'd only need one.

• • •

"I'm *starved.*" Lou said as she opened the door, then her mouth dropped when she saw him: Connor had an armload of peach and apricot blossoms wrapped in colorful tissue.

"Why are you still single?" she asked, unable to contain her astonishment, taking the flowers and searching for a vase. "I can't imagine how a guy like you could still be available."

"I undoubtedly have some fatal flaw," he said. "Your job is to figure it out before you decide to date me."

"Oh. That's right." She smiled. "We're not dating."

"Exactly. So, this evening we are not dating at whatever restaurant you choose. Because, while I might seem to have anticipated all your needs, I really am clueless about what gastronomic delights would please you. So, you're in charge."

"Gas-tro-no-mic." Lou sounded it out. "That's four syllables. I think perhaps I'm going to make an exception for a man who is able to use four syllable words in conversation, and date you."

"Good. Where to then?"

•   •   •

It was a progressive dinner she chose, her appetite for her favorite foods as piqued as her curiosity for this new man in her life. Lou led Connor on foot through the exotic, waterfront alleys of Guangzhou, past stalls teeming with epicurean oddities enough to squelch all but the most intrepid appetites. They passed caged monkeys and muskrats, centipedes crawling over one another in wire baskets, snakes coiled in huge jugs of oil; there were pig and goat and dog carcasses suspended from windows, whole pigeons and dried ducks, and a stench in places that did all but destroy Connor's appetite. Lou breezed through all of it unconcerned and took him to a small, odor-free shop where she insisted they had the best crab soup in China.

"I'm relieved it's crab," he said, when the waiter brought their bowls.

Lou had just put a spoonful in her mouth when the waiter brought a small plate of fried appetizers. "What's this?" Connor asked as he crunched into one.

"Oooh. Connor," Lou said, covering her mouth full of soup, trying to speak before he ate it. "Cricket, she said. "They always bring a complimentary plate to the table at this place."

He raised an eyebrow, grimaced.

She shrugged apologetically. "Sorry. Think of it as a pretzel."

"Hmm. A little nutty," he observed, forcing himself to chew it, swallow. "Is there any nutritional value to this?" he asked peering at a second one.

She giggled. "Loaded with protein."

He offered her the plate. "No thanks. Been there, done that. Get my protein elsewhere."

Next they took a cab to a traditional Chinese establishment on the banks of the Pearl River, with a view of the neon skyline. Dishes of eggplant, braised celery, and barbecued pork steamed for hours in clay pots, Hangzhou style, were brought to the table. Connor admitted he was relieved the food was recognizable, and delicious. A steaming plate of something curly and suspicious appeared between courses.

"What's this?" he asked, poking it with his chopsticks. "Looks like squid."

"Nope," Lou said, and whisked it away from him. "And we didn't order this."

"What is it?" he asked the waiter to whom Lou was handing the dish back.

"Wolms," the waiter responded.

"What?"

"Wolms," he repeated.

Connor cocked his head at Lou. "Worms, Connor. Worms."

"Am I being tested?" he asked.

"Not intentionally," she laughed. "Not now anyway. I already tested you. You passed or I wouldn't be here, whisking the wolms away."

Dessert they had at a small Bavarian café a short stroll from the Pearl: saffron custard and mangosteen, a fruit, despite his travels, Connor had never seen before: small and segmented like a tangerine, but with a hairy hard brown shell, like a coconut. Sweet and delicious.

"Lou," he said as they were scooping up the last of the custard, "I hope you won't mind. I took the liberty of planning an overnight trip for us to a park. Yong'll cover for you. You deserve some time off. Now, before you jump to conclusions, I want you to know I got us separate rooms. I just thought you might want to go somewhere to relax for a couple days and Yong said this place would be just perfect. Lots of walks, nice scenery. Out of the city. What do you think?"

"I think it sounds lovely," Lou said, patting some wayward custard off her lips with a napkin. "When do we leave?"

• • •

To Lou's dismay Connor would not come in to her apartment after dinner. He kissed her long and hard at the door and she could feel something that wasn't his wallet or keys pressing against her. But then he abruptly excused himself, saying she needed the rest if they were getting on a train the next morning. She was going to have to strip completely naked to get his attention. It was killing her.

· · ·

Yong insisted on taking them to the train station for the hour and a half trip from Guangzhou. He smiled and winked at both of them as they waved goodbye, clucking and fussing over them like a mother hen. "Have fun!" he shouted as the train pulled away. From Shaoguan, where the train stopped, it was another hour bus ride to the Danxia Shan Geopark. Neither Lou nor Connor had ever heard of it before, and there was no one on the trip to inform them as all those around them were speaking Chinese. Yong had been purposefully obtuse with their questions about the park and its history, saying only they would have a great time. They left their bags at the hotel on the grounds and took a shuttle ride in.

"Oh my God." Lou said, her jaw dropping as they entered the park. "Is that what I think it is?" she asked.

Connor looked in wonderment as well at the 60 foot tall hunk of natural sandstone rising out of the undergrowth. "What do you think it is?" he asked.

"A giant penis."

"I don't know if that's what it is, but I like the way this conversation is going," Connor grinned as they moseyed down the path for a better look.

"No wonder Yong was acting like a schoolboy," she laughed. From every direction they approached it on the path winding through the trees and hills, the red rock was an accurate replica of a penis. Down to the circumcision.

They were not the only ones giggling at the giant phallus. At each turn they encountered native Chinese, taking pictures and pointing. Eventually they ran into an English-speaking guide, who led them to another of the park's remarkable natural phenomena: a 30 foot high pair of labia.

"What does that look like to you?" she asked.

"Heaven," he replied. "Although, the proportions are daunting."

Connor took her hand as they strolled, laughing about how Yong had set them up. They visited the monastery on the grounds, and the tea house, took the tram to the top of one of the peaks, and wandered through the Chinese sex museum at the exit which showcased, among other things, collections of coinage used in ancient brothels, Kama Sutra carvings in ivory, and displays with names like, "Popularity of Dildo in Ancient China."

By the time they arrived back at the hotel, all traces of the intimidating distance that had so confounded their attempts to get together were gone. They fairly bounded off the shuttle, and there was no need, either of them thought, for two rooms.

● ● ●

The next several days were a blur. Lou had much work to do following the Longzhou outbreak: keeping track of the boys, their village, their parents, the quarantined hospital workers, conducting press briefings, networking with Geneva. But what she would remember of this time would be little of that. Outside of her ten and twelve hour days she and Connor were having the time of their lives romancing one another through the exotic wildness of Guangzhou. Connor arranged to stay for a while, moving his single suitcase into her apartment. Working on the developing avian story gave him a convenient excuse to remain, but both he and Lou knew why he was there.

Amid the babble of five million Chinese they heard all they needed to hear from one another. They told stories of their childhoods, of their families and friends, and former lovers. Talked of favorite places, and people and books, their careers and hobbies. They held hands and drank bottles of wine together, tried terrible Chinese martinis and interesting Chinese beers. They spotted one another at the gym, joined ballroom dancers on the promenade in the early mornings, laughed as they stepped on each other's feet, and strolled through the public gardens in the evenings.

Less than two weeks later even this bit of an interlude was interrupted by another call that came in the wee hours of the morning. Lou wondered dazedly, as she silenced the ringing fiend next to her bed, why nothing catastrophic ever seemed to happen before midnight. It was Yong with a new case: three hospital workers in Chongqing had come down with H5N1 after exposure to a patient with bird flu who had died the preceding week. Yong had already booked Lou and himself on the 7 a.m. flight to China's largest city. When she hung up she realized Connor was trying to open one eye in the glaring light of the lamp she'd just switched on. "Sorry," she said, switching it off again and giving him a peck on the cheek. "Go back to sleep." And she flew out of bed and into the shower.

When she emerged Connor had a fresh cup of tea sitting on the shelf in the bathroom for her. He had set her travel bag out in the bedroom and was sitting in the kitchen reading when she appeared, dressed.

"Can I get you some breakfast?" he asked.

She glanced at the clock. "No time."

"I thought you might say that. Here." He handed her a couple granola bars he was able to scrounge from her cupboard, and an apple.

"Thanks," she replied smiling and went on, cocking her head and eyeing him sideways, "Are you trying to take care of me?"

"If that's what the situation calls for," he said straightening himself up in the chair in mock defense. "I want you to know I'm not just another pretty face," he continued dead-pan, knowing full well his hair was sticking out in all directions and he still had pillow wrinkles on one cheek. "I'm capable of making you breakfast. Although I will say if given a little more warning I can come up with something a bit more appealing than that," he said nodding his head toward the granola bars she'd laid on her pack.

Maybe it was the interrupted sleep. Maybe it was hormones. Maybe it was because he offered her food which even in its humblest form signified caring to her. It was ridiculous she knew, but she was momentarily misty-eyed. And he caught it.

"What? Are you okay? Was it something I said?" He stood and came around the table to hold her.

Leaning on his solid frame she felt the words well up spontaneously inside her. They seemed to start in her chest and bubble up to
her lips where they almost escaped before they got to her head and she
stopped them. She jerked away, totally unprepared for the feeling. This
couldn't be happening yet. It was too soon, wasn't it?

Connor was now holding her at arm's length. Puzzled.

"I'm sorry," Lou said shaking the thought away and nuzzling back
into his shoulder. "I'm fine. I guess...I just have a lot on my mind." She
shrugged and picked up her back pack.

"Come on. I'm driving you to the airport," he said as he swung her
bag over his arm.

"Don't be silly. I can drive myself."

"Really? All this," he inquired as he swept one hand dramatically
from her pretty head to her toes, "and you drive too?" He opened the
door for her and they walked to the car together laughing in the twilight
before dawn.

There were those words again. Floating around in her head.
Banging up against the resistance of years of her history, blocked by
the detritus of former loves and hurts. How long had the syllables
been dormant, yearning to be felt, waiting to be spoken out loud, to be
cherished and returned? She looked hard at this man getting into the
driver's seat in his tee shirt and wrinkled jeans, mismatched socks and
loafers, stubbly two-day beard and funky hair.

There was no accounting for it. Nope. None. She let the words
coalesce in her head. Allowed the sentence to take shape in the silence
of her mind. *I love you*, she thought as he started her car and pulled out
into the early morning traffic.

CHAPTER 15

CHONGQING, CHINA
June 4

Things were a mess in Chongqing. Lou had the anxious admitting physician speed-talking in Chinese on one side of her while Yong hurriedly translated on the other as she was led down the institutional green hallway of Chongqing General Hospital to a windowless cubbyhole that would serve as her base for her time here. She entered the details of the cases into her computer as soon as she sat down, waving with her hand to slow Yong down as necessary.

The first victim, the *index* patient, was presumed to have picked up H5N1 through her job in the poultry industry. She came down with symptoms of the flu on May 18th but was not taken to the hospital until May 21st. The patient, who was only 30 years old and in otherwise good health, progressively worsened. On admission, which she had assiduously avoided for the first few days of her illness so as not to lose her job in the poultry market, she had lied about her exposure to fowl. Consequently there was no initial diagnosis of bird flu, and the woman stayed, without isolation, in a general hospital ward for people with respiratory symptoms. On her third day of hospitalization her color was so alarmingly blue that her sister, fearing for her sibling's life, notified the doctor of the patient's occupation.

The patient, who by then was on a ventilator, was moved to an isolation room with proper mask and glove protocols. The other patients in her former ward room, women with varying stages of pneumonia, asthma, and chronic lung disease, were placed in isolation as well. The poultry worker had died one week ago; five days after her death, the cause was confirmed as H5N1. The authorities subsequently raided the poultry market and confiscated all the fowl, pending assessment for disease. The usual attempts were made by the owners to hide stock from the officials. Nevertheless, even as the patient's cause of death was identified, no H5N1 was found in the inspected poultry. Amid huge popular demonstrations, the government decided simply to disinfect the area with germicidal spray and to vaccinate the animals rather than exterminate them. The source of the index case's flu remained a mystery.

The day after the index patient died, the aide who was assigned to the decedent's original ward called in sick to work. The next day one of the respiratory technicians who provided breathing treatments to all the patients in the respiratory ward came to the hospital on a stretcher with a high fever and cough. The day after that a nurse from the decedent's ward went to the hospital dispensary on her lunch break complaining of a headache, sore throat and cough. Her temperature was 103. Unfortunately, it had taken most of the rest of the week for the medical team at the hospital to realize that these three cases were connected and that all were suspect for H5N1. The three new patients had subsequently been isolated but not before they too had exposed any number of people in the early infectious periods of their illnesses. The results on the samples sent to WHO for testing had just been received early this morning and all three confirmed the presence of H5N1, prompting the early morning call to Lou and her subsequent arrival in Chongqing, the largest city in China. Thirty-two million people. More than one tenth the population of the entire United States in one city.

Lou sat at her desk assembling the pieces of the puzzle. The current set of facts strongly supported person-to-person H5N1 transmission. Until the full extent of the threat was ascertained Lou would be issuing the most stringent set of recommendations made to any area by the WHO yet. This would be the greatest test so far of Chinese cooperation.

She set Yong to interrogating each of the patients on all the public and private places they had visited since their symptoms began: grocery stores, noodle stalls, movie houses, laundromats, relatives' homes, anything they could remember. Fortunately all but the index patient were still able to communicate. He made notations of all contacts, getting addresses or directions to pinpoint their positions. Family members helped to fill in the blanks.

Next, Lou convened a meeting with the medical director of the hospital, the local health commissioner, the party chairman, and the chief of security for the city of Chongqing. They had outlined on a map the location of the poultry market where the deceased woman had worked, the location of the homes of each of the three additional victims, and the hospital. The nurse took a city bus to work regularly and its route to and from her house was traced also. Red dots and lines indicating all the possible contacts of the three *new* index patients and their connections were scattered over the city map. Yong's work with all these contacts, when complete, would target even more areas at risk.

The first goal was to identify and isolate anyone with symptoms, the second goal to quarantine, as much as was feasible, those who were exposed. The third goal was to provide osmavir to anyone with symptoms, or deemed at high risk for the disease by virtue of their exposure to one of the contacts. Lou bit her lip: the drug had proven modestly successful in reducing symptoms of avian flu and death rates under laboratory conditions in vitro; however if this H5N1 turned out to be a pandemic virus, it would be osmavir's first real test of effectiveness in the real world, in vivo. The chief of security had already subjected the families of the infected patients to quarantine. Lou advised osmavir be given to all intimate contacts of the four H5N1 cases. This would include family members present in the household up to three days before the development of any of the index patient's symptoms and all patients in the direct care of the aide, the nurse, and the respiratory therapist during the same period. The family members of the deceased woman, and the three new index cases were easily identified and consisted of no more than 25 people.

The hospitalized patients exposed to the four indexes were another matter. The patients at risk from the nurse and the aide were all on the same ward: 42 people. The respiratory technician, however, had treated over a hundred patients spread out all over the hospital. Compounding the problem was that several of the exposed patients had already been discharged.

Lou suggested tracing the location of the discharged patients from hospital records as well as broadcasting in newspaper, radio and television announcements. The Chinese party official informed Lou that they were very reluctant to use the media to encourage the discharged patients to return to the hospital. Lou pointedly reminded the man that the withholding of information in China during the SARS outbreak of 2004 was still a blot on China's record; an avian flu epidemic would make severe acute respiratory syndrome look like the common cold. If China wanted to participate in world commerce and tourism they had better show the world they were prepared to take whatever action they needed to rebuild credibility. The official might have taken offense at her remarks and the lack of finesse with which she delivered them if it hadn't been for Yong, who appeared to be very good at putting a tactful spin on her comments. The official indicated after some consultation on his cell phone that he would cooperate with the use of media.

They debated restricting all travel into and out of the city, a mind-numbing proposition considering the size of the population. Since a couple weeks had already elapsed since the poultry worker first got sick, and exposure from all four patients had potentially occurred during that time period, shutting down travel now would likely be of little effect. On the other hand, attempting to limit the spread of infection bought time for better assessment of, and response to, the situation inside and outside of Chongqing. In a perfect world, considering nothing but communicable disease, it was the right thing to do. Lou broached the subject of halting all egress from the city. The officials scoffed so dramatically in Chinese she had no need for the interpreter. It was not, after all, a perfect world.

Choosing a less contentious issue than the last two, Lou was able to ascertain that there was a local stock of at least 1000 doses of osmavir and that more could be obtained from the Chinese government within 24 hours if needed. This was good news as WHO had very limited quantities of the drug and wanted to reserve it for situations in which local authorities could not provide the medication. The faster the drug could be started, the more likely it was to be effective.

Police could make rapid deliveries of the drug over the next four hours. During that time hospital officials hoped to have identified all the exposed patients who had been discharged. Those who could be found would be served with medication and quarantine orders in a second wave, which Lou expected to accomplish within eight additional hours. Those who were not rounded up in the second wave would, she hoped, be made aware of the dragnet with the media campaign within 24 hours. Obviously they were wild cards. If exposed people did not voluntarily turn themselves in, their potential infectiveness could only be guessed at.

All people subjected to quarantine would be offered the hospital as a shelter if they chose. Each party involved in the planning thought this would be the best use of the limited resources and hoped people would take advantage of the offer. The quarantine would last two weeks from the most recent day of their exposure. The meeting broke up quickly then, with each member anxious to proceed to their assigned tasks and all agreeing to regroup and reassess the situation in twelve hours.

Lou started working on a written report to Geneva. After describing the details of the cases of the single deceased woman, identified in the official report only as Index A, and the three hospital workers, B, C and D, as well as the results of the meeting just concluded, Lou went on to share her thoughts with Dr.Bueller.

...There are issues in the current outbreak which give rise to optimism and those which are potentially devastating.

According to her hospital admission physical, Index A first developed symptoms on May 18th, presenting to the hospital on May 21st, when she was admitted. Due to her attempts to hide the poultry exposure 'A' spent three days in the general ward in a room with seven other patients before being isolated late on May 23rd after the poultry exposure was communicated to the attending physician.

Today is June 4th, twenty days after Index A is assumed to have started her infectivity period and thirteen days after she was isolated. By now one would have expected a local spike in respiratory illnesses and hospitalizations from respiratory symptoms if the viral strain were highly infectious. Indeed, if the strain were highly infectious it would have been expected that a full blown epidemic would already be upon us. All those whom Index A exposed have completed at least 13 days of the expected fourteen allotted for the incubation period of avian flu.

Not only has no epidemic of respiratory disease been noted in Chongqing, the poultry market is notably free of disease, as are A's co-workers and family members who have been quarantined since her diagnosis was confirmed, May 27th, the day of her death. Perhaps even more encouraging is that of the patients who shared the first ward in the hospital to which she was assigned, all of whom suffered from some type of respiratory diagnosis and would therefore be assumed to be more susceptible to H5N1 than the general population; none have tested positive for the disease.

There is certainly some room for doubt on the basis of these facts whether person-to-person transmission had indeed occurred between the deceased and Indexes B, C and D. But I believe after close questioning of the three infected hospital workers, that it probably has occurred, but that transmission required a large inoculum of viral particles. Each of the workers, B, C and D, described very close interaction with Index A during periods of intense coughing and expectoration of mucus. The respiratory technician described needing to clean his glasses after a particularly violent episode of 'A's coughing flung expectorant onto his face.

While I am inclined to conclude that H5N1 has been transmitted from A to B, C and D, it appears that the viral strain is still lacking in facile human infectivity, something for which we can be extraordinarily grateful. However, even assuming that very close contact with a large inoculum of virus is required for transmission of this strain, there is much to be concerned about.

Index B, a nurse's aide, was the first to become ill after A was diagnosed. After calling in sick to work on May 28th she remained at home taking care of herself until hospital authorities contacted her on May 31st and brought her in for evaluation.

The main exposure from Index C, the respiratory therapist, occurred at the hospital during interactions with his patients. The onset of his illness was acute on the morning of May 29th. By the time he was to report to work that evening he was instead brought to the emergency room with a fever and shortness of breath. He denies coughing until that day which means only his wife, daughter and parents who live in the home were exposed to his sputum. But if we look at the traditional onset of communicability as three days prior to the onset of symptoms, he may have exposed close to 200 patients at the hospital in his role as a therapist. In the 48 hours between the time C presented to the emergency room and hospital authorities recognized the possibility of H5N1 disease, approximately 40 of those patients had been discharged. The administrators here are working as I write to identify and isolate all the patients exposed, but the potential for widespread infection in the community exists should this H5N1 variant be more readily communicable than these three initial cases suggest.

Index D, the decedent's nurse, was actively coughing on the bus she took to work on May 30th She reports covering her mouth with her hand when she coughs but any of a number of passengers entering and exiting along the four mile route from D's home to the hospital might have been infected by her. Even with barrier protection from her hand, fomite transmission from sputum on her hands remains a valid concern. Since the bus ride occurred only five days ago we have a window of nine more days before the incubation period of anyone exposed on the bus route is effectively over.

B, C and D were finally identified as suspect for H5N1 and isolated on May 31st. The two week window for incubation from all exposure to the index cases will close on June 14th. If the viral strain is transmissible person-to-person, but not facile, at the very least we still have ten full days before we can rest easily that there are no more cases.

The threat of transmission is significant enough to warrant prophylaxis with osmavir to intimate contacts of A, B, C and D. Doses are being delivered for immediate use to household family members and the ward patients taken care of by B and D who are now at home. All patients who were under B's, C's or D's care and still remain in the hospital will be given treatment as well. We anticipate using approximately 300 doses, all of which will be provided by the Chinese.

Whether or not the current situation warrants vaccination of any specific population for H5N1 remains to be seen. With a finite quantity of vaccine available and unknown potential side effects we must be sure of its value in preventing more illness and deaths than it might cause before we advocate administering it. However, I believe we should be mobilizing WHO's doses of H5N1 for immediate use if necessary and recommend that you initiate the steps necessary to ensure its availability. Also give some thought to triage recommendations. Should we deem it necessary to use vaccine, the demand will far outstrip the supply.

In the worst case scenario, an infected person may already have climbed on a train or plane, carrying disease outside Chongqing. Further mutations occurring in each new case of human disease could make what appears in its current form to be a lethargic virus, much more communicable. We need to be alert for respiratory illness spikes in emergency rooms the world over. I suggest activating the major international airport infectious disease surveillance system immediately.

The sudden occurrence of three related cases of person-to-person transmission is certainly a worrisome trend for the H5N1 strain. We can only hope that this time H5N1 has made just another scary, but impotent advance into the human species. As always, I value your input.

Lou

CALIFORNIA
June 4

The words emanating from the car's radio hit Ken like bullets. They were exactly what he'd been expecting and he had a hard time maintaining enough concentration to finish the morning drive to Crossfire. His hands were shaking on the wheel when he finally pulled into his parking spot. Of course the details were sketchy. But he would fill in those blanks momentarily. He bounded up the stairs two at a time and burst into the lab, flushed and out of breath.

"What is it?" Carolyn asked, taking in his nonplussed condition.

"H5N1...Pandemic..." Ken muttered as he flew by her desk to get to his office and turn on his computer.

As he waited for it to boot up he noticed a gathering of people standing at his door, which he had left partly open in his hurry. The people who worked in proximity to his office, lab assistants, research fellows, grad students and receptionist, were huddled expectantly, trying not to disturb him but peering around the door, clearly anxious for some explanation.

He shook his head, still flustered by the report and said, "I just heard it on the radio...Chongqing...uh...China...has H5N1...person-to-person transmission...at least three health care workers with it...

hundreds of people quarantined...It's all I know," he stammered looking back to his computer screen. "I'm checking my sources now...I'll get back to you," he finished gruffly, dismissing all of them with a wave of the back of his hand as he opened his e-mail.

There was a bulletin from the Emerging Infectious Disease Network that confirmed the outbreak and related the salient details. The report had been filed by Lou Symington. After reading through the press statement Ken decided to call her; things would be at least a few hours further along since she released the report and he wanted an on-the-ground assessment from the front lines.

Lou got a message from her Guangzhou office that a very insistent Dr. Kenneth Culp wished to speak with her immediately. Although she had never met him, Lou instantly recognized his name. She was tremendously busy right now but she returned his call promptly thinking it a stroke of luck that the prominent H5N1 researcher was eager to speak with her just now.

"Dr. Culp?"

"Yes. Dr. Symington, thank you for returning my call." Ken said. "I just finished reading your press release to the EIDN, and I wanted an update. What can you tell me?"

"Well Dr. Culp, probably not much more than you read. I just put that copy out about two hours ago. We're still trying to nail down the patients who were discharged after they had been under the care of our index cases. It looks like we have almost forty people who were sent home after exposure but before the hospital identified the indexes as having H5N1. We've located most of them and placed them under quarantine. Medics are evaluating them now." Lou said.

"How many others under quarantine have developed symptoms?" Ken asked.

"None that I know of, but as I said, we have yet to evaluate everyone. We have histories, physical exams, blood and naso-pharyngeal samples on all the household contacts. A couple of them have gastrointestinal symptoms, but no one has a fever or a cough. The rapid tests for flu have been negative thus far. The blood titers won't confirm that for a few days."

Lou continued, "We are about half-way through evaluating another two hundred or so patients still in the hospital. Many of them were admitted with respiratory symptoms but none have had a positive rapid test for flu. Serum analysis is pending," she finished.

"What about the city? I didn't see anything about quarantining beyond the individual contacts of the index cases."

"No. I tried, but the government won't even consider it. We have put out an APB for all international airports to screen for fever and cough on passengers whose flights originate or connect through China. It'll be up to each country to restrict the movement of passengers who present with symptoms."

"I'm sorry to take up your time, but I am very concerned this outbreak may represent the beginning of a pandemic," Ken offered. "I want to be able to help."

"I appreciate that, Dr. Culp. We can use all the help we can get." Lou replied. "In fact I'm glad you called. Is there anything new you can tell me about H5N1? Anything from your research? Perhaps you have some insight that you've not yet proven or published? I'm desperate to understand this organism."

"I'm certain H5N1 is close to achieving pandemic form, although I haven't been able to demonstrate it yet," Ken responded eagerly. "I continue to manipulate the hemagglutinin proteins at various binding sites on the capsule, but I haven't created a mutation that can readily penetrate cells. It's the damnedest thing...the virus in vitro is able to reproduce easily enough but lacks cellular attachment properties... rendering it only minimally toxic...I see huge numbers of viral particles in the mouse tissue under the microscope, but all of it is outside the cells. There's very little cellular invasion."

Ken continued nearly breathless, "It requires a huge inoculum of virus into each culture to kill the tissue...the virus just doesn't spread from cell to cell with any robustness. Of more than a hundred manipulations in the past two years only two have shown any communicability and that was slight. The rest of the engineered changes have been completely ineffectual. It's frustrating," Ken said with a sigh, "...but I see that as just part of the process. We're sure to latch on to the secret of penetrability eventually. I just wish I could do it faster. I feel like I'm racing the clock and I'm running out of time," Ken admitted.

Lou paused to consider. "That's very interesting."

"What?"

"Your observations in the lab very much mirror what we've seen in the field," Lou responded.

"What do you mean?" Ken asked.

"Even though H5N1 is rampant and lethal in bird populations it lacks the necessary attributes to make the jump to humans. The couple hundred cases we've seen notwithstanding, it just hasn't shown the ability to adapt to mammalian species yet. Maybe it's just my hope Dr. Culp, but the Chongqing cases appear to be further examples of H5N1's inability to accommodate readily to people. I think each of our patients required a large inoculum to become infected. Maybe it will take another 100 or more years to mutate enough to be readily communicable."

"I think that is a dangerous assumption to make," Ken retorted, his tone suddenly brusque. "H5N1 has all the capability in the world to become pandemic now, and as many opportunities to do so as there are birds infected with it. Every bird-human interaction is another chance for mutation into communicability," Ken insisted stridently. "Why can't you people see that? What is right in front of you in Chongqing could be the real thing. What are you going to do about it?" he demanded.

Even through the phone lines Ken's anger was loud and clear and Lou was startled by the man's abrupt change in demeanor and instantly offended by his accusatory tone. There was a time she might have responded with equal animosity, but she'd found it sapped too much of her energy to engage in unnecessary argument. It took less effort to compose herself and turn the question back to him. "This virus is frustrating to all of us. What is it you think needs to be done?"

Ken, already in mid-breath, ready to launch into the next phase of his diatribe, felt the wind rush right out of his sails. He expected her to argue with him and she hadn't. She'd asked for his opinion. There hadn't been nearly enough of that lately, he thought resentfully. He paused, and in that brief moment didn't recognize himself. He preferred being sedate and controlled; these recent bursts of anger unnerved him. At least this one had evaporated quickly. If he had been an introspective man he might have remarked on the process by which he was able to calm down and resume his professional mien so adroitly. But he didn't evaluate the dynamics of Lou's strategy, didn't realize he had been disarmed. He was glad he was back in command. His illusion of self-control remained unchallenged.

"I think we need to be taking H5N1 as the serious threat it is." Ken said.

"I certainly agree with that. I'm sure you've been as challenged as I in trying to educate non-medical people on the complexities of the virus. Too many people in positions of power just don't get it."

"Is The World Health Organization guilty of that as well?" Ken asked calmly, but pointedly.

"I don't know what you mean." Lou said.

"I fail to understand why WHO has not advocated for widespread vaccination."

Now Lou was beginning to understand where his anger had come from: she'd forgotten Ken Culp was one of several experts calling for widespread H5N1 vaccination. "Dr. Culp there are 3 billion people living in the endemic regions. WHO has 500,000 H5N1 doses. Even if we were clearly able to identify H5N1 today as pandemic, it would be years before we could make enough vaccine for Asia alone."

"There will be 60 million more doses available in two months," Ken replied.

"And WHO would be happy to have those in stock," Lou responded. "We can't get the funds to buy any more than what we have, and we can't persuade wealthy nations to contribute more than a token amount of what's needed."

"They would pony up everything you need if they thought H5N1 was pandemic. WHO put H5N1 on the back burner by calling for a variety of vaccines."

Lou was trying very hard not to lose patience. She hardly knew where to go from here. There were so many arguments to be made she was having trouble holding onto a train of thought. It was enormously demoralizing to feel like she was trying to do her best and have her own peers criticize her for it. The bottom line was she was uncertain if she was right. No one would know the wisdom of their approach until the future unfolded. Precisely because she thought debate healthy under such uncertain conditions she did not shy away from it, but right now it was just too much.

She sighed with fatigue and discouragement. "Dr. Culp, your thoughts on WHO policy may prove correct: H5N1 may be the next pandemic. Maybe it has already started here, today, in Chongqing. But I humbly suggest that neither one of us, indeed no one, can predict that."

"Be that as it may, don't you see WHO would love to have those 60 million doses of H5N1 in our control should the situation here prove dire? Rationing those doses would allow us some time to contain the epidemic with quarantines and as much osmavir as we could lay our hands on. We can't do that without money. The international cooperation required to produce vaccine and turn it over to us does not currently exist. WHO is a bastard child of the wealthy nations. We receive just enough funds for them not to feel totally guilty, and not nearly enough to support us."

She took a different tack. "Consider this: if we announce tomorrow that H5N1 is pandemic, where do you think those 60 million doses being produced in California will go? To the U.S., that's where. The vaccine won't do a damn thing to stop the disease in Asia from spreading all over the world. But 60 million lucky Americans won't have to worry." Lou was getting angry now. "What if H5N2, the most lethal and communicable avian strain yet, arises in vivo again? If the world produces and administers nothing but H5N1 vaccine in the next five years, we will have squandered our limited resources on a poor bet."

"I do not doubt your sincerity Dr. Symington," Ken countered. "I'm just afraid you're wrong."

Lou had to end the conversation. "Dr. Culp, look, I'm sorry for losing my temper. I'm pretty stressed out here and I have several issues that require attention. I need to get back to work."

"So do I," Ken said.

"Despite our differences, I would be happy to discuss this further at another less hectic time..." Lou trailed off.

"Sure. Thanks for your time Dr. Symington."

Ken hung up more certain than ever that the World Health Organization was misguided. He could not deny that he deeply respected Bueller, Wataabe, Symington, and others he had spoken with: they were physicians or scientists of notable caliber, but he was beginning to see them as a small and ineffective group. Powerless really, without the wealth and leadership of nations. He conceded that the WHO had good intentions. The road to hell was paved with them.

CHONGQING, CHINA
June 4

Connor called Lou just before midnight. "You know you have to go to bed sometime," he said.

"How do you know I'm *not* in bed and your phone call just awakened me from the deep sleep I so desperately needed?" she asked.

"Two reasons. First, you would have called me to say goodnight. Second, you're not in your hotel room."

"How do you know that?"

"Which part?"

"That I'm not in my hotel room."

"Because I'm in your hotel room, and you're not."

"What are you doing here? I thought I left you in Guangzhou."

"A temporary situation which I have corrected. I'm a reporter, remember? This is a story. I'm covering the news. You were a little too distracted this morning for me to discuss my plans with you, so I just got here when I could. In the last nine hours I've pretty much interviewed everyone in the picture, except you, Dr. Symington. I'm still looking for an inside scoop from the chief WHO epidemiologist. Any chance she'll be in tonight?"

Lou smiled despite her fatigue. "Yes. I was actually just getting ready to leave. I could use some rest. It's been a long day and the next few aren't going to be any shorter. I'll be there soon," she said. "Oh, and Connor..."

"Yes?"

"No interview. I'm exhausted."

"No problem. I already filed the story."

"You're kidding? You filed the story without interviewing me?" she said with mock indignation.

"I thought sparing you professionally would leave you more energy for a night of wild sex with your favorite reporter."

She laughed. "It would if I were awake for it. How do you feel about necrophilia?"

It was his turn to laugh. "I'll sleep on it..."

• • •

Yong pulled Lou aside as she made her way out of the warren of cubby holes they were sharing as a base at the hospital.

"I thought you left already." Lou said.

"I was on my way out when I got a call from Guangzhou. One of the little boys died. I came back to tell you."

"Oh. That's terrible." Lou couldn't imagine what it must be like for his parents. "How are the others doing?"

"Two are on ventilators; the other two are stable but guarded."

"Did you ever get back to interview Chu-Wei?"

"I went back, but he was on a ventilator. The other boys are sticking to their story; they say he wasn't there. It's hard to tell. They're all so sick. Who knows? My gut tells me Chu handled the duck."

"Mine too," said Lou. "I don't think we're dealing with a communicable strain there." She transferred her back pack to her other shoulder and clapped her hand on Yong's shoulder. "Let's get some sleep buddy."

CHAPTER 16

CALIFORNIA
June 9

Ken withdrew the keys from the ignition, locked his car and trudged up the stairs to begin what was sure to be another disappointing day at Crossfire. The damned, *damned* virus. H5N1 eluded him like a child, toying with him, teasing him. Running away each time he got close. But it was not a game. It was evil: a predator, lying in wait for the world. Ken could feel the malignancy of H5N1 in his bones. The thing was ready to pounce, to tear mankind apart. Only *he* could see it; try as he might, and he was trying mightily, he could not capture it, hold it up for the world to inspect. He needed proof of communicability, and the virus would not cooperate. Its sterility under the microscope, slide after slide, tray after tray, mocked him.

It was the end of a week that had started badly, the news of H5N1 in Chongqing, the conversation with Lou Symington. Thoughts were whirligigs; concentration an elusive commodity. Ken was distracted, obsessed, driven. Nights were punishment, his mattress a slab where he lay pretending to sleep for June's sake. His eyelids were pasted-on pieces of parchment, artificial contrivances that closed but did not release him from wakefulness. Behind their thin facade he pursued rest both day and night, mostly failing but occasionally stumbling into troubled dreams.

In one nightmare he was locked in a dark room, trying to find his way out. In the distance he saw a glow and he followed it to a grinning virus the size of a beach ball sitting high on a shelf. It sneered at Ken as he tried to reach it, dissolved like water when he finally grasped it, and reformed itself a few feet away, where the whole scene continued to repeat itself. In another phantasm, his lab assistants aged into haggard remnants of themselves before his eyes, their hazard suits turning into gauze and encasing them like mummies, as they pressed their faces to the glass partition of his office between violent coughing spasms. Each gob of phlegm they spewed at him was a fresh accusation of inadequacy, of impotence, as they fell writhing on the cold vinyl floor.

In the most disturbing scene of all he was sitting at his desk looking through his electron microscope, scrolling through the fields methodically as he had been trained. Beneath his vision, in a single frame magnified 80,000 times, suddenly there appeared his beloved Moira. His dream-self paused to consider how amazing it was that she had been reduced to a nano-speck smiling impishly back at him through the lens. As he watched she began twirling around the microscopic field, bathed in the eerie green luster of electrons. With horror he saw viruses marching in from the perimeter of the slide. Close. Closer to Moira, dancing, completely unaware. His mouth opened but the scream was no more successful in escaping his lungs than Moira was at escaping the attack. While he flailed vainly on one side of the scope, she succumbed and disappeared on the other, consumed by the seething iridescent blobs. June had wakened him, shaking him hard as he flung his arms wildly in the bed.

After that, he stopped even attempting to sleep. He drank coffee day and night so that no small slumber would invite these dreadful visions to hound him. And somehow he got by. He developed clarity. His thoughts began to gel.

Ken drew the shades on the glass partition, and locked the door to his office.

He buzzed Carolyn and informed her there were to be no interruptions. None.

The situation was becoming desperate to him, to the world. Desperate times required desperate measures. Someone had said that. He couldn't remember who. It didn't matter. They were right. H5N1 was loose in the population and no one else could see it. Oh, the WHO was concerned but they were too tied up with financial worries, and rationing, and stamping out fires to be able to see the big picture. The big picture was a close-up: an in-your-face snapshot of human misery and suffering about to explode on the international scene. Ken was sure it was already too late to avoid a major loss of life, but it was not too late to make a difference in the sheer scope of lives lost.

The time to act was now. Every day he waited was another day lost to production of vaccine, to prevention: another half a million people sick. How many would die? Fifty percent of the population? Sixty? It was unimaginable. Society would cease to function. Cease to exist as we knew it. The world would be reduced to chaos. He had been reading everything he could about the implications of a worldwide epidemic. It was all in his files. Ken pulled out first one drawer, then a second, and looked at folder upon folder, hundreds, maybe thousands of articles he had collected, and congratulated himself on his thoroughness. Who else was keeping up with this germ like him? No one.

"Just look at this," he said to himself, slapping at the cover of the folder labeled 'travel'. Pandemic would create pandemonium. The first wave of illness would stop discretionary travel into the affected area almost immediately. But there were few circumstances under which the viral threat could be identified early enough to stop travel *out* of the hotbed of infectivity in time to prevent the worldwide dispersal of the opportunistic virus. Air and train routes carrying people with undetected infections would be responsible for a macabre game of chance in which certain localities were visited with the virus much sooner than others.

Ken shook his head over clipped articles on the use of quarantine. The military might be called on to enforce such a decision, but social theorists predicted that desertion in the ranks of all the armed services would be rampant. Even with adequate personnel, it was virtually impossible to ensure complete isolation of the affected area. There would always be desperate people who would find a way to leave. Cities were far too enormous and porous to keep citizens from escaping through the cracks.

And there was always bribery, a cynical author pointed out. The article described how the Great Wall of China had been remarkably ineffective in keeping out invaders who routinely bribed the guards for passage, allowing everything from single individuals to entire legions to pass through unhindered. Human nature had not changed these past thousand years Ken thought. People fearing for their lives would flee, and carry the virus to new havens. You could count on it.

Ken paced in his lair, scuffing a track between the file cabinet and microscope as he contemplated the pandemic scenario. The local areas hit first by the epidemic would shut down almost immediately with people hiding themselves away in their homes, afraid to venture out. Fear of infection and death would take precedence over lost income quickly as the number of people refusing to report to work escalated with the spreading of the virus. Electricity grids and water and sewage treatment plants would cease to function without personnel to maintain day-to-day operations. No one would willingly enter an infected area; there would be no deliveries of food or medical supplies, no oil or gasoline. Hospitals treating the sick would run out of masks and IV fluids and syringes, competing with the pace at which they ran out of nurses and doctors well enough or brave enough to participate in the care of the sick.

Shortages of goods would occur not only in the areas identified with avian flu outbreaks but worldwide as the panicked public rushed out to hoard everything they could. Due to the dependence on international labor and supplies, much of what flew off the shelves around the world would be irreplaceable because Southeast Asia, the likely origin of the pandemic, was a key player in the production of many everyday goods the West took for granted. As the pandemic spread, not only local, but national and international commerce would come to a standstill with the same scenes of hysteria and fear, greed and desperation repeated around the globe. Rioting and looting would begin when it was apparent that security forces were minimal or absent. Anarchy would ensue.

The WHO and the U.S. government each held half of the million doses of Avimmune that PharmaGlobal had produced last year. These would be used for first responders (and probably political heavyweights and their cronies), but these doses would run out quickly. Sixty million more people could benefit from the vaccine PharmaGlobal was poised to release. And hundreds of millions more had a chance to receive vaccine if other companies, seeing the demand, initiated production. It was possible to crank out hundreds of millions of doses every six months from facilities that would participate if they saw the need, Ken was sure of it. Within a few years the population of the world could be immunized and the threat from H5N1 would be gone.

Of course because H5N1 was already so widespread in birds, pandemic was likely to occur before it was possible to immunize everyone. That was one of the WHO's excuses for not proceeding: they couldn't immunize everyone so they decided not to ration the vaccine to anyone. But many more lives would be saved by trying to achieve global vaccination eventually than by sitting around waiting for the pandemic to proclaim itself. He scoffed out loud, "They act as though there will be a glittering billboard in Times Square announcing, 'H5N1 coming soon to a location near you!'" Not only are we *allowed* to predict the pandemic virus he thought, *we are charged* to do so. Our duty as experts is to protect the public from this threat, and to craft strategies which support that mission. To do less is to shirk our responsibility. Abandon the cause.

Ken picked up some of the articles he'd cut out in the past several days and shook his head sadly. One of the little boys died in Guangzhou last week and another today. Two more of the hospital workers died in Chongqing. The WHO could fret all they wanted about another avian strain he thought; it was H5N1 killing people now, just waiting for the right spin of the roulette wheel to jump into a new species. He hadn't proven it in the lab; but he was sure he would, and soon.

Sitting at his desk, Ken now realized that he couldn't wait for that, or rather the world couldn't wait. He and 499 other lucky people who'd been the first volunteers to test Avimmune were protected; but everyone else was not. Ken had a fool-proof plan to change that. He must open the eyes of his own country to the threat. Only if the most powerful nation in the world took up arms, could the battle be won.

And it had to be him.

It was destined to be him. He could see that now. Who else had the combination of knowledge and will, power and opportunity to fight H5N1?

No one.

Ken knew he was alone. And what he must do.

It would be simple. He needed to contrive nothing. His plan would only turn around the systems already in place so that they were to his advantage, or rather, to the world's advantage. Ken would make western society aware that avian flu was everyone's problem by planting a single case of H5N1 on American soil, creating the climate that would motivate leaders to address it. It would just be the visible enactment of what was truly the case. Nothing more. Avian flu was a global threat and therefore as much of an American issue as a Chinese, or Vietnamese, or Indonesian; America was just too blind to see. Until the United States government supported widespread vaccination, it just wasn't going to happen.

Ken would issue a wake-up call. That was all. One human case of H5N1.

The press, now just the lackeys of the latest trend, would have their attention seized by a new matter. He could see the headline blaring from the front page of the *Chronicle*: "Bird Flu Hits America!" The strongest government in the world would have to sit up and take notice when H5N1 appeared on their doorstep. Public hysteria in the U.S. would generate the dollars to crank up the industrial complex into producing as much Avimmune as it took to remove the threat. Other nations in addition to the U.S. would no longer be able to turn away from something they downplayed as an Asian problem.

It would be easy.

He was angry with himself for not thinking of it sooner. Regretted the delay in his brainstorm that could have saved more lives. Every day lost now was one day too many. Still, he felt his gut tighten involuntarily even now with the single additional feature his strategy would entail: his plan required the sacrifice of life. Just one life. He rationalized that it was a small price to pay considering how many would be saved, but he still would have ended all thought of it right then and there if it hadn't been for the remarkable coincidence that he was intimately connected to someone who wanted to die. Was desperate to die. Desired more than anything at this moment to die.

Indeed, the entire plan was conceived as a whole or it never would have occurred to him at all. H5N1 was not accepted as an active threat; Anna Wardman wanted to die. As the sleepless nights piled up, and his feet wore new patterns in the carpet of his den, the simple juxtaposition of the two separate thoughts that had been eating at Ken for months suddenly coalesced into a plan with purpose. His mother would have loved his reasoning, the cognitive process that linked two seemingly unrelated problems, the resolution of each dilemma inexorably intertwined and fulfilled in the commission of a single act. She could

225

never have imagined that in asking Ken to end her life, she would be instrumental in saving millions of others. She would be so proud of him, so privileged to be a part of it if she had known, and it calmed him, hardened him to his purpose to think of it this way.

He had spent nearly two years of deepening agony as Anna deteriorated, being unable to do for her as she wished. He would be able to help her now, but only because he knew that in helping her he would help all of humankind. He was humbled by the thought that his one small action might benefit so many, and he thanked a God, whom he believed in more and more, for the opportunity presenting itself so clearly.

Ken now understood the purpose behind his lifelong feeling of professional isolation from the scientific community. Years of struggling without the recognition he deserved, bending his will to grind out the research purely for altruistic benefit, had taught him to believe in himself, to live without the accolades of colleagues. When his opinions on H5N1 had been forsaken by the mainstream, this even after the bestowing of the Pritzker award, he had been thrown into a crucible. The flame, he found, had not burned him up but left him worthy and strong, able to recognize the uniqueness of his position and the power that lay in his grasp.

He spent some time going over the details of his design. When it first began to form in his mind, he threw one hurdle up after another. But each one melted away with the slightest thought. It was uncanny how much of his plan required no effort at all. Circumstances, coincidences, twists of fate not of his own doing conspired to smooth his way. As fast as his mind threw up new challenges, it handed him the solutions on silver platters. He couldn't shake off the feeling he was destined to be doing this.

First, the virus was readily available. There were no barriers to his removing a small quantity of live H5N1 from the lab. A single milliliter would never be missed. Ken laughed out loud at the virus; this time *he* would use *it*. If the H5N1 he studied would not demonstrate communicability in the lab, it would be equally impotent in making that elusive leap in a dying old woman. With no significant cough reflex left, Anna would be unable to spread the virus, even by direct contact, to anyone. It was perfectly safe. He would force the virus, hiding in its cloak of false sterility, to do *his* bidding. He would use his frustration with its weakness as a means to his own strength.

Ken chose one of the very first strains he had worked with. This particular batch had shown such limited capability to infect mouse cells that he had abandoned further research on it years ago and directed his research toward other H5N1's with more promising infectivity. Since they never destroyed any viral isolates, Ken was able to use the lab's index to locate H5N1, subtype A0100.07, and remove one cubic centimeter from the store of it last evening after everyone else had left.

Because it was not readily infectious, a large inoculum of the virus would be required to cause disease in a human. He pulled a glass vial from the rack on his desk and squinted at the single milliliter of clear fluid within it: ten billion viral particles should be more than enough to cause infection when applied directly to Anna's nasal mucosa. His mother's debilitated condition would ensure the outcome. If the mortality rate from avian flu with H5N1 was close to 100%, a patient with terminal Alzheimer's was not going to beat the odds. She would die, and bless him for his mercy. He was still not comfortable with his role as the angel of death, but for the fact that her end would mean the living of so many more. He wouldn't, couldn't, have proceeded under any other circumstances.

Second, it was critical to Ken's plan that Anna's death be recognized as due to influenza, and not just any influenza, but H5N1. Ken remembered the day they had signed Anna into the nursing home and the admitting nurse had explained to him and his mother that Cypress Arbor was part of the Center for Disease Control's surveillance network for flu. This meant that anyone with influenza-like symptoms of fever and cough would have a nasal sample sent as a matter of course to CDC in Atlanta and the offending virus would be identified in detail. Ken was counting on it.

CDC would uncover H5N1 in Anna's sample probably just before, or perhaps even after, her death. Epidemiologists would be all over the nursing facility searching for clues as to the source of it, which left him a final hurdle. The investigators would probably evaluate, perhaps even quarantine, anyone who had been in contact with her for two weeks prior to her death. Ken would be in that dragnet most likely, and he was initially concerned about his name being recognized, but there was a safeguard already in place, and his mother had inadvertently created it. Even through the veil of the Alzheimer's, or more precisely, because of it, she had protected her son. That hideous disease, which ate his mother alive and burdened him with the dilemma of euthanasia, would provide his cover. It was only fitting. What had happened was this:

According to an arrangement between Anna, a trailblazer in feminist thinking, and Ken's father, Ken had been given his mother's maiden name, Wardman, at birth. Anna had thought hyphenating the name too cumbersome; after all, she reasoned, if her son went into academics as she hoped he would, who would truly call him Dr. Wardman-Culp? It was long and ungainly. Anna had kept her own name during her marriage to James Culp and she decided she would like her son to share her name while he was growing up. James Culp would have been content to have his son keep the moniker Wardman forever, having no particular need to wrap his ego up in the boy's name. However Anna, for whom the concept of fairness trumped personal attempts to correct generations of sexism, thought it only right that Ken adopt his father's last name at some point. By mutual agreement then, she and her husband chose the age of majority. She would have her little boy for his first 18 years, his father and society could have him for the rest. Prior to registering for college, Ken changed his name legally to Kenneth Wardman Culp which had contracted over time to his current professional title, Kenneth W. Culp.

As was typical, on the day his mother was admitted to Cypress Arbor she was intermittently cognizant of her surroundings. The nurse collected demographic information for the chart, addressing Anna first to answer the questions as she seemed eager to participate. Ken, sitting at her side, filled in or adjusted the information as needed. Anna did pretty well with her full name and birth date, her marital status and former occupation. But the interview grew more difficult and she stumbled over questions about her medicines and drug allergies, almost coming undone over her social security number. She broke into tears as she struggled with the sequence of numbers before Ken managed to fish the card out of the bundle of papers he carried with him to read it off to the nurse. In her partially aware state it flustered and embarrassed Anna not to know something she knew she should have known. When Anna was done dabbing at her tears with the handkerchief June had quickly pulled out of her purse, the nurse moved on and asked what she intended to be an easy question.

"Who would you like listed as your next-of-kin?"

Anna's face lit up and she smiled all around the room before she said with confidence, "Why, my son, Kenneth Wardman, of course." She turned to Ken for approval, relief written all over her face that she could answer this one. June glanced at Ken who decided in a heartbeat that there was no harm it letting Anna's memory substitute for reality on this point. His last name was of no consequence to him in these circumstances, and at the moment it was everything to Anna.

Since that day he was known to the staff at Cypress Arbor as Mr. Wardman, a quiet, nondescript man, of unknown occupation, who visited his mother dutifully once a month. Being an introvert it was a lifetime of habit that he never talked of his work or boasted of his accomplishments outside his peer circle. Any investigators sent to the nursing home to evaluate his mother's death would pass over him easily after a few standard questions, unaware of his connection to research or the virus.

Even if they discovered his occupation it would just be another bit of information, and a respected scientist would not be nearly as likely a suspect as the hundreds of Asian employees at Cypress Arbor. Ken judged from the faces and the language skills he had witnessed over the past two years that many of the employees were immigrants or first generation Americans living with extended families that included immigrants. Ken knew it would take weeks to months for CDC to follow up all the employees who might have directly or indirectly infected his mother. In the end they would identify no obvious source for Anna's illness, and be left with an isolated case of H5N1 in the United States. No verifiable cause of her disease would ever be found and no one on the staff would be found to blame, but the inquiry alone would provide plenty of fuel to ignite the cause of vaccination in the eyes of the public and the politicians. Ken's action would be simple, harmless and effective.

Despite the ease with which he could carry this plan off, Ken would have readily traded someone, anyone, for the execution of it.

Execution. It was the right word, try as he might to shrug it off.

But the burden was his: he alone was in a position to comprehend the problem, to create a solution, to act with conviction. He picked up the vial and placed it in his breast pocket. It was so light he could not even discern it was there. Reaching across the desk he took the metal lid off a standard glass jar and removed a package of sterile swabs which he slid into his coat next to the vial. He stood up to leave feeling the full weight of his years and the responsibility of his task. His feet and his shoes were leaden foreign objects as he picked up one and then the other in deliberate fashion, making his way out of his office and down the path he had chosen.

CHONGQING, CHINA
June 10

Dr. Bueller,

Indexes B and C died last night. D is improving and expected to survive. All but one of the patients who had been discharged from the hospital after being cared for by the indexes has been located. None of the household contacts or the patients of the indexes show signs of infection. Within 3 days every possible exposed person in Chongqing, including those in the city at large and on the bus route of index D, will have passed through the two week window of incubation and quarantine. There are no spikes of respiratory infection in the city or out. All patients with fever and cough in the Chongqing hospital system have been tested for avian flu, and none had been found. In conclusion, no further outbreak of H5N1 is evident.

I'm returning to Guangzhou. I'm happy to proceed as you suggested with a series of press conferences to help build the case for preparedness.
Lou

On the flight back Lou pored over stacks of information she hadn't had time to attend to in Chongqing. She tried to read the newspapers she'd brought, but the articles chronicling the hype and misinformation surrounding the flu were too much to bear. She closed the paper and her eyes, trying to get comfortable with the inadequate airplane pillow. As she scrunched into the recess between her seat back and the window, she wondered if Connor had arrived back in L. A. yet. He had spent most of his time in Chongqing with Lou, returning to Guangzhou just before she did to do an update on the five boys. He had called her yesterday and told her he had exhausted as much coverage of the Chinese outbreak as he could justify and was going back to L.A. where he intended to begin the process of moving to a more practical location to continue their relationship. She fell into a deep sleep missing him terribly, and didn't waken until the jet's landing gear bumped the pavement.

PORTLAND, OREGON
June 10

As he walked up to the entrance of Cypress Arbor Ken was acutely aware of every oriental feature marking the people he encountered: body types, skin tones, and the shapes of eyes and faces. He heard snippets of foreign languages and far eastern accents in passing conversation. He saw a little old man bent to his tasks with gardening shears, a young man pushing a food cart stacked with empty trays, volunteers in their smocks guiding residents in wheelchairs and walkers. Many were Asian. They were all so different. There must be a dozen or more nationalities represented in just the people I see here today he thought.

He passed the nursing station and envisioned where they kept the kits they would use to collect his mother's nasal sample for the flu surveillance program. He saw telephones: at the ward clerk's desk, the head nurse's desk, and one tucked in the corner at a carrel where the doctors probably dictated their notes. He thought the nurse might use that one to call him when his mother died.

Ken saw the polish gleaming from the vinyl floor covering as he walked in slow motion to Anna's room, counting the doors on each side of the hall, noting the name plates and the personalized decorations identifying the occupants. He was drawn to the window at the end of the hallway, or perhaps he was avoiding entering her room, the door to which was conveniently closed. From his vantage on the fourth floor he could see the city below, not very far away, over the tops of the enormous trees. The crafted illusion of remoteness was exception-ally well done here. Of course that was one of the reasons Anna had chosen it.

His legs suddenly felt wooden from being confined in the car so long on the drive to Cypress Arbor. He'd had to drive because of the vial. He could not take any chances with security procedures at the airport. The test tube was glass, not metal, so it wouldn't have tripped the detector, but if he'd been searched, the officers would ask questions about the vial, or worse, it might be dropped. No. Ken had considered whether there was any way he could fly and he determined that option unworkable. In the end he had told June a lie, *Oh God another one*, and said he felt the need for a solitary drive up the coast. He left Friday, straight from work, so that he didn't have to take the virus home with him, and drove for a few hours before it got dark. He'd risen early this morning after multiple abortive attempts at sleep and completed the drive well before he had intended to be here. Hesitating at Anna's door, and then walking past her room once more, he decided instead to stroll the grounds first to stretch his cramped muscles. There was plenty of time for him to see his mother.

Opening the front door to escape, and selecting a path that would take him away from the hub of activity on the terrace, Ken thought how much harder this was turning out to be than even his troubled mind had suggested. As justifiable as it was, he recoiled from the performance that lay in front of him. He reviewed the logic, rehearsed the scene. It was the right thing to do from every angle he considered. Just one case of H5N1 here, in an Oregon nursing home, would become the catalyst for both national and international action. The countries who thought they had some kind of automatic, God-given protection, some hall pass exempting them from the realities of this biological opponent, would find out how flawed their logic was; if they needed to be shaken into action, he would do it. After this, the dawdling and the denial would cease. He was providing a safe scare, and was counting on the newspa-pers he despised to trumpet it to full hysteria for the clamoring public. If the government wasn't going to drive the response for pandemic preparedness, the people would. He slipped his hand into his breast pocket searching for reassurance, and felt the vial, safe and secure.

He caressed it: the staff of his leadership, the lightning rod of his courage. Ken Culp had the power to evoke change.

Simply.

Effectively.

He could do this.

Reaching into his hip pocket he felt the plastic bottle with the lethal dose of crushed sedative his mother had left in his care. He didn't intend to use it. Didn't need to. The H5N1 would be enough. He had simply brought the bottle along as a permission slip for the other deed he was about to commit. This, he admitted as he squeezed the container hard, clenching his misery around the terrible thing, this was the impossible task. There was no way around the deliberate ending of her life if he was to accomplish his goal.

He slumped on a bench at the side of the path and pounded his fist into its unyielding slats. "Why, why, why did you ask me to do this?" he cried to the woman haunting his head, the shell of a thing in her bed. He could foresee no time in his future when he would not be plagued with the guilt of her euthanasia, no matter how grand and glorious were the life-sparing results of his scheme. Ken Culp would forever be his mother's killer. It mattered nothing to his conscience that she wanted to die, that he bore witness to this fact in the bottle of sedatives she had researched, obtained, crushed finely by her own hand and delivered to him for safe keeping. "Until the time was right," she had said.

The time was now right.

Would never be more right.

But no matter how noble the cause, no matter how much this was the merciful end she desired, he would be marked forever by her death. Her murder. In the eyes of the law, and his own. It was too much. The taking of one life was too much. Too much. He couldn't do it.

He had to do it.

It was only one life. He would save millions. Other people had made decisions like this before. Others with less worthy credentials. Generals, ship's captains, presidents. Ken's motivation was pure. He had nothing to gain. He was acting to preserve the lives of countless people. A single small thing was required. He had to sacrifice the one life. Just the one.

VIRION

Clouds obscured the morning sun. Twenty minutes might have passed or an hour. He sat for a long time on the bench. Occasionally people walked by. They saw an old man, lost. Wooden. If they had seen him the week before, they would not have known it was the same person.

After a while Ken tried to stand, but the inertia of his agenda made a second attempt necessary. He made a conscious effort to pick up his feet and direct them back inside. If his senses had been alert on his arrival they were dull now. As he walked back to Anna's room he noticed nothing and no one, a dead man walking his own plank.

Anna lay on her back in the bed. With her eyes closed and her pale skin and no perceptible rising and falling of her chest under the sheet, she might already have been dead. But she wasn't. Her mouth was open slightly, with the drying crust of the last mashed meal evident at the border of her lips. Her parched tongue could be seen lying dully between her remaining teeth, yellow and brown with age and the derelict hygiene of the last two years.

It was one of those rare times she was allowed to be on her back due to the ulcers that continued to chew away at her tissue-paper skin. The staff kept her supine with the head of the bed elevated for an hour after each feeding to minimize the chances of aspiration. Anna would have been happy to develop pneumonia from a bolus of blended protein and cellulose, but her wishes were not in accordance with good nursing care, so day after day the patient and her caregivers were at well-intentioned cross-purposes. The nurses were winning the individual battles, but the patient would ultimately win the war, by losing it.

Stealing a glance down the hall first, Ken allowed the door to close behind him and placed a chair in front of it as an added precaution. Donning gloves and a mask, he quickly unscrewed the cap on the vial and with practiced hands tore off the paper exposing the sterile swab. He saturated the swab with the viral solution and pressed it gently, deeply into her right nasal passage, deftly repeating the process on the left. He broke the swab off and left both pieces in the now empty vial, recapping it. He strode to the bathroom and washed his hands and the vial first with soapy hot water, then finished with an antiseptic gel he had brought. He dried his hands and the vial, replaced it in his pocket and removed the chair from the door. The whole thing took less than 90 seconds.

234

Ken pulled the chair up to Anna's bedside, his heart thumping wildly, thinking how extraordinary that nothing looked different in this moment, but everything had just changed. He stared for a while at her, trying to see some trace of the act he had committed, looking anxiously for a sign from her that she knew, that she approved, and could find none. He wanted to hear her speak, maybe to mouth the words, 'thank you,' or at least, 'it's okay,' but he knew that even if she could say them, the words would not make it so.

It was not okay. Would never be okay again. Despite the nobility of his deed, done for her and for the world, he felt gravity pressing down on every fiber in him. His lungs seemed unable to expand without effort. Air was thick as mud. His skin was lead, his bones were rocks, his clothing, granite. With stunning clarity he saw Anna's misery transformed: it was his now. She had bequeathed it, he had taken it up. Her affliction would soon be over. His had just begun. He dropped his head on his chest, "Oh God in heaven forgive me..."

VIRUS: IN VITRO/
IN VIVO

*Between the fixed points of conception and death
the organism is . . . 'at risk' to the hazards of life.*
—Richard Fiennes, *Man, Nature and Disease*

PORTLAND, OREGON
June

There was no accounting for it. The change was unforeseeable, except that being unforeseeable was part of its nature. Under intense scrutiny in the laboratory, it would not perform: yes there were changes, some spontaneous, most configured intentionally, but nothing of consequence. In the lab the virus was incapable of invading its host. The organism had resisted scientific manipulation to communicability. But outside of the watchful clinical eye...

There are parallels. Any zookeeper can tell you about animals that are unsuccessful at adapting to captivity, those whose breeding skills disappear, for example, behind bars. Is a virus less complex? Is a glass test tube or a petri dish, full of rich media designed specifically for the growth of the microbe, different than the enclosure created to fill all of the pandas' or apes' perceived needs?

The naturalist observes far different behavior in animals in the wild. Why should H5N1 be any different? One might argue that there are only eight proteins in the avian virus versus millions in an ape, but another would counter that the laws of gravity apply to the falling

236

acorn as much as to the giant oak. So it is with science. The experts will argue both sides of a question until nature or the advance of knowledge proves one right and the other wrong. The discarded hypothesis either falls to the side forgotten forever, or is held up as yet another example of humankind's dim understanding of the world.

In the living laboratory of Anna Wardman a tiny fragment of the genetic material coding for the H5N1 capsule was lost in one of the many reproductive cycles, and the virus, spontaneously regrouping in its new environment, grabbed a chance piece of host protein to fill the gap. Out of the makeshift patch in the viral capsule sprung a new claw on the outside of the germ, a grappling hook for seizing and piercing the walls of the epithelial cells lining the respiratory tract of its host, and other hosts just like her. Despite the patient's markedly debilitated condition the virus was in the presence of abundant resources for its purposes. With plenty of host protein to avail itself of, the single muta-tion of one virion became two and four, and eight, and within a few days, millions.

• • •

The hypothalamus of the brain is located deep within the cranium. Among other things it regulates the temperature of the body, keeping it at a constant 97 to 99 degrees under normal circumstances. Elevation of more than one and a half or two degrees is usually an indication of illness, but the accumulated insults of aging may damage this glandular thermostat, making it less responsive.

Ordinarily it would take just a few days to develop the telltale sign of fever resulting from exposure to H5N1, but Anna's hypothalamus was, with the rest of her intracranial function, deteriorating rapidly and not up to the task. Her temperature remained steadfastly in the 99 range, not particularly notable to the staff.

After the H5N1 was thrust upon her, Anna's immunologic defenses recognized an assault on her system and gradually began building a white blood cell response, attempting to match the offending agent to some previously encountered one. Antibodies could be generated quickly if a similarity could be found. But there was no concordance of her immune system with the avian virus. She began to fight the infection with respiratory reflexes that had not yet ceased to exist with the rest of her.

First a clear nasal discharge appeared, her body's attempt to dilute and wash away the organism. This was accompanied by audible grunts as her major airways attempted to clear small bits of accumulating mucus without troubling the rib muscles enough to participate in a full-fledged cough. After a couple days these symptoms progressed to congestion in her nose, producing thick yellow mucus indicative of the white blood cells' presence at the site of the viral breach. Soon she developed a deep rattle in her chest, the first audible sign of a quantity of phlegm that threatened to choke her.

Anna's nurses trundled a machine to her bedside which they used frequently to suck the accumulating viscous material from her airway so she did not suffocate. Anna gurgled and coughed reflexively from the intrusive probe being stuck down her throat, as well as from the burgeoning fluids taking up residence in her chest. Nothing so large as a glob of phlegm made its way out of Anna's mouth and onto her care-givers, but a fine mist of infected respiratory droplets proceeded from her with each coughing spasm. With its newly acquired infectivity, the virus would not need a large inoculum for transmission. Since Anna had no fever and no history of communicable diseases, no precaution-ary measures such as masks were used. After all, pneumonia, the cause of death for most people in Anna's circumstances, is not catchy.

Between Ken's inoculation of Anna and her death, there were eleven nurses and aides in and out of her room, four respiratory tech-nicians, six orderlies, two maintenance workers, seven housekeepers, two ward secretaries, and one lost guest looking for a relative. The door to her room was open most of the time.

CHAPTER 17

On a crystal clear Saturday morning, one week after Ken had set his plan in motion, he was sitting in his den reading, or rather pretending to read the morning paper. Outwardly he was a paradigm of calm, but his demeanor was a purposeful camouflage for the turmoil within. Concentration had been a scarce commodity. His nerves were frayed from constant worry about what each day would bring to his mother, and the additional effort of maintaining his composure was sucking the energy right out of him. He had to restrain himself every moment from calling the facility to check on Anna. Was she ill? Was she suffering? Would the staff notice? Would someone send a specimen to CDC? Would CDC correctly identify the organism? Would the nursing home call him when she was sick, or would it be so fast they would only notify him after she died? How long would it take CDC to identify the H5N1, who would they send to investigate? How long would all these events take? Would anyone be quarantined? Would he and June be quarantined?

Night and day he obsessed over his unfolding scheme. He had set the wheels in motion, but the turning of them he could not precisely predict and now he found this bothered him mightily. There seemed so many more opportunities for his strategy to go awry than he had contemplated beforehand. He knew he would be unable to rest until everything fell into place as he had envisioned. The week that had just passed seemed an interminable stretch of time.

The telephone jangled noisily in its cradle, piercing his thoughts. He jumped visibly in his chair, before looking to see if June was around to notice. Forcing himself to let the phone ring one more time, he then picked it up as nonchalantly as his pounding heart would allow.

"Hello?"

"Hello, this is Penny Chan calling from Cypress Arbor. May I speak with Mr. Wardman please?"

Ken, feeling his pulse thrum in his veins, deliberately slowed his speech as he responded, "Uh...this is...Mr. Wardman."

"Hello Mr. Wardman, I'm the nursing supervisor on your mother's ward."

"Yes, Ms. Chan."

"I'm helping to take care of Anna today. I am sorry to bother you but I wanted to let you know she has taken a turn for the worse. She developed a temperature of 101 degrees last night and her breathing is very shallow today. She is coughing a lot and there's quite a bit of mucus We're having to suction her frequently."

"Well, I'm sorry to hear that...of course she's been going downhill for some time..."

"Yes, it's always sad to watch," said the nurse. "Mr. Wardman, I need to clarify something with you. Your mother has a 'do not resuscitate' order on her chart, and instructions that she is not to be hospitalized without your consent. I am calling to see if you want us to transfer her to a hospital, or continue to provide supportive care here."

"Well...I see...poor Anna...I guess you're never ready for this," Ken said taking a deep breath. Even though he expected these developments, the experience of it was still new to him. He was unsettled by his feelings and struggled for control.

"What do you think is the matter?" he asked, clearing his voice. June, who had now entered the room, was watching him intently. She would just think he was responding as a son might be expected to.

"Well, it looks like pneumonia. The doctor ordered an antibiotic."

"Do you think she will respond to antibiotics? I've heard pneumonia can be viral. Will antibiotics help a virus?" Of course he knew the answer to this question.

"No sir, they will not. It's just standard treatment here to culture a patient with a fever and a cough and start them on antibiotics."

"Oh. I see. So you're checking cultures?" He had to verify this.

"Yes. The results will be back in a few days."

"Then we'll know if it's bacterial or viral?"

"Well, we don't usually culture for viruses this time of year."

Ken was taken aback by this unanticipated response. "I thought you were a flu surveillance site."

"We are, but this isn't flu season. We usually don't start sending viral samples to CDC until October unless there are reports of flu spreading in the area sooner."

"Well, I'm a little surprised by that," Ken continued, trying to think quickly of a way to address this unexpected problem. "You know...my mother elected not to take any flu shots the last several years due to her condition...I just thought you might be extra vigilant on those patients because in any season they would be more at risk," Ken offered, hoping he wouldn't have to insist they send the sample. It might arouse suspicion and he didn't want to incur any, but his plan absolutely depended on identifying the cause of her death. It would be completely unforgivable if he had ended her life and there had been no resultant benefit to society. He never could have done it. The viral culture had to be sent.

He was lucky. The nurse took the bait.

"Well, that's a good point, Mr. Wardman. Most of our residents do take a flu shot...I hadn't realized Mrs. Wardman did not.

"I know my mother would be distressed if her decision to decline the flu shot caused anyone else harm." Ken replied.

"I appreciate your concern. We'll send off a sample right away," Nurse Chan intoned. "Mr. Wardman, about hospitalization?"

"My mother was very clear about not wanting any measures to prolong her life after she lost her mental capacities. Please do everything you can to see she is comfortable, but keep her at your facility."

"We'll take good care of her."

"Thank-you."

Ken hung up, relieved to be done with the conversation. He replayed the nurse's words over and over the next few hours and wondered if he should call back and ask if the staff was using masks. But he thought better of it, telling himself that he was just being paranoid. The virus he had chosen was harmless to everyone but his mother; it had been a failure in the lab. No, he concluded, the staff was not at risk and such a call would only arouse suspicion.

June brought Ken a fresh cup of coffee and settled herself on the couch across the room. She was pretending to read, but he knew she was watching him, had been for weeks, tip-toeing around, fussing over this and that. His mother was ill, dying. He shouldn't have to defend his distress to June. He ignored her.

June 21

Four days had passed since the phone call from Nurse Chan and Ken couldn't stand it anymore. A concerned son could call the nursing home without attracting attention, couldn't he? Perhaps he was arousing more suspicion by not calling to inquire about Anna.

"Hello Mr. Wardman," said Anna's nurse of the day. "She's holding her own but her pulse is a little rapid and her breathing is labored. We can't get her temperature below 100 most of the time."

"Is she coughing?"

"Oh yes, but not hard. She's very weak. She hasn't eaten anything for days."

"Are you taking precautions? Perhaps she should have a mask on..." he couldn't help himself; it was just common sense for goodness sake. Didn't they know that? What happened to standardized infection control procedures? Gowns? Masks? Gloves?

"Oh no, Mr. Wardman, that would choke her for sure, we've got to suction her all the time now to clear that mucus. Don't you worry about it, most people don't realize pneumonia isn't contagious."

"Yes, well, thank you for pointing that out, but I always thought it was better to be safe than sorry." *Settle down* Kenneth. *There is no way the organism is contagious to anyone but her. It would take a huge dose. Like the one you gave her.* Just let it happen. But how long was this going to take? He thought for sure she would be gone by now. What was left of her to fight this thing?

"Anything else Mr. Wardman?"

"I guess not," he said pausing, debating whether to ask about the cultures. He knew they wouldn't have the CDC specimen back yet or the whole facility would be in an uproar, but he desperately wanted to know how long it might take to get the results, a detail he had overlooked before. He couldn't stop himself, "Oh, did you learn anything from her cultures?"

"Let me check...She grew routine flora in her bacterial cultures and...the same was noted on her gram stain..." He could hear her flipping through pages. "It looks like that's it."

"Is the viral test back?"

"...Hmmm..." More flipping. "No. It looks like it was collected Saturday and sent out Monday. Let's see, that's just two days ago. It usually takes at least a week to get those back."

"Thank you for your time, nurse, uh...?"

"Wilson...You're welcome. Call anytime." And Nurse Wilson was sincere in saying that. As she picked up the chart and filed it away she thought how hard it must be to lose a parent to Alzheimer's and to be so far away that visiting was difficult. But just the same she was glad to be off the phone. All the staff on the ward would be extra busy today because two of the day shift nurses and one of the aides had called in sick. It was bad timing, but what could you do? Retrieving the medicine cart she had left in the hallway she began her rounds.

June 23

Ken was not asleep when the phone rang thirty six hours later. Anna was dead.

June reached over and laid her arm on his chest as he hung up. He shed no tears, but drew a deep breath and sighed. He lay there for a while without moving or speaking then turned away from her in the bed. Whether he slept or not after that she could not ascertain, but no sign of rest attended his features when he got up in the morning. His eyes were lifeless and the flesh of his face appeared to have sunk, draping over the bony prominences that not too long ago had captured the smiles and joys of a grandfather. He had all but abandoned Moira lately, and the rest of them. June thought she understood Ken's misery watching his mother deteriorate, but his reaction seemed all out of proportion to the end they had all foreseen for years. While Ken showered June wept for the changes in him.

He insisted on going to work as usual, despite her begging him to stay home. It was unnatural how he was driving himself. Ken asked her if she would make airline reservations for him to pick up his mother's things the next day at the facility and then he left the house clutching his thermos under his arm, the way he had every morning for the last thirty five years.

When he arrived back home June didn't even bother to tell him that she, Betsy and Moira were going to accompany him to Cypress Arbor. They ate dinner worlds apart and went to bed in silence.

June 24

Early the next morning Ken appeared startled when June was in the driver's seat of his car ready to take him to the airport. He did not argue with her. For her part June was brooking no dissention. She had no idea any more what to expect from her husband so the safest approach was to tell him nothing and take matters into her own hands. They drove without speaking until June pulled in to pick up Betsy and Moira. Ken looked at her quizzically as the two came out the front door toward the car.

"It's no time for you to be alone Ken," June said gently but firmly. "Betsy, Moira and I are going with you. That's what families are for."

He had looked at her then as though he intended to protest, but whatever he was thinking failed to escape his lips. The hardness of his face visibly softened and for the next few moments, before the girls got in the car, she saw flickers of the Ken she desperately missed pass over him as he met her gaze. His eyes welled up and he turned away, brushing the back of one hand over them to destroy the evidence.

Betsy opened the back door and Moira climbed in, pausing to reach her hand up and touch the side of Ken's face. Ken did not respond, but June took the little girl's hand and kissed it, saying softly, "Good morning Sunshine. We sure need plenty of that today. Your grandpa is very sad."

Moira nodded. "I love you Grandpa," she said and kissed him lightly on the back of his head before settling into her seat.

"I'm so sorry Dad," Betsy said after she closed the door, laying her hand on Ken's shoulder.

Ken drew himself up in the front seat and cleared his throat. He put his hand over Betsy's, patting it without turning around, and when he could trust his voice again hoarsely uttered, "Thank you."

June eased the car into traffic knowing she had made the right decision.

OREGON
June 24

As she wound up the driveway, June thought Cypress Arbor was even prettier in the Oregon summer than it had been in the spring when they first came two years ago. The mild climate encouraged all things blooming, and the gardening staff expertly fertilized, weeded and pruned the flower beds into dazzling displays of color amidst the stately evergreens. If ever a setting could wash away the blues, this was it, and she was pretty sure the designers of the grounds intended exactly that effect. She stole a glance at Ken and was disappointed but not surprised to see his thoughts were elsewhere. It had been a long time since anyone had spoken, deferring to Ken's mood. Betsy broke the ice softly, "It's beautiful here, isn't it?"

Moira, who had been biting her lips trying to maintain the silence in the car, piped up immediately, "Yes, we should pick some flowers for Grandpa. Would that cheer you up?" she asked.

Ken sighed wearily. "Oh sweetheart, Grandpa is so sorry. I haven't been much company have I?"

"It's okay. I would miss my mommy too, even if she was in heaven," she turned toward Betsy who hugged her, holding her head tightly to her breast. Moira raised her head and continued, "I think your mommy would want you to be sad for a little while Grandpa, but prob'ly not forever. Mommy always says she wants what's best for me. It's best not to be sad too long. When you're done being sad we can play again...I can wait."

June was relieved she had pulled into a parking spot. She couldn't even see anymore and reached into her purse to get a tissue as soon as she shut off the engine. Stepping into the sunshine they all felt their burdens lighten a bit.

It would be alright, Ken said to himself as he closed the car door. The virus had done its deed, and was now safely gone with her body. His mother was at peace. He had to take comfort from that right now, and wait a little while for the rest of his plan to come to fruition. It would take some time. He hadn't counted on how the minutes and the days of anticipation would weigh on him. He would try to lighten up; his family deserved it. He owed them that: they had weathered so much for him. Ken reached down and took Moira's hand and led her up the walk.

Cypress Arbor was its usual subdued buzz of activity for a Saturday morning. Ken was again impressed by the number of professionally-clad people of Asian descent bustling about with their elderly charges. As was typical in any nursing facility the sight of a child brought smiles and solicitations from many of the residents. Moira returned them as graciously as a beauty queen on a runway as she walked with her family down the corridors to Anna's ward.

On reaching the nursing station, Ken identified himself to the clerk, and told her the reason for his visit. The staff was expecting him and the shift supervisor came to meet them presently. Left to her own devices for a few minutes, Moira was making new friends with some of Anna's former hall mates in various stages of dress and dementia who were sitting in the common area. Ken was ushered to a conference room with the nurse and June fell in step to accompany him. Betsy walked the hallways while keeping an eye on her little girl, who was in no danger of escaping from the company of her new-found fan club.

Moira was entertaining the coterie of pleasant, if not entirely cognizant, white-haired residents when one of the aides who had taken care of Anna was pointed in her direction.

"Hello," said the aide walking up to Moira and temporarily interrupting the proceedings. "My name is Cindy. I helped to take care of your great grandmother." She pulled something out of a pocket in her smock. "Do you recognize this?" she asked, holding up the little stuffed bear Moira had sent with Ken several months before.

"Oh, yes!" Moira replied, clapping her hands together. "I gave it to Grandpa to bring here. Where did you find it?"

"Right in your great grandmother's bed. I'm the one who made sure it was tucked next to her. Your picture was on her table and your little bear was cuddled beside her. I knew as soon as I saw you that you were the one in the picture."

"I named her Hope," Moira offered helpfully as the aide handed her the teddy.

"That's a beautiful name. Your great grandma was lucky to have someone as special as you in her life," she said kindly, putting an arm around Moira who now clutched the little animal to her face, inhaling deeply.

"It smells just like her," Moira said quietly, rubbing the bear's soft mat of fur to the skin of her cheek.

"I'm sure she would want you to have it back."

"Thank you."

Smiling, the aide stroked Moira's head and returned to work.

Moira resumed her *tete-a-tete*, with Hope nestled protectively in the warm fold of her arm. From time to time she glanced down at the bear and smiled sadly, occasionally raising it back to her nose trying to discern the memory of a person she had barely known, but knew her beloved grandfather had loved dearly.

A little later Ken and June emerged from the consultation room carrying a small accordion folder and a tote bag. Betsy, who had stopped her pacing in a place that gave her a view of both Moira and the meeting room, looked forlornly at her father who was once again beset by grief. His shoulders sagged as though the bags he carried were filled with rocks instead of the few mementos that would be traveling back home with them. June took Betsy aside as Ken was heading for the elevator and told her that Anna's cremated remains would be shipped back to California the following week for burial. They gathered Moira up, still chatting away with her new friends, and left as unremarkably as they had arrived.

VIRUS: IN VIVO

OREGON
June 24

The virus exploded out of the attractive young nurse's nostrils accompanied by an aerosol of clear mucus, nasal debris and personal bacterial slime as she sneezed her way into the bank. One, two, three times: she always sneezed in threes. She covered her mouth and nose with her nicely manicured hand as a matter of course, behavior reduced now to rote by the proper manners her mother insisted on as she was growing up. She usually didn't need a tissue after she sneezed, just a quick sniff and she had forgotten all about it as she grasped the door handle. Handing her viral-coated payroll check to the teller, she made a deposit of millions of microbes to the bank. Her mind wandered, while she waited for the receipt, to what she needed to pick up at the grocery store on the way home. She was feeling a bit tired this afternoon. It'd been a long day. Maybe they'd go out for dinner. A nice inexpensive place just opened by the mall; her friends told her the food was good, for a buffet.

She made a pretty picture coming out of the bank, good legs, nice figure, long ponytail breezily swinging over her bright white nursing uniform. She pushed on the door to exit, then smiled and thanked the man in the UPS uniform behind her who rushed forward to hold it open: she appreciated the timeless courtesy. He too was still smiling, right hand awash with viral particles from grasping the door handle after her, as he popped the top of his soda back in the

248

truck. With the side of his hand he took a swipe of his itchy nose as he brought the can to his mouth for a good long drink. Every year at this time his nose and eyes seemed to bother him more. Drippy, stuffy, itchy. He made a mental note to get back on his allergy medicine as he drove away.

CHAPTER 18

GUANGZHOU, CHINA
June 26

From the time she had arrived back in Guangzhou, Lou had been besieged with additional reports of animal outbreaks of avian influenza in all its known iterations, relentlessly tracking its way to new locations in Asia and beyond. Thank God no new mutations had been reported since winter.

Africa was now involved in the bird epidemic with its north coast reporting H5N1 and H7N7 in both migrating fowl and domestic poultry. It would only be a matter of time before close living conditions with the birds, and poor sanitation, resulted in human cases. H9N2 had been found in Eastern Europe, and Russia had isolated all three types of avian influenza from one end of the country to another. North and South America had sporadic cases of the less lethal H7N7 and H9N2 in their bird species; together with Australia and Antarctica these four continents had not yet been invaded by H5N1. Nothing more of the lethal H5N2 had been encountered since the three men who died in Vietnam.

Lou had finally gained the additional staff WHO had promised her and her new roving field assistants were scattered from Indonesia to Siberia investigating claims. Dr. Wataabe had informed her recently of a breakthrough in making rapid vaccine. Cell-Ect Cellutions, a small U.S. biotech firm, had been successful at producing a batch of H7N7 in just two weeks at their New Jersey facility. Although the initial run was quite small it showed promise for mass production. It was currently being tested for efficacy and the scientific community was hopeful. Patent rights could be extended to other manufacturers if the process

250

was commercially viable, and flu preparedness would finally enter the 21st century.

Director Bueller had told her that money and supplies were still moving too slowly into WHO's hands. Obtaining rapid flu testing kits, face masks, IV bags and respiratory equipment for first responder teams continued to be a challenge. Despite verbal support from his board members, Bueller reported there was no movement afoot to actually purchase more H5N1 vaccines or to develop others as they had hoped, let alone for nations to hand inventory over to WHO for husbanding.

It was an international game of hot potato, with the wealthy countries continually tossing the problem back in the laps of the third world nations where the virus seemed to be making its stand. Of course no one in power ventured to articulate the reasoning out loud; it was all very hush-hush. But there were rumblings, rumors of the words actually spoken. As with the HIV epidemic, as long as the brunt of the disease was being borne by the overpopulated, under-endowed nations, it might be just what the doctor, Mother Nature, or God, ordered, depending on the source of entitlement of the speaker. International powers were beginning to address internal preparations but refused to take on the burden of prevention or management far from home.

The only resources being devoted to research were coming from private, academic and philanthropic funds: not nearly the magnitude of response WHO had hoped for, or adequate influenza readiness required. With a few notable exceptions there had been no major influx of government capital into funding research. The world was in a tizzy but without focus, without commitment, without leadership. The World Health Organization struggled valiantly to provide guidance, but its advice was largely ignored, recognized only when it was convenient.

Lou tried not to let the political aspects of her career get her down. There had always been people who were forward thinking and those who dragged everyone down with them. She responded by working harder, following every infection, every story, every lead until she was certain she had all the facts.

Closing the books on each case was satisfying, but under-reporting remained rampant and Lou wondered just how many infections and deaths in humans weren't even recognized. Life was so difficult, so cheap, and illness and death so commonplace and expected in many of the places under her authority, that Lou believed many cases of bird flu weren't even known. People got sick and died and no one thought much about it, let alone reported it.

Lou stood up from her desk and stretched herself out with a yawn, determined to force the depressing cycle of thoughts from her mind. She grabbed her backpack and pulled the door to her office behind her to go for a walk. It was impossible to get any work done when she obsessed about the uncontrollable details. As she hiked into the throngs on the pavement Lou easily shifted from one obsession to another, more pleasant: she really missed Connor. She missed him when she was happy, and she missed him when she was sad. If she was cranky, she thought of the wry humor he would employ to cheer her. If she was brimming with news, she wanted to tell him. She yearned for the depth of his mind and the rugged substance of his body.

Great, she thought, as though it wasn't hot enough outside she was creating her own heat wave. Chuckling she removed the shirt covering her camisole and tied it around her waist. Native Chinese always stared at her western face as she passed, now they peered unabashedly at her as she laughed out loud. Oh, let them, she thought as she beamed at each ogler. I have stared at them too as they stand in the squares every morning doing their Tai-chi...waving their arms and legs in ethereal slow motion engaging some unseen spirit. Each to her own she thought as she smiled at the curious strangers and continued on her way. It wasn't too long before the brightening of her spirit allowed her to return to more productive enterprises.

• • •

In her next life Lou was going to have a job without a phone. Or at least she would have a job without a phone that rang in the middle of the night. Had she done something egregious in a previous incarnation to warrant this? What bad karma was she being forced to face with this recurrent nighttime aggravation? All these thoughts raced through her head as she rolled over in the bed, untangling herself from the sheets to silence the jangling.

"Hello," she croaked, noting once again her inability to conjure her voice from a deep sleep at a moment's notice.

"Lou?"

"Well it's not the Dalai Lama," she responded sarcastically, trying to place the familiar voice...*Holy crap!* she thought as she realized it was Director Bueller. She sat straight up in bed.

"Oh, I'm sorry..." she stammered. "I had no idea...What is it?" she asked, alarmed.

"It's Hans Bueller..."

"Yes, I know. I'm sorry Dr. Bueller..."

"It's alright. Lou, I hate to bother you but I just had a call from CDC in Atlanta. They have a case of H5N1."

"Migrating birds or domestic?" she asked, all senses on alert.

"Neither," Bueller responded in measured tones. "Human."

UNITED STATES
June 27

Belief does not come easily. We always doubt ourselves, our eyes, doubt the technology, the process, the information in front of us. It cannot be. The technician at the Centers for Disease Control in Atlanta repeated the test. Twice. This took an additional two and a half hours.

The lab tech called his supervisor who then called the director, Dr. James Demint who placed a call to Cypress Arbor to instruct them to isolate the patient, and was informed the resident had died 4 days ago. Without identifying the specific results, Demint advised the director of the Oregon facility, Janalee Manson, to prevent anyone from entering or leaving the establishment. The astonished manager requested a reason and was told that someone would get back to her as soon as possible with more details. It was 2:30 in the afternoon.

Ms. Manson made an announcement over the public address system that did not go over well with the employees, who were coming up on change of shift. Unable to answer the immediate deluge of queries from the restive and the curious on her staff, she had to close her office door and post her secretary outside to avoid interruption while she met with the facility's single security officer to discuss how they might enforce the precipitous directive from CDC. They elected to place orange cones and signs in the driveways at both the front and the rear entrances, but since there was only one guard, he could not monitor both sites. Compliance would be largely voluntary.

The local police were called for assistance and Ms. Manson was told that the officers were changing shifts and that the police chief would need further information before deploying his force. Since she had no information to provide, Ms. Manson called the commissioner of the health department whom she was informed was busy and who would call her back presently. During these proceedings one of the residents had the temerity to develop crushing chest pain and the hapless director called the emergency squad for assistance, informing the ambulance personnel before they removed the patient, some eleven minutes later, that the nursing home would contact the Emergency Room when they figured out what was going on.

Concurrently in downtown Portland, Multnomah County health officials were being notified of the existence of a case of H5N1 and were ordered to quarantine the nursing home immediately and assemble a team of adequately protected public health workers to be sent to the scene at once. The county health commissioner called the mayor who called the police ordering them to cordon off Cypress Arbor. Two county health nurses, an epidemiologist, and three paramedics trained for disaster response were provided with masks, gowns and gloves and dispatched in one ambulance and one private automobile to the site. This took about an hour.

After the health commissioner made the other calls and sent his team, he spoke with Ms. Manson and advised her of the reason for the action. She was told to keep the information confidential until local officials could meet and decide on the best way to present the news in a way that would not incite panic. In Ms. Manson's mind however, panic had just found a home.

Over four days passed from the time of Anna Wardman's death until the first team of health officials arrived at ground zero to assess the situation. Seventeen days had passed since Ken administered the fatal inoculum. Over a week had passed between the time Anna's nasal swab was collected and the date it was processed in Atlanta.

In that period of time two of the exposed employees from Cypress Arbor, each of them with vague muscle aches and a low-grade fever, had nevertheless decided to continue with their upcoming travel plans because their airline tickets were non-refundable. Both boarded planes to domestic destinations exposing 632 people on the flights as well as a host of others in the airports they passed through, which included Portland, Salt Lake City, Houston, Tulsa and Toledo.

Seven infected employees continued coming to work at the nursing home even though they were ill. Four of them had low-paying part-time jobs without any paid sick leave; they had to come to work to sustain their incomes. The other three were nurses who knew if they called in sick someone else's job would be harder that day.

Six additional employees were at home in various stages of illness. Three had seen their health care providers for respiratory symptoms and exposed a number of others in the doctors' waiting rooms. Two workers had no health insurance and had delayed seeking care because of the expense. One had just been taken to the emergency room in Salem by her mother with whom she had been staying since she became ill. She was in the process of being admitted for pneumonia. One little girl, the great grandchild of one of the residents, carried the germ back to San Francisco.

Each of these people had family and friends who had been with them during the early days of their infections, the prodromal period in which symptoms are not yet apparent but the disease is nonetheless contagious. In addition to spreading it through close personal contact, there were protean opportunities for less intimate but no less significant community interactions between those carrying the germ and incidental passers-by: at eating establishments, schools, department stores, groceries, libraries, churches, banks and places of employment.

Health officials arriving at Cypress Arbor would take stock of the situation and transmit the initial information to CDC, whose chief epidemiologist and several supporting staff members were already on their way to a private hangar at Atlanta's Hartsfield Airport to fly to Portland and manage the scene. CDC would bring instant flu tests to check the sick employees. In several hours it would become apparent that a highly communicable form of H5N1 had entered

VIRION

into, and escaped from, an Oregon nursing home. It would not be at all clear how that had happened.

. . .

"Goddammit Hunt! Don't tell me about problems, tell me about solutions!" The president slammed both palms on the table and leaned forward, glaring at his HHS Secretary. "How in the hell did the goddamned plague arrive in the United States!"

Cyril Hunt sat across the great expanse of carved walnut that served as the president's desk in the Oval Office and let the man's anger ricochet around the room. The last statement was just another missile of rage, and not one requiring a response. Hunt couldn't possibly have given an explanation anyway. Pausing as long as he dared before speaking, he said in his most assuaging tone, "Mr. President we have five million doses of osmavir in government stock. My staff is checking on the availability of more through national and international manufacturers as we speak. We can potentially acquire another 10 million doses within a week and maybe twice that much within two weeks. In addition, the Justice Department confiscated 30 million doses from Viraban in April..."

"Big fucking deal! We confiscated them because they're no good!"

"Not exactly," Hunt countered, beginning to stretch his drawl out a bit to try to calm or at least slow the proceedings down. "It's half potency. In our tests of it, every pill is the same. The company intentionally diluted it, but by using twice the usual recommended dose the pills could provide protection for an additional fifteen million people," Cyril offered.

"Is the FDA willing to back that up?" he growled. "The last thing we need when this is all over is a class action lawsuit against the federal government."

"I believe the FDA will be agreeable." Hunt licked his lips out of habit, missing the cigar he was denied in this rarefied setting, the president being an intolerant non-smoker. "I also believe the executives at Viraban would be very happy to be allowed to contribute to the national cause."

"How's that?"

"As commander in chief you could override the justice department and authorize the company to resume production. We suspended their osmavir operations pending the investigation a couple months ago."

The president chewed on the idea for a moment before barking, "Do it. But send somebody in to watch the bastards. They're not going to screw the federal government."

"Done, Mr. President." Hunt always derived satisfaction from uttering these words. He didn't have time to enjoy it.

"Why the fuck don't we have vaccine?"

"Mostly because it doesn't exist yet Mr. President. WHO has half a million doses of Avimmune; we have half a million too. But PharmaGlobal will have another 60 million doses available sometime in the next four to six weeks..."

"Fuck four to six weeks! CDC says we need it right now! They're predicting half the population in the northwest will be sick by then. Do you know what will happen to me when people start dropping like flies?" he fumed. "What are you doing about it?"

"We are currently in negotiations to buy as much H5N1 as PharmaGlobal will sell us, which right now is 52 million doses. The CEO says they have an additional 8 million doses under contract to WHO and other foreign governments..."

"Bloody hell! This is a national emergency! If PharmaGlobal won't sell them to us we'll confiscate them..."

"Mr. President, they said they are sure they can renegotiate something with their other clients, but under the circumstances that will take some finesse..."

"Yes, I see, they want to extort a higher fee...Fine. Pay them extra, but the U. S government will not be scalped, goddamnit! I'll send in the fucking National Guard if they get too uppity."

"I'm sure we can work it out Mr. President. PharmaGlobal might be able to make as many as 80 million doses in another six to eight months. They want a confirmed contract for the vaccine with half the money up front and they'll pour all their resources into H5N1 production."

"Wonderful Cyril, just fucking wonderful. And how many Americans will be left to use it?" the president inquired, sitting back in his chair and quieting down for the first time since Hunt had entered the room. The president had been lashing out at him like a wounded tiger, but now he turned toward the window staring thoughtfully. Cyril waited. No one dared to interrupt the president's fugue. "How do we get our hands on the doses held by WHO?" he finally asked.

"Well, I think WHO would be happy to have a hand in deciding that, Mr. President..."

"Yes, I'm sure they would. They'll be all over us like flies on shit trying to run things, telling me what to do. We don't need them. CDC is in charge."

"As you wish..."

"Will they sell them to us?"

"I think they would *give* them to us, but they're definitely going to want to have some say in who gets it because rationing is clearly going to be involved. They won't give up control."

"What do they want?"

"They want to send a representative of their choice to the site to work with the CDC. They want you to authorize the CDC to fully cooperate in providing access to all information available."

"Is that it?"

"They also want a government liaison they can trust."

"And who might that be?" the president asked."I damn well know it's not you Hunt. They don't like your ass any better than they like mine."

"They have mentioned Michael Farrington."

"Get him in here," the president ordered his chief of staff who had been sitting attentively in a side chair taking all this in at the president's request.

Hunt cleared his throat as the man stood. "He doesn't work for us anymore."

"Goddamnit!" the president cursed again as he slammed his palm again on the desk. His face had gone purple with the latest explosion causing Hunt to wonder if he might next witness a stroke. "Find him and bring him here. I want to know what he knows about the WHO and why they want to work with him. What the fuck is the matter with the CDC?"

"Nothing is the matter with the CDC Mr. President. The WHO has more history with Farrington and they trust him. They want him involved in the process over here."

"Malloy, assemble the cabinet," he ordered the chief of staff who was now on his way out the door. "I want to meet in thirty minutes." Then leveling a glare at the HHS secretary he growled, "Hunt your ass will be sitting right outside this room until then, in case I need to chew on it some more. Dismissed."

"Of course, Mr. President."

•   •   •

Connor Mackenzie was in Los Angeles meeting with his boss at the Associated Press when a tip came over the wire: *CDC identifies H5N1 in USA. Sample taken from patient in Oregon extended care facility. Patient deceased. Facility quarantined. CDC officials en route to manage situation. No further details available.*

The intern monitoring the wire had burst into the newsroom looking for the manager who now burst into the office with the fax in his hand saying, "You need to see this."

The editor read it and handed it to Connor.

"Holy shit."

•   •   •

"Connor, seriously, you need to think about this..." Lou's thoughts from Guangzhou were running faster than her tongue could keep up. He had called her as soon as he got the news, to tell her he was going to Portland.

"We have no clue what's happening there yet...Multnomah's health department says there's a definite spike in respiratory symptoms among the staff and residents they've triaged at the facility. We won't know until CDC arrives with rapid test kits if it's avian flu, but if it is, you might get there and not be able to get out...Martial law could be invoked...It might be absolute chaos...You won't get vaccine...There isn't enough osmavir... You're putting yourself at risk...You can write the story from L.A." Lou was beside herself with anxiety, rattling off one objection after another.

VIRION

"Whoa...slow down there Doc," he said. "I had no idea you'd be so upset. Why is this any different from any other case I've covered, or that you've rushed into? Do you think I don't worry about you too when you go riding off to investigate these things? I'm not going to do anything stupid. This is my job. I'm an investigative reporter on the international health beat. I'm not writing a book report Lou, I can't do it from my desk," Connor said trying to soothe her.

"No, no. It's not the same," she said, "Please Connor, hear me out. Just listen for a minute."

"Okay, but slow down. Don't turn hysterical on me. I like the smart sensible girl in you. Show me some of that. I'll listen better."

Lou stopped short. He was absolutely right. How did he know just what to say to her? What had happened to her legendary sang-froid? She knew what happened to it; it was called love. It was turning her world upside down. She went on quietly, "Connor, I care about you...I just found you." She sighed heavily. "I don't want to lose you," she admitted as much to herself as to him.

"Lou," he said matching her earnestness, "You know I feel the same about you. But why is this case so different from what we did in China, or Vietnam? I don't break any of the rules. I don't violate isolation orders, I use the recommended precautions, masks, whatever, when I interview anyone suspected of infection. I'm conscientious."

"Connor this is really bad. There's a huge difference. The United States has no endemic bird populations carrying H5N1. There is no readily identifiable avian source for this infection. The patient was a nursing home resident with a terminal disease. She wasn't exposed to any chickens...or ducks or even...pet parrots. The only possible mode of exposure was human to human. And if H5N1 was carried by a person from an endemic area across the ocean it is very probable there have been additional exposures, and that they are widespread."

"Yes?"

"And depending on where the carrier entered the country, it's possible the whole west coast is already in trouble. You can bet CDC is conferring with the U.S. government right now about quarantine. The whole city or state may be under martial law by the time you get there. You may not be allowed out. We just don't know anything yet and

I don't trust the U.S. response necessarily to be appropriate, judging by their lack of understanding and cooperation with the WHO on the international scene." She was starting to speed up again.

"Do you think this is a pandemic?"

"I don't know. I don't have enough information yet, but on the limited facts available to me at this point it's entirely possible. I'm very concerned. The whole thing just doesn't gel. It doesn't make sense. And until I can put it together better I have to assume the worst case scenario."

"Wouldn't you like to know more?"

"Well, of course."

"Well, that's my job, to find out. Like you, I'm a public servant."

"Connor..." she pleaded.

"Lou, now it's my turn."

"Okay."

"I do not have a death wish. I am interested in enjoying many wonderful years in the company of my favorite doctor. But my career, like yours, involves occasional exposure to dangerous circumstances. Arguably, this may not even be the most dangerous situation I have encountered. At least the threat is identifiable. I can wear a mask, gown, gloves...on the airplane even, if you think it's appropriate. I am man enough to look like a dufus if it will protect me."

"Lou, someone has to tell the public the story, and preferably in a way that emphasizes the facts and minimizes the hysteria. If this truly is the start of a pandemic there will be all manner of crap hitting the fan, with lots of potential for misinformation, exaggeration and outright lying. Someone has to sort through the static and find the message. That's me. It's who I am. I can't just pick up my toys and go home because the game got a little scary."

"But what if you can't get out?" she asked, the fear in her rising again.

"Even worst case scenario, if it is the start of an epidemic, it won't last forever. I have osmavir, it's part of the protection my boss at AP was able to obtain, I'll take it with me just in case. Frankly, if this is the beginning of a pandemic it's probably better to be sick early on while we still have supplies and people to treat us."

"Don't say that! You could die! Even if you don't get sick, what if the public panics...and it's horrible...and there's looting...and rioting and..."

"Lou, you may be right," Connor interrupted, trying to quiet her across the miles. "It may create pandemonium but it's not an atomic bomb. None of this will happen overnight, but will stretch into weeks, months, maybe years. If that happens I'll have time to regroup, figure out my options. We're all in the same boat if this is a pandemic. We're simply not prepared."

"Yes, but I've been immunized by the WHO," Lou said quietly, "and you haven't."

"Yes, but you've only been vaccinated for H5N1. You're no better off than I am if another strain pops up. That's why you've been fighting so hard for better vaccine technology. Remember?" Connor sighed. "You know Lou, it's just killing me to argue with you from half a world away. But I have to say I feel like the luckiest man in the world anyway."

"What?"

"It's wonderful to be...well...so...cherished. There are 10,000 miles between us right now, but it seems like you're right beside me."

"Oh, Connor. I love you." There. Ohmigod. It just slipped out.

She barely had to time to consider how it had happened and whether it was premature and what he would think before he responded, "I know. I love you too."

Well then. There it was. It was the best and most wonderful thing and the worst to be uttered under such circumstances and so far apart. What would happen now?

"Please be careful," she said with an earnestness that carried through the wires, across the miles.

"I will. I'll call."

"Connor, wear the mask. Everywhere."

"Okay chief."

• • •

"Mr. Wardman?" said the voice on the other end of the line.

Ken, dozing peacefully in his chair for the first time in weeks, was momentarily confused by the use of his middle name. He shook the late afternoon nap from his head, then he remembered. It must be the nursing home. "Speaking," he said as he sat up and replaced his glasses.

"This is Evan Benner of the Multnomah County Health Department. I don't want to alarm you but we have identified a potentially serious problem here at Cypress Arbor. You may have been exposed to a dangerous infectious disease on your last visit here. I have a few questions for you.

"What?" Ken said, trying to muster as much incredulity as he could. "How's that?"

"Have you or anyone in your family traveled outside the country in the past thirty days?"

"No."

"Have you had any contact with live poultry? Do you own any pet birds? Have you been to the zoo or fed any ducks or geese in the last month? Do you own any livestock or live on or near a farm? Are you of Asian descent? Have you had any contact with Asian immigrants or travelers to Asia?

Ken answered no to all the questions as fast as the man could ask them. But he wasn't sure if he should say more, ask more. How should he respond? Should he be upset, concerned, curious, distrustful, irate? What was normal? He could hardly hear the man speak there was so much happening in his own head.

"Have you or anyone in your family exhibited symptoms of a cold or cough, or any fever in the past thirty days?"

"No," Ken said, then opted for curiosity. "Excuse me, can you tell me again what this is all about?"

"Anna Wardman may have died of a dangerous infection and we are charged with monitoring everyone who was in contact with her in the past two weeks. I'm sorry to be so abrupt but we have a lot of people to talk to and we must do it quickly."

"I don't understand...What do you mean?" Ken stammered, now playing dumb.

"When did you last see your mother?"

"June...ah...let me see...it was a Saturday... few weeks ago... yes, June 10th."

And is that the last time you were at Cypress Arbor?"

"Uh...no. My family and I were there just a couple days ago to pick up my mother's things."

"Who else was with you?"

"My wife, my daughter and my granddaughter."

"Do you know their whereabouts?"

"Well, yes. My wife's right here and my daughter and grand-daughter live down the road." This was working. He could feel it. He was responding normally now. It was getting easier to play along.

"Is anyone ill?

"No, no. No one is ill."

"No one has a cough, a fever, runny nose?"

"No."

"Mr. Wardman, I need the name, telephone number and address of your daughter and granddaughter so that I may continue my investigation."

"Is that really necessary? They haven't seen my mother alive since last Christmas. They only came with me to pick up her things...her body was already at the mortuary for heaven's sake."

"Yes, I'm afraid it is. I must also inform you that the Centers for Disease Control is recommending a quarantine of all individuals who visited the nursing home any time between two weeks prior to your mother's death and today. This means you and your wife, your daughter and granddaughter must remain confined to your homes until further notice."

"What?" This was really over-reacting Ken thought. There was no need to quarantine Betsy and Moira.

"Someone will call you back shortly to reiterate the details. Do not leave your home."

The man hung up after Ken gave him Betsy's address and phone number.

Ken was relieved for the first time in weeks. Other than Betsy's and Moira's inadvertent involvement, which he wished he'd been more mindful of at the time (he couldn't be too hard on himself, he couldn't think of everything), it was happening just as he'd planned. It was all going to be okay. He switched on the television and flipped through the news channels quietly. Nothing yet. He turned it back off so June wouldn't question him. He never watched TV.

GUANGZHOU, CHINA

By the time Lou got to her office, there were dozens of messages from Geneva in her e-mail, mostly one or two liners as bits of information were transmitted to headquarters and then relayed to her.

Discussions with the U.S. government had resulted in approval for Dr. Wataabe to go to Portland. He was already on his way to the airport according to Director Bueller who suggested that, depending on the gravity of the situation, the WHO might fly Lou in too. However they were very concerned that she not be sent to the United States unless they could guarantee she could get out. The uncertainty of the unfolding events made it impossible to predict exactly what might happen in the ensuing days, and the WHO did not want to tie up their chief epidemiologist indefinitely in America as she was still very much needed in Southeast Asia.

Information was scant: beyond the name and location of the nursing home, all that was known about the deceased was that the patient was a 93 year old female who also had advanced Alzheimer's. Dr. Wataabe had run a search of emergency room visits in the Portland area before he boarded the private jet to the states and found no acute blips for respiratory illnesses in the past two weeks; this was somewhat reassuring as there didn't appear to be an unrecognized epidemic. County health officials were on site at the nursing home and beginning to interview the staff and residents. Since the trip from Geneva to Oregon would take about eight hours, the extent of the threat should be much clearer by the time Dr. Wataabe arrived. He would talk with Lou as soon as he had more information.

The president was preparing a press release that would go out within the next few hours. Right now the only people who knew anything were the county health officials and the captive staff and residents of the nursing home. But they would be making phone calls out of their impromptu prison and rumors would spread like wildfire if someone didn't start managing the information soon. Lou hoped the authorities would be pro-active with the media; regardless, she would not be able to share confidential details with Connor.

After reading the messages Lou sat at her desk with a cup of tea watching the sunrise and pondering just how a bed-ridden woman in a nursing home in the United States might have acquired H5N1. It was a puzzlement.

UNITED STATES

The anchorman stared solemnly at the camera as he read the message off the teleprompter. "At six o'clock this evening the Centers for Disease Control in Atlanta issued the following statement: *'Through routine influenza surveillance a case of H5N1 bird flu has been identified in the United States in a former resident of an Oregon extended care facility. The patient was elderly, suffered from a terminal disease, and died four days ago. While the virus has been demonstrated in the victim's system authorities have not confirmed if the actual cause of death was bird flu. The nursing home, its staff and residents have been placed under quarantine until an investigation can determine whether there is any additional disease present. Local health officials are working with experts from the CDC who have just arrived at the scene.*

We urge the public not to panic. An investigation is being conducted with due urgency to determine whether any additional measures are necessary. The Centers for Disease Control will update the news services for dissemination of information as appropriate.'"

Betsy had called to tell Ken the news was on all the stations and he was relieved he now had justification for tuning in. He'd been turning the television on surreptitiously every half hour since five o'clock when he'd gotten the call from the health department.

Of course Betsy sounded alarmed. She was supposed to be, as was everyone else, but him. That was exactly the point. Even though Ken knew that it would soon become apparent that there were no other H5N1 cases, the alarm would remain. The public would insist on better pandemic preparedness and the U. S. government would be forced to act, coercing the rest of the world to follow. It was a magnificent plan. He was heady with enthusiasm now for how he had single-handedly managed to change something that the WHO and CDC and every other respected scientist could not. He became so excited that he had to restrain himself. He adopted a studied concern as June came into the room. She appeared to be undergoing her own transformation into panicked citizen as she listened to the talking heads drumming up their own theories. Soon they would be calling prominent experts in the field. He might be one of them. He hadn't thought of that. Dr. Kenneth Culp had better prepare a statement, just in case.

• • •

Connor did not wear a mask onto the jet, but he did put it on discreetly after he was seated; he hadn't wanted to alarm the flight attendants or do anything that might cause the jet or him not to leave the airport. He'd heard the CDC announcement on the news while sitting at the gate in the terminal and knew by the time he got off the plane in Oregon he would probably not be the only one sporting facial protection. People would begin going crazy immediately.

CHAPTER 19

In the first twenty-four hours following the call from the CDC to the Oregon nursing home, these things happened:

A handful of employees of Cypress Arbor simply drove or walked away from the facility against orders, and without therefore being caught in the initial dragnet of investigation and testing; they had pressing issues elsewhere and could not afford to waste their time sitting around the retirement home when no compelling reason had been provided. After the health department team and the police arrived, it was discovered that some of the staff were missing. Belatedly, officers were stationed along pathways around the perimeter of the grounds in addition to the driveways.

County officials identified 37 residents of the nursing home with respiratory symptoms or fever. All the symptomatic patients were moved to the same wing of the facility and placed in isolation. CDC arrived 2 hours later with rapid test kits and confirmed that nine had bird flu.

Nineteen of the 52 employees held captive at Cypress Arbor had respiratory symptoms. They were corralled into a large meeting room where they waited for evaluation. Seven tested positive and were immediately isolated at Cypress Arbor where CDC medical personnel began to triage them. The remaining twelve were isolated as well and given their first doses of osmavir because they had just been exposed to H5N1 when they were grouped together with the infected staff by the health department.

Attempts were made to contact all remaining employees and recent visitors by telephone. Squads of EMT's, paramedics and nurses were dispatched to private homes to perform rapid testing after a brief training session by CDC personnel. All employees already in their homes were advised not to leave, but there was not enough police manpower to enforce quarantine of that many people. Against advice, some staff members went to the grocery store, some to the bank, some to relative's homes or to pick up children from day care or school. By 11 p.m. another six employees at home had tested positive for bird flu. A handful of employees including two staff members on sick leave had not been located and bulletins were sent to all area hospitals to be on the alert for additional cases.

Officials from the CDC apprised the president of the situation in the wee hours of the morning when the blossoming status of the epidemic was apparent, even if the source of it remained obscure.

The president reconvened his cabinet at 6 a.m. It was a contentious session with health and human services, defense, homeland security, interior, justice, state, commerce, labor and transportation secretaries all weighing in on issues from quarantine, to the economy, to national security. There was little stomach among most of them, including the president, to adhere to the stringent dicta of a disaster plan recommended by the CDC and the WHO. It was not clear to everyone around the table that there was any major disaster in the works. Twenty-some cases of the flu were not enough to bring to a halt the normal functioning of a nation. To overreact would incite unnecessary panic, was the majority opinion of the cabinet, if not the consensus. The meeting lasted for two hours. When it was over an updated statement was approved for immediate release. It would hit the news at 8:05 a.m. eastern standard time and all hell would break loose.

· · ·

After Ken had been directed to remain at home, an unwelcome if anticipated consequence of his action, he had called Crossfire to say he'd be taking two weeks off. He had accrued massive amounts of time off over his long career; it was perfectly reasonable to use some of it to recover from the death of his mother, whose name no one ever knew. His boss had understood completely.

Ken had gotten up as usual without the alarm on this, his first, morning at home and taken his coffee in front of the television where he was now, he noted with satisfaction, rather expected to be by June. There was very little new information at 6 a.m. Health officials were not talking to the press yet. Mostly the 'news' consisted of the talking heads confabulating about where all of this might be going. He was disgusted by the amount of air time pure conjecture got. These people knew nothing. At least this time their ignorance would be useful.

He muted the sound and pulled out the paper instead. More of the same all over the front page. One case of H5N1 and the nation was wide awake. There had been a few hundred cases in Southeast Asia and no one over here gave a damn. Such self-centeredness. Such hypocrisy. The government was too selfish to assist the third world and too short-sighted to realize this was the only means to ultimately protect itself. Pandemic. The very definition of it involved the world. How did the U.S. come to believe it could walk away scot-free? Its presence was required in the battle, and it had just been drafted, courtesy of Kenneth Culp.

• • •

Connor got up before dawn, and drove the rental car to Cypress Arbor. Since the authorities had not been forthcoming with the location of the extended care facility Connor had been forced to do a little research before he left L.A. yesterday. It had not been difficult. He had one of the desk jockeys at the news bureau call every facility in Oregon offering to deliver free wheelchairs. The only one that turned him down was Cypress Arbor in Multnomah County, a stammering receptionist saying, "...the facility would not be...accepting any...uh...deliveries... uh...indefinitely." A call to a colleague in Portland confirmed police blocking the entrance to the home. It had taken less than two hours.

Connor knew he would not be able to gain entry to Cypress Arbor. He didn't even try. He simply cased the place for context, then went to the county health department where he found a couple other news agencies camped. Evidently he was not alone in figuring it out. Probably the employees of the nursing home had been leaking word with cell phones all night. Connor expected hours to days of a news black-out; as officials tried to assess the situation they would stonewall the press.

He took up a position in the parking lot with his comrades and pulled out his computer searching for a wireless connection. Finding one, he proceeded to do some research. This was the heart of investigative journalism and he loved it. The authorities could tell their story voluntarily or he would try to beat them to it. Within a couple of hours he had a list of all the deaths in Multnomah County in a 48 hour period surrounding the day mentioned in the original press release the H5N1 patient had died. There were almost sixty people. Only the primary cause of death was listed on the web site and none of the death certificates mentioned avian influenza. He figured it wouldn't be that easy. It would take weeks for a pathologist to complete an autopsy and confirm H5N1 as the cause.

It would take too long to research the addresses of sixty people. Connor needed to narrow his list down. He discarded twelve people under the age of 65 as too young to be called 'elderly,' the word used by officials in describing the victim. He was able to throw out over half of the rest, people who died of heart attacks, strokes, trauma or suicide, clearly not consistent with a 'terminal disease,' the only other clue the press release had given. That left about twenty people, some of whom did not even have a cause of death listed yet. Several of the certificates listed cancer, and there were a few infections he noted: sepsis, hepatitis, HIV. And pneumonia.

Connor knew from past experience that a common cause of death in the elderly was pneumonia. He thought it a decent probability that someone with a terminal condition *and* H5N1 would have died of pneumonia. Since presumably no one knew of the H5N1 at the time of death, or CDC would have released the information then and not four days later, the patient's death was very likely attributed by the doctor of record to pneumonia. There were four certificates listing pneumonia as the primary cause of death. Connor decided to start with these, and e-mailed the condensed list to his office assistant in Los Angeles to search for addresses.

His deductions were solid: within another hour he had identified the H5N1 index case as one Anna Wardman, resident of Cypress Arbor Care Facility, deceased June 23, 2006, cause of death: pneumonia,

secondary cause of death: Alzheimer's disease, which certainly qualified as a terminal condition. It was almost 9 a.m. Not a bad morning's
work, and it was barely time for breakfast. He scratched his two day
beard growth wondering where he should go from here.

Anna Wardman.

Anna Wardman. Her name rolled around in his head.

He wondered how she got sick. In a nursing home in Oregon. No
H5N1 within thousands of miles as far as anyone knew. But, this is the
west coast he thought. Huge Asian population here. Was somebody
smuggling diseased poultry? But then how would a bed-ridden patient
be exposed to that? Person-to-person transmission? Who was the person then? Had to be an employee. Unless Wardman herself was Asian.
Could it be that a family member exposed her? CDC was no doubt
way ahead of him in figuring this out. They ought to be; it was their
job. Lou might know as well, but she couldn't tell him. Professional
privilege and all that. He knew. He respected that. But it didn't mean
he wasn't going to do his damnedest to find out.

Anna Wardman.

He thought he'd heard the name before. He shook the idea out of
his head; after a while in his business everyone's name started to sound
familiar. Maybe he would cruise the hospitals for information. Contact
employees. Try the family of Anna Wardman. He wondered if she had
any, if they had seen her prior to her death. Maybe she had no family.
Died alone.

Anna Wardman.

He couldn't dismiss it; there was definitely something about the
name. He packed up his computer and went to get some chow. Driving
in the car, searching for a suitable breakfast, he heard the bulletin on
National Public Radio:

*The Centers for Disease Control has confirmed 25 additional
cases of avian influenza of the H5N1 subtype in staff members and
residents of an extended care facility in Portland. The CDC, in con-
junction with local health care personnel, is working around the clock
to identify, isolate and treat all suspected persons with the disease. The
World Health Organization is assisting in determining which citizens
will be given preventive doses of the flu fighting drug osmavir, and who
might be a candidate for immunization with H5N1 vaccine.*

After review of the information the president has declared a health emergency for the state of Oregon. All unnecessary travel into and out of the state is discouraged.

Connor acknowledged Lou's worst suspicion had been correct. A new form of H5N1 was out of the bag, this one apparently transmissible from person to person. Connor glanced down at the mask he had not been wearing most of the day, thinking it was overkill until now. It looked like he'd be using it more conscientiously.

A quick call to Lou confirmed the details of the White House statement. The tests were valid. The outbreak was real and potentially deadly. No one knew yet how it might have started but all the employees of the nursing home were considered suspect. She also affirmed what he knew must be true from his previous interaction with WHO and CDC leaders: both organizations were pushing for a much more aggressive response to the situation but thus far had been stymied by the government's unwillingness to cooperate. It seemed the administration was panicked about the possibility of causing panic.

• • •

WHO and CDC officials, tuned in to their televisions to listen to the White House press release, were aghast at the federal response. They had spent the night exposing the tip of a dangerous iceberg. In unison they had stressed to the president's advisors that a national emergency must be declared with all travel severely restricted and policed within the country, and international egress halted completely. Instead, the administration had chosen to characterize the threat as a state-wide problem, a decision it would later come to regret.

• • •

June saw the same trailer running across the bottom of the screen on the still muted television. "Ken, there's a news bulletin," she called out to him as she picked up the remote and found the volume.

Ken was standing at the window wondering why there was a car bearing a county seal parked on the street in front of his house. With a man in it. Looking at his house. They were really taking this quarantine thing seriously. Fine. He had no intention of challenging it.

He returned to the den where the announcer was saying, "We interrupt your regularly scheduled program..."

June and Ken sat together on the couch and listened in silence to the latest announcement. The doorbell rang, startling June from her intense focus on the television but Ken did not move. June turned to look at him as she stood up to answer the door, and was as frightened by his appearance as by anything she had just heard on the news. His face was drained of all blood, with a cold smoothness evoking plaster. His lips were slightly parted, blanched, dead strips stretched over disordered, aged teeth. His eyes were unblinking, with huge purple shadows beneath them created by the acute angle of the morning sun, which also had the surrealistic effect of bleaching his fading hair suddenly to white. So appalling was the look of horror on his face, so frightening the frozen features and form of him, that June gasped aloud and reached over to shake him, fearing in the instant before she touched him that he might actually have turned to stone as in some myth whose details she had long ago forgotten. It was flesh that gave under her grip as she squeezed, and not granite, but her husband was not of it. He did not seem to notice her.

The doorbell rang again. Torn, she backed away distraught from the immobilized Ken, and smoothed her shirt down over her hips on her way to the door. She looked through the window pane at a man wearing a hospital mask and gown and carrying a clip board in his rubber-gloved hands. His appearance was neither welcome nor reassuring. June opened the door just a crack.

"Mrs. Wardman?"

"Uh..." June was momentarily perplexed. "Oh...yes. Yes." she stammered, distractedly looking over her shoulder toward the den. "What...what is it?"

"I'm from the health department and I need to ask you some questions. I can do that from right here on the porch if you like," he added helpfully. The young fellow seemed none too eager to enter. "Is Mr. Wardman here?" he asked attempting to peer around June.

"Yes," June answered, wondering how accurate her response was.

"Good. Perhaps you should get your husband," he paused, "Or I can come in."

"I'll get him," June said and closed the door while she went to retrieve Ken.

The man who came to the door shepherded by June appeared to the health worker as a debilitated elderly man, who may not have had influenza by the look of him but certainly ought to be checked for anemia. He gazed into the distance and seemed not to notice his visitor.

"I'm sorry I just have a few questions..." the official said, hesitating as he ogled the detached being in front of him. Then he proceeded to ask a more detailed version of the same things that the Oregon official had asked Ken over the phone, only this time June answered the questions. Ken spoke not at all until the man pointedly asked him if he was alright. He'd had to repeat himself and move somewhat to get right in Ken's line of sight where he couldn't be ignored. Ken had finally looked the man straight in the face and said brusquely, "We have no risk factors for bird flu and no illness in our household. We will not violate our quarantine. Are you done yet?"

Chastened, the official said that he was, but for advising them that someone from the health department would be back soon to swab their noses and to draw blood samples. After Ken had withdrawn again, the official gave June his card to phone immediately if either one of them developed symptoms of a cough, cold or fever.

By the time June closed the door Ken was back on the couch methodically scrolling through channels looking for more news. His body was hunched forward with both hands gripping the remote tightly, the ghastly pallor of his complexion serving to highlight a feral cast to his eyes that bore into the television screen. The intensity of his communion with the inanimate monitor was unnerving to June who paced fretfully behind the couch hardly knowing what to do. She was concerned about the flu but she was more concerned about Ken. She had just determined to at least call Betsy when the telephone rang, startling her just as the doorbell had done. She skittered toward the phone, one hand over her breast, and picked up the receiver.

"Mom?"

June heard the fear in Betsy's voice immediately. "What is it honey?" she replied trying to steady herself.

"It's Moira. She has a fever."

. . .

Connor finished breakfast and was sitting in a booth at the diner on the phone to his assistant in L.A. who had been searching for information on family members of Anna Wardman, and employees of Cypress Arbor. He nodded for the waitress to pour him another cup of coffee as he jotted down the phone numbers of several employees to call for eyewitness information. You had to be very careful how much stock you put into an insider's report, especially if it could not be corroborated, but it was a start. The county, CDC and WHO hadn't admitted to anything except what was officially contained in the two press releases. It had been some fifteen hours since the first one.

Connor's assistant was researching Anna's place of birth for high school information, marriage certificates and any other clues as to her identity or the existence of any relatives. This would take a while.

After leaving the waitress a generous tip, Connor returned to his car and called all the Cypress Arbor employees he had phone numbers for and found a few who would actually speak to him. He usually encountered a mix of people in the course of an investigation, from types who were paranoid about their privacy being invaded, to the terminally shy and inarticulate, to those who were delighted to give information out for public consumption whether or not it was accurate. This story was no exception. Unfortunately he was not able to find anyone trapped inside the facility to speak with and he didn't have much to write about yet. He did notice that a lot of the employees' names sounded Asian. A few of the people he spoke with had eastern accents. He had quizzed everyone about recent travel outside the country and poultry exposure but had no admissions of either. And no one admitted being related to Anna Wardman.

Connor sat in the car wondering what to try next. He had brought a phone book with him from the hotel this morning and thumbed through it looking for the veterinary listings. There were a couple dozen. Checking his watch he figured they were open by now. He began calling, looking for any information on livestock or pet bird illnesses and found none. He tried the pet stores as well without success. He had the radio on quietly in the background in case there was another bulletin. He stewed for a while, drove back to the health department, drove by Cypress Arbor again. No change. Nothing happening.

He called Lou. He couldn't remember the name of the fellow who was the H5N1 researcher that had called and aggravated Lou so much when she was in Chongqing. He was pretty sure she told him the man worked on the west coast. Maybe he was close by and Connor could interview him on the breaking news. It might be more of a story than he currently had. Lou gave him Ken Culp's name but couldn't remember the name of the company he worked for, saying she was sure it was in California. After a few Googles Connor had it narrowed down to seventeen laboratories and hit the jackpot at the first one he called. Sort of.

"Crossfire Laboratory."

"Hello, may I speak with Dr. Kenneth Culp?"

"I'm sorry, he isn't in today."

"Oh, he isn't?"

"No."

"But he does work there?"

"Yes."

"When will he be back?"

"I'm not sure, but I think he said a couple weeks. Would you like to leave a message?"

No, no thank you. I don't suppose you are authorized to give out his home phone number?"

"No sir."

"Alright. Is there anyone else there who is qualified to speak about the avian flu virus?"

"Well, probably nearly everyone here but me. But Dr. Culp usually conducts any interviews. I'd be happy to leave a message."

"No...thanks. I'll get back to you."

Connor tried to call Lou to ask if she was familiar with anyone else at Crossfire Laboratory but she wasn't answering her phone, or she was on another call. He too got a call just then from L.A. His coworker had found Anna's place of birth, a small town in Northern California, not too far from the location of several of the research labs on his list, including Crossfire, and close to the manufacturer of H5N1 vaccine, PharmaGlobal. Connor made a snap decision to go to San Francisco. A quick call to the ticket counter at the Portland airport revealed that despite government discouragement, planes were still landing and taking off. He didn't know how long that would last but nothing was happening here. He might as well check out some different leads. And he would wear his mask.

· · ·

Betsy's voice was pinched with strain as she told June about Moira. "She felt fine when she went to bed last night. I didn't think too much about her sleeping in this morning. I figured she was bored, not being able to go outside and play or see her friends..." June could hear the hitching creep into Betsy's breathing as she fought to hold back the tears.

"I thought she just...turned over and...fell back asleep. But when she did get up she was flushed and her nose was runny...While I had... the thermometer...in her mouth she started to cough...she could barely keep her mouth closed long enough...to get her...temperature...It's 103...I don't know what to do... She looks miserable Mom..." poured out before she finally let go with sobbing.

"Okay honey. Calm down," June said trying to calm herself at the same time. She looked at Ken who was totally oblivious to the conversation, still flipping through channels, pausing to hear other renditions of the CDC press release as he encountered them.

"Ken?" she said. Then, "Ken!"

"He turned toward her, his bushy eyebrows knitted in consternation at her interruption of his data collection. He didn't speak, just looked at her, challenging her to say why she had bothered him.

"It's Betsy, Ken," June said, cupping the receiver to her chest and not knowing what to make of his accusatory stare. "Moira has a fever."

"Moira?" Ken croaked, the name of his darling grandchild the first sound to escape his lips voluntarily in hours.

"Yes, she's sick and Betsy's worried and doesn't know what to do."

"Betsy's always worried." Ken said gruffly. "Let me speak to her."

"Who...Betsy?"

"No. Moira," he barked.

Ken spoke to the little girl gently, solicitously. He could hear the stuffiness in her voice, the cough that interrupted her. He told her to be a good girl and go back to bed and rest. Then he shoved the phone back at June.

"What should I tell Betsy?"

"Tell her," Ken said, "that Moira has a cold. She's had colds before. Tell her to stop getting hysterical and take care of her. Tell her to turn off the television if she can't keep her wits about her."

The harshness of his response cut June to the core. Ken had never had model communication skills, but how could he be so insensitive to his own daughter?

She was about to ask what remedies Betsy had on the shelf when Betsy said, "Mom, I have to go, Jake says the health department is here."

• • •

Connor's first stop in San Francisco was PharmaGlobal. It was late afternoon but he figured someone of importance would still be around, considering the potential marketability of Avimmune in the unfolding crisis. He was right, and found the CEO willing to speak with him personally. Conner was ushered into the lush corporate office of a successful U.S. businessman, all done up in expensive fabrics, fine wood and grand views. All this, and his ship hadn't even come in yet, Connor thought, mulling over the profits PharmaGlobal was likely to reap in the ensuing months.

J.B. Vaughn shook his hand and attempted to appear concerned with the crisis, answering all of Connor's questions with a polish that belied his attempts to sound spontaneous. Connor thought he could almost see the dollar signs spinning through Vaughn's eyeballs like symbols on a slot machine as he spoke of the value of PharmaGlobal's likely contribution to fighting the disease. Connor could hardly blame him; it was probably a significant gamble to have produced the vaccine in the absence of a pandemic. Certainly no one else had done it. Still, the idealist in him was a bit offended that the forced gravity of the man's demeanor barely concealed his suppressed glee at his enviable business position. Connor was not inclined to take so much pleasure in the world's misery. He left the tony trappings with a rather sour taste in his mouth.

Connor checked his watch: it was now after five. There was no point heading to Crossfire Laboratory. Despite Lou's not having another scientist to recommend there, he thought he might still go tomorrow and see if anyone had the credentials and desire to comment on H5N1. If no one would speak to him he could at least obtain information on when Dr. Culp might be available.

Connor decided to go to the main library and look up Anna Wardman; he still couldn't dispel his sense of familiarity with her. "Bingo," he said softly as the computer screen of the card catalog lit up with references for Anna Wardman. It was one of his better hunches he thought, as a dozen or more tomes appeared: *Modern Medical Technology and Ancient Ethical Questions; Active Dying; Euthanasia: A Prescription for Our Times.* And more.

As he perused the list he suddenly remembered why the name was familiar. He had seen Dr. Wardman, a widely respected philosopher and medical ethicist, on the lecture circuit, had heard her speak at some of the health conferences he had covered early in his career. How old had she been? It was hard to tell. He conjured up a spry slip of a woman with penetrating eyes and a strong voice that belied her stature and years. He had little skill in judging the ages of people older than he. How long ago was it? A decade? More? She certainly didn't have dementia then. Could it be the same person?

What an interesting turn of events if true. He checked the publication dates of the books and found they were in keeping with Anna's age as listed on the death certificate. It might still be just the coincidence of a name. But in Connor's experience there weren't a lot of coincidences in life, just connections that hadn't been explained yet. Connor looked around the library for an unoccupied carrel and settled into a computer station to find out more about Anna Wardman.

• • •

The health officer would only allow one parent to travel with Moira in the ambulance to the hospital. Her rapid avian influenza test had come back positive and the results sent Betsy into a flurry of anxiety and tears. She and Jake went into their bedroom to discuss who would go along. Jake took Betsy's shuddering frame into his arms and held her tightly, trying to contain the fear in his own heart as much as the distress in hers. Much as he wanted to be with his family Jake knew that his anguish could not justify separating his wife from his daughter. They agreed it was Betsy who would go. As she quieted down he released her and, grim-faced, told her that Moira needed her to be strong.

Since they would all still remain under quarantine it would be impossible for Betsy to return home or for Jake to spell her at Moira's bedside. They packed a few belongings in silence, Jake blinking back tears as he searched Moira's room for something special to send with her to the hospital. He spied the teddy bear she had been carrying around lately and tenderly placed it in Betsy's bag, quickly wiping his eyes before he turned back to face his wife. Jake maintained his composure at the front door, waving to the back of the ambulance as it pulled away holding everything dear to him. When he was sure Betsy could no longer see him he dropped his face into his hands and cried.

CHAPTER 20

UNITED STATES
June 28

Anna Wardman had graduated summa cum laude from Smith College with a degree in philosophy, earning her doctorate in the same subject from the University of Chicago a few years later. Connor was unable to find out anything else biographical on either the internet or the pages of some of her books he had pulled off the shelf. If she married she had kept her maiden name, as not only her books but her death certificate confirmed. But how to be sure it was one and the same person? He did not have access to an address for Anna Wardman prior to her institutionalization at Cypress Arbor and he wasn't sure how to get it. The nursing home was incommunicado. He could probably call the alumni office of either of her alma maters in the morning and get up to date addresses on the author, but still, how to match that person with the 93 year old Alzheimer's patient in an Oregon nursing home without access to Cypress Arbor's records?

Connor was stymied and his usual response to that predicament was to sit on the information for a while and let new ideas percolate into his consciousness. Trying too hard to make something happen often paralyzed the whole process. His mind was better at problem-solving when left alone than when directed too rigidly.

Time for a late supper. Maybe some light reading. He flipped through a few pages of *The Meaning of Life, Death and Dying in a Modern World: A Conversation,* and decided to check it out.

• • •

"Dad, I don't know what to think. I'm so scared," said Betsy from Moira's hospital room.

Ken listened on the phone to his daughter's voice from the deep abyss of a well into which he had fallen the moment the news of the additional H5N1 cases had registered with him. He had no idea how long ago that had been. Twenty minutes? An hour? A day? What did it mean? He was still trying to figure it out. Using every brain fiber he possessed he was trying to understand how the news could be so wrong. There couldn't be twenty-five cases of avian flu, there could only be one. The one he caused. With the attenuated H5N1 sample. It required a huge inoculum just to give the disease to his mother. It had no communicable characteristics in vitro. In the lab. It could not have been passed to anyone else. The authorities were wrong. All wrong. But where? How? Was there something the matter with the rapid test kits? Was there cross reactivity of the test with another, common germ? Was something as banal as a common cold virus causing false-positive avian flu results?

And his granddaughter had been snared in the mess. She was a kid. With a cold. And they had carted her off to the hospital, no doubt scaring his daughter, who was excitable under the mildest of circumstances, out of her mind.

Things were spinning out of control. He needed to help the teams on the scene: this inadvertent spread of misinformation was causing mass mayhem. In his grand scheme there was supposed to be concern, alarm, even panic from people who panicked anyway. But misdiagnosis was not in his plan. How was he going to help without arousing suspicion? How could he get or give out information without putting himself in the limelight where his association with the nursing home might be noticed?

He didn't know. He needed to know. His mind was spinning: spinning out questions without answers; spinning around problems without explanations; spinning in circles of guilt, and away from fears that he refused to confront. He was very, very busy. But it was all in his head.

He looked at June from time to time when she wasn't watching. June didn't understand and he certainly couldn't tell her. He was aware of everything happening around him but it was as though he was viewing it all from a distance. June wanted him to calm her fears, explain things to her, but he couldn't when he didn't understand himself. So he remained active, but behind the mask of his face which bore no reflection of the frenzy inside.

"Dad? Dad?"

There was Betsy again. How long had he been holding the receiver? Why couldn't he hear her? She sounded so far away.

June had answered the phone in the den and had spoken to Betsy first, before holding the instrument out to him, but he wouldn't take it. Hardly recognized it. It was extraneous to his current mission which was comprehension. Comprehension of the data. He sat like a stone, refusing to accept June's offer of the receiver. After looking at him with disbelief, June thrust the phone at him, finally demanding with the fierceness of her gesture that he snap out of whatever had gripped him and respond to his child who was desperately in need of her father right now. He placed the phone closer to his ear.

"Dad?"

He could hear sobbing. Ken knew that if he moved his lips he could make a noise, but he wasn't sure what he would say, so he said nothing.

June, hearing Betsy's cries and choked to tears with her own anxiety and frustration, took the phone back from her impaired husband and managed to say, "Betsy, I'm here. You're dad is not...not well...I don't know what's the matter. I know he wants to be there for you but this whole thing has him so upset... I...I don't know..." She paused, trying to regain control. Swallowing her own misery with a tremendous effort of will, she went on, "Honey, tell me what the doctor said."

Betsy told her mother that someone from the CDC had met them at the hospital and repeated the avian test which was again positive. For the time being Moira seemed okay. Her temperature was 102 and she was stuffy and coughing more, but her chest x-ray was fine and she was not having any trouble breathing. Betsy said that the doctor started Moira on osmavir intravenously and assured her that Moira would have the best care modern medicine had to offer. From June's perspective Betsy was more upset about where things might go than with where they were. June realized that Betsy's fears were valid: they both knew about the fatality rates for H5N1 and had no illusions about advanced medical care being able to save Moira if the infection progressed. After all, Ken was an expert on it, had filled them in on all the scary details over the years.

Their talk turned to the inevitable questions that begin with 'why' and 'how' as they struggled with their anguish. Betsy's breathing calmed as she talked to June. The cadence of her mother's voice, the rhythm of the syllables rising and falling in familiar soothing tones quieted, at least for the moment, her rising terror.

•   •   •

Night fell. Late. Just past the longest day of the year in the northern hemisphere. Ken didn't notice. It was all the same to him. The seconds passed seamlessly into minutes, the minutes into hours. There were snatches of sleep. Purely unintentional. Sleep was not something he wished for. No friend. No comfort. The irrational themes that his mind casually accepted in dreams were too difficult to distinguish from wakeful reality. Nothing made sense sleeping or waking. Ken made no effort to change clothes or go to the bedroom. He lay on the couch, arms folded across his chest and waited in the dark, prayed even, not for sleep, but for clarity.

He was awake when the phone rang later that night, but did not answer it. June came into the living room where he'd been camped and handed him the portable set saying, "Ken, I think it's important. It's someone from the CDC asking for Dr. Culp." Ken blinked. "I'm sorry," June continued as she handed him the phone, "I didn't catch his name."

Ken sat up on the couch and rested the phone in his lap while he put his glasses on. He cleared his throat and his face resumed the engaged character of a human being. In the dim light June had switched on, she was able to recognize again the remote vestiges of a professional in her disheveled husband as he took the call.

"Dr. Culp here."

"Dr. Culp, Dr. James Demint, from the CDC. I'm sorry to disturb you on your vacation but I'm sure you recognize the gravity of the crisis unfolding. I'll come straight to the point. We've got two additional deaths in the past eight hours we think are directly attributable to the H5N1 strain in Oregon. You have the closest and most secure lab, with the best electron microscope on the west coast. Our team would like your help in looking at the pathology specimens from the lungs of the victims to confirm whether the cause of death is H5N1, and in making some assessment of the invasiveness of the organism at the cellular level. Time is of the essence. We need to have proof of the cause of death and an indication of the pathogenicity of the virus to enlist full governmental cooperation in fighting it. You're the expert on H5N1. Will you help?"

Ken could hardly believe his ears.

They called him.

To help.

With the slides in front of him he could dispel once and for all the notion that H5N1 was at fault here. He was being handed a chance to fix the things that were going wrong in his scheme. He could maintain anonymity as long as his picture wasn't published anywhere, and he would make sure it wasn't. They had always given him a hard time at the lab because he refused to have one taken for his file.

"Certainly." Ken responded. "You can count on it. When can you have the specimens here?"

"Within a couple hours. The jet is on the runway ready to take off with two of our techs, a doc from CDC and a WHO rep."

"I'll meet your liaisons at Crossfire."

"Great. Thanks Dr. Culp."

"Happy to help." Ken said with sincerity. "Uh...before you go Dr. Demint, I've been very concerned about what I'm hearing on the news. Is there anything else you can tell me?"

Ken was informed there were now thirty five confirmed cases, with seven people in serious condition in local hospitals in addition to the two deaths in the past few hours. Since the bulletins had been released by the government, hospitals and outpatient medical offices had been flooded with people presenting with respiratory symptoms, concerned that they had the avian flu and demanding prescriptions for osmavir. CDC was in the process of getting rapid test kits to area medical providers to assess how many of these patients were infected. According to Demint there was every reason to believe from these early indications that the H5N1 strain satisfied all the criteria for a pandemic organism.

Ken heard what was being said, but his mind refused to believe it, so convinced was he that malfunctioning test kits or some other unidentified fallacy in the process was just the latest snafu of the well-meaning but inept organizations entrusted with national and global health. He did what any person firmly entrenched in denial would do: changed the subject.

"Where do you think it came from?" Ken asked.

"We have no idea. We picked this up on our routine influenza surveillance for God's sake. The index case from the nursing home was bedridden, hadn't been out of the room for months. She had no personal Asian connections. The best guess is that she was infected by one of the employees in the nursing home, many of whom have close immigrant ties. By the way, I'm sending her tissue sample too. You can look at all three and compare."

. . .

June looked at Ken dumbfounded as he snapped out of his fugue state and carried on a perfectly reasonable conversation with the man from the CDC. Indeed when he hung up, he stood up and acted as though nothing at all had happened the past few weeks. His color was good, his features concerned but natural in appearance. Gone was the pallid specter of the man she'd been living with.

"I've got to go," he said.

"What?" June asked, "Where?"

"To the office." Ken replied as though surprised she didn't realize.

"You can't leave," June protested, incredulous. "You're supposed to stay here."

"Oh. That's right," Ken said, pausing on his way to the bedroom where he intended to shower quickly and change. "It doesn't matter," he shrugged, proceeding. "I have to go."

"You can't go."

Ken turned around and looked June full in the face. "Not only can I, I must. My presence is required. I'm an expert and they need me. Look out the window. There isn't anyone guarding the house. No one will stop me and I'll be back in a few hours or less. I won't be missed."

"But what about the outbreak? What about your infecting someone else?"

"June," Ken said with impatience, "I've been immunized, remember? I can't get it."

"Oh. I forgot," she said looking down, chastised. She smoothed the front of her nightgown. "Of course."

"Furthermore I'm not convinced there is an outbreak."

June looked up at him sharply. "What do you mean you're not convinced?" she asked.

"The tests are wrong. I'm going to look at the slides and prove it." And with that he continued his march to the bedroom, looking very much like the man he had been before his mother died.

• • •

WHO, CDC and federal officials met through the night to strategize. The WHO decided to make all of its doses of Avimmune available immediately for use in the United States. They were hashing out with CDC and the government how to ration the immunizations. Initial policy was also being set for dispensing osmavir which would need to be rationed as well, even though there was much more of it than the vaccine. A secondary response for vaccine administration was also being planned for the 60 million doses of Avimmune nearing completion at PharmaGlobal. State and local disaster teams were being placed on alert for the recommendations which would be announced at a press conference first thing in the morning. Everyone wanted an evaluation of the pathology slides before proceeding, and the appropriate CDC and WHO team members were on their way to Crossfire to complete that mission.

All the major news outlets had been invited to the hastily outfitted Multnomah County Health Department for a briefing to inform the public and quell whatever aspects of the spreading misinformation they could. There were rumors aplenty arising now with Cypress Arbor, health department and county employees calling relatives and friends with the snippets of information they had gleaned through their involvement in the crisis, magnified and distorted in the telling and retelling. Certainly just the facts the officials intended to present were going to be scary enough but it had to be done; there was no getting around it.

• • •

Ken sat hunched over the eyepiece of his electron microscope. He could have put the image on the computer monitor for the others present in the room to see, but he wanted to view the material alone first. He chose his mother's lung tissue to begin with, identified on the slide only as index A. How strange this turn of events, he thought as he adjusted the lens; who could have predicted I would be called to give an opinion on my own mother's death? He was appalled to realize as he settled in to focus that the scientist in him was eager to see how the virus appeared in his mother's tissue. Was that too macabre a thought for a son to have? He thought not; he was sure Anna would understand his excitement as he zoomed in on the specimen.

Scrolling through the fields he experienced a moment of triumph as he marveled at the pattern of the organism's presence: it appeared exactly as he had predicted it would from his mouse cell cultures. There were plenty of the characteristic avian particles clumped together in the interstices between the cells, but very few viruses actually penetrating the cells, and there was only minimal cellular destruction. Ken pulled back from the instrument to reflect on his experiment of one. His hypothesis was correct: it had indeed taken a whopping growth of the virus just to provide enough organisms to harm enough cells to kill his mother. If she had not been so debilitated already from the Alzheimer's Anna might even have survived it. In hindsight he was not surprised it had taken her so long to die after he had inoculated her.

Leaning into the eyepiece once more, Ken communed silently with his mother through the preserved flesh captured so vividly by the instrument. I wish I didn't have to be the one, Ken said soundlessly to the woman represented by the lung cells beneath him, but I am glad your suffering is over. He sighed quietly. For the first time since he had taken her life he entertained a hope that he too might find peace.

As he drew away from the optical, Ken looked again at the hands that had committed the act, trying to see them as blameless. He watched his fingers push the buttons that would allow his visitors to see the slide he had just scanned on a large monitor mounted on the wall of his office, and thought how they looked so benign. He panned the contents of the specimen for his guests, struck by the sense that his hands were foreign objects, no longer part of the flesh of him but robotic attachments taking direction from some source other than his own mind. Likewise Ken found he was able to speak to the CDC and WHO officials about the tissue findings even while he contemplated issues of which they had no knowledge. His voice seemed to come from other parts of him operating, like his hands, without conscious input.

After all those present in the room agreed that the index patient had a significant lung infection with H5N1 which she probably died from, Ken switched the monitor off again and returned to his private view through the eyepiece of the microscope, replacing his mother's slide quickly with Index B, one of the two subsequent patients who had supposedly died of H5N1. He could hardly wait to see the looks on the faces of these authorities when they realized their rapid tests were wrong. He flipped through the knobs on the instrument to bring the new slide into focus to prove to these men they were mistaken...and... and...snapped his head up...

... he pulled the slide back out of the instrument and checked the identification on it again, peering intently, adjusting to the reading distance of his aging eyes to be sure he was seeing it correctly. He looked at the box of samples the officials had brought and checked the label there... and...chose another slide marked Index B...he was sure this time...and focused...and...jerking away from the lens once more, compulsively repeated the sequence of removing the slide and checking the label again...and yet again.

Ken's guests were eyeing him quizzically while he frantically focused, viewed and replaced the different samples. He went from Index B to C with the same frenzy, then back to A. Ken was flying through the slides changing them in and out and strewing them about the desk as he discarded each.

As suddenly as it started, Ken's furious evaluation of the slides stopped. He pushed back from the scope and eyed the evidence cast haphazardly about him. He sat outwardly motionless, inwardly preoccupied by a massive, quaking upheaval. Worlds were clashing, all reason confounded, the horizon, pitching.

There are extraordinary moments in time, increments of definable existence when the magnitude of the unfolding event occupies every functioning brain cell. There is no room for extraneous thought; all consciousness overflows with the eruption. Time immediately becomes warped, alternately seeming to stand still or flee. In the instant of the revelation one can hear dust motes falling, feel the spaces between the seconds. Individual grains of sand can be seen to rush by the neck in the hourglass, cruelly taunting us to entertain vain fantasies of reversing the flow, pushing the grains back, unwinding the clock. The imagination flies into action seeking a path around the inevitable. The mind insists on reworking the scene. Playing it out another way. A happy ending. Wake up. Please, please, wake up.

By his hand.

By his hand.

Not one death. Not one. But many. Hundreds, thousands, millions. What had gone wrong? Oh God what had gone wrong?

To the others in the room Ken's cataclysm manifested as nothing more than a prolonged, and now uncomfortable silence from the man with his back to them. They exchanged glances before one of the officials spoke, rousing him. "Dr. Culp, may we see the slides?"

Ken was perceptibly startled by the sudden intrusion of sound. Something automated inside him switched on the monitor, removed one slide and mounted another as requested. It didn't matter which one, Index B or C. They were both the same, and vastly, recognizably different from Index A. Even a lay person could see the change. He scrolled through the samples one by one for them. He focused the instrument without even looking at the knobs, his eyes never leaving the monitor as though hoping he might discover some trick of vision or sleight of hand that was causing the unimaginable images in front of him.

The virus was there. All over the place. In between the cells, and more especially, inside the cells, filling them, digesting them, exploding them. He scrolled through each sample, the green nano-globules of virions refusing to go away, mocking him with their very existence.

A man with an extensive electron microscopy background of his own said, "It's not good," as he looked around at the others. He turned to Ken for confirmation and was astonished by the sudden change as the man faced him. Ken's face was gaunt, his features sucked back in a grimace drained of blood.

"No," Ken whispered hoarsely, "It's not,"

The people assembled from CDC and WHO looked at one another; H5N1 was distressing to all of them, but it seemed particularly unnerving to Dr. Culp.

Ken resumed staring at the screen.

Here it was right in front of him: the evidence that he had been absolutely right about the potential human infectivity of H5N1. The final criterion. He had been right. Right goddammit, and no one had believed him. He had tried so hard in the lab to create the strain taunting him from the monitor, the one invasive to humans. He was sure it could be done and yet he had failed to do it. Had not been able to coerce the virus, despite hundreds of attempts, to adapt itself to mammalian cells. No, beneath his watchful eye, his coddling, and care, the rich broths and nutrient-filled petri dishes, the virus had failed to perform. In vitro.

He had selected the most innocuous strain to use on his mother. It had shown no predilection for mouse cells. Indeed, like his mother's lung, the mouse samples had showed almost no cellular penetration. Who could have predicted it...away from his watchful gaze...in her... this mutation... this accident of nature?

His brain was screaming at the unfairness of it, blocking out the discussion going on around him. How did it happen? He had created that which he sought to create, but in the wildly uncontrolled living laboratory of life. In vivo. In the substance of the woman who gave him life he had unwittingly spawned this agent of death. He had finally illuminated the path of H5N1 as it shifted to pandemic form but the doing of it had not served to affirm his brilliant contributions to science, but had spiraled instead into an abomination of circumstances that utterly destroyed his life's work. Countless lives lost instead of spared.

Moira.

Oh God, Moira.

"Dr. Culp? Dr. Culp?"

The insistent voice chafed at his consciousness, reeled him back. "Yes?" Ken answered, feeling a staggering vertigo trying to rise from the abyss to the task at hand. With a mighty effort he summoned himself to the present, buried his inconceivable mistake, and determined he would resume the role he had played all of his life. Played flawlessly until now. Respected researcher. Acclaimed benefactor of human kind. A professional delivering sought-after advice.

That was all he wanted...ever wanted...to help prepare the world for what was coming...These people were here now asking for help. He would help. He must. Even if they vilified him later, as they must.

In this moment his voice was still respected. He would be all that he was trained to be. Now that he could see what had happened, understood that a mistake of unimaginable consequences had been made, made by him, he momentarily shut out the guilty son, the hopeful planner, the shattered plotter and put back on the mantle of scientist. Ken was fully engaged, his eyes alert, his hearing keen, his acuity focused.

"What is your view?" one of the men from the CDC asked.

Ken turned and faced them as he delivered his analysis in the self-assured cadence of a man with years of experience. "The organism has clearly been transformed by spontaneous mutation in vivo from an innocuous form in Index A, to a much more aggressive strain capable of extensive attachment and penetration of human cells, as seen in the tissue samples of B and C. At least the respiratory mucosa in front of us is remarkably susceptible to the shift in this strain of H5N1 as demonstrated by the profound changes between the lung epithelium in the first case compared to the subsequent cases. These changes have heretofore not been demonstrated either in vitro or in vivo, although I have long predicted them. Nevertheless I am stunned by the ease with which the virus has managed to mutate, apparently in the single incubation cycle of one individual, when it has been so resistant to multiple manipulations in vitro."

"I am forced to conclude..." Ken began choking on the words as they came out, his speech lagging a split second behind the thought that had already formed and consumed him. Finding it impossible to continue to face the others in the room, he turned back toward the monitor and delivered the rest of his comments to the inanimate particles trapped on the screen.

"...which should not be surprising to any of us...," but it was a revelation to him, something he knew he once knew, but had somehow misplaced...

"...that the virus has demonstrated it is...unpredictable," swallowing hard,

"...and highly adaptable."

Ken's mouth was set in grim lines as he forced himself to turn around again and address the men in the room in a solemn and controlled timbre. "I believe we have on our hands a highly pathogenic virus fulfilling the final criterion of transmissibility for pandemic, and I suggest we do everything we are capable of to stop it."

"Thank you for your help. We will not forget you Dr. Culp," the man from CDC said as he shook Ken's hand. They left immediately, bearing their slides and ill tidings.

In the ensuing minutes the struggling sides of Ken reassembled themselves inside him. He was finally whole again, allowing all the competing parts to recognize, take stock of, and judge the others. He was aghast, terrified, remorseful, ashamed, appalled; he was horrified that a part of him remained proud that his prediction of the virus' contagious capability had proven accurate, even as the rest of him recoiled in horror from the thought, beyond mortification, of the heinous wrong he had inadvertently wrought.

With calmness and clarity he had not known for days, weeks, months perhaps, he was able to see how the virus had led him astray, lulled him into complacency, turned his noble mission into a thing of unparalleled evil, made it into exactly that which he was working to avoid. He perceived now his mistake: the basic assumption he made was faulty. He presumed the strain was harmless because it had caused no harm in the lab. In vitro he had come to think of his virus as sterile. In vivo it had come to fruition. He had never thought of infecting his mother as an experiment, but it was the most successful of his life.

There was undoubtedly a philosophical lesson in all this. His mother would have found much to ponder, to magnify, to examine in all this, but he found he could not. And that was his second mistake he knew, to have allowed Anna's logic to inform his own. His mother had called it euthanasia. But he had never really believed it. He had committed murder and the weapon was H5N1. Each influenza death would be another. By his hand.

Oh God, but that was not my plan, he cried out as he pulled a shock of his hair through his fingers.

It doesn't matter, responded another voice, stilling the hand on his head. You will not be judged for your intentions.

Ken sat up and looked around him at what seemed now just the toys of his former existence. The microscope, the lab, the stacks of slides waiting to be assessed, the computer with its mega-memory and lightning-fast processor able to read the genetic code of the organism in minutes. His work had been turned into ashes. He had done it. Not alone. No, not alone, but in concert with the virus. An ancient bit of protein. Barely alive. He could accept his portion of the blame, unjust as it was, but who would call the eight-gene microscopic sequence to task for its role? To whom or what would the virion be held accountable? With all the DNA in his cells, he should have been smarter than the nano-bit of RNA. But it had won. He was beaten.

Ken spent a long time sitting there in the cool dimness of his office hoping to find some magical answer, some fix, some way to cope with the hideousness of what was happening. He had no cure to offer. Nothing more to sacrifice. He had donated his life and his mother's to the cause and it had all backfired. He would have liked to find comfort in tears. But they would not come.

His beloved Moira was sick. He might as well have stuck the swab in her nose himself, and into the faces of all the others who were ill. Those who had died. Those who would die. His name was, forever would be, linked with death.

Dawn, creeping in through the windows, roused him to move. What was to be done? There was no point in staying here. He had accomplished his final task, proving H5N1's transmissibility.

From the back of a deep file drawer he withdrew a small bag and verified its contents. He stuck it in his pants pocket and looked around at his office, then shut off the light and closed the door behind him.

We will not forget you Dr. Culp.

No indeed, you will not.

• • •

Connor got up early and grabbed a continental breakfast in the hotel lobby before heading out to Crossfire Laboratory. He entered the foyer of the building and was greeted by a pleasant receptionist.

"What can I do for you?" she asked.

"Hi, I'm Connor Mackenzie from the Associated Press," he said as he flashed his credentials. "I called the other day looking for Dr. Culp."

"Oh yes," Carolyn replied. "I remember you. I'm afraid Dr. Culp is still out of the office though."

"Bad timing for a vacation," Connor observed. "He's got to be glued to the TV with this avian flu thing."

"Well, Dr. Culp's not on vacation. He's taking time off for a death in the family."

"Oh. I'm sorry," Connor said. "Well, I was in the area and just thought I'd drop by and see if he might be in. Is there anyone else in the lab who might talk to me? Give me a researcher's point of view on the developments?"

"I'd be happy to call our director down to meet with you." Carolyn replied.

"Thanks. That would be great."

"Make yourself comfortable," the young woman said and pointed to some chairs as she rose to locate her boss.

Instead, Connor entertained himself by wandering the perimeter of the room reading the plaques on the walls. The certificates and licenses that were neatly framed attested to the brain power and professional standing of those who were employed at the facility. As he moved to the center of the room he encountered a large glass case whose position of prominence in the lobby bespoke the most prized treasures. He read the titles and the years and the names on the trophies, medals and statues lining the shelves to pass the time. A gleaming silver globe was distinguished by its conspicuous location in the middle of the display. Connor made out the words "Pritzker International Fellow" etched into the trailing curve of the orb. He leaned in to read the name engraved on the silver plate of the base. Reflections in the surface of the glass on the display case made it necessary for him to move around the cabinet to make the whole thing out. Moving backwards he read Culp first, then... W... then... Kenneth.

Kenneth W. Culp

W.

Really?

He moved to the diplomas framing the case. The curly formal scripts were hard to decipher. Each person in the lab must have had ten degrees he thought as he scanned over fifty of them looking for Culp's. There it was, Yale, PhD.: Kenneth W. Culp.

Damn. What's the W.?

And then he saw it on a certificate just below: University of Chicago, Anna Wardman's alma mater. Bachelor of Science, *summa cum laude* awarded to:

Kenneth Wardman Culp.

The receptionist had just reentered the atrium. "Dr. Neil will be right with you."

"Thanks," Connor responded coolly, despite the sudden increase in his heart rate.

He looked back at the display, calculating his next words carefully. "I do hope Dr. Culp will recover from the death of his...what did you say...brother?...soon."

"Well, yes, we hope so, but...no, Mr. Mackenzie...it was his mother who died," Carolyn replied correcting Connor.

"Really," Connor intoned. "Was it unexpected?"

"Oh, no. She'd been sick for a long time. Alzheimer's I think. He didn't talk about her much. He's not a real outgoing guy. Keeps to himself." She inclined her head toward Connor and said conspiratorially, "They all do. Research scientists are pretty quiet. Some days I have to talk to myself here just to have company," she giggled.

"Yes, I can understand that. Well, thanks for your time," Connor said and picked up his briefcase to leave.

"Wait, didn't you want to talk to Dr. Neil?" Carolyn said, confused by Connor's abrupt change in plans.

"Something's just come up. Sorry to trouble you..." he called over his shoulder as he swung through the doors and into the California sunshine.

Holy shit. Now this was news. What the hell had happened?

• • •

Betsy was shocked to see Ken walk into Moira's room at the hospital. He had donned the gown, mask and gloves required of all entrants so as not to attract the ire of the nursing staff, but his exposed features were still immediately recognizable. He invented answers to his daughter's questions, telling her he had been released from quarantine because of his previous H5N1 vaccine. There was no point in the truth now. Except that he was here to salvage something, something honest, something to leave them with: he didn't know what, just that he had to be here.

Ken moved to the bed and hovered over Moira, sleeping. Beheld her dark lashes resting on her silken, unblemished skin. Studied the button nose and the pink cupid lips he had cherished, the tender cheeks and the birth mark on her dimpled chin. With his eyes he caressed the delicate hands clasped on top of the blanket, rising and falling with each breath. He untied his mask and bent over, kissing her gently on the brow, stroking her hair as he stood back up.

With tears in his eyes he turned to Betsy and held her in his arms.

"I'm sorry. I'm so sorry," he said, weeping finally, the pain inside and all around him suddenly unbearable. "Tell Moira I'm sorry." He clutched Betsy tightly, unwilling to let go of all that he had too late discovered. "I love you. Tell your mother. And Moira," he choked into her ear.

Ken released her and fled the room, covering his face with the hastily stripped off gown until he got past all the people who might stare at a sobbing man.

• • •

Connor called Lou and filled her in on the details of his visit to Crossfire. There was no telling what the information meant except that they agreed that the connection between Anna Wardman, Kenneth Culp and H5N1 was not likely to be a coincidence.

They sat in stunned silence for long seconds across the miles trying to conceive of a benign explanation that would link the people and events, but neither could find one. Only awful theories arose in their minds, unbidden; there could be no justification for what they were able to imagine. It was unthinkable. The authorities would have to locate Ken Culp and question him. Lou made calls to Dr. Wataabe and Director Bueller while Connor went to work on a story whose ending he didn't yet know.

• • •

Ken drove around for a while after he left the hospital, not knowing where to go to do what he had to do. He wanted to go home. More than anything he wanted to go home, and to tell June, as he had told Betsy, that he loved her. Tell her he was sorry. He would have told her everything if he could have seen her. He would have trusted her alone in the entire world to see that there was good in him despite all the bad that would come, to know he had made a mistake, that he was not evil, that he was incapable of evil. He yearned for the forgiveness he might find in her generous heart. He longed to lie down in his bed, beside his wife, in the comfort of her arms and die there. Because he had to die. He must.

He could not even die from the disease he had unleashed. He would have rocked Moira in his arms pleading for the virus to take him instead of her but it would have been to no avail. He would survive the scourge and be forced to watch the consequences of his miscalculation. The hatred of the world would be a beam focused on him. He could not bear it. He could not endure the pain of watching his family trying to understand, trying to forgive him, love him, excuse him, justify him. Better to die. With some shred of dignity left. By his own hand.

If he went home June would try to stop him. If he succeeded in dying with her unaware by his side, she would blame herself. He could at least spare her that. No, he would not go home.

He drove as anyone distracted does, by rote, from years of habit. He could not have named an intersection or a route he traveled, whether he passed one traffic light or a hundred. By and by he found himself in a neighborhood he didn't recognize and pulled into a convenience market, turning off the ignition and finding momentary rest from the noise of the engine and the wheels rolling over the road. But there was no ease from the tumult in his mind.

Numbly he considered his next move. Everything was an effort. He released the steering wheel from his fingers and gripped the handle, pushing the car door open with a heave of his shoulder. Dragging himself into the store he struggled to remove his wallet to buy a bottle of water. The attendant, distracted by the television which was tuned in to the crisis, barely noticed him. The president was halting all travel out of the United States and severely restricting travel within. Ken turned sadly from the news and walked away.

Where to go? The indecision was nearly incapacitating. None of the places familiar to him would be safe. Betsy and June would be worried. Calling the authorities soon, maybe already, to look for him. Not remotely suspecting his crime. He looked around at the streets surrounding his parked car. It was a dingy place, inviting despair. Abandoned buildings, crumbling cracked sidewalks, falling down porches on dilapidated houses. A skinny dog trotting down an alley, a kaleidoscope of broken glass strewn on the pavement, a shredded plastic bag waving lazily among the weeds. Over the tops of old warehouses and between the peeling paint of tenements Ken could see the top of the Golden Gate gleaming in the morning sun. How often he had gazed at that bridge in wonder, a model of engineering and artistry. Today it was only another potential means to his end, and he was grateful to his mother as he turned away that he wouldn't have to use it.

He got in the car and cruised the tumbledown neighborhood until he found a satisfactory lot in which to park his car, somewhere it couldn't easily be spied from the street, but a place where he would eventually be found. He turned off the engine and leaned back in the seat so he could retrieve the package containing the bottle from his hip pocket. His hand shook slightly as he uncapped the powder and peered at it. Shook the container a little to gauge its contents. It didn't look like much in there. He hoped it was enough to kill a man. Hoped it wasn't bitter, that he wouldn't be sick.

"Forgive me," he pleaded aloud through the windshield, through the cloudless sky, and tipped the powder onto his tongue, washing it down with the water. He felt a moment of relief; it was neither bitter nor nauseating. He opened the front door and got into the back seat of the car and locked all the doors. Folding an old sweater he found there into a pillow, he laid down his head until all the horrible thoughts were erased by the hypnotic haze and he was no more.

EPILOGUE

Do you want to know what happens?

Do you?

I have no answer.

I'm nothing more than a strand of proteins. Just eight in all. A simple thing. You can't even see me.

But I am here.

Still.

And so are you.

We have survived.

And that is all the more I can say.

ABOUT THE AUTHOR

Mary Jo Groves, M.D. is an actively practicing physician and board certified fellow of the American Academy of Family Physicians. When she is not working as a hospitalist at the regional medical center, she can be found reading, writing, gardening, cooking, golfing, dancing, traveling, or recovering from the above activities on the front porch  with her husband and their love child, a Boston terrier named Tippy. MJ speaks at a variety of forums on medical issues of interest to the public. You can contact her for your meeting or book club, or follow her on the web at www.drmjisin.com.

• • •

Authors depend on reviews. If you enjoyed *Virion* I'd very much appreciate yours. Please log on to Amazon.com, BarnesandNoble. com, Goodreads.com or your own favorite site and rate this book. Thank you -- MJ Groves

BOOK GROUP
DISCUSSION QUESTIONS

1. There are 3 parallel perspectives in *Virion*. What are they and why portray them separately?

2. Do you see the virus as a remarkable construct of nature or something evil? Compare the survival mechanisms of the virus with those of humans. Which life form do you think is better positioned to last another million years?

3. What are the seeds of Ken's destruction? Are good people capable of doing terrible things? Can you create a different story for Ken— one with a better ending? Is it possible to recognize the seeds of our own destruction?

4. We expect money to motivate CEO, JB Vaughn. But what about Ken Culp? The WHO? How does the pursuit of profit in *Virion* serve society? How does it imperil society?

5. What rights should a business have to a monopoly on a medical treatment or device? What if that product is life-saving? Does it matter if the population it affects is small or large? What rights should consumers have? What should the role of government be?

6. Scientists think of their studies as objective: hypotheses tested by research. What factors influenced the research in *Virion*? Can

these factors compromise the validity of the results? Will you view the results of scientific studies differently now?

7. How does culture affect the spread of infectious disease?

8. If you were Anna's only child how would you have responded to her request to end her life? Would the request alone burden you forever, no matter what you chose to do? Can you imagine any conditions under which you would ask another person to end your life?

9. Pandemics have occurred throughout history and we are warned periodically that another is coming. Discuss the effect that hype has on raising or lowering your expectations of widespread disease. How well do you think modern media handle complex issues? How do you, personally, get detailed information? Do you think reporting is better or worse now than 10 years ago? How might media be different 20 years from now?

10. It's been said that a sign of intelligence is being able to hold conflicting thoughts in your head (presumably without going nuts). I don't know about the intelligence part, but I'm comfortable with competing ideas, perhaps because I was (my husband would say I still am) a debater. To win a debate tournament you must successfully argue both sides of an issue— in one round you will have to take the affirmative side of a proposition, and the next round you argue for exactly the opposite view. The judges decide at the end of each round which side wins. As the reader, you now are the judge. There are several debates taking in place in *Virion*. What are they, and which side do you favor?

11. Will we be ready for the next pandemic?

41688339R00189

Made in the USA
Charleston, SC
10 May 2015